The Seduction

Shirley Eskapa is the author of the bestselling non-fiction book *Woman versus Woman*, as well as the two highly acclaimed novels, *The Secret Keeper* (also available in Pan) and *Blood Fugue*. She was educated at the University of Witwatersrand, Johannesburg. She is married with three children and divides her time between London and Monaco.

Shirley Eskapa

THE SEDUCTION

Pan Books

London, Sydney and Auckland

First published in Great Britain 1987
by Century Hutchinson Ltd
This edition published 1988 by Pan Books Ltd,
Cavaye Place, London, SW10 9PG
9 8 7 6 5 4 3 2 1
© Shirley Eskapa 1987
ISBN 0 330 30165 9
All rights reserved

Printed and bound in Great Britain by
Richard Clay Ltd, Bungay, Suffolk

For Patrick Cosgrave
mentor and friend

PROLOGUE

An accident, as everyone knows, is sudden change.

An accident is also coincidence. It is even a riddle. But when that woman broke a leg or an arm or whatever it was, I did not know that I would have a story to tell, still less an accident – of destiny – to try to make sense of. After all, it was not my accident, it was someone else's, and when I was told about it – told that I would take her place, stand in for her – I did not so much as ask her name. Her accident was my opportunity... I was advised to take it, and I did.

Which is why I was outside her front door now, waiting to see – waiting, quite literally, to finger the messenger of my destiny.

Four months since her accident, and three months after what is now internationally known as my meteoric rise – and overtaken by a sudden whim to know her name – I discovered that she was called Ernestina Keynes. Of course I knew the name of the cookbook she had written. She was meant to promote Sixty Seductive Salads from Fifty-One States, but it was because of her accident that I came over from England, took her place and my book, Defending Wives, was promoted – coast-to-coast – instead. Naturally, if I had been a real writer, I would have known that the writer of Sixty Seductive Salads from Fifty-One States was also the poet. But I only found that out when I bought the cookbook.

Ernestina let me in; like a New Yorker, I now call people by their first names. She must have been seventy, at the very least. Still, she was dressed in a jogger's uniform, the severe top-knot of her grey hair softened by unruly wisps. Nothing soft about the way she looked at me, though. I don't suppose I will ever get used to that punishing glare of avid fascination...

She led me into her living room. An unusual room, to put it mildly – cages and cages of canaries, sixteen to a cage she said. Her numerous wall-hangings in scarlet and black consisted of startlingly erotic, exquisite lace and embroidered negligées. Apart from the canaries, the room was in black and reds, but gloomy for all that. Despite the bird stench, I managed not to retch.

'It was good of you to agree to see me,' I began.

'Why shouldn't I? I'm a star-gazer like everyone else. Who wouldn't want to see Emily Bradshaw in the flesh?'

'Oh, well...'

'Come on, you're a celebrity. Don't be so irritatingly coy!'

'Famous for being famous, you mean?' I said lightly.

'I don't mean anything of the kind. Irresponsible, ill-informed talk on talk-shows made you into a celebrity. I know why you came here; you came to play truth and consequence, didn't you?' She didn't wait for me to reply, but rushed on. 'Oh, it's all very well for you,' she said bitterly. 'Too bad for him, though. Words kill, and you killed him with your words.'

I said nothing.

Because I agreed...

The birds twittered. I felt I was caged with them.

'You, Emily Bradshaw, will defend yourself of course. You will claim that you cannot be held responsible for the death of some stranger out there, who tried to kill you.'

Right or wrong, it made no difference now. It was too late. We were in entire agreement, she and I, but telling her so would only release more venom. And, as the whole world knows, I've had more than my fair share of that. From somewhere an idea – a phrase – 'out-Nazi the Nazi' came to me. I made myself sound colder and crueller than she. 'I came here because I wanted to know something about Ernestina Keynes.'

'Oh, well, of course,' she said, softening at once. 'Be glad to help.'

'What was it you broke?'

'Broke, bankruptcy? What is this?'

'Your accident,' I said, almost shouting now. 'The accident that stopped you from promoting Sixty Seductive Salads from Fifty-One States.'

She broke into a cackling, echoing sound that passed for a laugh. The same sound, mimicked by a parrot, came from another room.

I had an hysterical urge to run away, but the urge to know the nature of her accident was even stronger.

Presently, Ernestina and the parrot stopped their noise.

'So that is why the mega-star has come to see an obscure poet like me. Curiosity about my accident. Am I right?'

'Absolutely. Perfectly.'

'There was no accident; I broke nothing,' she said, grinning. 'Nothing at all, except my word. The very idea of that selling carousel sickened me. I only agreed so Frontier would print more books, and they did.'

'No accident,' I repeated, stupefied. 'There was no accident?'

'It was an acceptable excuse . . . a white lie. An accident is an act of God . . .'

I could no longer control my retching or anything else, and I left at once.

Because that acceptable excuse had resulted in more than a million dollars for me.

But that, unfortunately, was where the fantasy ended.

For there was nothing fanciful about the rest – about millions made, lives lost, families destroyed . . . and all on the back of a real white lie.

PART 1
Early July 1985

Chapter 1

'So you *are* at home after all! Thank goodness I don't give up easily!'

'Keith! What on earth . . . ? Four o'clock in the afternoon?'

'You're surprised, of course. So am I!' He was standing beside her now, flourishing a champagne bottle, his normally pale face pink with exertion and astonishment. 'You've done it, my girl. You've done it! I bring you the kind of news any author would die for and you stand there holding a clump of laundered sheets, for God's sake!' He laid the champagne in one of the Grecian urns filled with drooping geraniums and tiny red roses and pricked his finger.

Grabbing the bundle of freshly laundered sheets from her, he picked up the champagne again and said, 'Sheets!' He began to laugh, and turned pinker. 'Lead the way, and then we'll sit down in your drawing room, if you please, where it's warm and I'll tell you everything. And stop looking so startled . . .'

They walked through the kitchen where Keith opened a cupboard, found two glasses and continued on his way through the adjoining dining room, up the narrow staircase and into the small drawing room.

Keith Summers was normally a man of few words and his uncharacteristic behaviour shocked Emily into silence. He was not the sort of literary agent who would flash champagne.

'Congratulations! Frontier Books are sending you to America. A coast-to-coast tour to promote *Defending Wives*! In three weeks' time.'

'Three weeks? But is the book ready? I haven't seen the cover...'

'Emily Bradshaw! Books are never ready – like cakes. And they have jackets, not covers...' He shook his head. Do you know what a coast-to-coast tour means? It means about twenty thousand dollars – perhaps more, who knows? Emily Bradshaw, a coast-to-coast celebrity. Television, radio, press.'

'Television! I'd be much too nervous.'

'Can you afford nerves, my girl?'

'I think,' Emily said slowly, 'I think I'd better phone Simon.' She looked at her watch, which was serviceable and dignified, like the rest of her.

'Simon? Darling? Keith Summers is here... drinking champagne... he couldn't get through on the telephone. He's telling me some amazing stuff about Frontier Books, a promotion tour in America and twenty thousand extra dollars for us. Do you think you could come home a little early? This sort of thing is hardly our scene... Yes, he did say twenty thousand dollars. The exchange rate? No, I don't know – he says he wants to talk to you. Keith?'

Keith had been sucking his wounded finger. Now he took the phone and spoke quickly. 'One-twenty to the pound sterling, as of this morning. Can't expect a solicitor to know these things... Super news, old boy! About fifteen minutes. Good...' He turned to Emily, the rapid reel of his excitement amplifying his voice and making it harsh. 'I think it would be fair to say it's a lucky break. An unintentional pun, forgive me! Frontier Books were about to promote a coast-to-coast cookbook called *Sixty Seductive Salads from Fifty-One States* and their author broke her back, or her leg. Anyway, there was some sort of break. The lucky thing is that their president saw your photograph on the jacket, and thought *Defending Wives* could easily be substituted. The segments were already booked.'

'Segments?'

'Television,' Keith said airily. 'Shows. Chat shows. Audience shows. That sort of thing...'

'Audiences?' Emily repeated. '*Audiences?*' She shuddered.

*

Simon came blinking in. He blinked when he concentrated, or was puzzled, but Keith explained and he understood at once. 'This is unexpected, Em,' he said again and again. 'I'm very proud of you.'

Emily smiled. But she was dazed... unfinished thoughts whirled and clashed. To contain herself she left the room – ostensibly to fetch an extra glass – and absent-mindedly began folding the sheets, sorting out the disorder of her mind. Presently Danny, their son, came in from school. 'Dad's upstairs,' she said. 'He came home especially early. Mr Summers is with him; go and say hello.'

A few minutes later, she came in carrying two glasses. 'Danny ought to join us,' she explained. It was her way of saying she would go.

'It won't be long, Em,' Simon said, 'only three weeks.'

He looked towards their valuable Ford Madox-Brown and Emily knew what he meant. They might be able to send Danny to Eton without having to sell the painting after all. That and the Chippendale desk were the only heirlooms they possessed; both had belonged to Simon's paternal great-grandparents.

Following his gaze, Emily bit her lip. She wanted to say she was terrified, that she couldn't possibly do this, or anything like it. She said, instead, 'I've never been to America. Nor has Simon...'

'That's true, you haven't. I'd forgotten that,' Keith said. 'Well, anyone who hasn't been to America isn't quite a part of the twentieth century!'

'You're going too far, Keith,' Simon commented coldly. 'I dare say there are still those among us who prefer quality to quantity.'

*

Rick Cooke, the outside publicist whom Frontier Books had engaged for the first time, pondered Emily Bradshaw's photograph. He was convinced it had been taken by an amateur, with some kind of inferior camera. Her bio told him absolutely nothing; so what if she had been to a British school called Cambridge where she met her husband, a lawyer named Simon?

She lived in London, so what was new? She was like millions of others, he thought. She could at least have lived in a castle, for Chrissake, but no: 'She lives in London, married, one child. First published full-length work; her real profession that of housewife.' It was this last which enraged him. 'Jesus, I'll go crazy!' he said out loud. Just his luck – that gal who wrote *Sixty Seductive Salads from Fifty-One States* had to go break a leg or a back. It didn't matter which. What mattered was that his plans had gotten screwed up. This British gal could screw up everything for him – if she was useless in front of the cameras, who'd smell bad in front of all those smart-assed producers, those tough bitches? Why, Rick Cooke, of course – not Emily Bradshaw. Frontier Books had been a lucky break for him.

Again he talked to himself: 'I put my fucking soul into all those fucking bookings for *Sixty Seductive Salads from Fifty-One States*. And this Emily can't even answer her goddamned phone!'

It was almost midnight and two Coke bottles were filled with cigarette stubs. He was trying to give up smoking and one of his authors had suggested this aversion therapy technique. So far it had only succeeded in making him smoke still more: it gave his self-loathing, self-disgust a tangible form, and therefore fascinated him. Too many shrinks had told him he had a low self-esteem for him to doubt this, but he was the sort who found solace and escape in his work – he enjoyed what he did and was dedicated, which was why he was still in his office and – infinitely more important – why he owned the business.

Rick Cooke had met his own deadline. He had been determined to be in his own business before he was thirty, and had made it when he was twenty-nine and a half; that was eighteen months ago. It sure had eased the pain of turning thirty, though. He was in love with Lorna, but terrified of commitment. Lorna was playing games – she had taken a teaching job in Hawaii. It was a last-ditch stand to get him to commit himself, and he saw it for what it was – and not only because his motherly secretary cued him in. Yet he did miss her. He wondered what she would make of this kind of book, *Defending Wives*. The blurb said that women had to work harder at marriage than men... Essential reading for every woman... Are women each other's natural enemies? It sure was controversial – a chat show producer's dream!

He laughed aloud, thinking that he hadn't had to read that cookbook, and he didn't want to read this one either – which was why he had decided to call Emily. He would use the standard ploy and ask her why she had written it.

He reached for the telephone. Still no reply. He connected with the long-distance operator, induced her to check the line and discovered he had had the wrong code and had been calling Germany.

The ringing tone must be different, he concluded, in London, England. They did things differently over there. He had never been outside the USA; not that he wasn't keen on travel, though – he'd pretty well covered his own continent, and was astute enough to realize that New York State was as different from Texas as, say, Holland from Sweden.

The phone was answered. 'This is Rick Cooke calling from the United States. I'd like to speak with Emily Bradshaw.'

Emily put down her glass of orange juice and wiped her forehead. 'Emily Bradshaw speaking,' she said primly, and added, 'do you know what time it is?'

'Twelve-thirty.'

'Twelve-thirty in New York; five-thirty in the morning in London,' she pointed out.

'But you're five hours behind us.'

'We're not behind you in everything, you know. We're five hours ahead of you. Everyone's asleep.'

'You don't sound asleep.'

'I'm not asleep, but everyone else in London is asleep.'

'Then why aren't *you* asleep?'

'Because I'm sitting in my kitchen drinking orange juice and counting sheets,' Emily said wearily.

'Sheets? Sheep, you mean sheep.'

'No, I said sheets and I mean sheets.'

'But sheep is what people count when they can't sleep.'

'I don't want to sleep.'

'Your voice – they'll love your voice over here. That's

something, let me tell you. It'll go over big over here! Even I love your voice.'

'The tour,' Emily said slowly. 'The author tour. Someone suddenly broke a leg, or a back. Something broke, anyway.'

'You're damn right. But it was an accident, you know. An accident can't be helped – don't you know that?'

'Of course. It's a mishap, that's what it is. I'd been thinking about it all night, but I couldn't find the right word... mishap...'

'Mishap or not, you really lucked out. It's a big tour we've got planned over here: twenty-one cities, coast-to-coast.'

Emily laughed nervously.

'I'll bet you're nervous,' Rick said. 'Don't be.' And then, on impulse, he added, 'Trust me.' A rolling lilt animated his deep American voice.

'I will,' she said seriously. 'I do. I do trust you. You trust the person who makes you laugh.' I'm exhausted, she thought, my defences must be down. Trust isn't something one talks about.

'Tell me about yourself,' Rick began. 'Your bio tells me nothing.'

'Bio? Oh, the biographic note, you mean?'

'Right. Why did you write the book? Did your husband cheat on you?'

'Cheat on me? Simon? Oh no, Simon isn't like that. He's a bit on the serious side, like me, I suppose. Very responsible. Very honourable. And he adores Danny.'

'And you? Does Simon love you too?'

'I'm very lucky,' Emily said. 'Yes.'

'So what made you write the book? You feel deeply about it, I can tell.'

Emily began to tell him. She had been obsessed, she said, she was certain of that now; she suspected it was because of her parents' divorce. Everyone involved came to believe, little by little – when it was too late, really – that the divorce had been unnecessary. Her mother gave way, gave her father to his girlfriend, Melissa, who was nineteen and didn't really want him either. By the time her mother realized that she could have put up something of a fight, it was too late.

It was a complicated story, she supposed. She didn't want to go into all the details now, because the real point was that when she herself had been the other woman, that wife – a woman called Norah – had had all the courage her mother lacked. Norah had come to see her; she'd been frightened off, actually, by Norah ... Norah and that man had stayed together and the last she'd heard was that they had two more children.

About four years ago, her great friend Marianne had had the same problem. Everyone thought Marianne should throw him out – everyone, that is, except herself. So in desperation, and wanting to help, Emily confessed the whole thing about Norah to Marianne ... and even about the way she had prayed every night for her father's girlfriend's death ... Marianne blasted the other woman out of sight; they had worked on a battle plan together.

And then something much worse had happened. Something tragic, really tragic. Emily and Marianne's close, really close friend, Penny, had been involved with a married man since she was eighteen. When his wife went away, she stayed with him and sometimes slept in the wife's bed too. Penny must have suddenly understood that he would never leave his wife, because one morning, after he had gone off to work, she had killed herself – slashed her wrists on the very same bed ... And that man and his wife were still married, still living even now in that same house.

So she had written the book because she hoped it might prevent needless divorce, but of course she didn't actually see herself as a real writer. Anyway, it had been done, which was why it was now six-thirty a.m. and they had been talking – or rather, she had been telling an absolute stranger things she never expected to tell anyone about – she had been talking for a whole hour.

It was terribly extravagant, wasn't it? But then, she supposed Americans *were* extravagant.

Rick could not recall when an assignment had intrigued him more than this one. Mega-books, mega-bucks, when you least expect them. Seize the moment and you'll make 'em! It would be tough, but he'd make it. After putting the phone down, he

15

studied her photograph again and then grabbed a magnifying glass. Emily Bradshaw, he concluded, was pretty enough but had no glamour. She had light hair and good bones, but smallish eyes and only half a smile. All of which could be fixed...

Easily.

Because of those legs of hers – those fantastically sexy legs.

Publicity shots. Somehow, he would have to get a great photographer all the way to London. And real quick, too. Now that he'd heard her voice and talked to her, he was certain she would be a hit. He imagined her on the *Virginia Byrnes Show* and shut his eyes, his mind reeling ahead.

'... and Emily Bradshaw, author of *Defending Wives*. *Good morning, Emily Bradshaw.*'

'*Good morning.*'

'*Emily has come all the way from London to talk to us about her controversial book. Now, Emily, wouldn't you say there is something demeaning about fighting other women over a man? Aren't you advocating a retrogressive step? A return to the Victorian era?*'

'*No. I'm saying there are very many excellent reasons for a divorce, but the other woman need not be one of them.*'

'*So, you believe it's OK for men to cheat on their wives?*'

Virginia Byrnes swivels her chair to face the audience in the studio, and the audience out there. 'You got to admit it, you guys,' she says with her famous chuckle. 'Emily looks more like a mistress than a wife!'

Rick Cooke made one of his instant decisions. If Frontier Books wouldn't pick up the tab, he would.

Emily Bradshaw would make much more than her own name.

He wished Lorna had chosen another time to play games. He missed her, he wanted to make love to her, he needed her. For the first time he thought that an apartment emptied of Lorna was not only inconvenient but... what? Unappetizing, unwelcoming, he decided, and worst yet, cold. *Freezing.*

About five minutes had elapsed since his transatlantic call to Emily. To confirm a hunch, he needed to telephone her once more. Still in the kitchen, drinking coffee out of one of Danny's old mugs with teddy bears on it, she answered at once. 'There's one thing I gotta know, Emily. Why did you leave all that stuff you told me out of the book?'

'Because it might have hurt . . .'

'That's what I thought.'

'I see. Then why—'

'I wanted to know you better. Well, thanks. Go to sleep now, OK?' He hung up. His mind returned to Lorna and his body tingled.

It seemed there was no alternative – he would have to make his way to a singles bar. He had never paid for it in his life and wasn't going to start now.

He decided on Hank's, the most businesslike singles bar of his acquaintance. There he picked up Kirby, who in another town was attractive enough not to have even known where the singles bars were located. After the usual decent interval of about thirty minutes or so, during which time he and Kirby played a real and mutually confident game of backgammon together, they transferred to her place.

Kirby told him she was a sales consultant to a new greetings card company. Rick accepted this and did not tell her than in his book, this kind of sales assistant meant 'a rep on the road'. Her L-shaped studio had been intelligently divided – louvre doors which almost stretched to the low ceiling formed a separate cubicle just large enough to hold a double bed. The place was neat enough, but aseptic as a McDonalds. Even her colour coordinations reminded him of a McDonalds: muted reds and yellows.

They took one another to bed and managed in a practised kind of way to forget, for a while, that they were two strangers locked in bodily intimacy, until for a few merciful moments they were joined into a single stranger.

They surprised each other by staying together long enough to share breakfast.

Chapter 2

The night of the long transatlantic phone conversation with Rick was to be Emily's only sleepless night.

The days that followed were bewilderingly hectic; life had become a perpetual rush-hour, so that she fell into an exhausted sleep just as soon as her head finally met the pillow. Up to then, Emily's life had been busy but disordered. There was no surfeit of time, just enough to allow her to believe that she led a life of luxury if only because she sometimes read a novel in the middle of the morning. This was the height of indolence, her mother said. Now, drawing up lists, planning menus, shopping, checking Simon's clothes, meetings with Keith – even the acquisition of an American Express card – all those petty details attacked and overwhelmed, and there was no time for reading and no time for thinking. Which may or may not have been a blessing. Emily was the kind of person who got on with things or rather, as she would have put it, muddled through. Making a fuss, however, would have been unthinkable. Because Simon had gone over everything again and again and his lawyer's painstaking solicitude and logic reassured her. He would manage. Ann, their Swedish *au pair* whom they had privately nicknamed Ophelia (when she arrived from Sweden, she had been pale, pathetic and helpless) would cope. Emily would give two days over to laying in a frozen store of Danny's favourite dishes; his Suzuki violin lessons would continue. Emily thought of the Brahms Lullaby – Danny's solo for the forthcoming children's concert.

The absurd details behind domestic chores were as comforting to Emily as an embrace. But every time her mind veered towards planning the kind of clothes she would need, she pulled it back. The advance had already been spent on – of all things in the world – the roof!

Though the decision to spend the entire advance on repairing the roof was entirely characteristic of the Bradshaws' uncompromisingly practical and even austere approach to life. They had toyed with the idea of splurging on a weekend in Paris, but in the end both agreed that it made more sense to spend it on something more permanent. Their terraced house in Chelsea, just near the World's End pub, suited them in the same made-to-measure sort of way in which they suited one another. Tall and slim, their graceful economical movements were as elegant as their combined predictable public school accents. Their house conveyed the same message as a club membership badge, aspirations linked more to the past than to the future because for the Bradshaws – and more than ever in this high-tec era – tradition equalled stability. Two rooms per floor, three floors and a basement, overall dimensions as narrow as a doll's house, made the place cosy, warmly welcoming and serene with domestic bustle.

The clothes, the tour, the book and the separation from Simon all merged, or rather collided in her mind; her very skull felt too small for her.

Now everything had changed.

Yet nothing had changed.

Because, when all this (whatever it was) was over, her life would resume its normal implacable rhythm.

And yet, other people had changed. Distinctly. Keith, for one.

Keith only agreed to read her manuscript because he had known Simon at Cambridge. He made it clear that it wasn't his sort of *genre*, but accepted it with all the world-weariness of his profession. Of course he had no intention of reading it himself, but gave it to one of his outside readers, who wrote a positive memo and suggested that it might be shown to an American publisher. Publishers are businessmen looking for bargains, and

Simon gave it to Gerald Grove of Frontier Books who happened to be on a buying trip (scouting for new books) in London. It might have been a line, a design of crockery judged unsuitable for the British market and then offered without any expectation of a sale, simply because Keith didn't want one of his customers to go away empty-handed... Somewhere, somehow, Emily sensed this, which was why she didn't quite regard herself as a professional writer. She was, however, a professional housewife whose minor hobby had been indulged by her husband's friend; looked after, humoured...

And if the author of *Sixty Seductive Salads from Fifty-One States* had not broken a leg, or whatever it was, Keith Summers would never had read *Defending Wives*.

At any rate, this is what Emily suspected...

Because she detected a note of resentment, a hint of envy, when he said again, 'Well, Emily, you'll be a coast-to-coast celebrity. How do you feel about that?'

But Emily only murmured. This was so far from anything she wanted, so distant as to be meaningless.

She was used to saying nothing. What would be the point of telling him that she felt as if she were going in for some elective, yet essential, surgery? Something was going to be corrected – the Ford Madox-Brown might not have to be sacrificed for Danny to go to Eton.

In so far as she thought of anything related to her tour at all, she thought of clothes, but could not bring herself to discuss this with Keith. Her mother was convinced that skirts and blouses would be right and Simon agreed.

She longed to get out of Keith's office and get on with the meals she planned to freeze.

And when she finally returned to Lamont Road, she found her mother waiting on the doorstep, brandishing a moss-green carrier-bag and a bunch of wilting daisies. 'I've been to Laura Ashley,' her mother exulted. 'They're having a sale. I think I've found everything you need!'

Emily sighed.

The cooking and the freezing would have to wait.

Fumbling with the key, because the phone was ringing and the new Labrador puppy Hal – a recent gift from Keith to Danny – was yelping, Emily let her mother in. She was still holding the door open for her when a man on a motor-bike screeched to a stop and a man resembling a 'Hell's Angel' called out urgently, 'Emily Bradshaw? Are you Mrs Emily Bradshaw?'

'Yes, I am Mrs Bradshaw.'

He brandished an envelope and she began walking down the steps, but her mother called out, 'Emily, it's someone from the United States! I think she said New Orleans, though heaven knows – she also said she's from something that sounded like half the alphabet.'

The messenger had left his gleaming machine and helmeted, black-leathered, was saying, 'Third time I been round your place. Air Courier Services. Sign, please.'

'Emily!' her mother said sharply. 'You're wanted on the telephone! Leave this ... this ... motor-bike to me!'

Emily might have been thirty-four years old, but she did as she was told. She went to the telephone.

The voice on the other end was Southern, or so Emily identified it. It was the first 'real life' Southern accent she had ever heard, and it delighted her; she found it absurdly touching. Her attention focused on this accent even more than on what the voice was saying. Suddenly she was aware that the woman on the other end sounded sharp: 'Didn't Rick Cooke alert you to expect my call?'

Habitually apologetic, Emily replied, 'I'm sorry, I was out.'

'OK, this is Jackie Stevens, producer of the *Virginia Byrnes Show*. You probably know we syndicate over forty states?'

'Syndicate?'

'Uh-oh ... we have a bad connection. I'll call you right back. Don't you move now – stay right where you are.'

Emily was about to say that there was nothing wrong with the connection, but Jackie Stevens had disconn—— ——an-while Emily still held the puppy and clutched th—— ——carrier-bag. While she had been listening to Ja—— ——mother had been gesticulating about wanting—— ——manilla envelope left by the courier. Emily ——

'Please do,' and then the phone rang again. Answering, she said, 'Jackie ...'

'It's not Jackie, it's Rick. For Chrissake, where have you been?'

'I ...'

'Forget it, forget it! I wanted to warn you. We've got a big coup. Jackie ...' his voice faded. 'She's already called you?'

'Yes.'

'Hell ...' His voice rose appreciably. 'Did you talk to her? Did she confirm the booking?'

'The connection was bad and she's going to telephone again. She told me not to move.'

'I'll get off the line.'

'Wait a minute. What is the *Virginia Byrnes Show*?'

'You mean you've never heard of the *Virginia Byrnes Show*? You've never even heard of the *Virginia Byrnes Show*?' Rick's voice rose higher with disbelief and he laughed briefly, bitterly. 'Authors fly in from Japan ...'

'I'm sorry,' she said, contrite. 'I'm new to all this ...' She sounded miserable.

'I'm sorry. I yell when I'm excited and I am *so* excited. Virginia Byrnes! Well, her show's almost as big as Merv's or Donahue's. Highest ratings, thirty million viewers. But I'll tell you about all that later. I wanted to warn you that the producer would be calling you for a pre-interview. Are you listening?'

'Yes. A pre-interview, you said.'

'I'd better talk fast. She'll be mad because your line is busy. OK? Listen – tell her yours is the first; no one has ever written about this before. Got it?'

'I get it – but I couldn't ...'

'Emily, I can hear you sighing all the way here in New York. Don't be shy and don't be modest. People here don't go for that. A producer gets a hint of shyness and thinks the guest will dry up. Got it?'

'Yes.'

'Don't louse this one up, I got a lot riding on it. As soon as I tell the other big shows that Virginia Byrnes has made a firm commitment, they'll all be screaming for you ...'

'But I thought the bookings had been made for the cookbook author?'

'True, but that was before I read *Defending Wives*. That was just an assignment. But this ... This is *wow*!'

'What does "*wow*" mean?'

'You're blocking the line. Jackie Stevens does not wait.' An emphatic pause between each word. Then, 'I'll call you when you're through ...'

Once more the phone clicked and the disconnected sound echoed Emily's own inner disconnectedness. Her mother giggled. 'What *can* "wow" mean, Emily?'

Emily laughed hysterically. To calm her – to distract her as she, Clara Rice, had done when Emily was a child – her mother hauled the contents from the Laura Ashley bag. 'Try them on,' she commanded. 'This is just like when you were a little girl. I always found what suited you.'

Once again, Emily did as she was told. But was conscious, all the while, of waiting for the phone to ring. She desperately hoped it would and yet at the same time, though with perhaps even more desperation, that it would not. For one thing, her mother hadn't read the manuscript. (Emily still did not have a copy of the book.) And how on earth was she going to disclose to a complete stranger the effect of her mother's divorce, with her mother right here in the room with her? Emily's reaction to the divorce had never been mentioned, let alone discussed. For a moment she felt like a thief caught wearing the clothes she had stolen from a close friend.

She could not possibly give that pre-interview while her mother was there.

Suddenly she understood that she dared not take the risk of ruining things before they had even begun. She was definite about this; so definite that, while pretending to check the phone, she unplugged it. There now, Jackie Stevens, you will think the phone is ringing and when there's no reply, you'll phone the operator who will test the line and report that it's out of order. She felt much easier now about trying on those blouses.

Her mother, Clara Rice, had long since settled – and not

without some satisfaction – on having herself described as the sort of person with 'more taste than money'. There had been a time when her tastes equalled her money, but that was before Tom had found his teenage Melissa and lost so much else, including his senses... It was no use having a huge alimony settlement if it could not be funded. She ought not to have prevented her lawyers from accepting the lump sum she had been offered in lieu of alimony. Tom had been so guilt-stricken *then* (as her lawyers had assured her) that he would have been ready to pay much more to lessen his pain.

'Well,' Clara said, looking at the blouses which should have been by Dior and not by Ashley, 'I may have been obstinate, but I wasn't weak-willed.'

Emily had heard all this before and she said, automatically appeasing, 'Oh, Mother! I prefer Laura Ashley's pure cotton to Dior's pure silk.' The royal blue blouse with its fluted ruffled neck and bow really did suit her. 'It's beautiful, just right. I'll use it again and again.' Though thirty-four, she had not yet succeeded in not blushing, in not rushing her words whenever money, or rather the lack of it, was mentioned. Now she said quickly, 'I can only afford one, though...'

'Oh Emily, what a mistake I made about that.'

Emily had a few proved stock responses to choose from and she said, 'I know. The alimony. It wasn't a mistake; you had your pride to consider.'

'I think, just this once, I'll have a meeting with your father – about this American trip of yours. After all, you are his only child...'

'If you do that, Mother, I will never forgive you. Never!'

'All right then, all right. Don't fuss. That charming salesgirl said I could bring them back if they didn't fit.'

'Does she expect you to return them today? Or did she say you could keep them for a day or two?'

'Oh no! Good heavens, no! Today... I promised.' Her mother looked at her pleadingly. 'You couldn't come back with me, could you, darling.'

'I have to wait for a call from America, remember?'

'Yes, darling. I remember now, though I confess I had forgotten. You are to learn the meaning of *wow* now, aren't

24

you? My memory's not as bad as I feared!'

Clara Rice set off at a slow pace to return the blouses. She knew her daughter well and had sensed that Emily wanted to be on her own. She experienced a tinge of self-satisfaction – she was usually right about Emily; she had been certain her daughter would agree.

And yet she had not been entirely successful with her daughter who, it seemed, had neither enough money nor enough ambition. Her house was tasteful, though rather traditional. As for the garden, Clara was given to describing it (over bridge) as '... really, really tiny. A jewelled patch in a patchwork quilt, and no larger than three larger quilts.' This tour of Emily's would provide quite a conversation piece and Clara began to relish the prospect. It would make a change from talking about her voluntary work for the League of Friends of the Royal Marsden Hospital as a conversation topic. She loved telling people about her amusing exploits as a volunteer maid, how during the hospital's auxiliary workers' strike she went down on her knees and scrubbed lavatories as well as floors.

But ... if only Emily would *do* something about the way she dressed: drab, sensible colours, pale lipstick and then only, Clara suspected, to appease her mother – and never a touch of mascara. Her hair should be lightened, but highlights cost the *earth*.

Her ex-husband could easily afford it. Yes, she would have to have a word with him. Clara was always looking for excuses to talk to him and she knew perfectly well that Sir Thomas Rice was not only her ex-husband, but her hobby.

Twenty years since their divorce – when she had been, as she now marvelled to herself, thirty-eight – and still she saw Tom as her husband. Well then, if not her husband, as *hers*. Tom was miserable with Melissa and unfaithful to her too. She knew all about him; she was exactly what her friend, Mags, said she was: a Tom-watcher ...

She was aware suddenly of tip-toeing instead of walking, and this on the Fulham Road, Chelsea! She was aware of this only because she glimpsed herself unexpectedly in the mirror of a shop window. She hesitated, paused for a moment longer and then, taken aback by her own unlooked-for image, stopped stock-still. Why, she looked years younger, years and years younger, she told herself, smiling into the mirror. Her cape, black and soft, fell into a perfectly graceful drape. Her usual serviceable black was flattering to her and undeniably chic, too. The pearls lay seemingly carelessly, yet within the correct range to complement the matched earrings that dressed her face. Her make-up might have been bought at Woolworths, but it was excellent.

Self-absorbed, almost self-beguiled, charmed by the very real hope of a meeting with Tom, and just as she was deciding that looks are all in the expression, but before she could even relate this thought to her assessment of Emily's looks, she felt a quick sharp tug at her elbow. She had just registered that when she heard a sound like marbles or pebbles rolling. Looking down, she saw a cluster of pearls. *Her* pearls. She thought she saw the 'Hell's Angel' messenger jump on that gleaming machine of his. She felt suddenly dizzy, felt herself begin to wobble, tried not to fall. Fake pearls, she thought – a blessing – and then realized that her handbag had been snatched. Mugging, she thought and was quite unable to stop herself.

'She's fainted,' someone said.

A mother pushing a pram with a twin girl and boy stopped suddenly and then, as if by reflex, went into emergency action. 'I'm a nurse. Get an ambulance. Watch my babies. this woman's dying. Heart attack.'

The nurse applied mouth-to-mouth resuscitation and thumped Clara Rice's ribs. The crowd grew.

'Stop it,' someone called. 'You'll break her ribs!'

The young nurse sweated, tried still harder. Her twins cried.

An ambulance attendant knelt down beside her. 'You did your best,' he said sympathetically. 'You did everything you could. We'll take her away anyway...'

A young man dressed in the punk uniform of the day, his ears flowing with safety-pins, his purple and orange hair cut rooster-fashion, waved the leaflets he had been giving out for Snippers' Stylists and wailed, 'I was watching her. I saw her looking at herself in the mirror, over there in that window. She looked so pleased with herself. I couldn't help watching her...'

26

Chapter 3

Emily was given the standard knock-out injection that doctors prescribe in these circumstances. The Laura Ashley bill was the only identification her mother had carried with her.

Though the injection controlled her hysteria, it did not send her to sleep. Her mind was fixated on the fact that while her mother lay dying in the gutter, she had been telling Keith Summers about that pre-interview. Worse, oh! uncontrollably worse, was that she had been enjoying a special satisfaction from the highly respectful, almost obsequious tones that Keith Summers had lately taken to using whenever he spoke to her.

Hating Keith was less painful than grieving for her mother. She had never liked Keith at the best of times, but she never hated him. Now she hated him even more than she hated her father's wife, Melissa.

Emily had asked to be alone, but wished Simon would come in to be with her all the same . . . or at least come and see how she was.

Her mind veered back to Keith and then to Melissa. The dreaded Melissa at her mother's funeral? Melissa who had ruined all their lives . . . Impossible! She must speak to Simon about this at once. She raced downstairs. 'Simon,' she said. 'Oh, Simon, I'm counting on you. We're not allowing Melissa – and that's final.'

'That's rather extreme, isn't it?'

'Extreme? How can you say that, Simon? How could you possibly imagine that I could bear to have that woman at my mother's . . .'

'Em, she's been your father's wife for more than a decade...'

'Trust you to remind me of that, Simon. I'm begging you to speak to my father, begging you. Tell him – tell him I'll make a scene. Tell him anything you like.' Emily put her head in her lap as if it were a pillow, but the harsh guttural sounds could not be stifled.

'I'll have a word with your father, Em,' Simon promised, patting her head awkwardly. 'Only, please, please, pull yourself together.'

Emily said she would pull herself together, and she did. She threw herself into informing all her mother's friends, and arranged a luncheon at her mother's small flat.

*

Sleepless, watching the dawn through the French doors of her kitchen on the day of the funeral, Emily astonished herself by telephoning Rick Cooke. Even more astonishing to her, perhaps, was that she called collect. She heard him answer the operator's, 'Will you accept the charge?' with, 'Sure. Be happy to.'

'You know what happened?' she asked.

'I'm sorry, Emily. It's terrible... terrible. What a shock! What's happening about...?'

'The tour...' Emily interrupted bitterly. 'The tour? Oh, I'll make it. I've fourteen days to go.'

'I was thinking of putting it back.'

'No need,' Emily said quickly. 'No need. That's not why I phoned you.'

'It's not?'

'No, I wanted to tell *you* that while my mother was dying I was giving that pre-interview. And I'm not going to tell anyone else – I can't.'

'You can't?'

'No, I can't. Because her last words to me were that I was to learn the meaning of "wow".'

'Now wait a minute, wait a minute. You're losing me.'

'You told me that before you'd read *Defending Wives*, the whole thing was merely an assignment. But after you'd read it,

28

it was . . . wow! Then, because of that producer from Cincinatti, we hung up. Now do you remember?'

'You were great. They loved you. That's why you're on the show.'

'Don't you see?' Emily repeated. 'Don't you see? I knew no good would come from having taken advantage of someone else's accident.'

'Emily, I know how you feel. Believe me, I do. And I get the feeling there's something else that's bugging you. You're not loading a guilt-trip on yourself about what happened to your mother, are you?'

'Oh,' Emily said, sobbing. 'I'm sorry, I have hardly been able to cry at all.' She struggled for control.

'Cry, Emily,' Rick answered in that deep and deeply soothing voice of his. 'Cry. It's good for you!'

'I've more control now,' she said. 'You see, I deliberately sent her away with those stupid blouses because I didn't want her to hear me give that pre-interview with that producer. Because it would have hurt her – and embarrassed me. And even worse, I knew I would give a bad interview! I can't lie to myself. I sent her away and I killed her . . .'

'Oh, Emily, you poor, poor girl! It's good for you to say those things. Listen, I'm going to ask you a very personal question. Do you believe in God?'

'I don't know, I think so.'

'If you even think you do, you *do*. Don't you know it's arrogant to blame yourself for an act of God? Listen, I haven't met you but I feel close to you. Don't do this to yourself.'

'I had to tell *you*. I don't know why I don't want to tell Simon, but I don't.'

'So you'll tell him when you feel ready to tell him. Did you get my flowers?'

'Yes. Thank you; I ought to have mentioned . . .'

'It's very, very early in the morning in London, I know that now. Now here's what I want you to do. I want you to go to the bathroom, fill the tub real hot, cover your eyes with a hot face-cloth and be kind to aching muscles.'

'How do you know about my muscles?'

29

'I've been through it. You've got a heavy day, and I'll be thinking of you. You'll go take a tub now? Right?'

'Right.'

It seemed odd to Emily that neither she nor Rick Cooke ever said goodbye. Odd, but somehow unimportant. She felt almost numb; it was not that her tears and weeping had been deliberately held back, but rather blocked and stopped – or perhaps the mechanism of release had been frozen. That the world went on, even that the bath-taps flowed, was something of an affront. Her mother's life seemed to have had no real effect on anyone or anything at all. A worthless struggle, and there was scarcely any comfort in knowing that it had ended painlessly.

Because Emily felt lifeless herself, though far from peaceful.

*

Maps and charts, ribbon-bright, contrasted glaringly against Rick Cooke's otherwise dreary office. He had gone back to empty Coke bottles for his cigarette stubs, but even accumulated filth failed to help him quit.

He had come to believe that little in life could really shake him any more. True, there were, and there would be, shocks as well as surprises – he expected disappointment the way he expected success. He'd eaten shit and made others eat it too. But Emily's phone call had shaken him. A dignified English lady like that – crying on the phone – Jeez, but it was mind-blowing. And yet he felt something for Emily: something deep and authentic and honest, the kind of feeling that was forbidden in his business. Not that feelings were forbidden, though; anger, for example, was all to the good – judiciously expressed, it could also be a powerful weapon. As for compassion, that, like all other irrelevances, could slow things up – and accordingly was outlawed.

Still, what sort of guy was she married to? The poor kid was guilt-stricken over having made her mother return those blouses, yet she couldn't even tell her own husband about it . . .

Compassion confuses, and this was one thing Rick Cooke would not tolerate. Dollars and cents were the most dependable, the most effective really. Also a refuge. Come to think of it, until her phone call he hadn't given as much as a single second to the possibility that Emily Bradshaw might not come. Now that would have been a real bastard...

If Frontier Books refused to pick up the tab for Emily Bradshaw's wardrobe and general reshaping, he had a deal ready for them. He would tell them they could cut back on first class and send her business class, which would fix two things at once – he would have got them to agree to send her business instead of first, and the difference between first and business was twelve hundred dollars, which would go towards his 'Reshape Emily Budget'. He would be utterly, brutally honest. No recycle, no package.

Rick Cooke had learned to trust one thing, and one thing only – his own instincts. Every time he disobeyed his instinct, he went wrong. His notepad, headed 'From the Desk of Rick Cooke', was crowded with air-fare arithmetic. On impulse he scrawled, 'Logic fucks instinct'.

The sound of Emily Bradshaw's voice had got to his instincts. For a moment, though, it seemed that his dreams were even too good for dreaming. But Emily Bradshaw was no dream; Emily Bradshaw was for real. As if to make her concrete, he moved to his typewriter and typed 'Logic fucks instinct' until he had covered half a page. Convinced he was on to something, he snatched the paper from the typewriter, stood up, went to the window, cursed because the fucking thing wouldn't open and sat down again.

He would get there, he would be out there, and when he did he would tell Frontier Books exactly where they could stick all their contracts. Every last one of them, too...

He was on sure ground – that bitch of a producer on the *Virginia Byrnes Show* didn't know it, but she had launched him.

Though Emily Bradshaw dominated Rick Cooke's waking and sleeping moments, neither he nor her books were of the smallest interest to Emily. She was too immersed in guilt. She felt more tied to her mother than she had ever been, which was why she now concentrated on the sort of time-consuming, mind-absorbing, essential details which attend every death.

It turned out that her mother had left definite instructions about a Sussex burial, and a service at the small church of her childhood. Emily made lists frantically, checked each line thoroughly, while those other lists headed 'America' were forgotten. Once she glimpsed one of the pages – for she kept all lists in the same spiral notebook – she turned the page fast and shut the book.

The days sped one into the other: she conferred with some of her mother's friends and placed a death notice in *The Times*. Everyone would have to drive down to the country for the funeral, so Emily felt it only right to invite them all to Lamont Road for a drink. All of this required her concentrated attention . . .

Which, as Simon and Keith agreed over lunch, was a mercy – that, and Danny's violin practice. It seemed nothing could deflect Emily from her dedication to Danny and his violin.

Emily had not mastered a musical instrument, nor even come close. She believed this was because she had never really been taught well enough to coordinate her fingers with what she read on the music sheet. It was three years since she had first seen a two-year-old playing on television and decided on lessons for Danny. She had no gift for music – could not as much as sing in tune – and it was this lack which she was given to describing as one of the greatest sadnesses of her life. Danny had graduated from the simple rhythm of 'Do you want a hot-dog?' and his violin no longer bore the bright yellow Sellotape which indicated where he ought to bow. The concert was only two weeks away, and he was to play the Brahms Lullaby.

*

Throughout, Keith Summers and Rick Cooke were in constant transatlantic touch. Both agreed that nothing at all would be mentioned to Emily until the funeral was over. And even then, they would wait for a day or two. Keith found himself not only following Rick's advice, but agreeing. He was mildly surprised at this, for he would never have predicted that not only would he fail to object when Rick called her a fragile piece of valuable merchandise, but also he would begin to see her this way himself. Books, and not authors, were considered 'hot properties'. Though now of course, thanks to someone's broken leg, things had changed. Keith would wait until the news of Emily broke in the States; Emily and *Defending Wives* would generate more publicity than he would even want to handle. 'Just wait until you start freaking out over all the tear-sheets and videos and tapes,' Rick told him. 'Don't let them see *Defending Wives* until we're ready.'

Keith had the world rights only because no one had judged the book important enough to query the contract. It was one of those wonderful ironies, he thought.

*

'Grief,' as Emily decided to tell Simon, 'ends dismay, cancels disappointment and eliminates delight.'

But she was shocked to discover that trivial emotions went on and on.

The day after the funeral, Emily fell into a dreamless sleep. She believed when she awoke that she had been conscious of herself sleeping even as she slept. Ophelia tended the doorbell and Emily slept through lunch, only waking when Danny was standing beside her holding an enormous cellophane-wrapped bouquet of white roses. Flowers had been arriving all that week, and whenever Danny was home from school he opened them for her. But she seemed to herself inexplicably impatient, so impatient that her fingers trembled and slowed her down. The card simply said: 'Thinking of you and wishing you courage. Please call me collect when you feel ready to talk. Rick Cooke.'

She found herself delighted and rapidly amended this to 'absurdly delighted'. A second bouquet . . . And she felt guilty, and could not stop herself from weeping in Danny's presence. To recover herself, she asked Danny to help her find an empty vase.

Then her father was on the telephone, inviting her to lunch at his club.

Emily had been fourteen when her father left to set up house with Melissa, who at nineteen was five years older than Emily but managed to look the same age. Twenty years on, Melissa still affected the trendiest gear and looked ridiculous. Emily hated her father's old-fashioned, well-cut suits, because when he was with Melissa he looked more like her doting father than her husband, which made Emily positively cringe. Since her marriage, Emily saw her father as seldom as civilized attitudes permit. Their meetings were always stilted and formal and whenever possible, Simon joined then; he diluted the atmosphere and eased Emily's discomfort.

Her father said pointedly, 'I hope, Emily, my dear, that you will grant an hour or two to a private lunch with me?'

'When?'

'Would tomorrow suit?'

'Certainly.'

'The Reform, then, at twelve-thirty.'

Emily had only left the house for a few minutes when she decided to go back and change. Thinking she would wear the royal blue Laura Ashley blouse her mother had bought for her, she remembered she had not paid her for it. What had happened to the other two? She would have to look into it. Had her mother returned them? She would simply have to force herself to go back to the shop and enquire... Though perhaps she would ask Simon.

Standing in the imposing, elaborately Italianate foyer of the Reform, Emily and her father sipped sherry. 'You look peaked,' her father said.

'I think I'm hungry.' This, in the context of their relationship, was a confession of intimate dimensions.

'Oh well, drink up and we'll go in to lunch right away.'

'Good afternoon, Sir Thomas,' the waiter said. 'Your usual table?'

Emily was hardly used to her father being called Sir Thomas. He had been knighted a year before – standard procedure, as Emily now reminded herself, for a senior civil servant, a Permanent Under-Secretary at the Ministry of Transport. She ought to have been proud, and would have been if her father's honour had not also elevated that tart Melissa to Lady Rice. This rankled even more than she had realized and she felt her lips tighten, which her father – who was not as insensitive as she supposed – observed.

'Feeling any better now, Emily, my dear?' he asked tentatively.

'No,' Emily replied. 'Worse, if anything.' She glared.

Sir Thomas sighed. 'You won't believe this, I know... I cared very deeply for your mother. I miss her keenly, keenly. She and...'

'I know,' Emily interrupted. 'Simon told me.'

Emily looked round and managed to catch the head waiter's eye. 'You'd like to order, Sir Thomas?' the waiter said.

'Oh yes,' Emily answered for him.

They settled back to wait for their food and Emily heard herself say, 'The last thing Mother ever did in this world was to buy me this blouse,' and then she blundered on about the three other blouses.

'I'll attend to that for you, Emily my dear. I've plenty of time...'

'No, don't. Don't do that, please! You'll take Melissa with you, and I couldn't bear that. It was a private thing between Mother and me!'

'I won't even tell Melissa. But I feel I must tell you, dear, that your mother didn't hate her.'

'Because she didn't hate anyone. She wasn't the sort who hates, was she?'

'No, she wasn't. She was the finest woman I ever knew.'

'Trifle late to be saying things like that, isn't it?'

'But your mother knew how I felt. I was devoted to her. I was always devoted to her, she never doubted that. The flat was proof, she said.'

'The flat? What about the flat? Tell me. Tell me how Mother's flat proves your devotion.'

'That's simple. I allowed her the use of it.'

'The use of it? But it belonged to her. She bought it and I went with her to choose it. We made dozens of visits before she made up her mind.'

'Your mother may have chosen it, but I paid for it, so of course it belongs to me.'

'I see.'

'I thought you knew. She didn't tell you?'

'Obviously not.'

'It was when you married Simon. She didn't want to live alone in the house after you were married, so we sold it and bought the *pied-à-terre* in Knightsbridge.'

'With the money from the house? But it was *her* house.'

'Half.'

'So you left her and kept half a house?'

'A small flat in Knightsbridge is far more expensive than an entire house in Kingston...'

'I know that,' Emily said irritably. 'That's obvious.'

'The entire contents, needless to say, belong to you. A good deal of awfully good stuff – some silver that belonged to my grandparents. We agreed, you see, that Clara should keep it. Melissa didn't mind.'

'Ah,' Emily said. 'How generous! Most charitable!'

Overcome by a fit of coughing, her father's soup spurted from his mouth. Within seconds the head waiter was at his side, proffering water.

'Emily,' her father went on as if nothing had happened, 'you're a grown woman and a mother yourself. *Do* be adult.'

'I'm sorry,' Emily said. 'I'm making things rather difficult, I know.'

'Perfectly understandable, in the circumstances.'

'I'll try to make things easier. To get to the point, precisely what do you have on your mind? The flat?'

'That's my girl,' her father said, smiling. Emboldened, he repeated, 'That's my girl! I told Melissa you'd understand. She wants me to ask you when you think you'll be ready to let her take over the flat? Start redecorating... do all those sorts of things you women do?'

'I haven't thought about it. I didn't know I would need to.'

'You're about to set off for New York, aren't you?'

'New York? New York? Can't think why I'd forgotten all about that. Can you?'

'Now, Melissa, you agreed to be adult.'

'I'm *not* Melissa, I'm Emily. Kindly do not confuse me with her. Please!'

'Now it's my turn to apologize,' her father said. 'I'm sorry.'

'That's perfectly all right. Tell Melissa I'll sort everything out after New York. I'm afraid I can't imagine how I can do anything before then. Quite honestly, I couldn't face all that just yet, even if I weren't going to America. Do you think she'll mind waiting just a *little* longer?'

Her father flushed.

Emily longed to tell him what a fool he was, what an idiot. Everyone knew Melissa was promiscuous; why, she'd even made passes at Simon! Melissa probably wanted to use her mother's flat as a private convenient love-nest. How revolting!

Parents should have the decency to keep their sex life to themselves. Stop this neurotic thinking, she told herself. Stop it. She would have liked to have been able to tell her father how uncomfortable, even painful, these infrequent restaurant meetings were. A restaurant father, she thought. Thinking out loud, she said suddenly, 'Stop it!'

'Stop what? Don't be rude, my dear. No need for that.'

'I *am* sorry. Do forgive me. I'm not myself; I was thinking out loud.'

'You've been through a hard time. But I'm going to ask you something. Of course, you don't have to answer if you don't want to. You were telling yourself to stop something, weren't you?'

'Yes, I was. I suppose I was telling myself to stop feeling sorry for myself.'

'Sound advice,' her father said, and turned to the subject of Danny's violin lessons, which was safe neutral territory and therefore fairly pleasant. 'I'd like to be at Danny's concert,' he said.

'Would you? Do you think you could bear it? Why?'

'Because you would have had your mother with you.'

'Yes. Please do come.' She leaned towards her father, and for a moment rested her hand on his arm. 'Thank you for that . . .'

Chapter 4

If Emily had been educated in America, she would have been rated a high achiever. But in England her above-average intelligence was attributed to luck rather than achievement, and she was regarded as one of those fortunate enough to be Oxbridge material. For some reason Emily, like many other gifted children of her style and country, perceived this kind of good fortune as undeserved – or more accurately, perhaps, unearned – and therefore as odious as inherited wealth. Educated in that civilized uncompetitive ambience of team spirit and fair play, her academic shine was as embarrassing to her as it was unfair to others. She tried to submerge it, or at least dampen it, but it stubbornly surfaced anyway. So she went to Cambridge and indulged her passion for the metaphysical poets, Donne especially. Emily half hoped that the sheer indulgence of a useless passion would wreak its own kind of havoc, its own brand of recklessness. The whole thing was at odds with her essential pragmatism and she felt schizoid sometimes. It seemed immoral to be enjoying what – in the last analysis – could only be defined as utterly without altruism. She was at that stage when the only acceptable objective was the reduction of real suffering like starvation, oppression and so on.

At any rate, her essay on Donne was published in the scholarly journal, *The Journal of Metaphysical Studies*. And yet she was quite unable to regard anything in her academic life as achievement; it had been too lucky, too self-indulgent to qualify as meaningful. Her only important achievement in her eyes –

apart from having given birth to Danny – was having learned how to drive...

Because handling a steering wheel, handling gears, co-ordinating clutch with accelerator, with indicator, and so extracting obedience from each instrument gave her a sensation of power that she never took for granted. Any other kind of power was altogether outside her grasp and irrelevant to her. If power corrupts, it also soothes. Emily resolved to drive out to Sussex, to the little churchyard where her mother now lay, unguarded even by a gravestone. *That* detail was still to be arranged...

After about fifteen minutes of intense driving, she remembered Danny and the violin and returned to Lamont Road.

*

Simon, it turned out, had been certain that Emily knew the Knightsbridge flat belonged to her father. 'Clara had the *usufruct*,' he explained. 'She thought your father generous, and was grateful. Your father, I'm bound to say, was in fact generous. He had no legal obligation.'

'But you're her sole executor and trustee. It was up to you to tell me.'

'I thought you knew,' he said wearily. 'I've already told you that. You ought to have known, Clara should have told you ...'

'Well, she didn't.'

'Because you and she were above talking about that sort of thing...'

'Not at all; I knew she was hard-up. The last thing she did was to choose a blouse for me. And she was going to talk to my father about it.'

'About her alimony?'

'Of course not.'

'Your mother never had much of a clue about finances. I'm afraid you're just as hopeless as she was in that respect.'

The injustice of this was too much for Emily. Who managed the family budget, made ends meet and was aware of what happened to every penny? Not Simon. But on this she was silent.

Instead, she said, 'You are pompous, Simon. You've always been pompous!'

'Oh, well, if you're going to go on like a ridiculous, hysterical female—'

'My mother didn't tell me about the flat because she couldn't face telling me. You knew about it, so she left it to you. Can't you see that?'

'No, I'm too pompous.'

They fell into one of their rare and accordingly disproportionately horrifying quarrels. To Danny's bewilderment, the rest of the evening was given over to a shared resentful silence.

Once again Emily was beyond tears.

Which was as well, for Simon despised tears. He considered crying to be undisciplined and extravagant.

Hours later, sleepless – almost breathless with the strain of her own unexpressed emotions in the dark, and distraught over what was to become of her mother's exquisite little flat – she rolled toward her sleeping husband. He responded at once, and urgently, which made Emily wonder – but only for a moment – whether he really had been asleep.

Simon's urgent response, combined with Emily's urgent need, resulted in something beyond the range of the statisticians' finite gradings. It was one of those landmark nights of a ten-year marriage, the kind of night which dissolves hurt and despair.

'Did I ever tell you that you are brilliant in bed?' Simon said over their beloved, junk-shop oak table at breakfast.

'Did I ever tell you, Simon?'

They had departed from their usual reticence, their usual decorum, and Emily felt awkward and clumsy.

*

But certain financial truths, sharp as jagged glass, surfaced after the Bradshaws' storm. Simon was a solicitor and, as Emily now realized – and, believe it or not, for the first time – it was only in America that divorce lawyers could expect to make what he called serious money. There was absolutely no possibility, none whatsoever, of Simon claiming a share of a client's settlement.

It was not done, and that was that. Emily supposed that her subconscious belief that her mother was fairly wealthy had led to a mistaken assumption of financial security. Apart from holding on to the Ford Madox-Brown and the Chippendale desk, and even though her advance on *Defending Wives* went on roof repairs, Emily – pragmatic though she was – gave little clear thought to long-range financial expectations.

Well, she was thinking clearly now. She would simply have to adjust to new realities.

Emily took out the neat lists which had been started before her mother's death, forcing herself to concentrate. The memory of the night before was in the stretch of almost every muscle. Well, she amended to herself and smiled, every relevant muscle. It was, after all, the sort of night that a woman is entitled to think about – or, as her mother might have put it, dwell upon. She hated the thought, but it seemed highly likely that her mother's death had freed the last of her sexual inhibitions.

Besides, she felt comforted.

Sometimes, when the need of the bed had been met so perfectly, the need for affection became less cruel.

But she ought to be doing something now. She must have forgotten what it was, but it was something she usually did at this hour. Absently she picked up the telephone and began dialling, then remembered what she usually did at this time: she always telephoned her mother. She stopped dialling, replaced the receiver and returned to her lists.

But it was hopeless; she couldn't concentrate. Recalling the buff envelope which had been delivered by that 'Hell's Angel' type on that fateful afternoon, she decided to study the contents now.

It looked like a travel itinerary to her. Page one was headed *Emily Bradshaw – Defending Wives – First week*. There were airport times, studio times, studio departure times, split-second timing between bookings, between cities.

She had just tried to telephone her dead mother. Still, something else made her anxious. The day she was to 'depart Heathrow 9 a.m.' seemed important. Her hands trembled as she opened her diary and she remonstrated with herself (as she often did): pull yourself together. Pull yourself together. There it was: 'Monday, August 7: Danny's Concert. *Brahms Lullaby*.'

Emily glanced at her watch. The entire morning appeared to have evaporated, because it was now mid-morning, eleven o'clock. Good! Instead of subtracting she counted all the fingers of one hand: five fingers, five hours: six o'clock in the morning in New York. She checked the papers rapidly, then dialled the long-distance operator and, as Rick had instructed, called collect. He had been thoughtful enough to include his home telephone number.

She listened, attentive and grim, while the operator asked if Rick would accept the charges from London, England. Rick sounded sleepy. 'Who is calling?'

'What is your name?' the operator asked. 'New York wants to know.'

'Emily Bradshaw.'

She heard the operator repeating her name and then Rick's voice: 'Emily Bradshaw? I accept with pleasure.'

'Go ahead,' the operator instructed.

'Emily, what's wrong?'

'I can't possibly leave on August the 7th.'

'You can't leave on August 7?' Rick repeated, sounding incredulous. 'Hang up. I'll call you right back. I'm going to take this in another room, OK?'

Emily hung up. She had woken him, she was certain, and disturbed him. Her phone rang at once. 'Are you married?' she asked, and then was altogether taken aback by her own question.

'No . . .' he replied.

'But you weren't alone and I disturbed you. I'm really, really sorry about that.'

Jeez, Rick thought, this lady sees through the fucking telephone. Lorna was still playing games, so he was with someone depressingly *new* again.

'What do you mean? You can't leave London on August 7?'

'I can't possibly.'

August 7 was cutting it fine enough – too fine, Rick thought. He had planned on her taking at least three days to recover from jet-lag, besides the make-up and wardrobe people he had lined up to work on her. To say nothing of the *coaching* he planned. But he forbore from mentioning any of this. The first show, which – just his luck – was a really big one, was on Thursday, 10 August.

'OK, OK,' he said, 'No need to lose your cool. How does August 8 sound to you?'

'Oh, the concert will be over by then.'

'Concert?'

'Danny, my son – he's playing Brahms' Lullaby.'

'August 8 will give us enough time. I don't want you to worry about that now, OK?'

'OK.'

'I'll call you again from the office. As long as you're sure you feel up to it?'

'Thanks, Rick. Thanks for everything.' There could be no doubt but that she really meant what she said. Waves of gratitude washed over her like hope. For some reason that she could not clarify, still less evaluate, she wanted to please Rick Cooke – wanted his approval, wanted him to be proud of her. Because, when he told her not to worry, she did just that.

It was odd.

For the astonishing truth was that each and every transatlantic conversation with Rick Cooke infused her with a benign sense of safety and, above all, of strength, her own strength.

Yes, it was odd. Distinctly odd . . .

For the first time, Emily wondered what Rick Cooke looked like. He was obviously tall and attractive, with a craggy face and deeply etched laugh lines.

Emily had never met a PR, or a publicist or press agent. Nor, for that matter, had she known anyone other than Keith who had met one either. This sort of person, and that sort of world, had no meaning in her own world.

Meanwhile in her own world – the world of Lamont Road, Chelsea – Emily was overtaken by her overwhelming need to plan, prepare and freeze the finest store of meals she could think of.

Now that the departure date had been finalized, she felt free at last to go to the street market where she could choose her vegetables.

At around twelve o'clock she returned. The phone was ringing – probably America again, she thought.

'Hi, Emily,' Rick said. 'Remember me? Wanna know why I'm calling? The good news is that one of our great photographers Sheila Lyall, is... guess where?'

'London?'

'And she's free tomorrow.'

'But I'm in the thick of things...'

'I know you are, don't think I don't know that. I hate to ask you, but Sheila will give you her entire day tomorrow. Do you know what *that* means? Do you know what Sheila *costs*? No, I guess you don't – you'd never even heard of the *Virginia Byrnes Show*!'

'I'm sorry...'

'Aw, forget it! Sheila's done all the greats, from Taylor to Shields. But – wait for it – she's going to fix your image. Clothes, hair, make-up...'

'My mother would have been so pleased,' she said drily. 'So pleased.'

'Sheila will be at your place at 8.30 am.'

'But that's before dawn!'

'I know,' he interrupted. 'Sheila told me, but she won't do it otherwise. You're going to Mr Ivan of Belgravia at 9.45 and they'll work on your make-up. And while all that's going on, Sheila will get to know you. She'll have an idea of your house, where she'll shoot you, what floral decor she'll buy next door to Mr Ivan. See,' he ended triumphantly, 'we're taking care of you over here... I'll call you tomorrow, OK?'

'I...'

'A little warning, though...'

'Warning?'

'You *must* tell her you're honoured, that she's the best thing that ever happened to you. Got it?'

'I got it.'

'I *knew* you would! It'll be a great experience. I'll call you tomorrow, OK?'

The phone disconnected.

Emily confronted her vegetables and began with the onions. How could she have chosen such limp and lifeless specimens? She considered returning them, but at once rejected the idea. Like all efficient housewives, Emily was flexible; therefore she could get away with onion soup, which would freeze just as well as onion tart.

Immersed in what she always called the therapy of pots and pans, she successfully deferred for the moment her entire future.

*

The doorbell rang.

Emily slipped off her apron and went to answer it. Susan Waddington, Danny's violin teacher, was standing on the doorstep holding a large cake-box. 'I'm sorry to disturb you, Mrs Bradshaw,' Susan said. 'I brought Danny's prize – it's a chocolate cake.'

'Of course you're not disturbing me,' Emily said warmly. 'Danny's thrilled to bits about his prize. And you baked it yourself, I know. Won't you please come in and have a cup of coffee with me?'

'Well, if you're sure—'

'I'd be delighted,' Emily said, as she took the box from Susan. 'To tell the truth, I could do with some company.'

'I was so sorry to hear about your mother.'

'It was a terrible shock.'

While Emily went to make the coffee, Susan studied the drawing room. One of her favourite games was predicting how the parents of her small pupils had decorated their homes, and she enjoyed testing how accurate she had been. She took in the room with one sweeping glance, from the soft, shabby chintzes to the one obviously valuable piece like the Chippendale desk, and concluded that she had guessed correctly. Some of her pupils were actually banned from the drawing room, but she had known that Danny was not one of those.

'What a lovely room,' Susan said enthusiastically when Emily returned. 'No wonder Danny's such a happy child.'

'Thank you; he is a cheerful chap.' Emily's face fell suddenly. 'To think he has to go away to school only next year.'

'Which one?' Susan asked sympathetically.

'Trevor-Winston School. His father and his grandfather went there. Cold showers every morning!' Emily shuddered. 'Danny's such a sensitive child – too sensitive, his father says.'

Suddenly Emily realized that she was pleased to have some company, even if it came from a woman she hardly knew. Susan talked about the rewards of teaching small children, and of encouraging in them a working knowledge of music. Emily guessed that though she and Susan were probably the same age, Susan's pony-tail and tight jeans made her look much younger. The music teacher was slim, almost boyish, and just as Emily was thinking that she hadn't had children, Susan declared how much she would like to have a family one day, only things hadn't worked out – she had never married and her biological clock kept ticking away...

Emily never felt comfortable when childless women mentioned their childlessness. It saddened her. She murmured a few encouraging remarks about several women she knew who had given birth to their first child when they were well over thirty-five. Then, more to change the subject than out of any real wish to discuss her forthcoming book tour of the United States, she said, 'I suppose Danny told you that I am going to America to promote my book?'

'Aren't you nervous?' Susan asked in her musical voice.

'It would be much worse if I knew people over there.'

'Oh? How do you mean?' Susan was thinking how nervous her concerts always made her, whether she knew anyone in the audience or not.

'I would be terribly embarrassed if I thought anyone I knew might see me. I couldn't do it then.' Emily paused to sip her coffee. 'You see, if no one knows me, I'll be doing whatever I have to do in private. People who know you are bound to be critical of you,' she went on slowly. 'But I'll be anonymous, you see. And Simon—' Emily stopped herself from continuing.

After Susan had left, Emily returned to the kitchen. It was always a good place for thinking. Susan's extravagantly tall chocolate cake looked delicious and she couldn't resist tasting a sliver of the icing. She must ask for the recipe.

Her thoughts returned to what she had stopped herself from

46

saying. For she had come dangerously close to revealing that in a way she was more nervous of Simon that she was of anyone. This was not something she liked to admit to herself, but she was sure that if this promotion was going on in London, Simon would have made fun of her, or else found some way to put her down. Simon was like that – he considered all publicity to be not only immodest, but vulgar. The legal profession was now permitted to advertise, but he was as much opposed to that as he was to all departures from tradition. And yet, now that she was being honest with herself, she was certain that though he had encouraged her to go on the US tour, he would have positively forbidden such a promotion in England.

As far as Simon was concerned, an American tour didn't really count. Simon probably hated Americans, Emily thought, because that was traditional too. She wished Simon was not quite so rigid.

Sometimes, Simon mistook sarcasm for irony, which was why – when the subject came up – he loved to disagree that America had sold its soul to materialism. America, he would say, has no soul to sell.

Emily thought of Rick Cooke – if anyone had disproved Simon's theories of American soullessness, that person was Rick Cooke.

She put the apple pie in the oven and sat down to write a formal note of thanks to Susan. It occurred to her that Susan had not asked what the book was about and perhaps she was just being polite. But it seemed more likely that she was involved with a married man. After all, that was what *Defending Wives* was all about.

Susan looked boyish, but then her make-up was so discreet that few men would have guessed that she was wearing any. She must be an amazingly kind and generous person, Emily thought, to have baked that cake. So why, she asked herself, did she have the feeling that Susan was not *quite* as kind as she seemed?

Emily shrugged, impatient with herself. For all that she was not the suspicious kind, she could not rid herself of the feeling that Susan Waddington was capable of being ruthlessly unkind.

*

Smoke from two cigarettes furled about Rick, and he realized he must have been smoking both at the same time. Shit, if only he could kick the habit. He'd wait until after Emily's tour. She, of course, had no idea of the kind of negotiations which had been going on even to begin to get her tour off the ground. Without Rick Cooke, she would not have had a snowball's chance in hell. When he had got the news that the *Sixty Seductive Salads from Fifty-One States* tour was cancelled, why had he immediately come up with *Defending Wives*? Because he'd done his homework, that's why. Because he read Frontier's goddamn catalogue and there, in a 'nothing' corner, he chanced to see her book.

Here's this gal, Sheila Lyall. Only one of the biggest names in the States, so naturally Emily's never *heard* of her! He felt miffed, almost bitter, because Emily was no more aware of what being photographed – and dressed – by Sheila Lyall could *do* for her, than she was aware of what the *Virginia Byrnes Show* meant. And none of this was costing her a fucking dime, either. Still, it was a coup to have got Sheila Lyall. Why, just to track down which photographer might at this time just happen to be in London, he'd had to turn into a fucking sleuth. And to think: if Lorna hadn't still been playing her games, and he hadn't gone to that new singles bar where he met Cindy who just happened to work at Cosmo – and if he hadn't asked a few idle questions – he would never have known.

But Rick was honest enough to admit to himself that this sort of thing was the name of the game which added momentum to his business. It set his juices running, made the adrenaline curdle and revitalized his instinct.

Shit, but he'd been following that instinct all the way. But all the way . . .

Chapter 5

'Hi, Emily, this is Sheila Lyall. I had to wake you to tell you that I'll be at your place at 8 a.m. and not 8.30. It's a heavy programme and if we start out thirty minutes sooner, we have a better chance of making it.' The hoarse baritone voice was businesslike yet impatient. It recalled Emily's distant but still dreaded gym-mistress, Miss Fordyce. A long-forgotten reflex was activated and Emily immediately sat up straight. (*Now then, Emily Thomas, sit up straight at once. This minute...*)

Emily said, 'I'll be on the pavement, waiting for you, at precisely eight o'clock.'

'Hold it, hold it!' Sheila sounded curt. 'I gotta examine your pad. Then check out the appropriate floral decor...'

'I see,' Emily said. 'Will you have time for a coffee?'

'Sure I will. See you!'

Emily turned to Simon. 'Americans never say goodbye,' she said. 'They cut out instead.'

The Bradshaws gave themselves up to a few extra, deliciously shared sleepy moments.

Because the freezing had gone well. *Boeuf en Daube,* Lasagne, *Poulet à la Provençale, Ragoût de Mouton,* as well as Onion Soup, *Ratatouille, Crêpes d'Épinards Gratinées,* even *Compote de Poire au Vin Rouge* – all clearly labelled with simple and precise instructions, these dishes were now stacked in perfect symmetry on the freezer shelves. Effective as a confession, the freezer and its contents eased her conscience about leaving Simon and Danny.

Last night – almost, *almost* pleased with herself – she had felt relaxed, expansive and particularly sexy. For his part Simon, though distinctly puzzled by his wife's unusually brazen ardour, was more than ordinarily masterful. Perhaps it was this feeling of challenge – Emily had never been quite so passionate – which gave him extra power that night. For the Bradshaws, two nights running was pretty exceptional. Whatever it was, though, barriers seemed to break, to move, to dissolve. Which explains why Sheila Lyall's phone call had roused them from an extraordinarily necessary sleep.

'Quite a night, Em,' Simon murmured. 'With one's own wife of ten years. Quite something, wouldn't you say?'

'Oh! Absolutely. Absolutely! You are incredible – I need to sleep for at least six more hours . . .'

'We'll have to get on, or we'll be late,' Simon said. 'Tell you what, Em, stay in bed for once and I'll see to breakfast.'

But Emily had no intention of staying in bed. Blessing Simon for his unusual offer to make the coffee, she leapt out and by the time the coffee was ready had already taken a quick bath and made the bed.

For it had suddenly occurred to her that Sheila Lyall might want to inspect her entire house. This was not as terrible as it might have been, because the Bradshaws were a tidy couple. For all that, a quick Hoovering of the drawing room and the bedroom carpets would not go amiss.

Sheila Lyall arrived ten minutes early, which was what Emily with uncanny accuracy had predicted, though for reasons that she could not possibly have identified.

However accurate her instincts, Emily was quite unprepared for either Sheila's size or her style. Even without her higher-than-high heels, Sheila Lyall would have been frighteningly tall and Emily felt herself shrivel. An up-to-the-minute scarlet duvet of a coat was flung over Sheila's shoulders, but as soon as she had crossed the threshold it was flung off. Slim but bosomy, her workmanlike black silk dungarees emphasized her curves. She had fashioned a scarlet and black scarf into a turban; both the scarlet and the black matched the coat exactly, Emily noticed.

'I made it!' Sheila said. 'Not a minute late.'

'With time to spare,' Emily replied. 'Fortunately the coffee is ready. It's in the drawing room.'

'I planned on starting out in the kitchen.'

Emily fetched the coffee tray at once.

'I prefer milk. You wouldn't have any Gitanes, would you? I'm clean out of them.'

'We don't smoke, but I just happen to have a packet. Someone left them here by mistake.'

Sheila puffed hungrily. She drained her milk in a single gulp while Emily wondered if she ought to offer something stronger. 'It's Stendhal today,' she said.

'Oh,' Emily said, 'Of course, make-up and all that.'

'No, goddamn it, *Le Rouge et Le Noir*.'

'Rouge? Make-up...'

'I thought you were a writer. Stendhal, you know, the French novelist!'

'How stupid of me.'

'Great stuff, Stendhal: "A novel," he said, "is a mirror walking along a main road." Maybe you never heard those words?'

'Well, I...'

'That's OK,' Sheila interrupted. 'Those words will stay with you for ever, and you will recall them again and again. Like today. Today is the day we remake your mirror.'

'Oh...'

'I see your bones are OK. Well, you're in my hands, I guess. With these hands stars have been made! Look at them.'

'They are lovely,' Emily said firmly. 'Fascinating rings.'

'Made to my own design. This one, for example, is a python's tooth set in ebony. This,' she went on, pointing dramatically, 'this is an Egyptian scarab, an antiquity. Here you see priceless jade. Gifts, tokens, call them what you will, all given as homage to these hands.'

Emily sat back. Everything about the woman, from her baritone to her jewels to her height, was bizarre enough to eliminate any embarrassment she might otherwise have felt.

Light touches turned Emily's head this way and that. 'I know exactly what I'll do,' Sheila said. 'Let me see your living room.'

Emily led the way.

'Cute house,' Sheila pronounced, 'but antiquated. Drab, dark beiges, dark browns. Built when?'

'About ninety years ago.'

'So recent? It seems older – architecture reminds me of Lutyens. Easy enough to check that out ... So what we need is colour, right? Burgundy sepia, burnt-orange. Bright ... Azaleas, cyclamen, geraniums in pots – I know exactly where to get those. Fresh flowers – roses, scarlet shaded down to baby pink, I think. I'll pick up some cushions. Ready? The car's waiting. Your puppy's darling. We'll use him – it is him, isn't it?'

Emily raced upstairs. Simon and Danny were about to go down to breakfast and Ophelia's kitchen dissonance clattered in Emily's ears. 'The woman's mad,' she said to Simon. 'Mad! I don't know how I'll get through the day ...'

*

A glittering Jaguar and an equally glittering chauffeur waited for Emily. Sheila and an assortment of cameras were on the back seat. Sheila snapped a camera case shut and Emily thought she caught the glitter of a flask. At eight in the morning? Impossible!

At Ivan of Belgravia, Mr Ivan, noted for his superior taste in all things and even for his superior knowledge in politics – so many of his clients were among the politically powerful – was going to attend to Emily himself. To anyone as unused to the professional world of beauty as Emily, Ivan of Belgravia was more frightening than exciting. The minimalist decor of the place made her gasp. Except for the glittering blue basins and the softly playing fountains made of Bristol blue glass, everything – the floors, the ceilings, the leather armchairs, even the uniforms of the hairdressers – was such a dazzling white that for a moment it seemed to Emily that Ivan had invented a new colour. Theatre-like lights illuminated the salon and the entire decor, and the people in it, were reflected in floor-to-ceiling mirrors.

'She's great material,' Sheila said to Mr Ivan.

'We'll see what we can do,' he murmured noncommittally,

while an assistant helped Emily into a white taffeta gown.

The scent of peaches wafted over and without thinking, Emily said aloud, questioningly, 'Peaches?'

'Shampoo,' Mr Ivan said airily. 'We only use fruit shampoos.' Their eyes met in the mirror as he raised a clump of hair and let it fall. 'Snipping away at your hair yourself,' he said disdainfully.

'Get rid of that fringe,' Sheila commanded. 'She's got a great forehead going for her.'

'Leave Madam to me, will you?' Mr Ivan snarled. 'I don't tell you how to take snaps, do I?' He cocked his head as he held up and caressed another fistful of hair. 'You can come and get her in another three hours,' he said dismissively, turning to Emily. 'You have beautiful thick luscious hair. It deserves to have justice done to it.' He addressed his assistant. 'Tell Carole I want her up here – and be quick about it!' He picked up his comb and gently passed it through Emily's hair. 'Don't worry, my dear,' he said reassuringly. 'If you don't like it, you can always change it. Carole's our best colourist.'

Mr Ivan spent some time instructing Carole and then Emily was whisked downstairs to another department where her white gown was exchanged for a blue one. The smell of chemicals was so strong that it burned her nose and almost before she knew it, an evil-looking black fluid was being applied all over her head with a brush that reminded her of a pastry brush. 'I'll be back in fifteen minutes to shampoo you,' Carole said. 'Would you like some magazines – *Vogue, Harpers, Cosmoplitan*?'

Emily shook her head, her heart pounding. She was so nervous that she was sure the alphabet itself would be hieroglyphics to her. Mr Ivan had said it could be changed and she hoped this was true, but her doubts mounted rapidly. Carole returned for an inspection and painted Emily's head once more. 'Five more minutes,' she said. 'It didn't take as quickly as I thought it would.'

The stuff was beginning to burn and to itch. At last soothing warm water was being sprayed over her head; then a sparkling white towel was deftly twisted in a turban and she was led back to her earlier seat.

When the turban was removed, Emily gasped in horror. Her hair was pitch-black and she looked like a witch – or Lady Macbeth. And because she wanted to scream, she was afraid to speak.

Now Carole picked up a strand of hair, threaded the handle of the comb through it carefully as if she were sewing, and then held the strand and the comb in place with one hand, while the other quickly painted it with a mauvish foaming substance. Emily shut her eyes to hold back the tears that threatened to humiliate her even further. She felt her hair being tugged, and rapidly opened her eyes. The strand of painted hair that Carole had been working on was now wrapped and sealed into a square of tin-foil.

Emily's voice trembled. 'Tin-foil?' she said.

'It has to cook. The foil raises the temperature.'

'I see,' Emily murmured. She should never have let herself in for this, she thought wildly. She should have insisted on knowing what Mr Ivan had in mind. It was torture; inside that tight tin-foil package, every hair follicle screamed. She saw the same thing was being done to another woman, who was having a pedicure at the same time. The woman's bracelets jangled. Emily was nothing like that woman, nor did she ever want to be. She opened her handbag and took out a handkerchief, crying quite openly now.

'It's the chemicals,' Carole said sympathetically. 'They do that to some people. Jane will do your manicure now.'

Emily sighed and submitted to the first manicure of her life. 'Cool pink, Mr Ivan told me,' the manicurist said, holding up a bottle of nail varnish.

Almost an hour later, Emily was conducted back to Mr Ivan. At this point she believed her hair looked like the prep-school tie that Danny would have to wear – black and gold stripes.

'Bend your head down,' Mr Ivan instructed, swinging her chair around. 'Over your knees, that's right.' He reached up for his scissors which were suspended from the ceiling. She knew her hair was being cut, but there was no sound of a snip.

Emily sat up, but kept her eyes tightly shut. She couldn't bear to see what was going on, and anyway it was too late for tears.

'Tired?' Mr Ivan murmured.

Emily nodded.

She didn't see him reach up for his blow-dryer. He worked silently, the drier moving like a bow over a violin. At last he said, 'You can open your eyes now. We're all finished, all finished.'

Emily opened her eyes and gasped. Illuminated with prisms of light, her hair sparkled and she could see at once that it had been made blacker so as to make the golden lights appear brighter. Her hair not only felt lustrous – it was the sort people longed to touch. Emily put up her hands to it and then trailed her fingers through, marvelling at how unbelievably silky it was.

'Sexy,' Sheila, who had just arrived, pronounced. 'Streaky and sexy. Your re-made mirror, remember? Wait till Mr Lawrence is through with you.'

'I can't begin to thank you, Mr Ivan,' Emily said warmly.

'Your hair is a gift,' Mr Ivan said, smiling. 'Not like those miserable heads I could mention who want to walk out of here looking ten years younger, and five years better.'

*

Back in the car again, Sheila telephoned yet another florist. She had bought everything except the orchid plants. Emily gaped at the telephone, but kept silent, concentrating instead on her newly manicured shell-pink nails. Not her style, but unimportant. Her hair, however, appeared not only to have acquired a new sweep but a new depth.

Sheila completed her phone call, lightly gathered a clump of Emily's brand-new hair and said, 'I bet you didn't know you had hair like this, did you? Now you look like you've got a mane.'

Another consultation followed, but this time in Bond Street where Mr Lawrence stood ready to wreak his particular wonders. Emily lay on the dazzling white couch, on the softest whitest towels she had ever seen. She did as she was told, kept her eyes closed and only opened them according to instructions. Eyebrows were tweezered into a wider sweep. Creams and colour were blended, worked into her skin. The subtle delicacy Mr Lawrence's fingers evoked was so soothing that she fell asleep for at least ten minutes, and but for the application of mascara and the need to open her eyes, would have slept on. As it was, she was unaware of the glueing of 'permanent' false eyelashes.

She felt half-anaesthetized, exactly the way she had felt after a pre-med before some minor gynaecological surgery. Indeed, it would not be too much to say that she half believed she was in an operating theatre; the towels, the lights, the surgically shaped couch, all were reminiscent of a hospital. The smell, too, because the tweezering had been preceded by application of an antiseptic surgical spirit.

And all the while the mirror was beyond her range of vision. She longed to snatch a glance at herself – at her eyebrows particularly. Emerging from her quasi-anaesthetic, a restless anxiety overtook her and she asked abruptly, 'Nearly finished?'

'You *have* been a good girl,' Mr Lawrence said. 'Five more minutes, and we'll give you a mirror!'

Emily almost trembled with irritation. And impatience. And curiosity. And more than a little anxiety. Her heart raced. Like a submissive patient, she said 'Is it almost over?'

'Sit up,' Mr Lawrence said. 'We'll give you a mirror.'

She sat up.

She looked in the mirror. She gasped ... and gasped again. She said, 'You *have* remade my mirror! Sheila said you would.'

'That's what we're here for, Mrs Bradshaw,' Mr Lawrence squealed. 'We don't always get such a fabulous result. Bones count, you see. I only enhance what is there, darling ... Not everyone has superior bones!'

Emily took up the mirror again and without embarrassment studied her own reflection. Her entire being was focused on that mirror. She was utterly unselfconscious, because she stared at that woman in the mirror in the way we stare at someone we know but cannot quite recognize. The blatantly beautiful woman stared back, steadfast though faintly enigmatic. The bones were there all right – prominent, strong and aristocratic. The skin glowed. But it was those eyes which drew – and then arrested – her attention. Those glittering sky eyes, wide and soft, projected an atmosphere of touching sensuality.

'Does madam approve?' Mr Lawrence asked sarcastically.

Emily dragged her attention from the mirror. 'I'm not sure,' she said seriously. 'Not at all sure. You made her beautiful, I admit.' It was clear that she was thinking out loud. 'Very beautiful. But a stranger, no one I know.' Then she brightened perceptibly. 'Of course, I couldn't do this for myself. It's just for today. For Sheila.'

Pointedly, Mr Lawrence drew off her surgical gown. 'You'll be back – for lessons. I'll underwrite that any time, darling.'

Emily was the shy, self-effacing kind for whom any embarrassment – however small, however private – is received as a major humiliation. And yet instead of being crushed, she now felt only slightly foolish. Her reaction was as new and as unexpected as her reflection. 'It's only temporary,' she repeated. 'A temporary change. For today.' Sensing Mr Lawrence's pique, she resorted to her impeccable manners. 'I am so grateful to you, Mr Lawrence,' she added. 'Most grateful.'

'Here's your photographer,' he said somewhat unnecessarily. Four camers swung from Sheila's neck, but the clank of her bracelets and the rapid click of her heels would have been quite enough to announce her arrival. 'Great job, Lawrence,' she said. '*Chapeau!*' She turned to Emily. 'They've got sandwiches waiting for you.'

'Ah ...' said Mr Lawrence approvingly. 'You're going to my almost namesake, St Laurent.'

As far as Emily was concerned, the next hour passed in a whirl of drifting space. Dresses on, dresses off ... and on again. An electric blue velvet dress with a wide purple taffeta sash caught Emily's eye and in spite of herself, she said, 'I love this!'

'Try it on if you like,' Sheila said impatiently. 'But you can't have blue; we can't trust blue on camera.'

Emily blushed, but put on the dress anyway.

'Doesn't do a thing for you, darling,' Sheila stated. 'Put this one on again,' she said commandingly. 'This sea-coral silk is really something. Lagerfeld genius, I guess. Then walk in it, then tell me how you feel.'

Emily walked out of the fitting room and stood in front of the mirror. 'It feels wonderful,' she said enthusiastically. 'Absolutely super!'

'Thought it would. You're a designer's dream, do you know that?' Sheila said – a little enviously, Emily thought.

Over the flowing coral silk, the low-slung belt embraced her hipline as snugly as a holster. Emily crossed the room with a long stride, her shoulders erect. Sheila watched with a professional eye, her mind racing. Sure, Lagerfeld padded his shoulders, but it was clear to Sheila that Emily's own broad shoulders had long pre-dated Komalo's gift to fashion. Her slender waist could easily be circled by two hands. Her hips swung forward naturally, Sheila noted, while her taut and concave belly and her firm high breasts meant that there would be no worry about underpinnings.

'Walk to the doorway,' Sheila ordered. 'I need to check the way the back falls. You've got to look like a million dollars.'

As Emily walked back, Sheila observed that she was already walking with something like the assurance of a top model – incredible what a perfect creation can do for a perfect figure! It was those hipbones of hers that were the secret, they protruded slightly. For as Sheila judged it, there wasn't a single vulgar extra inch anywhere. 'You'll catch the eye of the camera, even if it isn't focused directly on you,' she said. 'We'll have that dress!'

Sheila chose a silk coral shirt and a burgundy gabardine skirt, warm and ripe but not scarlet. 'You're the opposite of a scarlet woman, Emily,' she laughed.

'Oh, isn't this blouse sweet?' Emily said, holding up a classic navy-blue blouse.

'"Sweet" does not cross the Atlantic, Emily,' Sheila said scornfully. 'Now, if you'd written a book about blueberry muffins...' she went on, grabbing a burgundy satin blouse out of the saleswoman's arms. 'Divine. Put it on, Emily!'

When the clothes were handed to Sheila's chauffeur, Emily felt like an onlooker, as if all of this had nothing to do with her. She was following the chauffeur when Sheila called out, 'I still have to accessorize you.'

They went up Bond Street to Louws, where Sheila quickly

chose sinuously soft sea-coral pumps and a matching clutch bag.

'You're not wearing those graduated pearls of yours!' she shrieked. 'This long crystal and gold necklace is perfect.'

'I never wear fake jewellery,' Emily protested.

'You do now. I'm taking you away from your antique Laura Ashley look. Here, try this,' and she slipped a heavy gilt and crystal bangle over Emily's wrist.

'But it feels like handcuffs!'

'So what?' Sheila grinned. 'Fake Chanel, but who cares? It looks great.'

In the car on the way back to Emily's house, Sheila said, 'You're a photographer's dream. Every self-respecting photographer would sooner pick a model up off the street than get one through an agency.'

*

At Lamont Road, cords and lights seemed everywhere. A harassed but obviously exhilarated Ophelia was carrying mugs of coffee to two men who stood smoking in the kitchen. White umbrellas opened wide, looking as if they were in midflight because they were attached to high stands, and white lights had transformed the house into a temporary photographic studio, or a movie set. Or so it seemed to Emily. Because the kitchen was a florist, a fruiterer. Scarlet apples shone in a strange transparent bowl, a string of onions hung from the ceiling, carrots and red peppers were in a suspended basket, and a copper jug held coral, scarlet and pink roses in full bloom – yet all looked as if they had long been in harmonious and permanent residence.

'Let's check upstairs,' Sheila suggested, leading the way. 'Surprised, huh? What do you think I've been doing all morning?'

The drawing room, too, had been transformed. More lights, more umbrellas, and roses everywhere; some in highly glazed plum-coloured vases, others in baskets. A collection of burgundy Chinese baskets lay on the coffee table.

'It will photograph well,' Sheila said. 'You'll see.'

She turned to the chauffeur who had followed her, but clearly did not know why. The clothes were draped over his arm and he

59

might have been a clothes rail. Emily took the burgundy silk shirt and said, 'Perfect.' It was only then that she noticed a collection of ten small cushions, all ranged in the colour of a ripening strawberry. She said, 'Strawberry . . .'

'Ah, so you got it. I wondered if you would.'

'Amazing,' Emily murmured. 'Amazing.'

'Get ready,' Sheila instructed, 'and we'll start shooting. We're running late as it is! We'll begin in the kitchen.'

The house was quiet when Emily came downstairs. Sheila worked with her cameras: Leicas, Emily noted, and noted also – raising her new eyebrows – that she had been right about the flask so early in the morning. She wore the silky coral shirt and the burgundy skirt and felt good. It had taken quite an effort of will, though, to get herself away from the mirror.

'You look good, Emily,' Sheila said.

'Thanks.'

'Lights are wrong, but that's OK. I'll solve that one.' Sheila attended to her cameras. Then, 'Now, if you'll sit there – with the apples just so . . . OK? I sent that girl of yours away. She says you call her Ophelia.'

Once again Emily did as she was told. An excitement pervaded the kitchen, but there was nothing jittery about it. Rather, Emily felt only mildly nervous as if she were about to serve an aromatic new dish. Click-click-click went the camera Click-click-click went Sheila's high heels. Suddenly she thrust a rose into Emily's hand. 'There now, raise both your arms, right hand over left on top of your head. Hold it! Hold it! Hold it! OK. Drop them. Great, great, great!'

It was an hour before they ascended the stairs to the drawing room. Sheila still wore her scarlet and black head-scarf, but her exertions with the camera had loosened it and now a scraggly grey plait straggled down her back. Droplets of sweat gleamed on her upper lip. 'OK, now we'll have you on that couch. I want your legs, but not your shoes. So – you'll recline without them. Right?'

'Right.'

'Hold it. Your make-up needs fixing.'

Emily was astonished to see Sheila open a make-up case –

bottles, brushes arranged with a surgeon's precision. Once more, Emily complied. Leaving the eyes to the last, Sheila applied blusher and lipstick. 'Take a rest,' she said, sitting down firmly beside Emily herself. 'Lie back, rest your head back on me, and I'll work on the eyes. You're zonked.'

Yet again Emily submitted. 'I think I'm too tired to know I'm tired,' she murmured. 'This feels better.' Her head against Sheila's breasts felt comfortable, supported, soothed, almost renewed. They had worked well together, Emily thought, cooperating, even colluding. Except for her mother, it was years since Emily had worked in such close proximity with anyone, and the kind of friendship that springs up between colleagues was almost unknown to her. Before the real camera work had begun, Sheila's forcefulness had unsettled not to say unnerved her. But now, with her head resting so comfortably against those soft breasts, wellings of longing arose for her mother – even of hope for a substitute – for that safe, trusted mother-love, for those sweat beadlets on her upper lip especially.

Sheila said, 'Open up your eyes. Look up,' then 'OK, shut them.'

As Sheila's fingers trailed along Emily's brow, these long fingers with their hideous rings floated her into a further state of sleepy bliss. A strange feeling of physical delight stole over her. Her skin felt peaceful, so peaceful; peace seemed to reach every pore, every cell. It was like being in her mother's arms again. She wondered if perhaps this was what meditation felt like, and a moment later gave way to the heightened sensation of thoughtlessness, of thought suspended ... which perhaps explains why she failed to connect with her awareness of a subtly insistent, increasing pressure from Sheila's arm against her own breasts.

All the while, Emily's eyes were shut tight – sealed in pleasure. So she did not know that her own face was all but covered by Sheila's face. Then something – but what? – was pressing hard against her chin, her nose, her mouth. Then inside her mouth. A hard thick ... She recognized it. A tongue. A crazed tongue! Like skin retreating from a burn, Emily reacted. She was being attacked! Extra strength came to her and she forced the face away, but she was not strong enough for it returned at once. She heard the rip of silk, felt the pain of nails, squeezing nails biting into her breasts – and then, and only because Sheila's arm no longer pinned her down, she grabbed and pulled on Sheila's long plait. Sheila screamed.

Emily struggled and managed to leap free. In a flash Sheila was up and shaking her shoulders. 'You bitch!' she screamed. 'You fucking bitch whore. You led me on. I'll teach you!' She released Emily and took a step back.

Too shocked to move, shocked speechless in a way that later – for the rest of her life – she would never be able to fully comprehend, Emily stayed wide-eyed where she stood. 'Think you'll get away with this, bitch!' A face slap punctuated each word. Then Emily flew up the stairs into the bathroom and locked the door. Sheila followed, but was too late.

'I'll get you!' Sheila screamed.

The sound of the door rattling triggered Emily's memory and she remembered the panic button. She pressed it. The siren, the merciful siren, tolled through the house. 'Get out!' Emily shouted. 'Get out before the police come. That siren rings simultaneously in the police station.'

But the siren was not connected to the police station; it had been designed only to scare off an intruder. 'You'll be arrested, Sheila. Get out! In England the police are obliged to use handcuffs and they'll take you away. Get out while you can.'

The click-click of Sheila's heels was somewhat muffled by the carpet, but Emily thought she heard the front door slam. Even so, it was a while before she ventured out of the bathroom to check.

It was at least five minutes before she switched the siren off. Sirens often sounded in Lamont Road – mechanical faults, mistakes and the like.

She heard Ophelia return.

Emily changed into a dressing gown, then she checked the locks on all the doors. She heard Ophelia clattering in her basement room and called out, 'They'll be collecting all their lights and things, Ophelia. Let them in for me, will you?'

Something would have to be done about her face – her

aching, scarlet, swollen face. But what? Just what *does* one do with a battered face? Especially when one wants to keep the whole thing quiet.

Ah, *The Encyclopaedia of First Aid* would come to her rescue. In the context of poisoning, fractures and heart attacks, it seemed that beating, bruising and black eyes were unimportant. Why else would they have been excluded? She turned to *The Mother's Medical Dictionary*, but with the same result. There must be a remedy besides raw steak. But there was no steak in her freezer. The freezer? Her memory jogged to attention. Simon, alternative medicine, acupuncturist, treatment... 'Treatment will be helped by a pea poultice. Take a large pack of frozen peas and you will have a ready-made flexible ice poultice, that is easy to apply...' Of course, and though they never knew why, Simon had been helped.

Emily fetched the peas, took the phone off the hook and lay down. She was certain of only one thing. No one must ever know how near she had come to being raped by a woman. For all she knew... perhaps she... Such thoughts could not be completed, she dared not complete them. It was more than enough as it was. Because of those soft breasts. She had not known soft breasts could be so wonderful, so compellingly *soft*.

But her face! How would she, how could she explain her face? Her mind darted, revolved – it was all because she had taken advantage of someone else's accident, she had not even bothered to find out the name of the author of the cookbook. But an explanation for her face was beginning to form. Mr Lawrence... she was allergic to all that make-up. Allergies make one swell, make one redden. But a black eye? Black *eyes*? Eyelash dye. Of course, spilt eyelash dye! She would mask all the damage in a plaster of her own make-up. Her right eye itched, so she removed the pea-poultice and went to the mirror to look. And that was how she first knew about the false eyelashes. The ice-cold pack of peas had disturbed the glue and dislodged the eyelashes of the right eye. To think she had thought those lustrous long eyelashes were her own, as if Mr Lawrence's magic had made them grow. Emily laughed out loud.

*

Sheila Lyall burned. She had abandoned her cameras, left them in that house, beating it out of there and not stopping even to grab her exposed film. Her purse and coat, too. Because she had been booted out like a common thief. The police yet! God, why had she sent that chauffeur away? Now she needed a cab – but not as much as she needed a phone. She saw a phone booth and went inside but the smell of wine, of stagnant bad breath, made her nauseous. Goddamn it, she needed a drink! The phone worked and she was angrily grateful for that. Soon she was saying , 'Put my assistant on ... James, get your fucking ass right over to Lamont Road. Pick up my cameras. Yup – you heard right. My cameras, goddamn it! You can take that cunt of an assistant of yours to go get the rest of the stuff. Bring the cameras and the film. Don't forget the *film*, you bleary-eyed idiot! I want it at the Chesterfield immediately.' She slammed down the receiver, raised her hand, saw a taxi with its sign up, put her fingers between her lips and produced the piercing whistle she had learned from her brothers that long-ago summer on the Cape. It worked and the taxi screeched to a halt. 'Where to, Madam?' the driver asked. As soon as the taxi moved, she gave the finger sign to some of the people who had stopped to stare. Right now she needed a drink.

'The bell captain will pay you,' she said to the driver as she flew out of the taxi.

She barked an instruction to the unhappy porter, snatched a scarlet apple from the magnificent bowl in the hall and made her way to her room. She had no intention of eating an apple or anything else – she took it because it looked so good.

She needed that drink!

In her hurry to get it, she had forgotten to stop for the key. Frustration ran through her and she rattled the door; the noise attracted a maid, who let her in. The vodka was there, it hadn't gone! She drank her fill and felt better.

She really liked this Mayfair hotel. The bell captain would take care of the cab-driver without first checking with her; the hotel was one of the few places in London that met her standards. A pile of messages lay on her desk. 'Call Rick Cooke,' one of them said. Like hell, she would call Rick Cooke.

As for that snob, that whore, she would get even one day. The world turns full circle and her day would come. She was certain of *that*. She knew how to wait . . . She was also certain that she did not want anyone to know what had happened. That jerk thought the same way too, so no problem there . . .

Still, it was too bad that all the pictures would be in the kitchen. But they would be good shots, without doubt. One or two might just be great.

Right now, she knew what she had to do. Order another coral blouse to replace the one she had ripped, and have it delivered to Lamont Road. But it was after five and this was not New York. It was too late; the shop would be shut. She scribbled a note on her memo pad. Tomorrow she would take care of that.

Sheila did not believe that Emily Bradshaw was the kind of woman who made enemies. She lacked the guts, lacked the ambition for that – and was too dull, too much of a softy, besides. If she inspired anything at all, then – like all failures – she inspired indifference. Until *now*, that is. It really was too bad that things had got screwed up like this, because that naïve snob was going to have to learn a whole lot of things. Like she would need friends, allies. Like not to set the cops on a major photographer – who in their right mind would do a stupid thing like that? Maybe, just maybe, the girl didn't know what she could be . . .

Sure the snob had made a big, big enemy of Sheila, but work was first, was up front: way way ahead even of enemies, even of friends.

Then it struck her that there would be no shortage of enemies in Emily's life. The networks would take care of that . . .

Right this minute, though, the ball was still in Emily's court. So the girl was beautiful, so of course she had gotten all steamed up, all creamed up . . . So what? Not wanting to respond is very different from not responding. And she knew enough to know that the bitch had not been unresponsive. So she had been this way before, too often. She would wait until the snob was ready. And randy! She was good at waiting.

So maybe Emily Bradshaw already had a ready-made powerful enemy, and maybe not. Sheila was good at slamming doors shut, but not before they were wide, wide open.

*

Emily lay in her darkened, silent bedroom. From downstairs came the clicking sounds of movement, of equipment being snapped back into shape, of American voices... 'Jeez, she forgot her coat. And her purse! What the fuck's been going on here?' carried upwards. She longed for a cup of hot tea – even her throat felt raw – but thought it best to lie quite still under that pea-poultice. That and two aspirins had taken the edge off her raging, smarting face. Her shoulders felt as if they'd been crushed – she could only hope that they had not been blackened, but she was too afraid to look.

She would have scrubbed the make-up off anyway, even if nothing had happened. But how had she allowed it? Had she been... well, encouraging? And even if nothing had happened, she would have tied her hair back too. Hidden it. That way she would be her usual self – unremarkable and far from stunning. Because she did not want Simon to see her all tarted up like that; too unsettling for everyone.

Besides that different Emily Bradshaw, that temporary and unmistakably glamorous Emily Bradshaw, was for America where it didn't matter because no one knew her, and where she would be as strange and as temporary to everyone as she would be to herself.

*

'What's up?' Simon asked later. 'You're not ill, are you?' He disliked illness as much as he disliked tears. He began opening the curtains.

'Don't open the curtains, please,' Emily begged.

'Why ever not?'

Her sharp tone stopped him. 'It's my eyes,' Emily said. 'The make-up they used. I must have been allergic. My eyes!'

'You poor thing,' he said, coming closer. 'Poor Em!' He touched her cheek. 'Hot?'

'Yes, it affected my face too.'

'I wanted to know about your day. Tried phoning you earlier, but there was no answer. Keith tried too. So, I gather, did Rick Cooke. All wanting to know about your day. He's coming to have a drink with us.'

'Who?'

'Keith.'

'I can't see him. I'm sorry. I can't ... really see anyone. I haven't been able to face Danny.'

'Then he didn't practise?'

'No, darling, he didn't. I am sorry, but I took two aspirins.'

'Ah well, that explains it. Aspirin always makes you sleepy, we know that.'

'Yes.'

'Best to sleep it off, then. I'll deal with Keith.'

'And Danny?' she said anxiously. 'Danny's concert?'

'Leave it to me. I'll see what I can do.'

He tiptoed out, which considering her own deceit was unbearably moving.

In the bathroom mirror the swelling did not look too bad. The pea-poultice had helped and the swelling had been controlled by the ice-pack. There was no sign of a black eye either. Everything definitely ached and throbbed all over. But that was the least of it, that didn't count. Keeping it quiet was what mattered ...

She made up her mind that she would never wear the bracelet or the necklace.

*

The Kurt Lagerfeld package arrived at Lamont Road punctually at 11 o'clock, which conformed to Sheila's instructions. Emily contemplated the blouse. It was not entirely unexpected, and all through the long night she had debated the question of how she would react if and when it was delivered. Since there was no excuse for bad manners, the answer was obvious: she would say thank you. *What* to say, however, would depend on Sheila. And if Sheila was out, she would leave a message of thanks. She rather doubted, though, that it would be necessary to leave a message.

'Sheila?' she said. 'Emily Bradshaw.'

'Hi, Emily Bradshaw!'

'I want to thank you for the blouse. I wasn't sure when you would be leaving London, so I thought I'd better telephone at once.'

'That's OK. They sent the right size?'

'Oh yes, yes. I'm sure it is.'

'Good. Are you OK?'

'Oh yes, thank you. Fine . . .'

Sheila was silent.

'Look, Sheila, I'm sorry about yesterday, but . . . well, I feel I must tell you. That panic bell does not ring in the police station.'

'Huh – so you didn't set the cops on me?'

'No, I didn't.'

'But you would have, huh?'

'I don't know. I was frightened, I didn't really know what was happening.'

'I figured that.'

'When do you leave, Sheila?'

'This afternoon.'

'Well, *bon voyage*. And thank you. Thank you for everything.'

'See you in New York. The photographs are sensational!'

Sheila almost added that they were among the best she had ever done. One or two might well go on exhibition. Emily Bradshaw had better learn the meaning and the power of an acclaimed photographer of the likes of Sheila Lyall . . . She took another swig of vodka and milk. She was drinking too much again. Nervously, she fashioned and unfashioned her long scrawny plait while she studied, yet again, those contact sheets of Emily Bradshaw.

How would Emily react when she finally saw herself as Sheila had seen her?

Sheila's nerves started to jangle; hard-boiled or not, she trembled. The hell with what Emily would see in these pictures! Because Sheila saw – or rather, identified – something . . . that *je ne sais quoi* . . . that certain something in Emily that was precisely what the networks were looking for, TAN especially.

It was that same look – even in those amateur photographs – that had made Rick jump out of his seat to snatch up his magnifying glass. But of course, Sheila was not to know that. She saw the same aristocratic allure that Rick had seen. She saw further still: drawn, drowning in all that smouldering innocent sensuality of those wide eyes, she yelped: 'Jesus, Mary, mother of God!' because it was too much, she was freaking out. Rick Cooke's assignment or not, she would keep some of those shots herself.

More vodka and milk, her thoughts racing. Jeez! It was mind-blowing. A new look, the Emily Bradshaw look. Art Kristol, Entertainment President of TAN, and his wife Eartha had asked her to be on the lookout for a new face, for a new show.

It takes a little longer to spot the obvious.

Sheila could already hear the Kristols raving over the Emily look: 'Sure, it was obvious, Sheila, but it took the genius of a Sheila Lyall to bring the obvious out.' In Sheila's mind, Emily Bradshaw had already become her own invention. But there were no patents, goddamn it!

And a big piece of the action would go to Sheila Lyall . . .

But she needed to work in her own lab. Fast. Like right this second. She called the hotel operator. 'Get me PanAm,' she ordered, but the phone wasn't answered quickly enough.

She called the operator again. 'Get my office in New York. Number's on your records.'

No reply from there either.

'I rather think they'll still be asleep in New York.'

'What's the time over there?'

'Six-thirty am.'

'Get me PanAm reservations. New York.'

As soon as she was put through to New York, she said, speaking very rapidly, 'They don't answer the phone over here.'

'Where?'

'I'm calling from London. *No one* answers phones over here. What time is the next flight out of here?'

'To New York?'

'No, to Peking. Of *course* New York. Why would I call you? Get me on it. Sheila Lyall. Charge it to me or to *Chic Magazine*.

Same difference. Got that?'

She took another swig. She would just make it.

*

The really awful thing for Emily was that there was no one whom she could tell that she owed her sanity to a bag of frozen peas.

She might have been able to tell her mother. No, certainly not – it would have upset her too much. But at least the possibility would have been open to her. Penny . . . Penny would have been the one. They would have laughed – not about what had happened, only about the marvellous uses of peas. Ah, Penny, she thought for the thousandth time, you should not have done it . . .

Was she really so friendless, then? Rebecca, yes, she could conceivably tell Rebecca. She trusted Rebecca. After all, they had been at school together . . . Besides, Rebecca would get the point about the peas. Rebecca was at the Madrid Embassy, and had been for eight months. She thought she might phone Madrid, but it couldn't really be talked about, not on a long-distance call.

There could be no compromise. The whole thing would have to remain a strictly private episode – the two women were united by their secret. Emily could not help thinking that her mother would have been more fascinated than repelled by Sheila. Because her silks and her colours, her rings and her bracelets were distinctive and definite. She had created a style that others found memorable, a portable art form much admired by women like Emily's mother.

It is shocking at thirty-four to discover yourself friendless in the city in which you were born, where you grew up and where you still live. And equally shocking, perhaps, to conclude that you are lonely . . . She decided to write to Rebecca in Spain, and began at once.

She had only just settled when the phone rang. 'Simon!' she said.

'First tell me, how's the swelling?'

'Much better.'

70

'Good. We're going to give a dinner party the night before Danny's concert, which is only two nights before you leave.'

'Oh, I'll manage.'

'It's by royal command.'

'Ah, the senior partner.'

'And Sir Roger and Lady Wilbury, and the Campbell-Quines. It's something of a celebration, so black tie. The whole bit!'

'A celebration?'

'Senior partner's handing them on to me. My new clients would like to meet you. See you later. Glad you're feeling better. Bye, Em.'

Emily replaced the receiver, picked it up, dialled and then remembered. Her mother was dead. She put it down very slowly and went on with her letter, determined to finish it. That burgundy blouse would be perfect for the dinner, she thought; it would do wonders for her black silk skirt.

Only a week to go before Emily's departure date and Danny's concert, and she would not have said which made her the more nervous. In any case, there was little time to think, which was a blessing. Her ears thrummed with the precise rhythm of Danny's solo – she longed to be able to hum it, or even whistle, but she had never been able to carry a tune.

These days when the phone rang, it was most likely to be Rick Cooke, or another of those pre-interviews which usually had to be terminated abruptly because all hell was suddenly breaking loose in someone's office somewhere in America. She answered their questions concisely, and was unfailingly gratified by the reaction to her voice. 'I love it – everyone will be crazy for it, it will go down big,' and so on. She wished Keith wouldn't call her quite so frequently; she could not forget that she had been talking to him while her mother lay dying, and she hated speaking to him now. He had changed; there was something deferential, almost nervous, about the way he spoke to her, though he continued to call her 'my girl'. Emily put it all down to what she believed was a logical and well-founded anxiety about how she would cope in America . . .

Danny's solo drummed in her head all the time now. She

deferred all conscious thought of whatever might be in store for her in America, and immersed herself in domestic detail – which was what she had done during the long week before Danny's birth, when concentration on essential trivia prevented her from thinking about the birth and the pain that lay in wait for her. And so she did not give one conscious thought to the prospect of cameras, or lights, or film crews, or interviews. She had never seen the inside of a radio or television building, let alone a studio, to say nothing of never having crossed the Atlantic.

In any case – and thank the Lord – it would all be happening worlds away where she knew no one, and where no one knew her, so it didn't really matter...

Soon the dinner party was upon her. Everyone was taking a second helping of her roast beef, Ophelia was coping wonderfully and Emily was beginning to relax. Catching Simon's eye, she knew that he felt the same way. She was thinking how good he looked in his Oxfam dinner jacket, how no one would ever guess where it had come from... She had drawn her hair away from her face, toning down the highlights, and her stable black silk skirt did the same thing for the burgundy blouse. She looked the way she usually looked – the practical wife who makes do with what she has. The dinner was going extremely well; it turned out that Sir Roger knew her father, and the senior partner heard him say so too. Over the gleaming silver which she and Ophelia had polished together, over the camellias, she and Simon permitted another momentary meeting of the eyes.

'Lavinia,' Sir Roger called out to his wife across the table, 'did you know that Emily has written a *book*? She's going to America to talk about it on television!'

'A book,' his wife answered. 'How absolutely splendid! What sort of book?'

'It's about wives and families, I suppose,' Emily said, embarrassed. She added quickly, 'It's not being published here, of course. Only in America.'

'I know what you mean,' Lady Wilbury assured her. 'More their sort of thing.'

'Well, we must drink to that anyway,' Sir Roger said, raising his glass. 'Congratulations!'

The chorus of 'well done', 'congratulations', and 'absolutely splendid' made Emily miserable.

'If you're going to New York, you'll want to have your wits about you,' Mrs Campbell-Quine stated, her voice shrill. 'Corrugated streets. Rough. Like the African bush!'

'My wife was almost mugged. In our hotel, too,' Mr Campbell-Quine explained apologetically.

'Narrow escape, wasn't it?' Anna Giles, the senior partner's wife, turned to Emily. 'I do admire you – moving into the public domain. I couldn't bear it myself.'

'Oh, but I won't be. I'll be in America.'

'That does make a difference, of course,' Sir Roger agreed.

'You poor dear, you must be so nervous,' Lady Wilbury sympathized.

'I'm not thinking about it,' Emily replied. She wanted to talk about something else. 'I don't know anyone over there,' she added.

'Don't you? Lavinia, remind me to tell my good friends the Lerner twins about Emily. They'll look after her. I'll alert them to watch the TV. When does all this happen?'

'Emily's flying out there the day after tomorrow,' Simon replied.

'It must be a frightfully good book,' Anna Giles said.

'Should think she'll become frightfully rich!' Sir Roger laughed his most affable laugh. 'It's what the publishers choose to call a promotion. A heavy investment, what?'

'Oh, it's not like that at all,' Emily said hastily. 'It seems that someone broke a leg. At least, I think it was a leg...'

'What's that got to do with the price of eggs?' Sir Roger wanted to know.

'The writer whose place I'm taking – she broke something. She wrote a book called *Sixty Seductive Salads from Fifty-One States.*'

Now they all laughed. Now it was amusing instead of threatening – successfully reduced to the ridiculous. When they had recovered, Sir Roger said, 'You're filling in for the author of a cookery book? That must make things less terrifying.'

'Excuse me,' Emily murmured, 'The kitchen...'

73

She was shaking and it was safer in the kitchen. But she wouldn't think about it. There was chocolate soufflé to attend to. Danny's solo thrummed in her head.

When she returned, Simon had manoeuvred the conversation along to safer terrain and they were debating the merits of the Suzuki versus the traditional method of violin instruction. In her usual way, Emily joined in – she listened.

*

The children's concert was to begin at the end of the afternoon, promptly at 5.30. 'All fifteen children are to be assembled punctually therefore at 5 pm – and not one minute later.' Their music teacher, Susan Waddington, was adamant about this.

Notes, phone calls and messages via Danny had made punctuality appear to be the only difficulty the children would have to face. 'A wee bit of amateur psychology,' Susan explained. 'It deflects the focus of their concern!' At two o'clock Danny was already dressed in his new corduroy trousers, frilled white shirt – frills stitched by his mother, shirt from Marks and Sparks, not Oxfam – and black velvet bow tie (from Harrods). His grandfather was expected at three, and a taxi had been ordered for four. It shouldn't take more than fifteen minutes – twenty at the outside – to get to Belgravia, but even then one could be detained for hours on the King's Road, as Emily explained to her father. The concert hall was an art gallery in Belgravia, and Simon would meet them there and drive them home afterwards.

Sir Thomas was, as he would have put it, 'at the top of my form'. He brought small gifts 'to mark the occasion', he said: for Danny, a *Children's Guide to the Orchestra* and for Emily, Alistair Cook's *America*. 'It will amuse you on the plane,' he said. 'The girl recommended it in such flowery terms that I didn't dare tell her I'd read it myself. It's not the most recent book on the subject of America, but it is comprehensive.'

'Oh, Daddy,' Emily said. 'How very thoughtful!'

'You really mean that, I can tell.'

'Of course I do.'

'Would you like me to play my piece, Grandfather?' Danny asked, violin at the ready.

The familiar tight feeling across her chest – a sort of constriction of the lungs, that she experienced whenever she was with her father – tightened further and she crossed to the window to get some air. An audible sigh escaped and she sat down. 'No need for anxiety, Emily,' her father said. 'The boy will acquit himself well.'

The thin, squeaky notes sounded like chalk scraping and breaking on a blackboard, but note-perfect however squeaky, Emily thought with relief.

Sir Thomas clapped extravagantly. 'Bravo! Bravo!' he cried. 'Allow me to shake my young grandson by the hand.'

Now Emily's smile tightened too. He is so pompous, so like Simon, she thought irritably and disliked herself at once. Because she would so very much have preferred her mother... meanwhile her father, bow in hand, with wild, sweeping movements was pretending to be a conductor. Danny giggled with delight and his grandfather conducted even more wildly. The bow hit a vase of flowers and sent it crashing down.

Several quick thoughts jangled – producing, she could have sworn, a sudden streaking pain in her head.

Had her father smashed Danny's bow?

No, it was only her favourite crystal vase, another of her junk-shop treasures, which had been shattered.

'Bow undamaged,' her father said, reading part of her mind accurately. 'My dear, you look quite pale.'

'I'll fetch a dustpan and brush,' Emily said. When she returned she remembered to tell him that she had met Roger Wilbury the night before, and he was as pleased and as pompous as she had predicted he would be. It seemed that Roger Wilbury had acquired his title along, alas, with two or three others of equally dubious reputation.

'Oh,' said Emily. She would now hear a blessedly lengthy, blessedly harmless explanation. It would smooth things beautifully.

Danny left them to go to one of his electronic games.

Listening to her father's enthusiastic account of a safely boring tale, some of the tension left her chest and head and she felt almost calm.

Then came the mild flurry that always accompanies the

imperious piercing way in which taxi drivers jab doorbells. The traffic, the traffic ... 'Will we be late?' Danny asked over and over again. 'We promised Susan.'

When the Bradshaw party arrived, most of the pupils and their families were already there. Chairs and a stage were arranged in the basement. The paintings – neon-bright oils of sad, shrouded Iranian women – brought something of the theatre to the large, white-bright room. 'But the acoustics,' Susan Waddington said again and again. 'The acoustics are perfect.'

After Emily had introduced Susan to her father, he said, 'Miss Waddington certainly understands children, doesn't she?'

'Yes.' Susan Waddington and she were probably the same age, Emily thought. Susan fitted in with the children so well that she seemed more at ease with them than with her own generation. When she was with the parents of her small charges she seemed ill at ease and it was this awkwardness, Emily decided, which made her seem so much younger than she really was.

Each child had been given a solo, which meant that Emily had to suffer through eight of them before Danny's turn came. When little Fiona, who was only five, forgot her notes, she had to be led away crying hysterically, and Emily felt as much as heard her heart racing in her ears. She longed to take Simon's hand, but it might have seemed irrational. Public expressions of affection embarrassed him, and Emily did not want to annoy him. Finally, finally Danny was on stage, with the angelic earnestness of a chorister, each squeaked note perfect.

Now that the ordeal was over, Emily could sit back and let her mind drift in the direction it usually took these days – towards Rick Cooke. The curious thing was that though she had only experienced his warmth through a telephone, and across an ocean, it had made her see that Simon was somehow ... cold. Perhaps she had never understood this before because all the men she had known, or had so far been friendly with, had been no different from Simon. The warmth that came across the airways from Rick forced her to face up to an unpleasant truth about Simon – he wasn't too keen on private expression of affection either. Not that he was sexually cold – no one could have accused him of that – it was just that, for Simon, sex and affection did not go together.

Later that night when they were in bed, Emily said, 'Danny was good, wasn't he?'

'Note perfect.'

'Oh, he's not musically a very gifted child, I know.'

'He's not bad – better than both of us!'

'That's not the point. His musical ability is not really important. What counts is what it does for his confidence. The way he stood up there in that lovely gallery, in front of all those people! I was so nervous for him, I almost fainted.'

'But I knew he'd be note perfect. Didn't doubt it for a moment...'

'It's what it does for his confidence that counts,' Emily repeated. 'I couldn't do *that*. He won't be – like me – desperately shy.' She sighed deeply. 'I dread the thought of Danny going away to school next year. It's too cruel; leaving him for three weeks is bad enough. Do you know what Danny said when I told him about this tour?' She sped on without waiting for a reply. 'He said, "Twenty-one days takes hours and hours." He's so brave. It's cruel to send him away to prep school.'

'Trevor-Winston School wasn't too cruel for me. It didn't do *me* any harm,' Simon said impatiently. 'You're nervous,' he said more slowly, 'about tomorrow. About America.'

'Yes.'

'Oh well, no one knows you over there.'

'You mean I can make a fool of myself in public. In my own personal wilderness, so to speak?'

'Stop being silly. You need to sleep.'

'So do you.'

Simon turned over and though Emily switched off both their lights, she didn't even try to sleep. Images and memories shifted through her overcrowded mind. All that planning... Nothing had gone into her suitcase until it had been ticked off the list, but she must have forgotten something.

Lists of her itinerary were taped to the fridge, on Ophelia's wall and in Simon's office. Everything was organized, under control.

She would re-read her manuscript on the plane and take brief notes at the same time. And somehow, somehow she would have to prepare the kind of questions she would like to be asked about her book. 'We'll compare your questions,' Rick had told her, 'with my questions, make a final list and then package the press kit, OK?' The very idea of compiling one's own list of questions was too absurd for words . . . She wondered what the book looked like – every day she had waited, hoping it would arrive before she left. Once or twice, she came close to asking Keith for it, but stopped herself. She might have appeared vain or, even worse, it might have looked as if she thought her book was being promoted on its own merit, and not because of someone else's accident.

PART II
Early August 1985

Chapter 6

Rick Cooke had planned to meet Emily at Kennedy. Curiosity apart, it had seemed the natural thing to do, scarcely a decision, nothing tactical... Sure, he'd been straight with her – he had a lot riding on her, and had told her that. But once he'd started in on the idea of having some really good news for her – like getting her on *TAN Media News Show* – he couldn't leave his office, just in case they called him. So he consoled himself with the thought that in any case, Emily Bradshaw was already getting enough star treatment for a beginner. A limo and a driver, Jordan.

Now if Emily got a limo, Jordan *and* Rick Cooke, why, that might give her the right idea about herself... Rick Cooke saw it as a good sign when he even liked his own humour. He decided to find out how she was getting on in that limo. The phone rang, but Emily made no move to answer it.

'Ma'am, that's your phone,' Jordan said.

'The phone?' she said, picking it up. 'I thought it was the television.'

'Hi, Emily? Welcome to the US of A.'

'Rick! I thought...'

'Have you seen your book? Don't you just love it?'

'It's rather more... garish... than I...'

'Garish? What do you mean, garish? It jumps out at you, it will fly out of the shelves. Jackets sell; there's a big investment in that jacket.'

'It was incredibly thoughtful of you. A wonderful surprise!'

'They'll go crazy for your voice. Just crazy! So finally, finally, you and me... are... going... to... get... acquainted.'

'You sound like a commercial,' Emily said and giggled.

'Great! I like it better when you laugh. Now here's what I want you to do for me. Get in your hotel, take a shower and I'll be with you at five. That's in *ninety* minutes. Ninety. OK?'

As usual, Rick hung up without saying goodbye.

Was it her imagination, or did the doorman at the Pierre break into a slight run to open the door of her limousine? Jordan took care of the doorman and the bellboy. She looked around her room, went into the bathroom, changed into the softer-than-soft white towelling gown that was waiting for her and, dizzied by a large whisky, fell asleep.

Meanwhile Rick put in yet another call to the producer of the *TAN Media News Show*. Gail Carlton sounded more and more doubtful every time, which might just mean that she was getting closer and closer to making a commitment. Power games, all the time, people playing power games – everyone's trade-off.

Gail answered the phone herself. Another good sign, he thought. 'Rick? Hold it. I'll get right back to you. I'm just finishing up this LA call. Don't go away...'

'Anything you say, Gail. You're the boss!'

He could just picture her: a twenty-five-year-old princess sitting in her office, playing with the earrings she had taken off each ear so that she could play two power games at the same time. He could hear her saying, 'We're scrapping that segment. D'you think I don't know we made a commitment? The whole segment's been bumped is all I know...' She loves it, he thought; letting some poor dude down gives her a hard-on. He heard the 'tring' of her phone slice that call. 'Rick?' she said. 'Am I ready to give you a final decision on Emily Bradshaw?'

'You got it.'

'She in New York?'

'Just flew in. She's just hit the Pierre.'

'Great. We'll put her on tomorrow. On the 8.12 segment.'

'Tomorrow? Hell, she's doing the *Hal Morgan Radio Show* at eight.'

'Hal Morgan? Big deal. Big, *big* deal! Next thing you'll be telling me it's in the same league as *TAN Media News Show*. What are you, a loser or something?'

Christ, she was even worse than her reputation, Rick thought. The word 'loser' really got to him – pushed him perilously close to unprofessional conduct, like telling her where to stick her fucking show. Instead, he switched on his booking, louder-than-life laugh. It worked. 'I sure will have some explaining to do,' he said.

'No problem,' she said. 'You're experienced!'

Rick had not even approached Hal Morgan's producer. Tomorrow morning! August 10. He had allocated one day for adjusting, for getting over jet-lag, for getting to know Emily. And what about the fucking coaching he'd counted on giving her? There must be a catch in it ... Why else would the *TAN Media News Show* put Emily on? Someone must have axed *TAN* at the last minute. A sudden streak of envy shot through him and lasted long enough to inspire him: one day *he* would be big enough to cancel them at the last second. Which, even if that had been his sole ambition, would have been as effective as a whole pump of high-octane.

There was no time to get a cab and he ran all twelve blocks of the way to the Pierre ...

Only to find that when he buzzed her, she was asleep.

'You're asleep,' he said. 'Still *sleeping*?' he repeated, as if the very possibility were preposterous.

'Sorry.'

'OK,' he said slowly. 'Now here's what I want you to do for me. Get up. Get dressed, and I'll see you in the foyer in fifteen minutes. And here's what I'll do for you – I'll order a pot of English tea.'

Rick ordered his tea. Waiting to see her, he decided to do the next best thing and study her photographs. Sheila Lyall's pictures were great. That fucking dyke was tougher than tough to deal with; tough or not though, if his instincts were anything to go by she seemed insecure, like she was hyped-up about Emily ... like she was stalking her. Emily couldn't have been dumb enough to turn the woman into an enemy ... Sheila Lyall could easily screw things up ...

Emily wished she had not fallen asleep. It was a relief, though, to rush. It was a way of escaping thought.

She found Rick waiting at the elevator. He took both her hands at once and drew her a few steps away, then stopped to examine her. 'Hi,' he said. 'Hello! Welcome to the United States.' He let go of one hand, but grasped the other, and led her towards a small group of tables covered in stiffly starched ice-blue cloths. 'There it is,' he said looking out of touch, 'Your tea.'

A waiter held out her chair, and she sat down. 'Course, I had the advantage,' Rick said. 'It's like we're one half of a blind date. Hey, Emily, say something. Let me have that voice of yours – live. We've been living on tapes and telephones. Talk!'

Emily glanced at the tea-tray. 'Do you take milk?' she asked.

'Do I take milk? Did I hear right? I'm waiting for her to talk and she asks do I take milk in my tea? Let's get this over with. No, no milk. No sugar, OK?'

'OK,' she said, lifting the teapot. 'You didn't give me a chance to say a word, actually.'

'I guess I kind of freaked out. I got some great news, a half-hour ago.'

'Oh, really?'

'Yeah. A big show for one of my authors. The *TAN Media News Show*, no less. That's big. I've known authors fly in from London just to do a single segment of that show.'

'It must be a very important programme.'

'Level with me, Emily, please. Magic words like *TAN Media News Show* – what do they mean to you?'

'Not as much as such words should, I'm afraid.'

'You mean Keith didn't tell you? He didn't clue you in at all? Now, here's what you must do for me – listen, and learn, and let me be your teacher. OK?'

Speaking rapidly, Rick gave a precise explanation. 'In the US of A,' he began, 'there are four major networks. Which means that their networked shows – shows like *TAN Media News* and *CBS's Morning News*, *ABC's Good Morning America*, *NBC's Today Show*, reach viewers through all of North America. Some shows, like the *Virginia Byrnes Show*, are syndicated over as

many as forty states and compete for *ratings*. That's the key-
word: ratings. Right now the *TAN Media News Show* has the
highest ratings and that gives them a kind of temporary
monopoly. And if you get on one of the networks, you get
credibility. And, after that, the sky is no limit. Believe me. No
limit! Have you got it? If not, feel free to ask me any questions.'

'You've been very patient.'

'Patient? It's my job I'm talking about. Now, you want to
know why I'm telling you all this, right?' But it was clear that he
could hardly contain himself and he said loudly, 'Because Emily
Bradshaw is on the *TAN Media News Show* tomorrow morning
at 8.12 a.m.'

'Tomorrow? But ...'

'I tried to delay it. Believe me, Emily. I broke my balls trying.
Oh, excuse me ... excuse my language.'

'Please don't apologize. I like the way you speak.'

'Optimum would be to get you to adjust to the States, get
over jet-lag, etc. etc. But in this business we take what we can
get.' He stopped for a moment to light another cigarette. 'Gail
Carlton's made this commitment, and if she cancels me I'll go
right over her head – to the fucking president. I've had guests
waiting in the Green Room and then, two minutes before
they're due to go on, they're bumped.'

'Green Room?'

'That's the room where the celebrity guests wait to go on the
show. "Bumped" equals "cancelled".'

'I see.'

'You're learning. You're learning. Good. We got a lot to get
through before tomorrow morning. Now tell me right off, what
happened to the glamorous Emily Bradshaw in Sheila's
pictures?'

'Oh, they used false eyelashes, for ...'

'Whatever they used, it's great. Hey, wait a minute,' he said,
raising his voice again, 'Don't tell me you aren't going to use
those eyelashes? Don't answer. No problem – we'll fix that. Just
one or two or maybe even three phone calls.'

Nothing about Rick was the way Emily had imagined it
would be. Without any form of amplifier, even his voice

sounded different. He was younger than she had anticipated; possibly younger than he looked. He could have passed for thirty-six, but she had the feeling that he wasn't quite thirty... He had the anxious expression of a male model and there were no laugh lines, only worry lines. But he was elegant, he walked gracefully and his impatiently mobile hands were slim and strong. He was attractive, even good-looking in the conventional way of an American actor who plays the role of an educated American diplomat, or businessman. Neat, sparkling with correct hygiene, correct teeth. Clean, Emily thought. Clean-cut, without a hint of grime about the fingernails, the darkened edges that were like dark rings under the eyes of every man she had ever known – Simon, Keith, her father. Clean as a clone, she thought, without knowing why. Then she amended this: not merely clean, but as her mother would have put it, immaculate.

It was safer to think about Rick Cooke; it was a way of postponing tomorrow, or pretending, almost, that it was all going to happen to someone else.

And when Rick slumped in his chair and announced that he had fixed it, that hair and make-up people would be at the hotel at 5.30 a.m., because he wasn't going to bet on the TAN people giving her enough time, she still did not quite believe that this was all happening to her. She got through the dinner, got through the evening, only because dread mingled with disbelief and cut her off.

All will, it seemed, had absconded.

Rick sent her up to her room at ten, ordering her to go to sleep because right now she was bushed – she'd better be fresh in the morning...

Her bed had been turned back. Golden rosebud chocolates with long green stems waited on her pillow – compliments of the Pierre – and a package wrapped and bowed in glittering burgundy paper lay close by: compliments of Sheila Lyall, Emily guessed correctly.

Extravagant burgundy handwriting on a pink envelope: 'Ms Emily Bradshaw'. The card said, 'Hi! Emily Bradshaw! Welcome to New York. You'll be on the run, so here's a small supply of panty-hose to keep you running. Good luck! Sheila. P.S. Call me?'

A small supply! A veritable shop, Emily thought, as she flicked through dozens of panty-hose in dozens of colours. Imagine having to take the time to choose which particular shade of beige or blue – even black – one would wear. She wished Sheila had not done this; it was embarrassing, though probably useful, yet designed to obligate... 'Call me?' Memories of Sheila's baritone plunged her into sudden panic. She would not call. A simple 'thank-you' note would do. She began at once. 'Dear Sheila ... It was most kind ...' crumpled the page. Began again. And again. Drafting a thank-you note? Emily could scarcely credit it. She gave up, ordered a wake-up call for 5 a.m. and, still wide-eyed at 2 a.m. drank a small bottle of port that the Pierre had provided. When the phone rang she thought she had only just fallen asleep, but sprang to attention anyway. Discipline... *When all else fails, Emily* (her mother had said) *turn to discipline*. The phrase echoed and soothed, gave Emily that false, willing feeling of having been with her mother all night long.

*

The beauty people took over and took Emily to the real world of synthetic and therefore identifiable glamour.

Emily stared at her newly transformed reflection. She decided that Mr Lawrence's subtle use of colour deceived people into believing that hers was a remote and delicate beauty – a clean, natural loveliness which owed little to cosmetics.

Mr Christopher's style, however, allowed his skilful use of make-up to be obvious. She had a shinier look now – her lips gleamed with lip-gloss, her cheeks sparkled with a glittering rouge that gave the effect of crushed sequins. And yet, surprisingly, though her make-up was obvious it was not tarty or vulgar. She looked hygienic rather than clean, healthy rather than delicate and accessible rather than remote.

Emily could not help smiling at her American transformation. The strange thing was that Mr Christopher's approach was less subtle, but more honest. It seemed there was nothing shameful about showing that you had gone all out to do the most for yourself. Certainly, Mr Lawrence had made her more glamorous than she had ever been, but nothing like as glitteringly glamorous as she was now.

Then, there in the real world, she signed – with a nonchalance that she hoped would conceal her horror – travellers' cheques for 250 dollars. *What would Simon say?* Once more she was saved from any anticipation of her immediate public ordeal. Was she really expected to spend two hundred and fifty dollars of her *own* money? Pragmatism overcame embarrassment; she would discuss it with Rick, would be absolutely forthright, and though she wasn't sure if she could either ask, or insist on getting the two hundred and fifty dollars back, she would make it abundantly clear that even if she could have afforded it, she was not mad.

'Jeez!' Rick said a little later, when they were in the limousine. 'She's going on the *TAN Media News Show* and she's thinking of the beauty bills. You look great, Emily. It's an investment... Christ...'

'I can't afford it, and that's that.'

'OK, OK, I'll talk to Frontier. It's tax-deductible, anyway.'

'You have to *have* it to deduct it. I haven't.'

Soon, too soon, Emily thought, they were at TAN building. Rick flashed her credentials. Now security guards, bullet-proof windows, signing in, stickers with her name – all reminded Emily of a hospital admission procedure. It also felt like that. Then the Green Room, orange juice, coffee, Danish pastries. It's a six minute-segment, to be shared with a psychologist and a social worker. Two hundred and fifty dollars on *hair* for two minutes, Emily thinks, and says so to Rick.

'Thirty seconds on TAN at prime time – people sell their souls! You're getting a free commercial that runs to thousands for *seconds*, and you're stuck on two hundred and fifty dollars?'

'Emily Bradshaw for make-up?'

'Me?'

'You Emily Bradshaw?'

'Yes.' A small laboratory. Brilliant lights. 'We're ready for you. Sit down.'

Another voice: 'Emily Bradshaw?'

'Yes.'

'I'm Lily Owen. I'm here to take you to the studio, OK?'

'Certainly.'

Doors, corridors, tunnels, red lights, ON, whispers, flex, cameras, tip-toe... Lily Owen whispers instructions, 'Right, you'll take the seat to the left.' A smile from the anchorman, the great Ed Gray. More instructions... They'll make you up. Quick. *GO*. Wait. Leave your purse with me. There you go – break a leg!' An atmosphere of absolute urgency. Emily is seated, a miniature microphone is hooked on her lapel which must, surely *must* be transmitting her wildly thudding heart – that louder and louder, deafeningly loud thrum-beat. She wants to get up and run; *what* is she doing here? Why is she doing this? 'We're on!' Which camera? Where must she look? She has no idea.

'... and Emily Bradshaw, author of *Defending Wives*. Good morning, Emily Bradshaw.'

'Good morning.'

'Now, wouldn't you say there's something demeaning about women fighting other women over a man? Aren't you advocating a retrogressive step? A return to the Victoria era?'

'I'm not advocating anything at all. However, my primary concern is to put an end to needless divorce.' Then the segment is over, *over*. Emily stands up to make way for the next guests on the next segment. She, the psychologist and the social worker are being led back to the Green Room.

'Emily Bradshaw? Hold it one minute, OK? The executive producer wants to see you!'

'Why?'

Dread, more dread. And what is this, sweat? She touches her neck and yes, it is wet and sticky. She wants to sit down, but has been told to wait in a dark corridor that seems to be a cut-off segment. 'Emily? Noel Whitanski. Glad to meet you.'

'Thank you.'

'Darling, wanted you to know that that was a great segment, darling, great! Congratulations!'

It was over, *over*... The ordeal was over, and that was all that mattered.

Noel Whitanski turned and was gone. She was alone. She

looked to the left and to the right of what appeared an endless corridor, or tunnel, and had no idea which direction to take, but began walking anyway. She felt lost, alone, depressed; the hair at the nape of her neck was sticky and she longed to get out, to escape into real air. She quickened her pace, then the rapid click-click of her high heels reminded her of Sheila, and she moved too fast for her high heels and tripped. She sat on the floor, glanced at the ladder running down her tights, got up, saw a cleaner and slowly walked the other way, towards him.

'The Green Room, ma'am? Miles away.' He pointed her in the other direction. 'It's that-a-way,' he said.

'I'll get lost again, I'm afraid.'

'Saw your show. You talk good. I'll walk you to the Green Room.'

Rick was beside himself. 'Where did you go? The ladies' room?'

'I got lost.'

'You were great. They even used my prepared question. That was great. *You* were great! I wanted to call everyone, tell 'em she's *on*! She's on! You were beautiful, just beautiful. They loved you.'

'Do you mean that?'

'Do I mean . . . ? Are you crazy or something? The executive producer wants to congratulate you. That hairdresser is a genius!'

Rick was almost running and it was difficult for Emily, in those high heels, to keep pace with him. She stopped still. 'I can't afford it,' she said.

'What can't you afford?'

'The hairdresser. I'm not a lunatic.'

'We'll work something out.'

'I *can't* afford it!'

'Forget it. I'll fix it, leave it to me. Right now we've got interviews lined up with the *New York Times, Post, Women's Wear Daily*. Never, never keep a journalist waiting. Then we'll just make the *Ann Sweeting Live Show*. That's a radio phone-in. Fifty thousand watts, hits millions, OK?'

The game was on, the tour began and Emily was on starter's

orders. A tight schedule – time strictly for the job in hand and not a second to waste. Each compacted second hurtled her into this new world where perpetual emergency flourished, where alarm was never absent. So Emily flew into emergency gear and performed. These people respected her and took her seriously, and demanded that she do the same for herself. It was *her* book the interviewers and producers held in their hands for a flash of calculated seconds. And at every studio there was evidence that some researcher had read some pages. Paragraphs, sentences, marked with pencil or pen. Even whole pages painted over with magic marker.

Rick's plan was to have Emily hit New York for three days, then on to Philadelphia, Washington, Chicago, Cincinatti, through to Houston – twenty more cities in twenty days. By the eighth radio interview, Emily could no longer remember when – or what – she had said.

It was all congealed in a mad rush where getting to the next interview on time was the only thing that mattered. Sometimes phone-in shows that were scheduled for one hour overshot their time. Once or twice Rick granted desperate callers a few extra minutes to hang on Emily's words. Not that Rick gave a damn about the caller's problems, it was just that he could accumulate still more bookings because out there they were mad for her; crazy for her.

Defending Wives had touched a raw nerve, or found a gap in the market, but whichever way you looked at it, it had caught on out there and people called in. Many of them introduced themselves by saying they were first-time callers. Jake Williams was one of those...

Chapter 7

Jake Williams was certainly not the type to pick up a telephone and talk to strangers; wasn't the talkative kind, anyway. He was far too introverted and far too bitter to waste words. He and his wife Kate, and their small son Andy, kept themselves to themselves. They had everything they needed: a house, a mortgage, two cars and an annual vacation. Jake earned enough to make it unnecessary for Katie to go to work. When Jake was two years old, his father left home and his mother never looked at another man. She supported Jake on a cashier's salary and did not go on welfare. A gentle woman – but not without ambitions for him – his mother had a few inflexible rules. The first was that grace was said at each meal, and the second that the people she worked with should call her Mrs Williams and not Mary. She wanted Jake to be like those classy people in the movies, so he was not allowed to call her 'Ma'; she was his mother and would be called 'Mother'. Also, he grew a beard like Ronald Colman. Because one day Jake was going to join the ranks of the professional man. Men who used brain and not brawn; and wore dark suits. Men who were not truck drivers like Jake's father. Early on in his career, when he was in seventh grade, she met with his teachers and laid out his future. Jake was going to be an accountant; he was going to be a senior corporate executive.

But in the event, only half of the plan had been carried through. Though Jake graduated as a registered accountant – the disciplined world of arithmetic matched his overall rigidity

– he did not become a senior corporate executive. He chose instead to satisfy his other – and more urgent – needs. He needed to be a loner, needed security and also needed power – a combination which could be more than satisfied by the Inland Revenue Service. There he could be certain of a secure, independent place in the chain of command – and this whether his fellows thought him a nice guy or not. Because he did not want to have to be a nice guy, he became a tax collector, an IRS Agent. He had found the way to command the only kind of respect he cared about – the kind that goes with fear. In every drugstore, books and magazine articles advised ordinary men and women on how they should dress, talk and even smile in his presence. Reading this kind of thing made Jake smile and Jake did not smile often.

If only his mother had lived to see his diploma, he would have been able to smile more often. He could not forgive her for having died when she had, in the way she did; going about her normal daily business, harmlessly crossing the street, getting killed by a drunk driver. In one fell swoop he had been cheated, robbed of his hard-won sense of achievement. If his gentle mother wasn't there to witness it, then there was nothing *to* witness. Her sudden death at such a time wiped out all the joy that he had worked and waited for, and he became a kill-joy.

Katie knew this and tried to understand. She put up with his occasional rages, counting herself lucky that he beat her so seldom and that, in marrying her, he had put thousands of miles between herself and her family. Besides, Jake was so different from her family – neat and clean and, in spite of his beard, so hygienic. He was fanatical about his underclothes, changed twice a day and always kept a spare in the real leather attaché case that she had scrimped and saved to buy. True, Jake was not an easy man – but then, which man was easy? His household standards were rigid, and in fulfilling them Katie found a sense of security. Jake's moods may have been black, but his house sparkled.

Jake didn't really like the world; Katie could understand that and even sympathize. But she could *not* understand why he didn't seem to like little Andy. She could make no sense of her feelings. Jake was dedicated to the boy, and spent hours teaching him boxing. But there was something ruthless about his determination to make Andy into the sportsman he had never been – he wanted him to be tough, but thought he was 'yellow'. Sometimes he said Andy was a loser. It was this that Katie found so disturbing, even frightening. He had never struck Andy, nor yelled at him, but sometimes when he was with the child his voice was cold, yet seething with something frighteningly like hate. Unable to understand this, Katie thought there was something wrong with her for thinking that way, and blamed herself for it. But it was his voice, and the look in his eyes, that sometimes made her feel that he didn't like Andy. 'He doesn't like him,' she would say to herself, but as a question only. She dared not go any further.

The morning that Jake heard Emily in his car, on the *Anne Sweeting Show*, was the morning when Andy's boxing had been useless. He turned on the radio to take his mind off things. He liked Emily's voice and was beginning to relax when he heard her say, 'Men can never be certain that they are in fact the father of their child; we women have the advantage. A woman may not even know who the father is, but she always knows – and with absolute certainty – that she's the mother . . .'

'Are you saying that this is one of the reasons men respond differently to sexual jealousy?'

'It is to the male reproductive advantage to be as promiscuous as possible.'

'Men are more promiscuous than women?'

'Well, they certainly have been up until now. In order to ensure their biological or genetic survival – that is, the survival of their genes – and because they could never be absolutely certain, they were obliged to be promiscuous.'

'I see. An interesting theory. Feminists will have your blood for this. Before we take our first call, let me tell everyone out there that I'm talking to Emily Bradshaw, author of *Defending Wives*, and that part of what we have been talking about concerns the fact that simply by giving birth to a child, the mother knows . . . Wait, let me put it this way. The act of childbirth is absolute proof of maternity. But you're saying there is no absolute blood test that can prove 100 per cent that a man is the genuine biological father of his *own* child?'

'It does sound incredible, I know. But at the present time no such test exists. Yet. When such a test is available, we can expect changes.'

'Just one moment, we have Norman Maitland from Portland, Oregon.'

This was too much for Jake Williams. He slammed the radio shut and although he was at least fifteen minutes away from his office, swung his car into a parking garage, left it, grabbed his transistor radio and raced to a call-box. He knew that number well – WXOY was his favourite radio station and he had heard it so often that it had become as familiar to him as some of the commercial jingles which sometimes entered his mind without his permission.

Jake could not recall having felt anything like the kind of fury that now engulfed him. This was the dirt that was polluting America, forcing fathers to think their own sons might be bastards. A pro-life supporter like himself was being made to believe he was not Andy's father! He was going to call that number and get through to that woman. If they put him on, that is. He got through, told the operator the nature of the question he wanted to ask and waited. And if he got to work late, that would be too bad. He was on hold and meanwhile, he had to listen to an angry spic: 'You're trying to tell me I don't know I'm the daddy of my kid. Hell, man, I *know* I'm my kid's daddy. My kid's not blond – my kid's dark like his daddy. I don't need no blood test to tell me I'm my kid's daddy...'

Jake could hear the caller furiously bang something, probably a table, then the interviewer's voice again: 'Norman, I think Emily was trying...'

Norman cut in again. 'Hell man, what *is* this shit?'

'Thank you, Norman, and God bless electronics. We don't allow obscenities out there, Norman. And now we have Chrissie Parker calling from...'

Jake could barely contain himself. He desperately wanted to talk to this woman. This Emily... As he tugged his short beard something stirred in him; he did not know *who* Andy looked

95

like – he had never known... Because his son was not only yellow, but pale, blond... He and Katie had brown eyes, but Andy's eyes were grey...

'Well, that's it from WXOY. We're going to have to make sure to have Emily Bradshaw, author of *Defending Wives* – currently on sale in all bookstores now – come join us for another session. Emily Bradshaw will also be appearing on the *Virginia Byrnes Show* at noon on Friday; that's in two days' time.'

Jake stormed away from the phone, unaware that his radio was still on. He passed a bookstore and went in; he located *Defending Wives* immediately, but could not resist looking at the latest tax manual.

'Sir, would you mind turning that thing down?' one of the sales assistants asked.

'Sure, OK. Sorry, I forgot.' Jake put down the tax manual and bought *Defending Wives*. He was going to be late, but he was also going to read that book even if it meant sitting in the john to do it.

*

Emily was exhausted. Three days of this and she could barely remember which shows on what station... The callers – all those people out there calling her – and though their questions and their loneliness spun around her head, Norman Maitland's thumping on a table in some unknown sitting room was an insistent drum in her ears. Oh, why had she brought genes into it? That man had sounded so agitated – he might even thump his own wife.

Emily was in a state of sleep deficit, heavily indebted, yet here she was at past midnight sitting bolt upright in bed, trembling, waiting to watch herself on *Nightguard*.

Now for the first time, she too would see exactly what all those ordinary people out there would see. Waiting, she had decided not even to try to sleep, but to attend to the problem of her hair instead. Madeline Star, the presenter of the *Woman-to-Woman Show*, had actually shown her how her hair could be managed with a cordless, heated curling gadget called a gas

96

wand. But finding the time to buy one was the difficulty. Because she would not ask Rick for help – she still burned at the way he had given her back the 250 dollars ... crumpled notes mainly, and no envelope. Humiliating! The familiar and therefore friendly sight of the two crossed keys on the lapel of the concierge signalled that help might be at hand. The concierge, though, was a Frenchwoman and, it seemed to Emily, forbiddingly efficient. She said, in a rush, 'Do you know where one might be able to acquire a magic wand?'

'What is that?' the porter said impatiently. 'A magic wand?'

'For hair ... it uses gas.'

The concierge sighed, clicked her tongue, let out her breath and shrugged her shoulders – all this with consummate grace. Overcoming her diffidence, her natural inclination never to trouble anyone – least of all someone who was meant to serve – even if it was absolutely essential, Emily said, 'I'm doing a television show in Washington tomorrow morning. I've just done one called *Nightguard* ...'

'*Nightguard?*' the concierge interrupted. 'You were a celebrity guest on *Nightguard?*'

'Yes.'

'My favourite show. Bill Hotspur – he's so good-looking, so 'andsome. You have a problem with hair? So you need a *coiffeuse.*'

'No,' Emily said firmly. 'I need a magic wand.'

'So I send the bellboy to every drugstore and *voila*, you will have one. But if it was me, I would have a *coiffeuse*. So why are you on *Nightguard?*'

Emily explained, agreed to sign a copy of *Defending Wives*, and went up to her room to wait for her magic wand.

Once she had it, and the blow-dryer the concierge had deemed necessary too, she spent the entire night learning how both instruments should be mastered. She was successful, and felt the same kind of triumph as when she had finally passed her driving test. She turned her head more slowly now, and delighted in running fingers through those cleverly cut layers and layers of her own gleaming, silky hair. It made her like herself more, which should, she thought, have offended her sensibilities – but it did not. Which was odd, because she had always despised synthetic women with synthetic hair, and considered them contrived and artifical. But *her* beautiful artificial hair made her feel more alive and, accordingly, more real . . .

About fifteen minutes to go before *Nightguard*. Her heart raced. Should she phone Simon? What time was it in London? About six in the morning – too early. She was also hungry; should one ring room service? She was about to do this when suddenly, in that strange lonely room, she heard the sound that is the most familiar sound to everyone, everywhere – the sound of her own name: '*Nightguard*, and in fifteen minutes, Emily Bradshaw, author of *Defending Wives*, will be with us.' It was too much, really it was too much. She laughed out loud – she thought, who would have thought it? But of course, no one knew her over here, so it didn't matter.

She gave up all thought of calling room service.

So it was that drunk with fatigue and dizzy with hunger, but acutely alert none the less, Emily watched herself on *Nightguard*. She studied herself and the presenter, Bill Hotspur, and coldly noted the way he laughed falsely, cutting through her answers with rapid-fire questions that were more like statements. She assessed her own conduct with the same cold objectivity, even though she was seeing herself on the most expensive mirror in the whole world. She saw herself listen carefully, and answer thoughtfully, fluently, looking so authoritative, professional and experienced. She was amazed. She was none of these, she knew. She had not performed, she had been herself . . . 'Just be your own kind self, darling,' her mother had said when she went to that distant Cambridge interview, and she understood now how long she had carried that advice with her.

How she ached, at this moment, for her mother.

Her mother had always wanted her to *do* something with her hair. Well, something had been done and, as a result, something had happened. She now looked expensive. Also valuable . . .

She could be certain, now, of sleep.

But her phone rang. First Rick. 'Emily, you were great . . . *great*. Mind-blowing dignity . . .'

Then Sheila: 'Darling, you looked gorgeous.'

Then the concierge: 'Madame, you were *magnifique* on the show. *Magnifique!*'

Emily thought, Oh my God, I love this. I actually *love* all this. I'm even glad to have heard from Sheila Lyall. What's happening to me?

Chapter 8

A stretch limousine, long and sleek, rolled down Fifth Avenue, and even that rutted street was smoothed. The Lerner twins, Leon and Milt, were indulging their favourite hobby – looking at their New York real estate, when the traffic was slow and they could see more clearly. It was their custom, whenever they acquired a new office complex, to have all the lights switched on at midnight and remain lit for two hours, as a kind of salute to their drive past.

It was a custom which had begun in 1960 when they had acquired what they called their first 'serious' project – undercapitalized and banking on leverage – a real skyscraper, seventy storeys high. Leon's wife, Ruthie, had hit on the idea, 'extravagant', as she said, 'but a gesture', and the four of them had embraced it as they had always embraced one another. The combined Lerner families – twin brothers married to the Barnett sisters, only a year separating Ruthie and Marcie – made a perfect partnership. Leon specialized in risks and called it foresight, while Milt specialized in arithmetic and called it planning. Their wives saw themselves as soul-mates and behaved in such a way that, had they not been sisters, destiny would have brought them together and made them best friends anyway.

They were lucky because they knew they were lucky – their friendship was real, but also blessed, sanctified almost, because it had been tied and sealed by the same real blood. Everyone wanted to know the secret of their success. The answer was as simple as it was unassailable – trust, utter total trust put them way ahead. Without that trust, Lerner for Enterprise (the pun on 'four' being Ruthie's idea), now internationally known as LFE, would never have taken off.

Of course they made enemies – but then, as they liked to say, 'Show me the man who has no enemies and I'll show you a loser.' It was inevitable, and they didn't like it, but it was one of those things you learn to live with and it brought them even closer. They both knew that bucks couldn't buy happiness, but knew even better how much happiness too few bucks could provide. Their father – Max Lerner, senior – incurable optimist, had fought and lost against several bankruptcies; the boys had been registered for private schools in New Jersey, but never even got to the door.

The only time they saw their father's optimism falter was when they volunteered for Korea. True, it was their duty, just as it had been his duty in the Second World War. It was also the only time they saw their optimistic father weep. When they got to Korea, commissions were applied for and approved. But they hated military life and resigned officer cadet school, yet after sixteen weeks' training in field artillery they graduated as trained killers anyway. The war ended while they were still in Korea. They saw combat as corporals and, like all other menials in the forces, called themselves 'dog-face'. Much, much later when a pet-products business was included in a complicated package deal, they kept the product, and thought of calling it *Dog-Face*. It would have been a whimsical, fanciful thing to do – after all, they went in for gestures like illuminating their buildings – but the idea had been vetoed by both their wives. Ruthie hit on *Canine-Chow*, Marcie amended it to *Kay-Chow*, and *Kay-Chow* it became. Though it took off and was now one of the biggest pet-food companies, it remained their only venture outside real estate.

They got out of Korea and into school. Their father had his Vikings back again. They worked summers and nights, but did not in the end graduate. Their mother, a secretary and book-keeper to real estate developers, brought them a deal. The twins quit school – heresy as far as Mr Lerner's wider family was concerned. But it was an offer they could not refuse to make. Leon saw the potential and evaluated the risk, and Milt did the arithmetic. It proved to be an invincible formula, but did not, in the end, save them from the real and the terrible risk that is both the penalty and the point of life.

*

True the newest building was illuminated tonight. Four people rode at the back of the line – but only two were Lerners. On the hundred and twentieth day of the hostage crisis, Ruthie and Marcie had flown in their own plane to their beloved compound at the Hamptons. Their plane crashed and they had been killed instantly. Useless, useless to talk about it – who, who has not suffered grievous loss? *Who?* So they never talked about it, but talked about their wives ... and because they were men, they needed women, and because they were tycoons there was an embarrassment of choice. Still, they did not go in for teenage starlets and shocked everyone by forming a regular relationship. 'No new wives, no new kids, and no women who are kids,' said Leon, and Milt of course agreed.

Besides, there was that vow ...

The vow they had made to their wives, that they would never re-marry. And then, when both wives died like that – together, and at the same time – they had repeated that vow to one another. This way the vow was made to the living and not to the dead. This way, and for these twins, the vow would live on.

They were not about to desecrate the memory of their wives with any new kids who might come in conflict with their own. They had trusted their wives, they were tycoons and therefore vulnerable. But trust was the one luxury they could not afford; vasectomy, therefore, was the only valid safeguard. Leon with Wendy, a former model and personal shopper, aged thirty-eight and the divorced mother of Karen; and Milton with Arlene, a former interior designer who had no children and had never been married. They were lonely women, chic too, and though they could not in any way be compared with Marcie and Ruthie – because no woman anywhere in the world ever could be – they were presentable.

The newest LFE acquisition, illuminated, beamed a salute to its new owners, the Lerner twins. 'So what else is new?' Leon thought wearily. 'What's it all for? So it's lit up – life isn't worth a candle.'

No Ruthie, no Marcie. Though maybe, just maybe, wherever they were, they saw the lights flashing upwards to meet them. Crazy thinking. But a glance at Milt's energetic puffing of a cigar told him his brother was thinking the same way. Milt passed him a Scotch, leaned forward and flicked on the television. Afterwards Leon would never be able to get over how he and Emily had met. If it hadn't been for her voice, that gentle kind of soothing – *sympathetic* – sound, he would have switched it off and switched on that long midnight of his. As it was, Milt leaned forward again to change the channel.

'Hold it!' Leon said. 'Hold it . . .'

'. . . the tragedy of needless divorce, if just one needless divorce . . .' And then, 'Emily Bradshaw, author of *Defending Wives*.'

Leon looked at Milt again. 'That's the woman Sir Roger Wilbury telexed us about . . .' he said. 'Good-looking, too. He neglected to mention that in his quaint way.'

Milt squeezed Arlene's knee. 'You gotta meet him.' Then he mimicked Sir Roger's accent: 'Quaint fellow, what?'

Already busy with the telephone, Leon was saying, 'I'll call the office and get hold of that book.' Now Wendy and Arlene exchanged a glance. Later, much much later, though not in terms of the passage of time but in destiny's terms, Wendy would say, 'I knew it then – I knew it all. The second before Leon picked up the phone. It was a gut feeling . . .' Yet she had been able to listen, though with a smile that hid the freeze-burn of every nerve, while Leon made that call. 'Hi, Willy? Yup, it was all lighted up – great. OK. Have Charlie go down to the bookstore and pick up a book called – hey, Wendy, what's that book . . . ? *Defending Wives*, Wendy says. We got a telex about the author, Emily Bradshaw.'

And yet there was no reason for Wendy to feel so agitated. After all, there was nothing unusual about Leon's calling his office like this, just after midnight. It was the way Leon and

Milt ran things: never wasting a minute, never postponing the smallest task, their fanatical attention to what others would have regarded as trivial was legendary. They knew the names and the details of every doorman who worked for them, for example. The trade-off? The quality of the doorman added to the prestige of the building, and the prestige added to the value. It wasn't difficult – they had enough of the right kind of infrastructure to keep their corporation running as smoothly and as efficiently as their limousine. Of course, you didn't have to be a graduate of the Harvard Business School to know that the faultless efficiency of LFE was because it was private – no nosy shareholders, no bureaucracy. If you could be private, you could afford to be personal. They were big on the 'personal touch' and said so. They preferred not to talk to journalists on principle, but on the rare occasions when they did, it was the personal touch that would be emphasized.

So Wendy listened to Leon and watched Emily. Or rather, to be more accurate, Wendy assessed the woman on the small screen who had suddenly invaded the night. Expensive, she thought, very expensive . . . The merest glance had been enough to tell her that. But that was as obvious as the glamour that went with it. There was something else, something behind that serious smile, those serious eyes, that phony voice. *Bitch!* she said to herself, bitch! Except that she could tell this woman was not a bitch and the voice was not phony, which was why she had that gut feeling.

The limousine pulled up outside the Lerner building in which Milt lived, when Emily's interview was just ending.

'That was quick,' Milt said. 'I'm bushed and Arlene's bushed.'

While Milt was helping Arlene out of the car, Wendy held Arlene's eye for an extra moment and then they were gone. The limo rolled on.

'I guess I'm bushed, too,' Leon said. 'I feel . . .' He stopped. 'I'd like to be alone tonight.' He leaned forward. 'Hey, Mike,' he said, 'we'll drop Mrs Griffiths off first, OK?'

He has such wonderful manners, Wendy thought. He's letting me off first! Typical. My luck. Milt had to switch on that fucking television . . .

Wendy managed to carry it all off gracefully. She stared at herself in the elevator, but saw Emily instead. Rage began to build, a furious rage the like of which frightened her. She didn't know where to put herself, she couldn't handle it. Even the key in the lock was holding her up. Then she was in her bathroom, frustratedly hurling bottles into the sunken tub . . . It was going to be an awfully long night, whatever she did. Then she heard, 'Mommy? I thought you weren't coming home tonight.'

'Karen – ah, baby, baby, forgive me! I'm so . . . so mad. I even forgot you were at home tonight.'

Wendy put her arms about her daughter and didn't try to stop the sobs that wrenched her soul.

'You and Leon fight?' Karen asked, sounding bewildered.

Wendy pulled herself together. 'Oh, no, baby, no. I'm sorry. I'm a bit overwrought, I guess. Let's you and me go to bed now, OK?'

'Together?' Karen said. 'In your bed?'

'No, darling. I'll be OK. Don't worry. Promise? OK?'

This was bad. She had forgotten about Karen, what with that bitch and her talk about needless divorce.

Bitching about that Emily Bradshaw would get her nowhere. She – Wendy Griffiths – was a kept woman, and like all kept women could be returned. So Leon had done just that – returned her to her own empty, empty bed. She was crazy about the guy and he knew it. But he didn't know how much she *adored* him. He had been honest with her and from the beginning had told her he never wanted to marry again, because he still loved a dead woman. His brother was the same. She had understood then that if she wanted to keep him, she would have to go along with it. Arlene had exactly the same problem – the brothers had made sure the girls knew all about that vow of theirs. And poor Arlene didn't even have a child of her own. No chance of one for Arlene as long as she stayed with Milt and his vasectomy. At least *she* had Karen. But right now she wanted Leon's kid . . . She was losing her mind, that's what she was doing. What about Leon's vasectomy? The terrible thing was that Leon probably thought it was only his money she cared about.

There must be a way to make him know the truth of what she felt about him, and for him.

She would keep on trying.

She would never give up.

She set about cleaning and creaming her face. She wondered how she would look on television.

*

The next morning – or rather the same morning, since she had watched herself at 1 a.m., Emily was on the plane to Cleveland where she would spend a day and a night; Chicago the next, then back to New York on Friday for the *Virginia Byrnes Show*.

How long had she been away? Time and space had lost all meaning for her, but she must write to Simon, and to Danny. How had she *not* written to them before, nor even telephoned? She answered her own question. She had not telephoned partly because her tight schedule had left her too exhausted to accommodate the time difference between New York and London, but mostly because she had feared that if she was unsuccessful in hiding her enthusiasm for America from Simon, she would be inviting his sarcasm. She simply could not face the thought of listening to his pompous talk about quality versus quantity.

Emily felt a sudden stab of loneliness, but for Danny and not for Simon. She was guiltily aware that being away from Simon's constant criticism was unexpectedly liberating. She longed to hear the sound of Danny's voice, but at the same time she was afraid that if she did speak to him, she would want to fly back to London immediately . . .

She was self-conscious about beginning with, 'Hello, darlings,' but there wasn't time to write two letters. She wanted to tell them about the *TAN Morning News Show*, about a stranger called Norman Maitland banging on a table somewhere in response to something she had said about paternity, about the way she had watched herself on *Nightguard* – but she did not. Because she might have sounded boastful and because, spinning on a crazy, temporary carousel, she was very far from Lamont Road. Her momentary life as a celebrity guest might make her seem not only further distant but boastful, even alien . . . Instead she wrote about her transatlantic flight, the chocolate rose-buds on her pillow, the way she had sat at the back of a limousine watching television en route to the airport; she wrote about things that were strange, but not intrusive, as if she sensed that something in this new temporary 'celebrity guest' could spell disharmony. She began telling them how much she missed them and then, like all inexperienced liars, was overcome by guilt. She had not missed Simon nearly as much as she had thought she would. Then she asked detailed questions about the puppy, the violin lessons, even about Simon's new clients.

It was while she was sealing the envelope that it occurred to her that her public life was her secret life. At this moment she was on hold, suspended, and Lamont Road was almost a . . . memory.

Dick Seagrave, the author's escort who had been laid on by Rick, waited to meet her. After almost three years of driving authors from TV station to radio station, to newspaper offices, he knew that Emily's schedule was uncommonly crowded.

'Traffic's bad,' he said when he met her. 'I alerted the TV station.' He took her overnight bag and began walking fast. 'Don't worry about a thing,' he said. 'We'll make it . . . I caught you on the *Ann Sweeting Show*. You were good. That Maitland guy – one of those crazies, huh?'

Emily adjusted her pace to the slight run that seemed to come so naturally to everyone else. As the day rushed on she would adjust that run from slight to full, and would quite literally race at emergency pace through doors that would be held open (sometimes even by executive directors) to speed her on her way.

Once again that atmosphere of permanent emergency, of time compressed, split into segments which must be filled and clamped with surgical precision. Ten-thirty a.m., two shows later, each maddeningly distant from the other, and, 'You were great, Emily, just great . . . Ratings will be great . . . Could you help us? We'd love to have you on our midday news segment!' Could she? A rapid glance at Rick, enough to have him check his schedule. 'OK. But we'll have to *run*.'

Everyone working, cooperating – and all, *all* in the name of segments. Exhilaration, optimism, America, where the impossible was welcomed as a challenge, where professionalism and enthusiasm are one, where immediacy galvanizes seconds. How could Emily not respond with·the same urgency? They pulled her in, expected no less than the maximum – a minor, temporary capillary only, but essential to the moment, part of the whole. How could she *not* respond to a society who turned a chauffeur like Dick Seagrave into a coordinator whose participation was vital, also? Above all, how could she not *connect*? After all, she was in America, where class does not insulate.

So, for the first time in her life, Emily felt connected instead of isolated, switched on instead of switched off. She had come from the old world of exported enthusiasm to the new world that had claimed it. She was exhilarated, uplifted. The need that she and everyone she knew had grown up with – the need to pretend not to try – had gone. Because she was in the new world where trying – yes, even trying for excellence – is natural and honest.

She would be herself, not her understated self. Which was a private liberation of such overwhelming intensity that there could be no telling of it, nor of what it might bring.

Emily had never parked on a yellow line, never broken a speed limit, never knowingly broken the law. Yet she was saying, 'We won't make it if we don't go faster ...'

'Never break the speed limit, ma'am. Cost me the better part of a hundred bucks if I do.'

'I'll take care of that ...' said Emily, adjusting her vocabulary as well as her principles.

'You will,' Dick said, eyeing her shrewdly in the rear-view mirror.

Emily was rolling her hair with her cordless magic wand. She paused. 'Sure will.'

The phone rang. 'Rick? No, we're not on our way to *ABC*. We fitted in the *Eye Witness News* on *CBS*, isn't that great?'

'Forget it. Turn around and get your ass over to *ABC*. Tell Dick to call when you get there.'

'I can't, I've given my ...'

'What is this? Elaine Nash, the producer of *Doomitive*, is

108

waiting to call you at *ABC* for a pre-interview.'

'*Doomitive?*' Emily said, her voice rising. 'I'm already committed to *Eye Witness.*'

'You're committed to *Eye*... Jesus, I'll have a heart attack! I'll call *Eye Witness*. That's my problem, not yours. But put Dick on...'

Dick pulled off the road, smiling sympathetically. He said, 'The people you promised at *CBS* would do the exact same thing in your place. If an opportunity comes, you *grab* it! No one respects anyone for losing an opportunity.'

Elaine Nash did not call. Emily saw this as poetic justice and felt somewhat better about the whole thing. Even so, nothing in the world would have induced her to tell Simon what she had done. Still, she felt – tainted...

All expenses paid – meals up to thirty-five dollars, everything except what she wanted most – to call London. But hotels add 60 per cent to the phone bill. She would call London anyway.

Dialling direct, she imagined Simon fast asleep in one of the striped nightshirts she always bought him. She smiled.

'Simon?'

'Em? What's wrong?'

'I think I miss you. How's Danny?'

'Everything under control.'

'Do you miss me? Does Danny miss me?'

'I told you, everything is under control.'

'Danny's not fretting, is he?'

'Did you choose to wake me up at this ungodly hour merely to ask me that?'

'I'm sorry, Simon.'

'How's it going on that vulgar continent?'

'Hectic. Very, very hectic.'

'Well, what did you expect?'

'This call is expensive. I suppose I should say goodnight.'

'Good morning.'

It was thoughtless of her to have woken Simon, Emily told herself, but Danny was all right and that was the main thing...

*

Chicago, and this time Mary O'Sullivan was to be her escort. 'Apologies – a Cadillac only, limo in repair at last minute – but we got lucky, I grabbed hold of a Cadillac with a phone.' Mary said she was a political activist. Sharing is caring . . . a pro-lifer, hoping to adopt one herself, a black little girl hopefully. Black kids, after three or four generations on welfare . . . She was keeping a diary on what it was like, waiting . . . Mary's voice droned on and on.

Finally, finally the TV station. 'I'm Mary O'Sullivan and this is my celebrity guest, Emily Bradshaw. For *People are Talking* – I'll sign her in, right? It's OK, I'm familiar with the way.' Then, 'Follow me, Emily.' Emily followed. A buzz in the corridor. 'That's your audience, Emily! Put your head down, and I'll get you through this mob . . .' Emily obeyed. Mary's voice even more officious, those wide hands pushing shoulders: 'Step aside. Out of the way! I have our celebrity guest.'

The Green Room. Mary's chatter. Make-up. *Peace, perhaps?* No chance. Mary would like to be in on it. Mary likes to share . . .

Over, *over* and on with the next. Lunch? No time. Five hours later. 'I'm fainting with hunger, Emily. I stopped by and got us hamburgers. Eat.'

They were on the way to do a major radio show, a prime time hour phone-in with Professor Finkelstein, a major professor of psychology. Sudden tears of gratitude and guilt. Only a moment earlier she would have happily drowned. Emily ate shamelessly, like a hungry person.

The phone: Rick. 'Emily, put Mary O'Sullivan on . . .'

Emily closed her eyes and concentrated on her hamburger.

'Change of plan, Emily. New York. PanAm has the new ticket. Rick said to tell you in this order. One, he's fixed it with Professor Finkelstein. Two, you're having dinner with Art Kristol, the vice-president of TAN. Three, the limo will come get you at twenty-one hundred hours. Four, Rick's meeting your flight in person. Five, count your lucky stars. Got it?'

'Got it!'

'I better get your autograph.'

'Mary?' Emily said, 'could I ask you a very great favour?'

'Sure.'

'Could you stop the car and let me get to the back seat? I've got a dreadful headache; I actually need to lie down.' Because she wanted to cry, because suddenly she was exhausted, and worse – *afraid* – and *alone* . . .

Mary turned on the radio. 'And on our panel Professor Alexander Finkelstein, professor of psychology of the University of Chicago, and Emily Bradshaw, author of *Defending Wives*, will be talking . . .'

'Did you get *that*, Emily! Great . . .'

Silence. Emily closed her eyes.

*

Jake Williams spent far more time in the john poring over Emily's photograph on the dust-jacket than in his office. He had been certain that she would be at least as old as his mother, but instead she was probably about thirty-two – his age, exactly. Which made him even angrier, for now he could not dismiss her as a dried-out, feminist crank. She should have looked like that, but instead she was like a movie star. And he really respected movie stars, Nancy Reagan especially. They were classy, and his mother had thought so too.

She had no right to look like a movie star! He could have understood if she had been the sort of woman no man wanted to touch. But this one was sexy, *fuckable*! Look what she was doing to him, driving him to think in profanities . . . It was unforgivable – another foreigner polluting the American way of life, making fathers believe they were not fathers. A man who can't believe his own son is his own flesh and blood, can't believe, can't trust anyone. A she-devil getting away with sowing the evil seeds of suspicion and hate. And getting away with it because she knew every living man wants a movie star; wants what he can't have . . . She wanted to show men something about not mixing lust with fatherhood . . .

Lust . . .

Oh God, look what was happening to him looking at her! He reached for the lavatory paper but it was too late – all that hot, spurting, spilling sperm.

His clean undershorts were in the attaché case in his office. Ugh! The *shame* of it! The sin and the power of it; sex. Katie pregnant, unmarried – 'Jake, I could have an abortion...' He had not been her first man. Sin and shame. So he became a pro-lifer and stayed one, and watched Andy's hair turn lighter, not darker. There was a damned good reason why Katie had put off taking Andy to be fingerprinted on Missing Children's Day... She was dumb enough to think that fingerprints were a kind of paternity test...

Jake turned to the index of *Defending Wives*. There it was: 'Fathers, biological'. So, she hadn't only said it; she'd put it in writing.

He heard two men enter the men's room. They were laughing and kidding the way he never could, talking about the biggest tits on the newest secretary which must have weighed a pound each.

Again, the sin and the shame and the power.

He waited until they had gone, then left the men's room and decided to quit work for the day.

At the barber shop there was more filth, more disgusting, evil magazines. *Pornography*. Everyone knew how the porn merchants evaded tax. All that filth, even though the hygiene of the place was safe. Combs sterilized, clean towels, antiseptic smell, the place even gleamed like a hospital. *AIDS, gays*; nothing was safe, you couldn't even trust hygiene.

He felt himself sweat. He and the barber, Stan Rothwell, had a lot in common – both were pro-lifers and Stan was an active member of the local Right to Defense Committee: 'So I had this guy from the Civil Liberties Union, saying pistol permits are given too freely. You got to be joking, I said. Muggings and murders on the streets. Every forty seconds a murder, something like that.'

'Forty-five seconds...'

'Forty-five, is that right? You would know that exactly. So let me tell you, I lost a customer...'

Jake interrupted savagely. 'Turn that thing down...'

'What?'

'The radio, for God's sake!'

'OK, OK. Keep your hair on,' Stan laughed at his poor joke.

'Sorry, sorry, my sick humour. Your hair's improving – see the change for yourself.'

'Don't give me that. At a dollar twenty-five a drop of that Hairgro stuff!'

'How d'you calculate a dollar twenty-five a *drop*?'

'Easy – twenty-two drops makes—.'

'Don't tell me. Don't tell me now. You get a special deal. Wouldn't want my other customers to hear . . .'

'That woman they were talking about on the radio. The one they interviewed five mintues back. Heard her on the *Anne Sweeting Show* . . .'

'But you made me turn it off.'

'We missed her anyway. They just said what had been on already, so I asked you to turn it off. What are you making such a big deal of it for?'

'Hey, Jake, what's biting you?'

'That woman, Emily Bradshaw, did you catch her show this morning?'

'Naw, I prefer to listen to my customers . . .'

'You're not wrong. Filth – even on the *Anne Sweeting Show*.'

Filth was Stan's hobby. If he didn't have customers, he couldn't provide an oasis of hygiene on West 88th Street. But if he didn't have those porn magazines, he wouldn't have any customers. The human being had an animal base. He had tried explaining this to Jake, many times. Jake was different from most of his customers – he never talked about women, only about filth like muggers and murderers and junkies. Stan had never forgotten the way Jake had freaked out the time he had started to talk about Sam Smollen, the rapist. He had ordered Stan, in a cold vicious whisper, to shut up and never say that word in his hearing again. 'What word?' Stan had asked. But Jake only shook his head.

The interlude with Stan helped Jake. The hygiene soothed, even though he had not yet changed his undershorts. This woman, Emily Bradshaw, had upset everything, like she had disturbed more than his routine. He had never ever quit the office early like this. And he wasn't going back home today; he couldn't face Katie or Andy.

It occurred to him that he looked upon Stan as a friend, a true friend. But Stan? Did Stan feel the same way? Hey, wait a minute, he was no homesexual – what was he thinking about a *true* friend like this for? Something was wrong if he was thinking like this. He was a loner because he wanted to be a loner. He'd had a friend once, a long time ago, when he was twelve. He shut his eyes – he would not think about Brad.

Why didn't Katie take Andy to be fingerprinted?

Everyone cheated, that was what that woman had said on the *Anne Sweeting Show*; they cheated through their taxes, they cheated through their wives, they cheated on the whole system. What she said about tax evaders was true, as he well knew. Tax evaders – dirty, crooked tricksters. Catching them and getting the better of them was the closest he had ever come to feeling almost holy, a little bit like a human god dispensing legal justice. Con-artists trying to take him for a fool . . . And his own wife, also a con-artist, cheating on him, and on *Andy* . . . The pain of this was exquisite, beautiful; he could bring it on again just by thinking of Andy. It gave him a high.

Because Katie must have cheated on him. He'd find out who it was. He knew how. He wasn't an IRS agent for nothing.

Chapter 9

'Now here's what you must do for me,' Rick had said. 'Doll yourself up with extra, *extra* care, OK?'

Sometimes following instructions, Emily thought, can be really wonderful. For once, in these past crowded days, there was time, luxurious time; she had taken a deliciously long and glorious bath and then a short sharp shock of a shower, and now felt as refreshed as if she had just been skiing down a slope of the crispest snow. For she was dressing for a command performance, dinner with the president of TAN. At least, she now knew what TAN stood for: *Trans-American Network*. The whole thing was ridiculous really. And mad. 'There'll be no stopping you now – not if he takes a shine to you. It's mind-blowing. An invitation to dinner with Arthur Kristol!'

All this, to sell books.

But the way Rick talked, books were almost irrelevant.

Meanwhile, dressing in her room that overflowed with roses was, well, almost sinful it was so ... Emily didn't know quite what it was ... *Welcome to New York. Looking forward to tonight*. Arthur Kristol hadn't bothered to add his name, which although strange was American and rather nice, really. And the dress ... the dress looked as good as it felt. Whatever else she was or was not, Sheila Lyall had known, that day in London, how to choose the right dress. The colour was wonderful, a turquoise that was green and not blue, yet if it had been in any other fabric than the softest, purest, silkiest satin, it would have looked garish. And yet it had a sheen to it, but this was so discreet that it was almost hidden; almost secret.

She would adopt these primary, bright positive colours and give up the beiges and khakis, all those neutral colourless shades. Panty-hose... She remembered she had not sent the thank-you note to Sheila. Oh God, she thought, disgraceful. Now it was too late to call. She would write... but not tonight.

The phone buzzed. 'Limo's waiting, Mrs Bradshaw.'

She could actually feel the sweep and flow of the silk against her legs. Oh! The cut of that skirt. It made her long to go dancing; apart from the odd charity ball, she could not remember when last she had even thought of dancing. The first thing she noticed about the man who came towards her was that he was unusually tall.

'Mrs Bradshaw?' he said rather formally. 'Good evening. I'm Leon Lerner. The car's right outside.'

'Good evening,' Emily said and held out her hand to shake his. After all, this was America where chauffeurs had the quaint habit of introducing themselves by name.

But yet another chauffeur waited and held open the door of the limousine. This one merely said, 'Evening, ma'am.'

Soon Leon Lerner was seated beside her.

Above the television set, a glimmer of champagne and two crystal glasses.

'Care for some champagne?' Leon asked.

'Thank you, yes.'

She took a sip. A wall of tinted glass window was rolled into position and privacy was secured.

The atmosphere was so formal and so, well, daunting, that Emily laughed nervously. It struck her that it was ridiculous to be sipping champagne like this, at the back of a limo, on her way to dine with Arthur Kristol. That is, if it was Arthur Kristol. Perhaps there had been a change of president, a sudden *coup d'état*? What she was about to say would possibly sound silly, she knew, but then to say the champagne was excellent was too banal and probably even sillier. So she said, 'You must forgive me. I thought you were the chauffeur...'

Whereupon Leon Lerner laughed. Both Leon and Milt were famous for a certain laugh of theirs, the laugh which came only when they considered something excruciatingly funny. He stretched out his legs to accommodate the kind of chuckled sound which is so hard to convey to those who have not heard it because everyone who hears it begins, without quite knowing why, to laugh with it. Of course, Emily was caught up in that laugh and with its accompanying release.

When they had regained control of themselves, he said, 'You thought I was the chauffeur? Oh, that's rich! That really is rich. Wait till I tell Art about this one!'

'Arthur Kristol? Must you? Rick would never forgive me.'

'Who is Rick?'

'Rick Cooke, my publicist. The whole thing is desperately important to him, you see.'

'I see. You mean, not important to you?'

'It is important, but more important to Rick; it's his profession.'

'But not yours?'

'Not altogether.'

'Of course I know that. Well, you can be forgiven for thinking I was a chauffeur. You hadn't met me before. But I met you, you see, the night before last.' He pointed to the TV screen. 'Right here.'

'Oh, on *Nightguard*?'

'You were great,' he said. 'Telegenic. Highly, highly telegenic.'

'Telegenic? That's a new word for me.'

'Me too. Don't think I heard it before myself. Must have made it up!'

'What time did you watch it?'

'Around midnight ...'

'That means we were both watching at the same time?'

'Seriously, though, you are telegenic. That's why I called Art Kristol to set up this dinner.' The limo stopped. 'We're here,' he said. 'I'll tell you more later.'

Art and Eartha Kristol were waiting at the Four Seasons Restaurant. Leon said nothing about Emily having thought he was a chauffeur; his silence, and their secret, created an intimacy between them which might not otherwise have been there.

Occasionally Leon caught her eye, and she caught its only-just-suppressed twinkle, and though they ate and talked Emily found herself straining after it and made no attempt to hide her own. Besides his thigh rested, as lightly as another hidden twinkle, against her own surprisingly alert thigh. Did he mean his thigh to rest there like that? Was he aware of hers as she of his? Or was it her imagination? She couldn't tell, but rather felt that she was mistaken and making too much of it. Meanwhile she was all too aware of Leon's touch, frighteningly aware.

The Kristols told her about the Lerner twins, about the tragedy which had befallen both of them, about the kind of husbands they had been to the kind of wives they had had. Emily heard about Leon's two daughters, Robyn and Jenny: both at Vassar, both presently doing their year abroad, in Italy. Surprisingly there was no embarrassment in any of this, on anyone's part. They wanted her to know, and assumed – quite rightly – that she would want to know, too. Emily found this stimulating beyond words – talking about someone, praising him in his presence, even referring to all his anonymous donations, his sponsorship of the Burn Research Institute and the Philip I. Bailey Hospital and the Barnett-Braudie Foundation. She had not come across anything remotely approaching this kind of flagrant candour before. Leon didn't seem to mind – perhaps it was because the Kristols said 'they' so often, instead of 'he', as if Leon were only half of everything they said. Or as if they were not all talking about Leon, but about his brother, Milt; it seemed as if the two were interchangeable.

'Were they identical twins?' Emily wanted to know.

'Not quite. Milt's lost more hair than I have. You've got to meet him. He's a character.'

Emily had no doubt but that she would. And then, suddenly, they were talking about her.

'You know, Emily,' Eartha began, 'you've only just hit New York and I've already heard about you from two different sources.'

'Amazing,' Emily said, meaning it. 'Who told you about me?'

'A dear friend of ours called Leon Lerner!' Everyone at that table laughed. 'And another friend...' Emily felt herself being assessed... 'Sheila Lyall.'

'She took some incredibly good photographs of me,' Emily said, making herself sound enthusiastic. 'Incredibly flattering, I must say—'

'They're not flattering,' Leon stated unexpectedly. 'I have them on my desk; Rick Cooke sent them to me.'

'I'm not sure I understand,' Emily said, sounding bewildered.

'I had a telex about you from Sir Roger Wilbury, remember? Then I saw you on *Nightguard*, called your publisher, who put me in touch with Rick Cooke, who sent me your photographs.'

'We've been looking for a new face for a new show,' Eartha said crisply. 'Sheila thought we ought to take a look at you.'

'Have you got an agent?' Art asked.

'In New York. No. I mean, yes. Rick Cooke.'

'Do we know Rick Cooke, Art?' Eartha asked. 'More to the point – should we?'

'What a babe in the woods this kid is,' Leon said, openly delighted. 'What a find. Rick Cooke is a hired publicist and she calls him an agent!'

'Excuse me for being rude,' Emily said – coldly, she thought, 'but what on earth are you talking about?'

Leon gave out his famous laughing laugh. (Later, Emily was always to remember this moment and that laugh. She would think of it whenever she thought of him – which would be all the time.) Now, as if suddenly taken aback by the sound of the laugh, and therefore compelled to remark on it though in the way of one who speaks to oneself, she said, 'Leon Lerner has a laughing laugh.'

'Why shouldn't he?' Eartha said sharply. 'What else is a laugh?'

'A laugh is not always a laugh,' Emily explained slowly, seriously. 'A laugh is sometimes an instrument.'

'Yes, a laugh can be a weapon,' Leon said. 'I agree with Emily.'

'I talked to Rick Cooke when I set up this meeting,' Art said, hoping to lead the talk back to the point not only of the conversation, but of the whole evening. Answering Leon's summons had meant that another very important dinner had been cancelled. Art was not going to waste tonight.

Which was how Emily first heard that a TV campaign would be waged around her, with a budget running to several million. She was going to do the commercial which would launch the newest vitamin-enriched vegetarian dog food. It seemed the product had not yet been christened – a brand-new name was still in the works.

'This is a new departure for me,' Emily said brightly and, she hoped, lightly. 'I'm not sure I quite ...' she floundered, but went on. 'It seems not really ...'

'We'll be making you an offer you can't refuse,' Leon put in softly. 'Mega-bucks ...' He went on firmly, 'I like the way you look. I'm not offering this to you because you wrote a book. If I'd only seen you – on TV – in the audience, that would have been enough!'

Art said smoothly, 'Rick Cooke is not exactly a heavy-weight.'

'But he's very kind,' Emily replied urgently. 'Such a warm and kind man.' She wanted to tell them about the way Rick had spotted her book tucked away in the corner of the Frontier catalogue, about the author of *Sixty Seductive Salads from Fifty-One Different States*. But she managed to stop herself. 'Don't sell yourself short, Emily,' Rick had taught her. 'In the USA modesty doesn't pay. Never forget it.' Instead, she said, 'Rick's sweet. He's always saying, "Now, Emily, here's what I want you to do for me."'

'She's adorable,' Eartha said. 'Adorably British!'

'Yeah,' Art agreed, 'she is.' He turned to Leon. 'You were right, Leon. She is great for that new product. Keats! How about that, huh? Keats Eats. A romantic British poet, images of the British countryside. "A green and pleasant land".'

'Not Keats.' Emily said, quite unable to stop herself in time. 'It was Blake – not that it matters, of course.'

'Blake?' Leon said. '*What is it men in women do desire? The lineaments of gratified desire.*' Now in unison, Emily and Leon: '*What is it women do in men require? The lineaments of gratified desire.*'

'Most impressive,' Art commented.

'I went to a no-name school, freshman year. Blake. The full extent...' He turned to Art. 'How about Windsor?' he suggested. 'Emily reminds me of Princess Di; that's what I thought when I first saw her. I wanted to be sure...'

'Brilliant, Leon, brilliant!' Eartha said, sounding ecstatic. 'Prince Charles has endorsed health foods, alternative medicine.'

Art let out his breath slowly. About twenty million, he reckoned – on a new product, sewn up... He said, 'Isn't that Governor Peerce with Senator Hallon coming towards us?'

Emily heard herself being introduced as the daughter of Sir Thomas Rice. Ah, well, she thought, *politics*... But how did they know about her father? Keith Summers, she supposed.

Or Sheila Lyall.

She shuddered.

For the first time that evening, Emily looked around the restaurant, conscious of taking in the scene. It was bound to be something to write home about. Suddenly her throat caught. Could that be Frank Sinatra? Her entire being tingled – which made her furious, for she wasn't that sort of person at all. Both she and Simon were no less contemptuous of those who courted the famous than they were of the famous... Nobel laureates excepted, needless to say. And here she was with a catch in her throat, all a-tingle because she wasn't absolutely certain that it actually *was* Frank Sinatra. And she would not ask. Another famous face, this time belonging to a personality she had long admired, and with unusual obstinacy too. Now this famous face was worth an open query: 'Isn't that Richard Nixon?' she asked.

'Where?' Leon said, squinting. 'I can see Frank Sinatra.'

'To the left of him, I think...'

'Yes, that's the man all right.'

'He let your side down, didn't he?' Emily said sympathetically. 'It always seemed to me that he was treated too harshly.'

'Americans don't see it that way,' Leon replied shortly.

Emily looked away... and straight into the eyes of Sheila Lyall. Sheila positively glittered. She wore a dazzling jewelled and beaded turban, Chagall-colours sparkling as she bore down on them. 'Hi, darlings,' she greeted them. 'What illustrious

121

company you keep. Emily Bradshaw *and* Leon Lerner!'

Sheila sat down beside Emily and – as if unable to help herself – grasped one of her cheeks and pinched hard. 'You need more colour, girl,' she said – menacingly, Emily thought.

Emily's cheeks burned, raising memories of that other time, so successfully repressed that until now it had seemed an eternity ago, if at all . . . Desperate for control, she bit her lip against the present terror and the present humiliation. Then she did something she would never have dreamed herself capable of; she moved her left hand to Leon's thigh and, digging her nails deep into his flesh, squeezed as tight as she could. She saw him wince.

But he got the message. 'Nice meeting you, Miss Lyall,' he said, standing up. 'We have to go.'

'Right this minute? I am disappointed.'

Leon said, 'Forgive me, Emily, but the people I have waiting for you would find me guilty of flagrant unpunctuality. Nice to have met you, Miss Lyall. Good night.'

Emily rose to leave.

'Talking of discourtesy, darling,' Sheila drawled. 'You did receive my gift of panty-hose?'

Now Emily flushed. 'Thank you. I'm sorry, I meant to write. But the schedule . . . I do apologize.'

As soon as they were out of earshot, Leon said, 'I'm taking you to Regines. You'll find it amusing, I think . . .'

'You are very kind. But really, I could go back to the hotel.'

'I told Milt we might drop by . . .'

He took Emily by the hand and led her away, and she was grateful and more than that. Because Leon Lerner had saved her.

*

At Regines they joined Milt and Arlene who had obviously been expecting them. Was she being touchy, or was Arlene rather curt, rather smouldering? Yet she showed particular curiosity about Emily's father, so Emily told her a bit about the ceremony that went with the knighthood . . . and then the music softened, and slowed, and Leon asked her to dance.

'Hey, Leon!' Milt said, chuckling. 'Before you lead your lady away, I need five minutes . . .'

'Later,' Leon said with the same chuckle. 'Music's just right for an old man.'

'Oh,' Emily said, embarrassed again. 'Please . . .' But he took her hand as she hoped he would and they threaded their way to the dancers. He stopped and said, 'Something tells me that heavyweight dyke made a serious pass at you?'

Emily nodded.

'And you took it personally?' He didn't wait for a reply, but went on, 'Nothing personal about it. New York's full of her kind.'

For Emily, then, came a welling of gratitude. Also relief, as when Danny had been note perfect. But something else besides, which for Emily was most startlingly unexpected: an awareness, a sensation of her own sensuality – so strong, so extraordinarily bodily that it positively tingled.

And all this even before they began to dance.

Emily the tall woman, whose height the sales director at Yves St Laurent had pronounced as 'perfect for clothes' . . . yet Leon towered over her, as Sheila Lyall had towered, but without the help of heels. Why, Emily wondered, *why* was she thinking of Sheila and Yves St Laurent now? She supposed it was the dress, the feel of the fall of the silk against her legs, a swish on the skin, *her* skin. Delicious! It made her feel nude under the dress, as if there was no underwear, nothing between her skin and that silk.

'I'm old-fashioned,' Leon said, pressing closer. 'This is my kind of music.'

'Mine too.'

They were swaying rather than dancing and Emily stopped. Arms flung about shoulders so massive, hugging him required a clasping of her own hands. Here she was, hugging a completely strange man in a strange country, gloriously dismissing prudence, manners, convention . . . and finally obliterating self – or, at any rate, the self she had known.

Irresponsible, but altogether exquisite.

The hug was returned, with equal force.

And yet, though it was a hug of affection, it was also a hug of the love of life. It was perceived by both, though differently. Neither expected to feel the love of life – Leon had not expected to feel like this *again*, and Emily had not expected it *ever*.

'Let's go,' Leon suggested.

Milt was very obviously put out. 'You're not going? Got to check something out with you . . .'

'Tomorrow,' Leon said.

As they were leaving, Emily heard, as she knew Arlene meant her to hear, 'Leon's hit bad *this time* . . .' *This time?* Emily thought. This time? We'll see . . .

'Where to, Mr Lerner?' the chauffeur asked.

'Home.'

Emily wanted to say that she didn't do this sort of thing; that she didn't go to the home of a strange man; in fact, she didn't go with men at all, ever. And not only because she did not want to, but because she had never been tempted, not even slightly. She was arguing with herself, pointlessly she knew. It was useless to remember now that men did not intrigue her, that sex did not engage her, that men and sex were not her scene, that sex with Simon was more than sex if only because it was all she had ever known or wanted, for the release and the comfort was shared and even. She stayed silent and was pleased because it didn't really matter what Leon would think of her; it was what she thought of herself that counted.

But in that shared silence, the altering, unpredictable rhythms of the hand on her knee, were annihilating thought. Unless, of course, the registering of sensations can be said to be thought, in which case she was dominated by thought.

Then doors and doormen swept open and Emily and Leon swept through, swept on, swept upwards until they were in Leon's bedroom. The bed (royal blue suede matching the walls, Emily noted, even with what was left of her housewife's eye) had been turned back, but no pyjamas were laid out. Instead, Leon's ubiquitous champagne. Ah, so she'd been expected then . . . Leon saw her see. 'Cato insists,' he said. 'Cato did this, every night for twenty years, for his previous boss. I humour him.' He picked up a glass. 'Would you?'

'Yes,' Emily said. God, she thought, it's obscene, *waiting* . . .

Leon moved toward the lamp and placed his hand on the switch. 'Shall I?' he asked.

'If you like.'

He left the light on and then, businesslike, he switched his attention from the lamp to her zip.

He was standing behind her, so she could not help him with his zip, which she ached to do. Courage! She swung round, found the zip-pull, was too quick. The zip caught . . . stuck. A brief tearing sound as Leon ripped the zip apart. 'The rip of a zip,' she said. Whereupon Leon laughed that wonderful catchy laugh of his.

And so it was that they fell into bed laughing.

Almost as they hit the sheets, though, the laughing stopped.

And in its stead there were other sensations, other movements, inner laughter, inner anger, inner passion. Womb and breast and skin and chest. And for Emily, sounds, new sounds, sounds unheard before because unsounded ever. A struggle of sound, womb to throat, perfect fit, tight inner grip, perfect movement, utter unity, rhythm increasingly desperate, womb to throat, ten toes hugging his waist, tongues twisted, everywhere wet. Then, desperately, 'Are you getting there, Emily? Are you getting there?'

'Yes.'

'When?'

'Now! *Now!*'

From Emily a final scream, hoarse and guttural, womb to throat. And from Leon a whistled cry, prick to chest to throat. Tears, sweat, juices, wetness everywhere.

They slept like that, uncoupled, for about half an hour. Emily was the first to awaken. She lay quite still, so as not to disturb him, staring at the heavy, brass-framed photograph which was under the lamp he had wanted to turn off. It was in colour and fairly recent; the woman's hairstyle, though not at the forefront of fashion, was still being worn, so it was impossible to tell when it had been taken. It was Ruthie, she knew. The Kristols had told her – it now seemed months ago – about Ruthie. Of course they had not told her about Ruthie's extra-large, extra-compassionate brown, almost black eyes. There was a sadness in those eyes, but an intelligence too; a sort of intelligent sadness. Emily decided they were *Jewish* eyes. It struck her, then, that Ruthie must have been Jewish. Was Leon also Jewish, was that what it was? Or if not altogether, then partly perhaps. She and Simon had met a few Jews, of course, at school and at university, though they had never been on anything like intimate terms with them. But none of this was really relevant to the shocking fact that here she was, naked, still in the arms of the man who had taken her to a place that until now she had not believed existed, staring into the eyes of his dead wife. Staring, not so much out of curiosity as of pragmatism, as if she believed Ruthie's eyes were teaching her something about herself – something she had always known, of course, but never quite faced. Then she knew she was jealous of Ruthie, jealous of those eyes, so jealous that she moved away impatiently . . .

. . . Which woke Leon, who was wide awake at once. 'You are something, Emily,' he said. 'Quite something. The bathroom calls.'

Emily needed the bathroom, too, but couldn't bring herself to move.

'You're a thirsty woman,' he said, pouring the champagne. 'And I'm a thirsty man.' He got into bed beside her, picked up the long cigar which had been lying beside Ruthie's photograph and asked, 'Would you mind very much?'

'No. I love the smell of cigars.'

'You do?' he said, plainly delighted. 'You do? I've got a theory about women who love cigar smoke.'

'Tell me.'

'They love men.'

'Oh . . .'

'I don't mean they're promiscuous, don't get me wrong. But they like men. They're sympathetic . . .'

'You're serious about this, aren't you?' Emily said. 'I suppose your wife loved cigar smoke.'

'She certainly did.'

He put down the champagne glass and the cigar, picked up a mouth spray, used it – two short bursts – put it down, took Emily's glass, put that down and then kissed her. It was a long deep, luxurious, intimate kiss and she felt as if she had been kissing him for years. He stopped. 'You're an excellent kisser,' he said. 'Want more?'

'Yes.'

So they made love again, and it was not the same as before. Because this time the wrenching, racking explosions hit Emily too quickly. 'Rest,' he said. 'Rest awhile. You'll come again, you'll see.' Still inside her, he rested too and they stayed still and very quiet. She moved almost imperceptibly, but he picked up at once. 'Ready?' he asked. 'More?'

'More.' It came out in a moan and she moved frantically; his hardness was driving her wild, his movements were subtle, deft, which forced her to follow, forced her to wait, and then he accelerated, and she was allowed to fly with him, and her body ripped apart, and nothing and no one mattered, only the ripping.

This time it was Emily who rushed to the bathroom. The pressure on her bladder which had so intensified sensation clamoured for release.

She gulped the champagne thirstily when she returned. Still thirsty, she said, 'Ordinary water is what I'd like.'

'Of course,' he said. He flicked a switch, a drawer slid upward and a gleaming jug of iced water was at her side.

'The age of America,' Emily commented.

'The age of electronics, you mean.'

'No,' Emily said, 'that's not what I mean. America is... dynamism; efficiency is everywhere. Efficient hedonism should be a contradiction. But not in America, it's not.'

'Never been fucked by an American before?'

'No.'

'Then I'm the first.'

'Yes, in more ways than one.'

'I know that. How long have you been married?'

'Ten years.'

'First outside fuck? First time you made love to someone who's not your husband?'

'Yes. I'm glad you put it that way.'

'What way?'

'Making love. This is pillow talk, isn't it?'

'Yes.'

'Were you faithful to Ruthie?'

'My wife?' he said sharply.

Emily knew she ought not to have mentioned Ruthie by name. 'Yes,' she said, 'I meant your wife.'

'No, I was not absolutely faithful. I had the odd screw, here and there. Nothing serious.'

'Nothing serious, *you* say. Did you love her?'

'I loved her. I still love her.'

'Tell me about her.'

He took a long draw on his cigar. 'I'd like to tell you about her,' he said. 'She was an exceptional woman, I guess. Everyone loved her. The Kristols were not exaggerating when they said that tonight. Ruthie and Marcie both, everyone adored them and they adored each other. Sisters! No one ever saw sisters who were also best friends the way those two were. At least they died together. Marcie wanted to die – Milt knows that, doesn't even try to deny it. We all knew that . . . But Ruthie . . . not Ruthie.

'Not that I blame Marcie, not really. She wanted to die. Some people say there are no accidents, only death wishes, but I can't work it out. Marcie wanted to die because of what happened to Martin. Their only son! He was like my son, you know. Martin was the only son in the family. The four of us even shared our kids . . . We don't know why he did it; he wasn't into drugs, he was at Yale, but he did it. Hanged himself on a tree. Found by a student out jogging on the campus – bumped into, I should say. Marjorie Boyle collided with his dead body – been in an institution ever since.

'My wife was taking her sister to the Hamptons for the weekend. Marcie and Ruthie were trying to get over it. Crazy. Who gets over such a thing? *I* haven't gotten over it. So the girls flew ahead in our Lear-Jet. And the rest you know. Did I love her, you asked. Yes, I loved her. Thank God I loved her. And she gave me two wonderful girls – both at Vassar now. They're in Italy together – having a year abroad.

'You know something, Emily? Ruthie would have liked you; she would have approved of you.'

There was a silence, then Emily permitted herself to speak.

'Thank you for that, Leon. It's probably the greatest compliment I've ever had in my life.'

'You're damn right it is!'

'May I ask why she would have liked me?'

'Because you're a lady. Nothing to do with your father's title, either. But she was gentle; she hated aggressive females. I think she was a bit tougher than you are, Emily. Ruthie would have fixed that dyke, Sheila, for example.'

Emily shuddered.

'She made a pass and you felt attracted and repelled at the same time, right?'

'Only I didn't know it at the time.'

'Want to tell me about it?'

So Emily told him about it, about her flaming face and the poultice of frozen peas, about setting off the burglar alarm siren, the hairdresser, the make-up, the burgundy cushions in her living room, the carrots and fruit in her kitchen, and finally about shopping at Yves St Laurent. Which led to her telling him about the Laura Ashley blouses, and her mother setting off to return them and dying on the street, of all places, on the Fulham Road. 'And she would have been so pleased about my hair,' she said. 'But she didn't live to see it. This will sound silly to you, I know, but I can't begin to tell you how it kills me. It actually hurts...'

'Don't tell me,' Leon said. 'I know too much about it. Trifles like that hit hardest.'

As if it was something she had suddenly remembered, though it had been troubling her ever since they arrived at his apartment, Emily said, 'I hope no one's been trying to reach me tonight, because I've never been incommunicado before. It's very irresponsible, actually...'

'I know it is. But let's not think about it. Let's think about this,' he said, his fingers skimming her nipple. 'Look at it. Watch it stand. It likes this. Look at the other one, untouched, but standing up and waiting. Marvellous breasts. Beautiful, beautiful!'

She felt practised with him, as if they had been making love for years. Because they had intermingled parts of their histories,

129

as they had intermingled all of their bodies. Now his lips travelled her breasts, her chest, her waist, her stomach . . . and he switched off the light and moved all the way down, till he found her toes, till each toe had been sucked and stroked, and then tongued his way up her calves, her thighs – only then was that writhing, waiting epicentre, still virgin to the tongue, tongued. The better, the more to feel, she must see. She raised her head to look and the sight of that silver-grey hair between her legs led climax into climax. 'Please,' she yelled, 'please put it inside, *please*!'

He raised his head once to say quickly, 'Not yet. Not yet. Wait!'

'No, I *can't* wait. Please, I *beg* you!'

'You begging me?'

'Yes.'

He entered her then and filled her, and she felt as if a lifelong leak was being stoppered, and at this moment sealed. No other moment mattered. Her entire body met and worshipped his every thrust, until that whistled cry of his was met with yet another new sound of her own. When she could speak, she asked, 'What time is it?'

'About five a.m. You'd best be getting back. Horatio will take you.'

'Horatio? Your chauffeur? At this hour?'

'That's right. He's on nights. I have an apartment for him in the building.'

'I'd rather call my own taxi, if you don't mind. I'm not exactly keen on being despatched like a used package. I should have thought you'd take me back yourself. After all, you yourself collected me.'

'Tell you what, you're right! Thanks for the lesson in manners. Emily's a good name for you. The name of the woman who taught manners to America is Emily Post – did you know that?' He laughed then, and that wonderfully contagious giggle filled the room. The force of the laugh shook his entire body and he stretched his legs and slapped his thighs. 'Tell you what your next book should be, *Fucking Manners* by Emily Bradshaw.' He laughed again. 'Emily Post, you are good for me! I haven't laughed like this in years.'

Though Emily had not exactly seen the joke, she had joined in the laughter for the sheer joy of it. She wanted to remind him again that she was not a real writer, but it was too late; she must get up, she was suddenly anxious about Simon and Danny. Perhaps they had been trying to reach her?

A Porsche was waiting for them. He must have arranged to have it brought round while she was in the bathroom, Emily thought. Which was very thoughtful, really. Even touching. He wanted to know if they could meet for lunch, but Emily had an interview with the *Post*. 'Emily Post,' he said. 'From here on in, I'm calling you Post. What about tonight? I'll show you New York.'

'You're all the New York I want to see.'

'Do you mean that?'

'Yes.'

'You're doing the *Don Cordow Show* at ten, right? Till eleven. And the *Virginia Byrnes* at noon?'

'Then the *Post* at 1.30, a syndicated cable taping at 3.30, and at six . . . I've forgotten which alphabetical combination it is. I still haven't learned the meaning of W or K, or whatever . . .'

'It's not important.'

'I know.'

'We're important. You and I are important. I'll be out there, rooting for you. Remember that. Or will you be too preoccupied with crackpot callers to remember me?'

'I'll never be too preoccupied for you.'

'Good. I'll catch you on the *Virginia Byrnes*. I'll watch live and video it for you, OK?'

*

When Emily reached her room, she was compelled to push hard against the door and practically force it open. A pile of envelopes had collected, messages; she scooped them up and could make out some of the computer-printing through the transparent slats: NO REPLY . . . URGENT . . . CHANGE . . . SIMON . . . The phone was ringing. Oh God, she thought, dear God, please . . . She answered the phone and at the same time tore the message which read: SIMON TRIED TO CALL YOU AT THE AMBASSADOR EAST IN CHICAGO. NO PROBLEM. HE WANTED TO

131

She was so engrossed in her reading that she did not immediately reply until she came to the end of the message. Leon was saying, 'Post? Are you there, Emily Post?'

'Oh,' she said, 'it's *you*. Oh, God bless you!'

'Hey? What's going on there? I left you less than four minutes ago.'

'Where are you?'

'In the car.'

'I found all these messages. Simon tried to call me in Chicago – he didn't know Rick cancelled . . .'

'I'm the culprit. I suppose you knew I called Art Kristol and suggested the dinner?'

'No, I didn't know. I am pleased, though. Chicago? I'd forgotten all about Chicago. Six messages from Rick Cooke!'

'Tell him there must have been something wrong with the phone.'

'I hadn't thought of that. Yes, I will.'

'See you tonight, Emily Post.' He hung up.

The phone rang again. Rick. 'Your line was busy. Where've you been?'

'Phone was out of order.'

'But I got the operator to check and recheck,' Rick said, sounding puzzled.

'Human error,' Emily snapped. 'Are you sure Simon and Danny are OK? I'll call now. It's about 11.30 a.m. in London.'

'He'll be in the country for the day and Danny's going with him. That's why he was trying you in Chicago. So, how did it go?'

'What?'

'Your meeting with Art Kristol. What's wrong with you?'

'Oh, that. Sorry, I'm confused. They brought a man called Leon Lerner . . .'

'Leon Lerner? Leon *Lerner*? You sure you got the right name? Leon Lerner? That's one big, big name in this town.'

Rick sounded highly emotional, Emily thought. It was strange, but she believed he was close to tears and for some reason she wanted to laugh. But because she dared not, she said nothing.

132

'Hey, Emily, are you there? Have we got cut off?'

'No.'

'Then you did say Leon Lerner?'

'Yes. By the way, just *who* is Mr Leon Lerner?'

'About the biggest real estate billionaire in this city is all Mr Leon Lerner is. Big in pet-foods, too. Ever heard of *Kay-Chow*?'

'They talked about that last night. I rather think that's why I was invited . . .'

'Whaaat?' Rick interrupted, actually screaming. 'This is fuckin' mind-blowing!' He calmed down. 'Did they say anything about a new product?'

'The vegetarian dog food, you mean? Yes.'

Needless to say, Emily thought, neither she nor Leon had mentioned dog food. Too busy. Too fucking busy all night! . . . She chuckled.

'It's no joke,' Rick said impatiently. 'They probably want you to launch it.'

He sounded emotional again. 'Jeez, Emily, d'you know what this could mean?'

'Rick, forgive me. It's too early for me.'

'I'll come and get you for the *Don Cordow Show* and we'll talk about it. OK?' He hung up.

*

Emily's first thought was for her hair. Tangled and matted with sweat, it testified to the realities of the night. She wished it could be left as it was. She had expected to feel overcome by a pleasant lethargy, expected to long for sleep. Instead, she was charged with enormous energy, a high-voltage charge, as if that part of her electrical system which had lain dormant had now been switched on. She had only been half-alive, now she was fully alive. Even the cold water against her scalp was exciting and her switched-on body tingled everywhere. Her muscles should have ached, but vibrated instead. She laughed aloud. The memory of the spent night, combined with the anticipation of the night ahead, was enough to produce a tingle, also a tumescence down there between her legs . . . Leon's grey hair . . . Jumbled thoughts, but all so deliciously stimulating – her first lover had become her only lover, her only real lover, ever. Leon was warm and confident, and above all friendly because he was American. His easygoing grace was his own, and natural; he had not been crafted by his school as Simon had been. He was not dependent on Simon's kind of processed Etonian charm. As far as Emily was concerned, Leon was a self-made man. Leon was his own man, sure of himself and super-competent . . . True, she was away from home. But could this have happened, say, in France? Oh, no – they have the same voltage, America has a lower voltage . . . So good to be light-headed, light-hearted like this, thinking ridiculously silly thoughts. So good to have been carried away. The only problem was that she wanted more, and still more; that creamy pulse between her legs was insistent, determined. She would have to be careful, very careful – she would need to wear two pairs of knickers if she wanted to make sure of no leaked stains on her skirt.

Emily rejoiced in her tight schedule, because the night would come sooner.

Her hair looked good and she was proud of the way she was managing it. It struck her that she had not even asked why Simon and Danny had gone to the country and that made her feel uneasy. She would phone them after the blasted *Virginia Byrnes Show*. What on earth was Simon doing, taking Danny out of school to spend a day in the country in the middle of the week? She hadn't even had the brains to ask Rick for details. And what if Danny had really needed her last night?

She had gone over the top, she told herself furiously – lost her senses, which was not only risky but downright dangerous. At the same time her skin still quivered with – and thirsted for – Leon.

She would have to pull herself together.

She would not be ruled by her body.

Emily wished she had never met Leon – it was too much of an upheaval. Yet she had to admit that he had infused her with a certain strength. She knew, now, what she must do. She would fly home tomorrow and, come hell or high water, Danny would not go to the Trevor-Winston School. She would fight Simon over that – to the death, if necessary.

Her mind reeled back to the pile of messages telling her that

Simon had been trying to reach her. She was grateful for those messages – they had carried reality.

The *Virginia Byrnes Show* would be the last she would do. From the outset this particular show had provoked a generalized sense of unease. After all, if that producer had not called London when she had, Emily would not have felt so desperately intimidated about speaking frankly in front of her mother and therefore would not have sent her to change the Laura Ashley blouses ... The *Virginia Byrnes Show* had already cost her her mother. Emily tried to stop herself from thinking like this; it lacked reason, smacked of superstition and was not like her at all. Even so, unease gathered like premonition, the nameless facts of the nameless future.

Chapter 10

The Lerner brothers usually worked together in the same office. Two large desks, faced one another. They had had these desks for ever – almost since day one. Ruthie had found them, discarded rejects left behind in Fawcett's building – the very building on which their dramatic turn of fortune had been based. It was not that these desks, known as partners' desks, were especially valuable. They were Victorian, though, and Ruthie had spotted that behind the green paint. It was Ruthie, and later Marcie, who added the personal touch to the foyers of their giant buildings. At first they shopped for copper vases or Mexican pots or African baskets; these seemingly insignificant acquisitions added a certain distinction to the vast halls, which might otherwise have been impersonal and filled with standard chill. It was only when their men became mega-successful that they began attending auctions at Sotheby's and Christie's.

Of course the twins had separate offices as well. These were necessary for separate meetings, but unless there was such a meeting the brothers spent all their time together, in the same room.

Today Leon had flirted with the idea of not going in to the office at all, of staying in his own apartment to listen to Emily on the *Don Cordow Show* in private. But Milt would have been worried, would have assumed at once that his twin was ill. Even since Leon's by-pass surgery, three months after the crash five years ago, Milt had been nervous ... far, far more nervous than

Leon. Milt of course had expected to have had his own heart attack by now; after all, they were identical twins and this might well have happened. But it had not. All his tests had thrown up was that he had three instead of two kidneys.

Leon was in his private office, waiting for the *Don Cordow Show* to begin, when Milt stormed in. 'Are you crazy, or something? Cancelling our meeting with Western Insurance?'

'Cancelled? I didn't cancel the meeting; I merely said I couldn't attend. They don't need both of us.'

'You know they'll read more into it. They'll think you're against . . .'

'I know that. I also know that I am going to watch Emily Bradshaw, live, on the *Virginia Byrnes Show*!'

'We could video it.'

'But I said I'd watch it live, and I will. And before that I'm going to listen to her on the *Cordow Show*.'

'She's married, she's a married woman. You know that decision we took: no married women.'

'I know. But she's not American and she doesn't live here. She lives in London and she'll be going back very soon. Too soon. Meanwhile, do you mind?' Leon raised the volume of his radio and checked the tape. Yes, it was all running smoothly. Milt sat down and Leon sighed and handed him a cigar. He would have preferred to be alone and Milt sensed that, but could not leave – it would have been too great a departure from their established habits. He flicked a switch. 'Two coffees, please, Miss Palmerston.'

Don Cordow had announced that Emily would be on his show, and meanwhile Leon was compelled to suffer through the commercials. Suddenly, he looked at his identical twin with the greatest curiosity – with more interest, even, than when he had looked at himself in the mirror that morning. He wanted to see – hoped he would see – in three dimensions, what Emily saw. For apart from a slight jagged scar over Milt's left cheek, the face he stared at was his own; and good-looking enough in a rugged sort of way, Leon noted with special pleasure, to do a shaving commercial. Better-looking now, perhaps, than he had ever been. That is, if one thought mature, distinguished looks were attractive. What did Emily think? Milt's hair, thick and straight, unstyled, was old-fashioned. His was the same – it would stand reshaping. He said, 'I think Gionni's a bit *passé*.'

Milt was mystified. 'Gionni?' he said. Leon was twiddling with his hair. 'Oh, Gionni the barber, you mean. Boy, you've been hit bad!'

'Hold it,' Leon said impatiently. For Emily's voice was filling the room, spilling over Giacometti sculptures, bouncing off the Rothkos – that clear, delicate sound which from the very first had touched or set off something almost religious inside Leon. And listening now, listening with his entire body, he knew that even if he had not been alerted by that introduction from Sir Roger Wilbury, even if he had not seen her on TV, her voice alone would have sparked an intense need to meet its owner. He felt a kind of indulgent, slightly stupid smile spread over his face. God, he thought, I'm like a lovesick teenager!

Milt barely heard what the voice said, because the sight of his brother's sickly smile was so infuriating. He could not remember when last he had felt so irritated, or so disgusted, or so sickened – and all at the same time. A grimace escaped and scampered over his face, which was picked up by Leon.

He thinks I'm a fool, Leon thought, and he's not wrong.

Now Emily was saying, '. . . the unforgiving heart is the immoral heart . . .'

'Too true,' Leon murmured, 'too true. Wouldn't you agree, Milt?' The commercials were on again and Leon could not bear not to talk, indeed needed to talk. 'Milt?' he said again, because Milt was silent. 'Wouldn't you agree that the unforgiving heart is the immoral heart?'

'I don't know,' Milt said. 'I suppose so . . . Haven't thought about it much lately . . .' Undisguised sarcasm, but Leon let that go.

Lovesick cunt, Milt thought. He remembered something: their father's warning, long ago when they were both *real* teenagers: 'Never come between a man and his moll.' Recalling this long-ago warning was a warning in itself, because this time this moll *would* come between the two of them. He was so certain of this that it might just as well have been an established fact.

Leon's excited voice cut across his thoughts: 'The lines are jammed, Don Cordow said. They're crazy for her out there. Hundreds of callers!'

Emily was saying '... no, I don't think I said that. What I did say was that paternity tests can prove that a man is *not* the father. In other words, there is no absolute test that can conclusively prove positive paternity.'

'Does that mean, ma'am – excuse my ignorance, ma'am – but are you saying that I can have a test that will prove that I'm not the father, but that there is no test to prove that I *am* the father of my son?' The caller's quick, heavy breath came over the air with a whistle, his anger unmistakable. 'You see...'

'Well...' Emily said, fumbling, because the voice sounded menacing. 'Of course new tests are being devised all the time. My information may be out of date.'

'You have not answered my question,' the caller snapped, his voice hard and angry. 'You sow the seeds of suspicion in a man's mind...'

'That is not her intention, caller,' Don Cordow slipped in smoothly. 'Emily was explaining why the male response to sexual jealousy differs from the female...'

'She's saying I can't prove I'm my kid's father...'

'Oh, please, don't take it like that,' Emily said urgently, making her anxiety all too apparent. Now it was her long, sighing breath that came through.

'Go to hell,' the man said furiously. 'I hope you rot in hell!' He hung up.

'We get those sometimes,' Don Cordow announced in his deep, fruity voice. 'My apologies to Emily and to our listening audience. Next caller is David, calling from Queens...'

'That guy sounded dangerous, if you ask me, very dangerous,' Leon said.

'If you put yourself up front, you're asking for it,' Milt said irritably, which wouldn't help any; he'd have to be more careful than that. Quickly he went on, 'She handled it very well. Didn't lose her cool.' But if Leon heard him, he gave no sign.

'See you later,' Milt said lightly and left the room.

Cancelling meetings arbitrarily, sitting there drooling like a kid – meant trouble. Big trouble. Shocked, Milt realized that this was the first time in all his life that he did not know how to handle it, how to manage the situation. Because their relationship had never been handled, or managed, or worked at. Each knew what the other thought, even before he thought it. For example, Milt knew that Leon had been thinking of his poor Martin's suicide when they had been talking of unforgiving hearts ... Right now, though, he could not predict what sort of changes were about to befall them. And what this could do, God forbid, to Leon's health – Leon's heart, for God's sake! Milt began to feel a tightening of his own chest. He was certain that Emily Bradshaw was unaware of Leon's condition. The scar that ran down the centre of his hairy chest, from throat to waist, was covered by his chest hair, and the same was true of the jagged scars along his inner thighs and calves. Because Leon was such an excellent healer – damn it! – there was virtually no scar to feel. He touched his own scarred cheek – nothing to feel; if he wore a beard, there would have been nothing to see either.

Emily Bradshaw was fooling around with a cardiac case, and it was about time she knew it.

He knew how he would tell her – how he would, as they say, broach the subject. He would mention the Philip I. Bailey Hospital, named after the cardiac surgeon who had performed the triple by-pass which had saved Leon's life. Named after Dr Bailey, but the Barnett-Braudie wing was funded by the Barnett-Braudie Foundation, the maiden name of Ruthie and Marcie and their mother, Bess Barnett. God, how he needed both girls now ... More than ever now. Crazy, because if they were alive there would be no Emily Bradshaw to consider.

The Philip I. Bailey Hospital, affectionately known as PIB, was Leon's special baby. He knew the names of almost every orderly, to say nothing of every doorman. That was the Lerners' special trade-mark, remembering names, anyway. He had a special relationship with the ambulance attendants; because of the heartlessly, unforgivably callous way he had been treated – though almost dying – by some of them. Since then he had sponsored several studies into the particular stresses to which ambulance attendants are subjected, though as he later said, he hadn't really needed any studies to confirm how underrated and overstressed they were. But the extent of the injustice had at least been documented. And when Leon wanted to buy out the Hill Ambulance Company, Milt had gone along with it.

Yes, this was the way he would go about telling Emily about Leon's heart condition. He would begin by asking her about ambulance services in Britain... She *had* to know she was fooling around with a cardiac case. Some women were afraid of that; it could turn her off...

Sure, telling Emily about the Lerner brothers' philanthropic activities would offend his and Leon's Jewish principles, or what was left of them. Because when the girls had been killed in the crash, they had dropped a lot of that ritual – Friday nights, and so on. All that was left of their ancient tradition was the Talmudic teaching that he who gives in secret is twice blessed, yet Milt was prepared to blow even this. For the life of him, there was no alternative that he could see.

*

'I'm afraid I've ruined that man's life,' Emily said to Rick. 'I upset him terribly. I must get his name and write to him or something. Don Cordow's going to see what he can do...'

'Aw, he's just a crank. An air-head,' Rick said quickly. 'You were great. Great! Didn't I tell you they'd love you?'

'I didn't get his name, but I'll get the tape. I have to!'

They were walking quickly. It would take at least fifteen minutes to get to the TAN studios and the *Virginia Byrnes Show*. Twenty minutes for make-up, though she would probably have to wait now until the other guests were through. Two psychologists, the interview... Rick was anxious, as usual.

'I wish I knew where Simon was. In the country with Danny on a school day? It's probably about 4.20 in London; I could call now.'

'But we're late and the limo's waiting. I see it. Good!' An idea struck him. 'We'll call from the limo!'

'You can call London from a car?'

'Sure. It's new. Some limos have them and I ordered the best. Frontier Books pick up the tab.'

But at Lamont Road, there was no reply. 'Now you see why

you should have had an answering machine?' Rick said, sounding aggrieved.

'Just a moment,' Emily said. 'I'll try his office.' No reply there, either. 'It's Friday afternoon in London,' she explained sadly. 'Everyone leaves early; all good Englishmen, anyway.'

'Yeah – I heard about it. From Keith, your agent. What a jerk he is! I needed him one Friday, waited till two o'clock your time. Course, he'd left for the afternoon – left at noon, his secretary said, to go to the country. It was Friday – I thought I'd bust a blood vessel, I can tell you. And then Keith has the nerve to preach about the civilized British . . .'

Emily laughed. 'I know what you mean,' she agreed. But Keith seemed distant and unimportant. That caller had unnerved her and she said, 'I didn't like the way he sounded.'

'Who, Keith?'

'No. That man.'

'Don't think about it. A crackpot. I should have warned you about them. He should have been screened out by the radio station.'

'There was one the other day, Norman Maitland. He thumped the table – about the same thing.'

'Leave out that genes stuff next time.'

'I did, this time. That's what troubles me, you see. That man was calling about what he'd heard me say on the *Anne Sweeting Show*.'

'You're right, I remember now. So many callers – it's hard sometimes to get the order of things. Leave it with me, will you?'

'I feel awful about it. Really, really, awful . . .'

'Forget it. We're here now.'

This time it was Rick pushing through the lines of people waiting to go in. 'Great audience,' he murmured. 'You'll wow them. You'll be a wow!'

Emily, who was now superstitious about the word 'wow', wished Rick had not used it.

'Make way. Step aside. Put your head down, Emily,' he called out. 'Step aside, madam, for our celebrity guest here.'

He loves this, Emily thought; he loves the attention. She

found it endearing. It was so very different from the way she imagined it to be when she was in London. There, people did all they could to draw attention *away* from themselves. Still, she had to admit she rather liked the curious animated looks the audience directed towards her.

To think she had never had the remotest inkling that she would love being in the limelight... so many unsuspected depths were now exposed. She seemed to think more clearly when she was in a rush of stretched nerves. Because these depths had been exposed and then – well, celebrated, by America. And by Leon.

Then the Green Room and a sudden attack of excruciating nerves. Because Leon would be watching, she felt self-conscious. She wished he was with her now. Then she felt guilty about Simon and, spying a telephone, decided she would call him collect. But no sooner had she begun than Rick said, 'They're ready for you in make-up; now here's what you can do for me...'

Emily laughed – that phrase of his always helped. But Rick continued, 'I'll call Simon when you're on. Find out where the hell he went to! OK?'

'OK.'

In make-up the girl said, 'You look beautiful, Emily Radiant. Like you just got hold of a great new lover!'

Emily was helpless against a sudden spreading blush.

'Why, I do declare, she's blushing,' the girl said happily. 'Haven't seen anyone blush since I left Alabama.'

It was too much for Emily. She felt... she didn't know what she felt, except that inexplicably tears began to well. She confided, 'I'm nervous. I'm nervous of Virginia Byrnes.'

'Seen her?'

'No.'

'She's a tough cookie.'

'That explains it...'

'Close your eyes, please. Explains what?'

'Why I'm frightened.'

'Sixth sense? Are you psychic?'

'No.'

'Good. See, if you were psychic, I'd have got frightened too. Like you had a premonition of disaster, you know – catastrophe.'

'Disaster? Catastrophe?'

'You bet. I believe in it. I'm a true Southerner. My cousin, Louise-May, now she felt jittery for no good reason, and sure enough her son was visiting Los Angeles. So when she heard about McDonalds, no one needed to tell her her boy caught his . . .'

'McDonalds?'

'You remember that shooting? More than ten killed by a crazed gunman.'

'Yes. Saw it on the BBC.'

'Bad news sure goes round the world. You're all done now, and you look great. Took your mind off things, didn't I? I'm going to watch your show myself.'

'Thanks. Thank you,' Emily said, but sounded doubtful. She was nervous and she was frightened, and all that talk about premonition and prevision had made her more nervous, more frightened. Utterly unnerved. That man, that poor father. What had she done? *Oh, what had she done?*

Chapter 11

When 'Reservations' told Simon that Emily had not checked in, that her reservation at the Ambassador East had indeed been cancelled, Simon too experienced a similar unease. It was not like Emily to be incommunicado. In fact, it was so unlike her that Simon felt constrained to phone Rick. It was four o'clock in the morning in London, and Simon had wanted to let Emily know where he and Danny would be the next day. Not to have told her would be unthinkable – and besides, he missed her.

Thus it was that Simon heard that the show with the professor in Chicago had been cancelled, and that Emily was not at the Pierre in New York. Then, when there was no reply from Emily's room at the Pierre either, there was no alternative but to call Rick again. Which, even at the cheaper rates for ungodly hours, was not exactly chicken-feed.

'Leave it with me; she'll get the message,' Rick said, adding, 'She's going over great. They love her over here. Course, the *Virginia Byrnes Show* will make or break her. We got a lot riding on that one. That's one hell of a great gal you got...'

'I have to agree,' Simon said. 'She's a splendid organizer. Tell her I said so; she'll know what I mean.'

Which was no exaggeration, Simon thought. He missed her, though. Ophelia had taken off, claiming a sick aunt in Sweden; she had been away for two days, which was why Simon had been obliged to ask whether he could bring Danny with him to the meeting at Sir Roger Wilbury's house in the country. Highly irregular behaviour, highly irregular; but the old boy had been most sporting about it, most sporting. Once Danny was with him there would be no need to cut the meeting short so as to be in time to collect him from school. In any case, an unexpected day in the country would be quite a bonus for both of them.

Danny asked if he could take his violin with him and, remembering what Emily had said about the boy's confidence, about his not being shy, Simon agreed. 'We'll leave it in the car, though,' he said. 'Then we'll assess the mood of the house and take it from there.'

'I know what you mean,' Danny said seriously. 'Old men can be cantankerous.'

'Who told you that? Mummy?'

'Yes, Mummy. About Grandfather.'

'Yes. Well, of course you won't say that to Sir Roger...'

'That would be tactless,' Danny agreed.

He's very grown-up for his age, Simon thought; he supposed it was because Danny was an only child. He enjoyed the boy more and more, and though he missed Emily fiercely – and far more than he had anticipated – he had not expected to find so much pleasure in the companionship of his young son. It must be a sign of age, he decided, though he didn't really feel thirty-eight, going on forty.

Sir Roger proved to be an exceptionally congenial host. Wellingtons were laid on for Danny and a stable-boy was deputed to show him round the farm. This way their meeting could go ahead without any disturbance, then Danny would join them for lunch and afterwards there would be more farmyard activity for him. 'A fine and healthy day in the country,' Sir Roger said. Lady Wilbury had gone up to London, so it was men's day.

Sir Roger has only recently retired and was disarmingly frank about how pleased he was to have a real working day ahead. Trusts and covenants and wills were to be put in order. His grandson was presenting difficulties, some sort of cult, alas! But young Roger would not be disinherited. Sir Roger had heard of people who de-programmed these youngsters. All this was the main reason for having requested the meeting.

The house was unusually cheerful – probably because the

colours were unusually sunny, Simon thought. There was something almost tropical about the yellow walls, the orange-pink Oriental rugs, the cyclamen couches. They were seated in Sir Roger's study, which went so strongly against Simon's expectations of the conventional very shiny or very dull leather, that he was constrained to remark, 'What a delightfully cheerful room!'

'Glad you think so,' Sir Roger said, openly gratified. 'We spent some time out in the colonies. Natal. Lavinia dedicated her life to imparting the appearance of sunshine. Succeeded mightily, I think. Talking of success, I had a cable from my good friends, the Lerner brothers, about your good lady.' He crossed to his desk. 'I have it here,' he said. 'Thought you might like to see it. Now where the devil is it? I'm forgetting myself. Would you like a drink? Gin?'

'Thank you.'

Sir Roger poured the drinks, and then remembered that he had not shown Simon the cellar. So they set off on a tour of the Jacobean house, so lovingly restored, and the cellar was indeed ancient, the original barrels gleaming in the gloom. The tour went on for about thirty minutes and it turned out that the Wilburys had only moved in three months ago – it had taken a little over a year to complete the restoration, which was not the same thing as reconstruction – no, not at all. Restoration was tax deductible in America, but not in Britain, of course. The Lerner twins had done the most amazing restorations, made quite a name for that sort of thing, made the most of tax benefits. Then he remembered the cable and just as suddenly recalled that it was in his pocket. He became agitated and turned his pocket inside out; his jacket was so old that the pocket seams were frayed and ragged. To the extent of a shabby hacking jacket with leather patches at the elbows and wrists, Sir Roger was conventional. So it was there, among the ancient bottles of wine, of port, of cognac, under a naked light bulb in a damp cellar, that Simon read Leon Lerner's lengthy cable:

DEAR SIR ROGER, THANKS FOR YOUR KIND MEMO RE EMILY BRADSHAW STOP WILL DO OUR BEST TO MAKE HER AUTHOR TOUR OF OUR COUNTRY AS PLEASANT AS POSSIBLE STOP YOU MIGHT BE

INTERESTED TO KNOW THAT SHE LOOKS LIKE A WINNER STOP
CAUGHT HER ON NIGHTGUARD STOP HIGHLY TELEGENIC STOP
ALWAYS GOOD TO HEAR FROM YOU STOP CORDIALLY YOURS LEON
LERNER.

'My word,' Simon said, 'Who *is* Leon Lerner?'

'Americans,' Sir Roger said loftily. 'Americans are extravagant communicators; they go in for public relations instead of
old-fashioned good manners.'

'I see.'

'Actually, Leon Lerner's not as crass as his cable.'

'I hope I didn't imply...'

'Of course not, old man,' Sir Roger cast his hand lovingly
over his leather log-book in which the contents of the cellar had
been painstakingly recorded with the ancient quill which had
belonged to his grandfather, and said, 'Come on up, and I'll tell
you more about the fascinating story behind the Lerner
brothers. You've heard of them, of course?'

'No.'

'Soon put that right. We'll have a glass of Château
Carbonnieux '75 before lunch. It's waiting for us now.'

Seated in his study once again, as they sipped their wine, Sir
Roger began his tale of the Lerner twins. 'You would never guess
they were American,' he began. 'They don't wear their trousers
just that little bit short; I suppose it's because Gieves and
Hawkes make their suits. Rather good-looking, one could say
striking. A bit like elegant film stars.' He laid down his glass
and smoothed his woollen tie. 'Perhaps I may be forgiven for
being rather more than somewhat prejudiced in their favour.
Tower Life made a great deal of money through them. I was
chairman at the time, and I don't mind telling you that it did my
image no end of good.' Looking around the room, he made no
attempt to conceal his delight. Then he gave a short laugh.
'Didn't do my lifestyle any harm, either! I had a hunch that Mrs
Thatcher would make it, so we concluded our negotiations with
the Lerner brothers only the week after she was elected.
Anyway, we bought Sutherland Centre for around 60 million in
'79 and sold it for just short of 100 million in '83. Not a bad
deal for our pension fund, wouldn't you say?'

'Not at all bad,' Simon agreed.

'The last time I saw them in New York, I asked how they felt about it. I was under the mistaken impression that they would have regretted losing out on a profit of 40 million dollars. I remember them looking at me as if I was slightly crazy, Leon especially. "No one ever lost money taking profit", he said. "We didn't lose. We were happy with the deal when we made it, and we're very happy now. Looking at it any other way would be the essence of greed."'

'Sound thinking,' Simon said. 'Almost philanthropic.'

'Oh, I wouldn't worry about them,' Sir Roger said shrewdly. 'They're tough tycoons. Low profile, but tough.'

'Most un-American,' Simon sneered.

'Quite so. They don't give interviews and most of their philanthropy is done anonymously. I had our company people check them out and it turned out that they *are* the Barnett-Braudie Foundation. Big in hospitals, too. Also medical research. Burns, especially. Part of the reason you're here today is the Barnett-Braudie Foundation, I suppose.'

'Oh really. How so?'

'I admire the way the Lerner brothers structure their affairs. Learnt a lot from them – and however modest, my estate could benefit by adopting some of their methods. But we'll leave that until after lunch. First, we must find that young son of yours.'

The dining room was a sombre wine colour, as if tropical brightness was considered unsuitable to dining. The lunch table, though, was a gleam of silver and china on burnished wood.

'Shepherd's pie!' Danny exclaimed. 'My favourite.'

'I'm so pleased,' Sir Roger said, 'though I suspect we're doing something of an injustice to Mouton de Rothschild '71 by serving it with shepherd's pie! By the way, how did your concert go, young man?'

'Note perfect, Father said,' Danny replied shyly.

'Note perfect? Can't do better than that, can we?'

'Susan – that's my teacher – says it's only part of music. I brought my violin with me; it's in the car.'

'Perhaps then we can have a short concert after lunch. Very civilized, what?'

So Danny brought his violin and tuned it, and though his thin but recognizable music didn't quite fill the room, it was pleasant enough. A profound contentment swept through Simon, and just as he was deeply pleased with his son, so he was deeply pleased with the work which had brought him to this pleasant cheerful room on a day when Danny should have been at school. He had the feeling, though he was not a sentimental man, that Danny would always remember the day, that it would be one of the highlights of his childhood for ever...

Danny chattered all the way home, and they decided they would make bacon and eggs for dinner. Simon would do the eggs and Danny would do the bacon. Neither felt like one of Emily's gourmet specials. First, though, they would watch the news.

A telegram lay on the hall floor. Simon read it, and smiled. The contentment of the day now reached a new peak. MISS YOU BOTH STOP WILL PHONE TONIGHT STOP LOVE EMILY. Danny read it too. 'Yes,' Simon said, 'you must stay up and wait for Mummy's call.'

It was seven o'clock, so Simon decided to have a whisky and soda and to watch the news in the drawing room. Danny was feeding the puppy in the kitchen and Simon could hear his hysterical yelps downstairs. They really ought to have taken the puppy out with them, he thought. He turned on the news – he preferred Channel 4 anyway.

It was one of those moments when everything in his own world felt so good as he rested his ankle on his knee and sat back to watch.

And it was not a nightmare...

The telephone began to ring.

*

Katie Williams began counting her blessings just as soon as she stopped being Katie Jenkins. That was six years back now, on her wedding day. On the face of it there wasn't that much to count. She was married to a moody, taciturn man, a loner who wanted little to do with the neighbours or anyone else. The Williamses had no social life, but they were a family and had no need of – and no time for – strangers. But Katie's gold wedding ring, thick and heavy, matched Jake's and meant the world to her. It encircled her past, or some of it, and she counted her blessings through her past. Through her foster-parents, with Katie as their Cinderella, taking abuse from all of them, even their obese ten-year-old hyperactive son. Four years of that, of the four Irish setters which jumped on her and knocked her down, of their filthy kennels and filthy house, with Iris, her foster-mother (foster-money, Katie used to think to herself) using the payments for Katie in order to buy more and still more cheap wine sold in gallon drums. Oh, the shame of it, and the humiliation of not having clean clothes; of not being allowed to use the bath tub. And worse – oh much worse – Peter, her foster-father ... Pete, who loved rubbing his unshaven cheek against hers, harsh stubble against her ears, her neck and ... But here Katie would stop her memory; she did not need that bundle of disease to count her blessings against ... there was enough bad luck without that monster.

Jake knew very little about this. She was still too scared to tell him more, for she might give away too much. To be kept, a terrible secret must be hidden inside other secrets.

Jake had given her a new bathroom and it was the pride of her life. He bought the bath at a sale, white porcelain with bright yellow rosebuds, and a basin to match. Sometimes Katie took as many as four baths a day. She bought bath oils and bath essences and bath salts at the supermarket, and Jake allowed her this luxury. Of course, she had to make a note of every cent that she spent on every item, but Jake was an accountant and worked with figures, so this was only natural. Jake's mother had considered trousers and jeans unladylike and never wore them, so it was only natural that Katie didn't either. Katie looked older than her twenty-six years; she was too thin, and glowed with hygiene rather than health. This immaculate look was mistaken for coldness; the neighbours believed she thought too much of herself and too little of them.

Only natural too was Katie's way of understanding things; it was a ready and simple explanation that could make life simpler. Above all, peaceful ... it was peace she craved, and she could have set her clock by the time Jake came home, the absolute predictability of his presence more than making up for the unpredictability of his moods. Certainty was her security. And when he was at work there was privacy, and cool rooms, and the bathroom. Best of all, though, was the television for the soothing, loving voices in the pain-killing commercials which gave out such sympathy, such kindness. She felt cherished. She felt safe, alone in her disinfected house, safe and hygienic. It was a good clean, safe life and she guarded it with a ferocity that surprised her ... because her other stinking relatives did not know or care whether she was dead or alive. She hoped they believed she was dead.

Katie had no friends. The world was full of enemies. And yet, she was not lonely. The stillness of the house could be broken at any time she chose; she had only to reach out for the television dial and conversation and laughter – in fact, every human emotion – was inside her own safe living room.

Sometimes she would go over and over bits of what the celebrities and hosts had said, how they had looked, what they had worn, what their expressions had been. She had developed a special interest in and relationship with Dr Joan Barnes, a psychologist who had her own show called the *Doctor Joan Barnes Show*.

So it was only natural that her vigil of dread began when Jake was only ten minutes late. Everything was ready; the house sparkled and the tuna casserole was in the oven. Anxiety turned into panic, but slowly. And even then it was a panic that took the form of paralysis, as if she had been hypnotized into acute recall of those long-ago waiting times when her real father had been late, when her mother had first begun to call the police and the hospital, until her mother had finally stopped calling because he had gone. And before long her mother had gone too, and that was when Pete and Iris Chesser and their Irish setters came into her life and all but ate her alive.

She managed to feed Andy, but didn't touch the casserole. Then she put him to bed and the nightmare wait continued, as if there had been no interval between *then* and now. Her six years with Jake had been nothing more than an interlude, a long intermission from a longer nightmare. Then she knew that she had always known the waiting nightmare would continue.

Except that Jake's father had abandoned him, too.

And here there was no hope.

He would never do this to little Andy; she must have been crazy to think he hated Andy.

He must have been in an accident and right now was probably in an emergency room somewhere. But she would not call a hospital. Bad news travels fast and she would have heard. But she did not want to hear. Jake always carried his ID. All night she stayed in front of the television set, dozing, waiting, hoping, praying.

She set a deadline. If, by tomorrow night at midnight, she still had no news, she would call the hospitals – until then she would do nothing. Jake would be home anyway.

Andy was a comfort and she kept him close beside her the next morning. The *Virginia Byrnes Show* was one of her favourites; you met brave ordinary people and they gave you courage as well as companionship. Andy wanted to switch channels, but as usual he wanted to please his mother more than he wanted to please himself. He was a quiet child, and shy, and because he was affectionate Katie was convinced that he was happy. When they went shopping and crossed streets, it seemed nothing made him happier than slipping his hand into hers. And yet they behaved differently, she and Andy, when Jake was around. Some instinct forced a restraint, a caution between them, like clandestine lovers afraid of being caught. In a way, Jake was as suspicious of Andy as he was of everyone. But it was better not to face this, because this was *not* natural.

Andy sat on her lap and together they waited for the show to begin. 'You didn't change, Mom,' Andy said. 'You were wearing the same dress yesterday.'

'It's not dirty, is it?' she asked, alarmed. Nothing unusual about Andy's noticing this; he even noticed a slightly different hairstyle.

'No, it's not dirty.'

'Good.' Katie withdrew Andy's thumb from his mouth. 'Don't do that, honey,' she said.

'I forgot.'

Suddenly Katie threw Andy off her lap, pushed him so roughly that he howled. But in her desperate dash to get closer to the screen, she paid no attention to him. She thought she had seen Jake in the audience, but she must have been mistaken. She was seeing things. Beards – so many men grew beards.

It couldn't have been Jake. Only, something in his expression was horribly close to the way Jake sometimes looked at Andy.

The celebrity's voice was consoling. 'I'm sorry I pushed you, Andy,' Katie said. And then, to distract him, 'She's a pretty lady, isn't she, Andy?' she asked. 'I'm going to make us hamburgers for lunch. OK?'

She felt calmer now.

And then Emily Bradshaw jerked backwards, and blood spilled on the blouse.

*

Leon Lerner waited for the *Virginia Byrnes Show* to begin. He too felt inexplicably fraught, tense, uneasy. Which was not like him at all. Besides, that minor quarrel with his brother hadn't helped. They did not quarrel, or only very very rarely, but Milt's demanding once more that he go to the Western meeting had tried his patience too far. 'No,' he had said. 'No, my final answer is no.'

'But it's a serious deal.'

'So?'

'Let me remind you how big a bundle we've got riding on Western Insurance.'

'Nothing wrong with my memory,' Leon said, supremely irritated, almost spitting out the words. 'It's only a deal. We've done plenty, we've got plenty, we'll do plenty.'

'You've lost your senses, Leon.'

'I know. That's why I'm alive again. I know I've lost my senses. Now let me remind *you* I'm going to watch *her* live . . .'

'OK. Have it your own way,' Milt said, disgusted. 'If you want me, I'll be in the board-room!'

At last, at last, she was *on*. There she was, a slight smile acknowledging her introduction, showing perfect, perfect teeth.

Sure he'd lost his senses. He was in love – what the hell was wrong with Milt? Couldn't he *see*? The camera was on her again, full-face. Telegenic? An understatement. And just as beautiful in the flesh, mind you. The flesh. Her flesh. He felt a rumbling between his legs, an erection. 'Stop it,' he said out loud. 'Behave yourself!' But he would tell Emily about this kind of misbehaviour. She would approve...

He watched the audience watch her. They seemed to be smiling widely, indulgently, and sat forward in their seats; they loved her too. Yes, every one of them concentrated on her; their interest showed, their enjoyment sparkled. Not a bored one amongst them. He was quite objective about wanting Emily to promote the new *Kay-Chow* product. Milt would have to agree when he watched this video. Virginia Byrnes was giving her a hard time and he didn't like her voice, metallic and rasping. 'No, *ma'am*!' she said, 'no *sir*, that's what you're saying *now*. That's not what you said in your book!' Emily looked bewildered. 'All that casualty of ecstasy stuff you wrote.' About to reply, Emily leaned forward animatedly.

And then – and almost in that same second – to the sound of a single gunshot she jerked back, slumped back, blood spilling bright against her bright pink blouse. Screaming, Virginia Byrnes screaming, everyone screaming. Leon, in Fawcetts Building, roared; people roared in houses, in apartments, in hotels, in caravans, in limos, all over the State of New York people roared.

The screen went blank...

Then jerked back to life...

A panicked floor manager switched to a jangling commercial.

Leon touched a dial on his phone and called Hill Ambulance. 'Got an ambulance on the road anywhere near West 55th Street? If you have, divert it from wherever it's going. You have? It's on 52nd Street now? Send it to TAN. Use sirens. This shooting there on *Virginia Byrnes Show*. It's moving there now?'

While talking, he had flicked another switch. His secretary came in and he handed her a scribbled, 'Get my car. On the double.'

He hung up and ran to the elevator. Ran to the limo. Ran up the hospital steps. Ran through to emergency. 'Stop at once, you can't go in there . . .' a nurse commanded angrily. 'Oh, Mr Leon, sir. Sorry, I didn't recognize you.'

'You got Emily Bradshaw?'

'Yes, she's right in intensive care.'

'Thank God!'

'Are you all right, sir?'

'Of course I am.'

Suddenly an enraged, anguished voice boomed through the corridors. 'Look, I gotta know if she's going to make it. I gotta call her *husband* in London, England!'

'Bring that young man to me. Better still, take me to him.'

'Who are you talking about?'

'The man who's shouting.' Though Leon was already walking in the direction of his voice. 'Rick Cooke?'

'What's that to you?'

'I'm Leon Lerner.'

Whereupon Rick Cooke broke into hysterical sobs and an astonished Nurse Mills watched as the great Leon Lerner took the weeping hysterical, blood-stained man in his arms. 'Get him something, nurse – a tranquillizer.'

'I'll go call the doctor.'

'Guy in the ambulance said you'd sent him,' Rick wept. 'Kept right on saying he was on special orders from Leon Lerner . . .'

'Did she hear you? Did she know that?'

'I don't know, she couldn't speak. They put up an IV, said something about an artery. Oh, my God, my God! I'll kill him. I'll kill him!'

*

It was not unusual for Arlene Scott and Wendy Griffiths to spend the day in one another's company. Watching television during the day was, however, distinctly unusual. But they simply had to watch Emily on the *Virginia Byrnes Show*.

As soon as Milt had left for the office that morning, Arlene – not waiting to call Wendy – rushed over to her apartment to tell her all about Leon and Emily and the brief time they had spent together the night before.

Arlene and Wendy had been friends for only a little over a year now, yet it was as if they had known one another since childhood. Their friendship began almost as soon as they met, probably because each sensed a useful ally in the other, which therefore permitted them the luxury of trust. After all, they had a lot in common; they were in love – obsessed, as they freely and frequently admitted to one another – with two brothers. Wendy had been going with Leon for about two months and had known both Lerner wives, which gave her a seniority of sorts, like an older sister. She was in fact almost ten years older than Arlene, had been married briefly, and her daughter Karen was sixteen. Arlene had never been married and Karen became her honorary niece, so between the three of them a steady, strength-giving loyalty flourished, like kinship.

Leon and Milt made it clear – indeed, had never even tried to pretend – that marriage neither was nor ever could be a possibility. And this was so from the very outset. The Lerner brothers had wanted to be honourable, and had spelt matters out on a take-it-or-leave-it basis. Arlene came from an old New England, landowning family – the Scott Park had been donated by her grandfather to the State of Massachusetts – and their disapproval of her relationship with a man like Milt, who was not only twenty-six years older than she was but two years older than her own father, amounted to outright rejection. Which was, to say the least, hurtful, but not nearly as hurtful as it might have been if Wendy had not been there to comfort her. But, as they assured and reassured each other, they had one another. This was their security, the security of absolute trust.

Wendy had never had the advantage of a real family to fall back on, let alone an old family. She had made her own way, and when she met Leon had managed to move from sales clerk to personal shopper at Bloomingdales. She took care of Karen, and the child support she received was erratic, but she managed. She worked at weekends too. She had been Ruthie's and Marcie's personal shopper, which was how she met Leon.

Wendy's stunning crowd-stirring looks were of the rare kind which would attract attention even at sixty. Naturally elegant, her stately walk was worthy of a concert platform and the smile lines about her soft brown eyes seemed an extension of her long, curly lashes. Her looks, her pert profile especially, shared something in common with Emily's present looks, even though Emily was blonde and she was brunette. Arlene, though undeniably attractive, was less striking, for hers was the attraction of youth, athleticism and exuberance. Arlene was a graduate of the Rhode Island School of Design, and had met Milt while she was writing a thesis on Corporation Parks.

Their future, it seemed to them, was as intermingled as their present. For if, say, Leon married Wendy, it seemed logical – indeed, inevitable – that Milt would marry Arlene. Arlene and Wendy were as open with one another about this as they were about everything else. For example, they discussed again and again the possibility that their shared obsession might in fact double – that is to say, worsen – their obsession. And then again, perhaps they were trapped because they wanted to be trapped. Who could say? But as things stood now, both Wendy and Arlene had stopped working. Their new career was to be available, wherever and whenever, and in case ... just in case they might be needed ... Of course, they each owned their own apartment – given to them by the brothers, who stayed over sometimes, though more often than not it was the women who stayed at the men's places. The brothers lived separately; as close as they were, they each needed their own space. And it was well understood that in this space not a hairpin, nor any other shred of evidence, was to be left behind ...

For they were free agents, all of them. Leon and Milt were unfailingly courteous, even courtly. They were old-fashioned enough to decide to be gentlemen, and were agreed that the gift of apartments did not entitle them to expect the girls to be at their disposal, which of course meant that the girls were not entitled to expect any more from them. Arlene had no need of their money; she didn't even have that as an excuse, she knew, and was seeing a shrink to try to get her head straight. Wendy, on the other hand, could justify her obsession on the grounds of her daughter's education ... But Wendy didn't have a real excuse either, because Leon had set up a small but adequate trust for Karen.

They were hooked, and in common with countless women

through the ages, it was the mystery of why they were hooked that was so gloriously overwhelming. So when Emily had sensed Arlene's chill, she had been all too accurate, but she had been quite wrong about believing that she felt the chill only because she was 'touchy'.

Arlene played things down and did not say a word about the electricity which had crackled over Leon and Emily – indeed, over everyone who was even near them. It was the first time Arlene had censored her comments and she did so now because she couldn't face this herself, couldn't face it any more than she could bear to hurt Wendy. The important thing, as she stressed over and over, was that Emily had not impressed Milt; he couldn't stand her, couldn't stand anything about her. 'Because,' Arlene said triumphantly, 'Milt believes she's a phony!'

'Why? What's Leon doing with her if she's a phony? The boys hate phonies.'

'Milt says she talks like a phony ...'

'But she's British.'

'Not her accent, Wendy. Come on – Milt's used to that. What she says ...'

'Things like "How fantastic America is, you Americans ..."' Arlene mimicked Emily's accent. '"Next to America, Europe's a suburb. Only in America ..." and then she goes and has the nerve to tell us every boring detail about her afternoon at Buckingham Palace when her father got knighted Sir Thomas Rice.'

'So she's an aristocrat? Even worse!'

'Hell, she's no aristocrat. Milt says it's standard procedure for civil servants before they retire. A knighthood costs less than a gold watch, he says.'

Arlene had changed into a pair of Wendy's jeans and a sweatshirt. About a half hour before the show was due to begin she suggested a Bloody Mary. 'So you *are* concerned about Emily Bradshaw!' Wendy said accusingly. 'We do not drink in the mornings.'

'Didn't sleep. It'll pick me up. Milt was in such a black mood last night ...'

'I wonder what your shrink will have to say about this new development?'

'Which one?'

'Vodka,' Wendy said and giggled helplessly. 'I'm glad Karen isn't seeing us now.'

'Course we wouldn't be having Bloody Marys if Karen was here.'

'I'm going to video the show,' Wendy said. 'I've a hunch we shall want to see it again.'

'Hell, she is beautiful,' Wendy said. 'The blouse is great, such a great colour.'

'It's a Yissel,' Arlene said, hoping Wendy would laugh. Yissel was the nickname for Yves St Laurent: YSL. But Wendy couldn't manage a laugh. Suddenly Arlene yelped, 'What's wrong with us, for Chrissake? Emily Bradshaw is a married woman!'

'So?'

'You know married women are taboo. You know that, Wend...'

'I know. But rules are made to be broken.'

'Hey, wait a minute. See the guy in the front row? With the beard? I never saw such a twisted mouth. Like a snarling dog.'

The camera zoomed back to Emily. 'I'm only interested in her,' Wendy said, moving closer to the television set.

'She could be phony; I don't know. She sure is feminine though – sexy legs. She's leaning forward, but she's not forgetting to display her legs...'

And then there was a single shot, and Virginia Byrnes screaming, and pandemonium, and blood spurting high and soaking the blouse, and then a blank screen, and then the jangle of a commercial. Wendy and Arlene screamed too, and clutched one another. Wendy began to bite her nails. 'If God is good,' she said very quietly, very clearly and very deliberately, 'Arlene, if God is good, Emily Bradshaw will die.'

Arlene couldn't answer this, or rather the only way she could answer was with a hug. She said, 'I'd better call Milt.'

'OK.'

Arlene was already pushing the buttons, then she said, 'He's in a big meeting. Think I should call?'

160

'You have to.'

Arlene had to do some quick, urgent talking about an absolute emergency. 'The woman we were with last night was murdered,' she said finally and Milt's secretary agreed to put her through.

'*What?*' Milt said, his voice rising. '*When?* Stay right where you are, Arlene! Is Wendy with you? I'll get back to you. And ... uh ... thanks. Thanks for telling me!'

'He was pleased I called,' Arlene said. 'He said so. Said we must stay right where we are.'

*

Contacts are the art, if not the secret, of success. Sheila Lyall took this art seriously and elevated it to a skill. Networking was the new word for contacts and Sheila thought it singularly appropriate. As she saw it, the only contacts worth having were those who already had their own contacts. Incremental contacts, she called them.

Accordingly, she was now watching the *Virginia Byrnes Show* with Eartha and Art Kristol, in Art's penthouse office at TAN. It was a piece of cake, really, once she'd seen them dining with Emily the night before. A phone call to Constance Reilly – one of Eartha's more intimate and even more secret friends – had done the trick. Sheila had a few photographs of Emily in her portfolio that she had been holding for the right person at the right time. And who could fit the bill better than the president of entertainment at TAN, Art Kristol?

Sheila Lyall was in the very building in which the shooting had taken place ...

Which was how the world came to see Sheila Lyall rushing alongside the stretcher carrying Emily to the ambulance which had arrived within three minutes of Leon's call. (Needless to say, the violence with which she had forced her way through was not caught on film.)

Therefore, the first interviews given about Emily Bradshaw were by her friend, Sheila Lyall, who had spent a pleasant day with her in that 'darling house' in Chelsea.

Sheila Lyall's photographs suddenly became incredibly valuable, for she owned the copyright. All in all, a lucky break, which surpassed even Sheila's extravagant expectations of what an incremental contact could mean.

*

Katie screamed and screamed.

'It's only television, Mom,' Andy said. 'It's only the television.'

'Shut up, Andy! It's *live. Live!*'

The screen went blank, then came one of her beloved commercials.

Katie sat very, very still, seemingly paralysed, yet her entire being was beamed on that screen. When Andy changed the channel, she screamed, 'Stop that! Don't touch it!' She had to wait. 'I gotta watch this,' she said, her voice coming out in a hoarse whisper. 'I gotta stay with it.'

Andy huddled against her, close up to the screen.

When the screen came alive again, the cameras had been moved from Emily and were now focused on a man surrounded by guards, which made it difficult to see him. 'The gunman is . . . The guards are waiting for the police,' the announcer was saying frantically. 'We do not yet know the extent of her injuries, but she appeared to be hit in a major artery. The guards are stepping to one side in a few seconds and we'll have this freak on camera!'

Katie held her breath, sure there must be something wrong with her. If she could think, even for one second, that it might be Jake, then she must be going mad.

Still, she could not let her breath out.

Then he was on camera . . .

Katie saw, and when she looked into the glazed, shocked eyes of her husband, her immediate instinct was to hold Andy's eyes against her, to hug his eyes away, to protect him.

'It's not your daddy, honey,' she crooned. 'It only looks like him. I was right not to call the hospitals,' she murmured. 'Bad news travels fast – I was right about that, too.'

'I'm hungry, Mom. Can we have that hamburger now?'

She went to the kitchen. She had control in the kitchen; the kitchen would control her head.

She needed to get her head straight. *Fast.*

Katie made the hamburgers and French fries, and even a salad. She concentrated carefully, had Andy taste the hamburger mix, set the table in the breakfast nook and then sat down to an unusually formal meal for the middle of the day. Andy spoke the simple grace: 'For what we are about to receive, may the Lord make us truly thankful,' and seemed to enjoy it.

Katie knew, with dreadful certainty, that this was to be the new pattern. And for many, many months – perhaps, for ever – Andy would be the head of the household, for she liked to have a male in charge. Outwardly calm, she listened and joined in with his amiable chatter, but inwardly her mind was engaged in arithmetical calculations. What would they do for money? If Jake was convicted, what would her situation be? Would something like a widow's pension apply? Or would there be nothing? Jake was an accountant, so he and he alone knew how much of their house was mortgaged. But she recalled him having said they'd got it at a bargain price, through one of his mysterious contacts. Or could the government take the house away? Did they do that sort of thing to murderers' wives?

Emily Bradshaw might die, might already be dead.

They finished lunch. 'Let's have a nap. Andy?' she suggested. 'Promise, promise you won't move.'

'I promise,' Andy said nervously. 'Don't be mad with me, Mom.'

'Sorry, son. My head aches.'

'Oh . . .' How easily kids are reassured, Katie thought. It's not fair!

Only when she put him on his bed, she could not resist a long compulsive, rocking sort of hug. Tighter than tight, she clasped him to her like a poultice, or a blood transfusion. The louder heartbeat of a child ticked its own strength against her chest, and his tender sweet-smelling – though not quite baby – skin offered that immemorial comfort that mothers live by . . . or die for.

Andy was almost asleep when she left him. But Katie did not want to die. Not yet. What she wanted was prayer. She took the phone off the hook, then went to her room to pray, in peace, for a while. There was not too much time left.

But it was not for herself, nor for her husband, nor even for Andy that she prayed. It was for Emily Bradshaw, for the life of an intimate stranger whom, even if this tragedy had not intervened, she would have treasured as a lifelong friend. As far as Katie was concerned, she and Joan Barnes were friends. It was Joan's voice that attracted and soothed her. It was like President Reagan's voice, sort of humble but firm, good-humoured and *kind*. Emily Bradshaw's voice was like that, too, though quieter. Katie would have listened for that voice, and Emily would have become one of her friends. She willed her to stay alive, and tried to find the words to pray.

Meanwhile, and with increasing dread, she waited for the police.

*

London 7 p.m. New York, 2 p.m.
Gunman shoots British writer live on New York television show

That was the first news bulletin; others were to follow, but Simon knew at once that it was Emily.

He watched, paralysed.

He watched his wife jolt backwards, watched her blood gush, watched her enter the ambulance, watched Sheila Lyall's brief interview, watched her arrive at the hospital, watched a brief excerpt from *Nightguard*.

The phone rang . . .

It was Sir Roger. 'My dear, dear fellow,' he said, 'I'm most frightfully sorry. Just saw it. Anything I can do?'

'I've no more news than you . . .'

'I'll telephone the Lerners. I don't want to block your line.'

The phone, the doorbell and the puppy yelping all at the same time. And he hadn't told Danny. But he had to answer the phone first – it might, it *must* be New York. Instead it was his father-in-law, who was about to alert the British ambassador to the UN in New York. He put down the phone and on his way to the kitchen to get Rick's phone number, he bumped into Susan Waddington. 'I heard it in the car,' she said. 'I came at once.'

'I hadn't thought of the radio,' Simon said, speaking rapidly.

'Excuse me.' He raced downstairs to turn it on in the kitchen.

'Does Danny know?'

'No.'

'Would you like me to tell him?'

'Please.'

It was impossible for Simon to dial out, because as soon as he replaced the receiver it rang again and again. Much later he found out that it was Keith who had called Fleet Street. Eventually it was Susan who took over, spoke to the operator and had all calls diverted except for those from New York. Meanwhile the radio kept him informed, and he knew that Emily was still having emergency surgery.

His drawing room was filled with people. Keith had thoughtfully brought some drink with him and it was he who dealt with journalists and photographers. Even his senior partner turned up, with more whisky. Simon stayed in the kitchen, but the party-like sounds carried downstairs.

Simon felt murderous. At last, about forty-five minutes after he had first heard the news, Rick was on the line. 'She's going to make it,' he said, speaking very calmly. 'She's still on the critical list, but she will make it. I know she will.'

'*You* know?' Simon said disgustedly. 'And what do the doctors . . . ?'

'Dr Charles Cowan, the surgeon, is right with me. I'll put him on.'

'Your wife has a strong constitution. The bullet was removed, the major vessels sutured, but we have put in a tracheotomy as a precautionary measure only, just in case there's some swelling . . . She's had six pints of blood. Her condition is, of course, critical, but we find her progress satisfactory. Rick Cooke here would like a word with you.'

'Simon? We've got reservations for you and Danny and anyone else you would care to bring, on the Concorde which leaves Heathrow at ten tomorrow morning.'

'I see.'

'I guess you're stunned. If Emily's father wants to join you, TAN will pick up the tab.'

'Who did it?'

'A crazy freak.'

'For God's sake, every idiot knows that.'

'Sorry, I guess I'm not myself. A man called Jake Williams. No previous criminal record, not even a driving offence. He's an IRS agent.'

'Why?'

'Why's he an IRS agent?'

'I can't make head nor tail of what you're saying. Is there anyone else I could talk to?'

'TAN's Entertainment President, Arthur Kristol.'

'Mr Bradshaw, Art Kristol...'

Finally Simon was brought up to date. Art concluded his account with, 'Mr Bradshaw, we'd be happy to accommodate anyone you might care to accompany you.'

The next morning, a crush of journalists at Heathrow. On the plane with Danny, Simon tried to sort out the sequence of the night before. Enormous kindness, he was sure of that, but besides kindness, there was something else. It seemed too simple at first, atavistic and too cruel to be possible. So it was a while before Simon was certain that all of them – everyone who had been in his house last night, yes, even including his senior partner – had positively fizzed with excitement.

He felt bitter about this and equally bitter about his own reaction to it. He had encouraged Emily to go and he would not flinch from facing up to that. A sense of guilt nagged, but resolutely he stopped it raging. Danny's excitement was only natural and therefore forgivable.

But he would never forgive those others. *Never.*

Last night that physical fizz of excitement had been felt viscerally, deep in his bowels. With his lawyer's logic he knew why, too. That excitement was the signal of change. Like a green light, it gave the go-ahead to run away with their lives.

He should be focusing on the gunman and not on the likes of the press and Keith Summers. But that would be even more pointless; Jake Williams was obviously insane...

Ophelia had called from Sweden, excited and weeping. She had seen it on the Swedish news...

He felt exposed, and raw. Violated. The press... last night, then this morning at Lamont Road, at Heathrow.

Emily was on the critical list, the Lord be praised, out of danger. Why then did he sense disappointment among them? Of course it would be more interesting, and that much more poignant, if he were now going over to claim her body. He felt *angry* – and with himself, most of all. He had encouraged Emily to go... One thing, however, was certain: as soon as she was well enough to travel, she would be on a plane and back in Lamont Road. The rest of this crazy stunt would be cancelled.

But amongst all those sightseers last night, it had been Susan Waddington, the violin teacher whom he scarcely knew, who had come to his rescue.

Just as he would never forgive the others, so would he be grateful to her. For ever.

He wished she was with him now. He wished he had thought of Susan when TAN said he could bring anyone he liked along with him.

It occurred to him that *Defending Wives* must by now be a best-seller. But it did mean that there was absolutely no reason why Emily should continue with her tour. Which, in his opinion, was the only positive factor in this entire mess.

All anger left him. He felt easier, and confident. Because of course she would agree with him.

*

Keith Summers was making the most of the shooting. His phones and telexes were jammed with offers from publishers all over the world – newspapers wanted to serialize *Defending Wives*... even Greece had put in an offer.

Which is to say nothing of the frenzied activities of the press, who were hell-bent on finding out why Emily Bradshaw had been shot. That she was the daughter of a senior government official, Sir Thomas Rice, made matters all the more pressing, not to say alluring. Why had she been shot? And what was the book about?

But where was the book?

Who had seen it?

Had *anyone* read it?

Here Keith Summers was under intolerable pressure. Because neither a copy, nor a manuscript, was in his possession. Believe it or not, but it was the truth. Of course no one believed him, so the astronomical offers (from the *Express,* the *Daily Mail*, the *Sun* and the *News of the World*) soared higher and higher. The *Daily Mail* topped everyone; their offer was signed at £150,000 and Keith felt obliged to accept it. At the same time he signed with ITV. *Defending Wives* was being sent over by special courier – reprints in hundreds of thousands were being rushed through. For once, a genuine case of a real rush.

All Keith had was the small item in Frontier Books' catalogue.

In any case, teams of journalists were despatched to find out why this had happened. One of the most enterprising proprietors of a weekly magazine had deputed their most glamorous investigative journalist to be on the same plane as Simon Bradshaw and son. Thus Christine Slater, having staked out Heathrow, was on the same flight as Simon. Unlike him, however, she was not averse to travelling first class. Simon and Emily, though essentially stalwart supporters of the Conservative Party, had always found the entire notion of first class one of the excessively tasteless aspects of conspicuous consumption. Indeed, on the admittedly rare occasions when Simon had been despatched to meet with one of his tax exiles, he had made his thinking abundantly clear. His clients thought him eccentric and did not offer to make up the difference in fees. They were, if anything, slightly put out; one of them categorized this kind of thinking as socialist and found a new attorney, who had no awkward scruples about first class.

There is no doubt that had Simon known what was going on in London while he was so uncomfortable travelling first class to New York, he would have been even more nauseated than he was already. For he and Emily had always objected to jumping on the band-wagon of other people's sorrows, tragedies and even their milder misfortunes.

Christine waited about half an hour before she made her first approach. And even then it was to Danny, not to Simon. She had seen his violin case before they boarded; she had also seen

168

Susan Waddington, who taught her nephew, Neil. But Susan knew she was a journalist, so Christine took great care to keep out of her line of vision ... She went to the lavatory and on the way back to her seat just happened to trip over her trailing shoulder strap, beside Danny's seat of course. Naturally Danny rose to help disentangle her and as she seemed quite shaken he offered her his seat, an offer which Simon was bound to endorse. She accepted prettily, took a while to recover and said nothing for a few moments, merely resting her head against the seat and closing her eyes. She accepted a glass of Perrier though, then opened her eyes and apologized for having been so clumsy.

'Not at all,' said Simon gallantly. 'It could happen to anyone.'

'Can't imagine not being clumsy,' Christine said, twinkling. 'I suppose I'm doomed to be clumsy for ever. I was like that at school. No hope for me.'

'I wouldn't say so, if I were you, you know. Self-fulfilling prophecies and all that.'

'Oh,' Christine said, 'wouldn't you? I'm a dreamer – a day-dreamer. Was your small son carrying a violin or did I dream that too?'

'No,' Simon said, 'you didn't dream it.' He laughed delightedly; then a wave of shock hit him, he stopped his laugh and continued, 'He played Brahms at a recent concert.'

'Not the concert Susan Waddington arranged at the Gallery?'

'Yes ...'

'Well, the world is made up of 2,800 people. Someone told me that once and I believe it now. And all those 2,800 people know the same people. It's a network, I'm convinced.'

Christine saw Simon wince at the word 'network', but affected not to notice as she continued, 'Tightly spun, wider than the old-school-tie connection, but there it is. My nephew, Neil Bailey, played pieces from Mozart.'

'Of course, I remember him. Very talented,' Simon leaned over to shake her hand. 'I'm Simon Bradshaw,' he added. 'And that young man is my son, Danny.'

'Christine Slater,' Christine said, smiling sympathetically. 'I would have been at the concert myself, but I had flu. We would have met then, I suppose.'

Encouraged somehow by her sad smile, Simon said, 'It seems so long ago, that concert.'

'I can understand that. Too well, I'm afraid. I saw the news last night, and the papers too this morning. *The Times.*'

'I saw the news, too. That was how *I* heard about it!'

'You must be joking. That's too cruel. Beyond belief, almost. I'm very, very sorry. I think *The Times* reported successful surgery.'

'Oh, did they? I've resisted reading the newspapers for news of my own wife. It's true, though, that she had surgery. The bullet – I can't believe I'm using this word, bullet – but the bullet just missed her sub-clavical artery and shattered her shoulder. She's in plaster, of course, and lost a great deal of blood. I'm told that her life was saved because an ambulance was diverted from another case, paramedics were with her within minutes and put up a saline drip, which apparently adds volume to the blood consistency... at least, I think it's consistency.'

'*That* saved her life? Americans call it an IV.'

'So I gather,' Simon sighed.

'I don't think we have that system in the UK. I don't know, though.'

'Well, I was assured that that had made the critical difference. And the tourniquet too, of course; they applied a tourniquet, you know.'

'Did you say an ambulance was diverted from another case?'

'I imagine Emily's was the greater emergency,' Simon said cryptically.

'Oh, I don't doubt that for one moment!' Christine agreed quickly. 'But how could that be arranged?'

'By the proprietor of the Hill Ambulance Service, no less. He was watching the show and saw it all.'

'Amazing. Incredible! What luck.'

'Yes, it is. And the network you spoke about earlier – same thing here. The man who diverted the ambulance, Leon Lerner, he's called. Just yesterday afternoon I was in the country with a client who showed me the cable he'd received in response to *his* cable about Emily's projected tour. It was from Leon Lerner! Actually, my client doesn't know that yet; he'll be pretty chuffed about it.'

'Indeed. You must be a lawyer, so I shan't ask who it was.'

'You're not wrong,' Simon said. 'It's just one of those things. We happened to mention her tour at dinner and Sir Roger took it up at once, said he'd tell his good friends about her. And, my goodness me, to think of what might have happened if he had not . . .'

'Well,' Christine said firmly, 'Thank God he did inform his good friends. That's all that counts now!'

'Don't tell me.'

'But to shoot her! Over a book! It boggles the mind!'

'Doesn't it just? The kindest, most thoughtful, most sensitive woman, Emily.' As he shook his head, his incredulity glowed.

'I suppose that's why she wrote the book,' Christine put in quickly.

'Probably,' Simon agreed vaguely. 'A friend's suicide was one reason. A wife, and the "other woman".'

'That's all in the book?'

'Part of it. Most of it. Emily said she'd mailed a copy of the American edition.'

'I assume it's out in the UK, then?'

'That's just the point. As far as I know, it hasn't found a British publisher. I believe Keith thought it unsuited to the UK market. Haven't given that much thought, though.'

'Understandably not!' Christine said in tones of absolute conviction. Simon sighed and she went on, 'Where will you be staying in New York?'

'Not the faintest idea. Trans-American Network – TAN, you know – are arranging all that.'

'I wanted to know if you'd mind if I rang you later for more news.'

'Of course not. I dare say TAN could put you in touch with me.'

'Good luck,' Christine said. 'I'll ring you if I may, but I'll leave you now. Take care. I'm praying for you.'

And then, openly emotional, she left . . .

But not without stopping to have a few words with Danny. 'I believe you know my nephew, Neil Bailey,' she said.

'He goes to Susan? Yes, I do know him.'

'Well, I'm his favourite aunt. Because I'm his *only* aunt!'

'Oh, yes. I know about you. You were supposed to come to the concert; Neil said so. We all hoped so, because you're a newspaper woman, aren't you?'

I've blown it, Christine thought. I overdid it! But, speaking urgently, she said, 'I know you've had a dreadful shock. But would you mind if I asked you what I would normally only ask of a grown-up?'

'No, I wouldn't mind.'

'Then please, please, may I ask you to *please* not tell your father that I'm a journalist?'

'Why ever not?'

'Because it would only upset him more than he is upset already. Besides...' Here she stopped meaningfully, expecting Danny to press her to continue, but the boy was silent and Christine was forced to go on without any prompting, 'You see, Danny,' she said, dropping her voice to a conspiratorial level, 'your father told me he objected to the press. It would only make things worse for him, knowing that he'd talked to *me*. Can't you see that?'

'Yes, I can. I won't say anything.'

'Do you promise?'

'I promise.' Danny picked up the book he had been reading.

'I'll leave you now,' Christine said. 'Promise? Scouts' honour?'

'I already did, but I'm not a scout. Too militaristic,' Danny stated.

What had happened was unfortunate. But she could phone in that exclusive to her paper. It was a weekly, so they would probably negotiate a highly lucrative deal with one of the dailies of her choice. Certainly it would do her reputation no harm. On the contrary, it would add greatly to her name, which was already quite well-known in any case. And, as she told herself, she had behaved scrupulously. She had told Simon Bradshaw her real name. If he had been less snobbishly – more widely –

read, he would have known that name. After all, he was not uneducated, he was a lawyer – Cambridge trained, Eton too – and probably spoke to her so freely because, in addition to her nephew and Susan Waddington, her voice proclaimed her own Roedean background. Besides, Simon Bradshaw was a lawyer. Christine had depended utterly on her divorce lawyer and he had let her down, or so she believed, and she had acquired a limitless, if unprofessional, hatred for that profession.

But she could see nothing unprofessional in her conduct of a few moments ago. Nothing at all. Fact was, she knew an English woman, Tess Norton, who was features editor at the *New York City News*. Not a bad idea for a US exclusive. Not bad at all. But she would be scrupulous; she would call her own paper first, from Kennedy – and then, and only then, Tess Norton.

*

Leon Lerner was still in the clothes he had been wearing for the twenty-one hours or so which had struggled and sped along since he witnessed her shooting on television. He could not bring himself to say 'Emily', not even to himself – 'she' and 'her' was as much as he could manage. His butler had thoughtfully brought along a change of clothing – Leon was known for his fastidious and immaculate tastes – but he had not been able to handle more than a shave. He was uncomfortable in his strangely rumpled and creased clothes, but however peripheral, physical discomfort seemed for the moment to be singularly appropriate.

It was evidence of his own inner suffering.

Sure, he had lost his senses. All his senses. As usual, Milt had been right. But if losing one's senses brought one's highest administrative faculties into the sharpest focus, then so be it. Again and again he recalled Dr Cowan's words: 'Diverting the ambulance very probably saved her life. She got saline and plasma, as well as a tourniquet, otherwise she would most certainly have died from excessive blood-loss. Leon, yours is the kind of quick thinking that saves lives.'

It was this last bit about quick thinking which Leon treasured beyond words. She would live and *he* had saved her, saved her life. It was awesome and enthralling and disquieting and even confusing... Life is time, he decided. We measure life in time. They say time is money, but time is life. Less than ten hours before her blood spilled and splashed over that pretty pink blouse of hers, he had held her in his arms and they had spilled and splashed over one another. Fifty-five years old, and in love; and with all the turmoil of a budding adolescent. Logic, reason, rationality, suffering – all, all irrelevant to life's force. Life's love. Life's loving. Yes, this was Leon Lerner – noted, respected and envied for his cool restraint, his low profile, his business genius. Leon – the level-headed calculating risk-taker – risking his all, his reputation, his life's blood, on a woman, the televised image of a woman he had had the nerve, or the courage, or the madness, to fall in love with, a stranger even before he had met her in the flesh – the soft, soft flesh – only last night.

It was the first time in his life when he had not wanted to be with Milt. He had wanted only to be near, close, to Rick Cooke whose shirt and jacket bore her blood, for it was Rick who had had the intelligence and the wit to try to staunch her bleeding with pressure from his hands and then, only moments later, the ambulance attendant had applied the tourniquet. Oh, his boundless, boundless gratitude to Rick Cooke! Grateful even for the sound of Rick's weeping – the sound Leon could not permit himself to vent... Of course, Rick was in love with her too. He had sensed that at once, but did not resent it – he felt infinitely more privileged, that was all.

Because he had to admit it, to himself at least. She was so beautiful on television that he was star-struck, and up until that terrible moment of the shooting he had loved her image – her telegenic image that was being watched by millions, perhaps because it was being watched by millions – even more than he had loved her in the flesh. Because of the indescribable intimacy of watching her, of studying her every movement in the intimacy of his private office, while she could not see how closely he studied, how closely he watched. Nor would he have wished her to see, or even to sense, his overwhelming pride that this glorious, glorious telegenic artefact was his, had been his, had been – only the night before – fucked to kingdom come! And when she was thrown back so cruelly, he had felt as if his newly-grafted coronary veins must pull back, must snap away, must give. But they had not. *And he had thought quickly.*

She had been in surgery for two hours.

After that, dressed in a surgical gown himself, watching blood and life-giving droplets flow into her veins, waiting, hoping she would come round to recognize him, give some sign – however fleeting, however small – of the night before.

But she would live. It was such a small hole – both Rick and Dr Cowan said so – so small, as if a dirty stick had been pushed through her flesh. Fortunately, however, the bullet had not exited through that same flesh; the speed of *that* would have left a large messy, gaping hole and put her survival in greater jeopardy. And it had missed . . . just, just, only just missed . . . that vital axillary artery, but her shoulder joint had been injured and was now in plaster, and it would be a long while before she would regain the full use of her right arm.

Again and again, he whispered, 'It's Leon, I'm right beside you. Squeeze my hand if you hear me.' But there was no response, just hours and hours of silence, and the electronic ping – that cash-register beep – of her cardiac monitor, and blood taken and measured, and soft sounds of nurses and doctors, and clinking sounds of machines and instruments, and from her the blessed, blessed sound of breath. He made countless pacts with God . . . *If* she would live – then . . . At one point he was ready to give her up, yes even *that*, but that was when he felt a slight, light infinitesimal pressure on his hand. She recognized him! It was hard not to yelp, still harder not to weep. He could not pronounce her name, but repeated, whispering. 'You are going to make it. You'll be out of here soon. Simon and Danny are on their way. They'll be here, right beside you, real soon.' Again and again the same words.

About ten minutes after he had received the message that Simon, Danny and Rick were in the limo, he left Emily to make certain that all his arrangements – his precise logistics – had been carried out accurately.

Leon was confident that his own initiatives would not be

misinterpreted. She had been shot, live, on national television; it was an international incident, her father was a senior government official and Leon was a senior member of the New York corporate scene. It was right and proper that the finest resources had been put at the disposal of the Bradshaw family.

Sir Derek Partridge, the British Ambassador, came to the hospital. He expressed gratitude on behalf of his country, his government, himself, Sir Thomas Rice and the rest of the Bradshaw family. 'But journalists and TV people caught us coming in and I was obliged to offer some sort of diplomatic non-speak. But it would be most unfortunate if Simon were obliged to deal with that heartless mob...'

'That's under control, sir.'

'I can't imagine how they could possibly escape detection.'

'My people have it in hand.'

Sir Derek raised his eyebrows.

'Of course,' Leon lied smoothly, 'their plans are classified. Even from me.'

The ambassador raised his eyebrows again. 'Indeed,' he lied back. 'Top secret, excellent planning.'

Suddenly Leon's rumpled suit seemed not only inappropriate but undignified, as well as disrespectful.

'By the way,' the ambassador asked, as if it were an afterthought, 'any idea why she was shot?'

'No, no one's told me,' Leon replied, amazed that he himself had scarcely given it a thought.

'Our people are working on it, too,' the ambassador said ponderously. 'They tell me that so far the gunman hasn't uttered so much as one word.'

'I believe he's at Bellevue – the institution for nervous disturbances. But do your people have any idea as to *why* he would have elected to murder a woman like...' Leon could not go on.

'Like Emily Bradshaw?' the ambassador finished for him.

'Why, yes, of course...'

'A theory that he might have been one of the three who called in about her selfish gene theory? It seems he doubted his own paternity. But that's only a theory, mind.'

'Of course.'

'It's believed that he's called Jake Williams – of all things, an IRS agent.'

'Now *that* does surprise me!'

'My people, too.'

'Well, thanks for the information. I'll be back shortly.'

There were bound to be all sorts of weird theories, Leon decided. But this one made sense. If she died, the man should get the electric chair. Now, at last, his anger inspired him. Once he had met Simon Bradshaw he would get in touch with Cliff Miller, the brightest mind in the legal world. Of course, Simon was also a lawyer, so he would set up the meeting which he was sure Simon Bradshaw would most definitely expect.

But he, Leon, did not know Simon Bradshaw. And so he had no way of predicting that Simon's only concern with Jake Williams was that he should be locked up as long as his wife had to stay in this violent society of assassins, of Oswalds and Hinkleys. In any case, Simon Bradshaw was against capital punishment, and he would make all that clear at once . . . but not before having announced his intention of getting his wife back to Lamont Road, and civilization, as soon as the doctors agreed.

Meanwhile Leon Lerner, spruced up and changed, had rejoined the ambassador to wait for Simon Bradshaw. Because in all of Leon's fifty-five years of dealing, of negotiating – years and years of bland outmanoeuvring, outfacing, out-talking, years of awe and envy on the part of his enemies as well as his well-wishers, years in those corridors of power that led to re-zoning and profits, a real-estate revolution in which he had met with and sometimes even lost out to competitors – he had never before had to deal with or even consider a truly significant rival. The climb, or rather the march to the top had not been easy and of course there had been anxious moments – even one or two not unimportant failures – but then there had always been other successes to compensate, which led occasionally to even luckier deals. But now, for the very first time in his life, there was no possiblity that failure or adversity might spur him on to greater or luckier alternatives.

Failure, here, was not to be contemplated. Because he wanted Emily Bradshaw – there, he had got the words out – he wanted her as much as he wanted life. His quick thinking had given her life, had sustained her breath and her soul, and in some strange way it had bestowed a sense, if not exactly of ownership, then as if in saving her he had also re-created her. He had won the right to go ahead, he had secured the option he now held in his own hands. All of which is perhaps another way of saying that he was in the grip of an emotion which knew no pity. He would bend every resource, move every available and unavailable power to claim her as his own.

True, Simon Bradshaw might be a force to be reckoned with. Certainly he was a significant rival.

Every man has his price. Leon had learned this early in his career and he too had a price. Yet, even so, he could also be a killer. He had his daughters after all, and he had Milt, and these attachments put him well within the range of ordinary mortals.

The conclusion, therefore, was as obvious as it was clear: Simon Bradshaw must also have a price.

Chapter 12

Emily improving. Out of danger, the message read: *Rick Cooke waiting to meet you at exit, and before customs and passport control. Wearing a dark brown suit and red tie. This way you will be incognito. You will avoid the press hordes. Follow me. Cordially, Rick Cooke.*

This was the message that was given to Simon when he got off the plane.

Cloak and dagger, he thought. Well, well! But it was distaste mixed with gratitude. When he met Rick, he did as he was bid, and all was accomplished most skilfully. He was given the VIP treatment and certainly managed to escape the press.

On the way to PIB Hospital, Rick filled him in on Emily's physical state. 'Vital signs functioning well. Shoulder chipped but set. Miraculous escape – bullet just missed major arteries. Effects on arm not yet known, but if it had hit the cervical cord, it would have been a different – and terrible, terrible – story.' Rick's voice kept breaking. He held himself responsible, because it was he who had randomly selected Emily's book from that Frontier catalogue, and for no better reason than so as not to lose out on the bookings he had made for *Sixty Seductive Salads from Fifty-One States* ...

Rick was first and foremost a publicist, and he could only pray that it would never get out that it was he who had given the press all the details of Simon's and Danny's arrival ... Now he was even grateful for Leon Lerner's amateur methods of eluding journalists.

When Rick spoke of Leon Lerner he became even more emotional. For not only had Leon saved her life – saved it, man, saved it – but he had had Governor Reed fix things for Simon. It was thanks to Leon Lerner that Simon was not now having to face the press. The newspaper women were the worst, he was convinced.

Danny spoke up then. 'Sir, you did say newspaper women, didn't you?'

'Yes, sir, I did say newspaper women.' Rick turned to Simon. 'You could accuse me of being sexist, if you liked. But, so help me, that is what I did say.'

'Dad,' Danny said, 'I think I have to break a promise, Dad.'

'That's serious, of course, but you wouldn't do that lightly, I know,' Simon said, responding at once to his son's unusually concerned tones. 'We are in an emergency situation, and emergency situations warrant emergency measures.'

'But we already talked to a newspaper woman! Christine Slater. She made me promise not to tell you.'

'But... did she tell you, Danny?'

'No, but Neil told me. He was hoping she'd come to Susan's concert, we all were...'

'So she deceived me.' Simon's voice was frighteningly icy.

Danny felt afraid. 'I didn't know what to do. I promised her.'

'You did the right thing, my son. You are perfectly right to have told me.'

'I know that, Dad,' Danny said.

Simon was now fully recovered. 'Is that a television set?' he asked Rick. 'If it works, I'm sure Danny would love to watch it, wouldn't you, Danny?'

'In a *car*?' Danny said. 'Moving! Would it really work?'

'Sure,' Rick replied, switching it on.

'Christine Slater may have done us all a great service,' Simon said to Rick while Danny fiddled with the TV channels. 'A great service. She's confirmed my resolve to have Emily come home to Lamont Road, where she belongs, just as soon as she's well enough to travel!'

For once in his life, Rick stayed silent. He said nothing. But he doubted, he very much doubted that Emily would agree. He

had watched her change before his eyes, and up to now he had
believed this was because of the impact of America. She had so
often referred, so admiringly, to the running pace: 'Running
short distances,' she said. 'Even if you don't know where you're
going. You get there faster. In the long run, of course, it's simply
enthusiasm. Not enough of that where I come from.' And
besides, there was Leon. Something in that man's behaviour
told him that something had happened between those two.
Something magical, which her brush with death made more
rather than less magical ... Simon seemed so controlled, so laid
back, so unenthusiastic. He wasn't mad at anyone, not so far as
Rick could see; he hadn't even asked about the gunman. Well,
he didn't understand these Brits, that was for sure. He'd keep his
fucking mouth shut. He began asking about the Concorde, the
service and so on ... Harmless, civilized topics.

The phone rang and Rick picked it up. Danny sat bolt upright
and turned off the television, his eyes sparkling with
wonderment. A phone in a car, just like he had seen in *Starsky
and Hutch* and *The Streets of San Francisco*.

'Mr Lerner ...' They listened closely to Rick's responses, as
thoughtfully he repeated what Leon was saying. 'Her
temperature's gone down ... The press and television are
everywhere ... We're to stop at West 55th Street, where we'll be
met by an ambulance ... Mr Bradshaw and Danny will
relocate ... Like patients ... Yeah, I've got it ... I'll stay with
the limo, then catch a cab and go in the usual way ... Hold all
their luggage ... God, Mr Lerner, sir, you've thought of
everything. Press and media at the hospital, from all over the
world. I'll tell him. OK. A hospitality suite prepared for him at
the hospital ... Thank you, sir. Mr Bradshaw sure will
appreciate that – goodbye, sir. Excuse me, I didn't get that ...
the British Ambassador (here his voice rose appreciably) is
waiting to receive him ... Of course, sir. I'll tell him
everything ... I've been relaying it all along. Like a
simultaneous interpreter ... (Here Rick permitted himself a
small giggle.) Thank *you*, sir ...'

'The ambassador is at the hospital already?' Simon asked
incredulously. 'It's two p.m. in London, but only nine a.m. in

New York. Or am I mistaken about the time?'

'Life begins sooner in the US,' Rick told him.

'That's because you started later,' Simon snapped back.

'She's a legend,' Rick said breathlessly, sounding at the same time as if he were offering an incantation of utter wonderment. 'She's a legend, and a super star now.'

'She's a sensation, you mean. Surely she's been sensational- ized. *I* call it scandalous!' He looked at Rick coldly and it was clear that he had summoned great self-control as he went on slowly, 'Emily will be as appalled as I am about all this. She despises this kind of violation and would never have gone in for this sort of promotion in the UK. She only agreed because no one knows us here, which made it more or less a private matter for us...'

'National television? Privacy on national television? You've got to be kidding!'

'Not at all. No one *we* knew would have seen it – certainly no one in our world. Now of course she's on the BBC, ITV – you name it, she's on it.'

'But national television is news. National television makes news. National television made Kennedy, made Reagan. Everyone knows *that*. Even your Queen resorts to national television, only with satellites it's global television now. No one turns down a chance to go on national television. Your own prime minister requests some of our people – and she makes sure that she sees herself on the monitor first and adjusts her own make-up, too. If she's not above it, why should you be? We're crazy for Maggie in America. The media is already likening Emily to her...'

Rick cursed himself. His mouth-zip had come unstuck. Why, this man, this Simon Bradshaw, was a third-rate piece of shit!

'Not all of us share your enthusiasm for Mrs Thatcher,' Simon said starchily. 'Nor for national television nor global television. Some of us have real lives to lead, without the aid of an eternal falsity such as global television. Emily despises this – it leaves her speechless with contempt!'

Once again Rick remained silent. For Emily had changed in the US... that was self-evident and undeniable. Very simply put, she had blossomed out as a woman. Or, to put it another way, she had caught something: infection or virus, it made no difference. He knew enough to know there was no more a cure for the perfumes of fame than for its poisons.

He had set something in motion ... or the Frontier catalogue had done it. He was overwhelmed once again by a sense of awe, verging surprisingly on fright, at what *he* had caused, by what had already come to pass ... and as terrifying and euphoric as a premonition, by the unknown unquantifiables which lay ahead. After all, Emily was young, beautiful, glamorous – as Rick saw it, a dignified *lady*. At the height of her powers, of her sensuality, but by no means peaked. It was not as if she was a dried-out fifty-year-old bag, though for that matter even *that* had been changed. And by what? By national global television, that's what. Like Joan Collins, mega-desirable at fifty plus. And this shit of a husband, this Simon Bradshaw of Emily's wanted to stop it all – cut her down, put her down, bring her down to size, that was what this punk was planning. A personality clash, to add to his problems. He wants her back in Lamont Road! Doesn't he know her right arm might be paralysed?

It was crazy. Simon should have *hated* Jake Williams – that would have made sense. But no, he hated the media instead, listen to him, and right now he was going on about Christine Slater: 'Con artist of chequebook journalism. Took undue and absolute advantage of our predicament. Heartless! But she won't get away with it, you may be assured of that.'

'This is where we part company,' Rick said. 'That's your ambulance.'

'So this is what we are reduced to. *Fugitives!*' Simon exclaimed furiously. 'Come on, Danny, we're off. We're in hiding in an ambulance. Incognito. In disguise!'

'I say, Dad, what fun!'

Once in the ambulance they were bedded down and wheeled through the emergency exit. Soon they were in the hospitality suite which had been hastily arranged for them.

Dr Cowan waited to receive them; Sir Derek Partridge, the ambassador, was there too. It was now about twenty-four hours since the shooting and less than twenty hours since Simon had watched the Channel 4 news. However enraged, he was forced to concede to himself that it was all a bloody marvel of the miracle of electronic and physical communication. Which meant therefore, all things being equal, that Emily would be on that Concorde the very instant it was safe for her to travel.

And on this Simon was absolute and adamant. So far as he was concerned, there was no alternative. He was resolute, he was firm and reasonable. This was *his* decision, his *final* decision and there would be no turning away from it.

Simon would take his wife, Emily, back home with him. Back to Lamont Road. And, if needs must, by the sheer force of his own will.

*

From Whitehall to Washington, it was generally agreed that Sir Derek Partridge was a diplomat of uncommon charm and skill. His constantly unruly hair – thick chestnut, even at sixty – was decidedly boyish. Sir Derek put this to good use; it added an air of raffish eccentricity, a kind of humorous wisdom to all his bitter, world-weary dealings with the UN. For one thing, it disguised his contempt for that failed world institution which he believed was hell-bent on destroying all decent values, all civilized history. As he saw it, all that was good and worth preserving in the kingdom of the world owed every distinction to the United Kingdom.

His patriotism was boundless *and* emotional. The trouble was that his emotions about America and the Americans were ambiguous to say the least. For one thing, emotion and diplomacy are mutually antagonistic and, for another, confusing.

Sir Derek was convinced, after the Falklands certainly, that though diplomatic life was unpredictable it had run out of surprises. He waited to welcome Simon and Danny in the hospital room which had been made available for this purpose. Two motionless bodies lying under green sheets were rushed in on stretchers.

The sweet heavy, somewhat high smell of ether had entered

the room with the stretchers, and though all this drama took only a few moments Sir Derek felt surprisingly nervous.

'OK, boys,' the attendant ordered. *'Move!'*

Simon and Danny struggled off their stretchers. But for once Sir Derek's diplomatic reserve failed him, and he found himself shaking with laughter. Laughter, in these circumstances... well, it was beyond him.

Simon, meanwhile, all but tore off his counterfeit hospital blankets. 'Forgive me,' Sir Derek said, regaining control of himself, 'I wasn't expecting you to be quite so injured!' Arms outstretched, he strode forward to greet Simon. 'Derek Partridge,' he stated. 'May I present Mr Leon Lerner?'

'How do you do, sir,' Simon said and Danny followed his father at once.

'But you must be Herbert Bradshaw's son!' Sir Derek exclaimed delightedly. '"Boots", we called him.'

'I certainly am,' Simon agreed with an awkward smile.

'Went to school together. Same house.' Sir Derek turned to Leon and by way of explanation, said politely, 'Recognized his buttons.'

'Buttons?' Leon repeated, bewildered. *'Buttons?'*

'Regiment,' Sir Derek amplified airily. 'He's one of us!'

'I see,' Leon answered, thinking these Brits are crazy. But he said firmly, 'Mrs Bradshaw's condition is quite stable.'

'I was rather curious about that myself,' Simon responded, looking at Sir Derek. 'I had hoped to have medical details from the doctor in charge...'

'I believe he'll be joining us shortly,' Sir Derek said hastily. He inclined his head towards Leon. 'Your "classified" system really worked, Mr Lerner. Excellent disguise! My congratulations.'

'Glad to be of service.'

'We're enormously grateful to you,' Simon said very formally. 'You've done so much for us...'

'The doctor claims she owes her life to Mr Lerner, you know,' Sir Derek said soberly. 'He diverted an ambulance which was already on the road to another emergency. You see, he was watching the show when it happened.'

'You took an ambulance away from *another* emergency?' Simon did not trouble to conceal his astonishment.

'Mr Lerner and his brother are the proprietors of this hospital, for which the Lord be praised!'

'Imperturbably British or not,' Leon said with a light laugh, 'I'm sure you'd like to see your wife at this time, Mr Bradshaw?'

'Thank you. Please call me Simon. Yes, I would like to see my wife.'

Leon conducted him to the small, private intensive care unit where Emily lay, but he left Simon to go in alone. For Leon, this was a sacrifice amounting to martyrdom. He couldn't bear it and would have sworn his heart and its grafted vein supply burned. *He* burned.

Rick was waiting for him in the office that had been placed at his disposal.

'Was I ever glad to see someone!' Leon said warmly, clapping Rick's back. 'Beats me, that's all I can say! They talked about buttons and ties before they even *mentioned* her condition.'

'Don't tell me,' Rick said, almost shouting. 'He was more concerned with Christine Slater than he was with Emily, for God's sake!'

'Christine Slater?'

'A journalist who conned him on Concorde. He hates her guts!'

'That's understandable. They show their emotions differently, that's all.'

'I don't think they have any,' Rick said bitterly. 'I've just been talking to her British agent and you wouldn't believe the deals he's doing. Astronomic, even by our standards.'

They were interrupted by a secretary. 'The ambassador says he would like to have a word with you,' she said, smiling at the phrase. 'That means he wants to talk to you.'

'I know that.' Leon laughed shortly. 'I'll see him right away, of course.'

'Well, sir, I wanted to thank you once again for your quite remarkably innovative assistance,' said Sir Derek.

'Not at all,' Leon said lightly. 'Though I wish I could say it's a pleasure...'

'My people are taking the Bradshaw baggage and so on.'

'Oh,' Leon said, 'I thought they'd be quite comfortable here.'

'Indeed they would have been. But they must stay at the Residence. Home from home, that sort of thing.'

'Of course.'

'We'll stay in touch.'

Leon and Rick were interrupted by the arrival of Dr Cowan. 'Hi,' he said briefly. 'What sort of a son of a bitch is that, anyway?'

Leon and Rick exchanged a glance. 'Mr Bradshaw, you mean?' Rick asked.

'He comes in, stays less than five minutes, then says when can he get her back to London. I said she'd be woozy most of the day. So he didn't see any point in waiting around, he said.'

'You mean he's not with her right *now*?' Leon asked.

'No, sir, he's not! Wanted to know when I thought she might be more awake. More awake? Christ, she's in a heavily drugged sleep . . .'

'What did you say?'

'What did I say? About when he should come back? Around 5 p.m., is what I said. Pretty arbitrary time, though. But then *he* was so arbitrary.'

'How is she now?' Leon asked. 'Do you think *I* could have a look in?'

Now Dr Cowan and Rick exchanged a brief, shrewd glance. 'Sure, come with me.'

On the way to Emily's room, Leon said casually, 'See that I'm informed when Simon Bradshaw hits the hospital again. He's staying with the ambassador.'

'OK.'

Once in Emily's room, Leon drew up a chair, sat down quietly and stayed beside her for three hours. He watched the droplets of blood flow into her veins, watched the speed at which they dropped and alerted the nurse when he correctly assessed that the speed had slowed. Other suspended plastic bags dripped other vital fluids. She lay quietly, as if under a tree, and Leon saw the bottles and bags on their drip-stands as the tree of life.

And she looked, he thought, so gentle, so delicate, but serene and pale. Once or twice she opened her eyes, but didn't speak. She seemed to shut them again – too quickly, Leon thought, as if in retreat . . . Each time she opened them he knew new terror. He had already been drawn in and drowned by her deep blue eyes, but now – because of the temperature – they were fever-bright and startlingly, brilliantly blue. A luminous blue against the white, white face and white, white pillows. And clear, clear as ink on a blank page. An abstract painting, Leon thought. Because what was she thinking, or dreaming? How much did she know of what had happened? And, God forbid, was her mind torturing and tormenting her dreams with the horror of what had happened?

Far from being resentful that Simon had declined his hospitality, Leon was delighted.

Towards lunchtime, about twenty-six hours after the shooting, Emily gave signs of being alert enough to want to know what had happened. He saw her lips move, bent closer, tried to lip-read, listened intently and was able to make out numbers. She seemed, for the moment, to be thinking only in numbers.

Her brainwaves had been perfect throughout and he knew her brain was unaffected. But it was some time before he was able to determine that she was trying to convey a telephone number: 730 9624.

He had the nurse check, she wanted to call London.

So it was from Leon that Emily heard that Simon and Danny were already in New York. But she was deep in anaesthesia and he couldn't be sure if it had registered. (Later, though, she would swear that she had heard him. But that would only be when she would also say that she wished they had not come . . .)

But Leon would move heaven and earth before he would allow Simon to take her home just as soon as she was fit for travel.

He did not yet know how, or even what he would do. But, as he said over and over to himself, 'Leave it with me . . . Leave it with me . . .'

Because Leon Lerner turned to himself for help, the way other people turned to him.

Chapter 13

'Do you realize what will happen to us if it gets out that an ambulance was diverted from *another* emergency?' Milt asked.

'I checked that out.'

'Good boy! *I* didn't have the nerve. No, I'm *not* kidding! I didn't have the nerve.'

'You'd better get a hold of yourself,' his son-in-law dared. 'Absolutely no problem with that ambulance. It was on its way to a suspected myocardial infarction which turned out to be a false alarm.'

'Don't worry about me getting a hold of myself,' Milt said coldly. 'You are aware that if that patient had died we could have been sued for more millions?'

'Why do you think I checked it out?'

'Sure. At least I can rely on you...'

Wayne knew better than to utter a word or a syllable against Leon. He had long since learned to monitor his every gesture in this respect. He merely said mildly, 'Remember, it's only twenty-six hours since that poor girl was shot, you know.'

'Less than forty-eight hours since we were all at Regines,' Milt agreed. 'I tell you, Wayne, he's got it bad! I feel it in my bones. That woman's no good for him. Even before the accident he cancelled a Western Insurance meeting.'

'But it wasn't an accident, the woman was nearly murdered! You can't blame Leon for being... uh... preoccupied when the woman he'd been with the night before was nearly *murdered* the next day!'

'She'll bring us no good,' Milt muttered.

'Uh, how's Wendy taking all this?'

'Wendy? She's all right. You know we've got a deal with the girls. Free agents, the lot of us...'

'Free as air,' Wayne agreed. 'It's tough on her, though, she's a lovely woman. So is Arlene,' he added hastily.

'They're good girls, Wendy and Arlene. Safe, you know? Sort of ... disciplined. Ladylike, if you get what I mean. They know the score. They were ready to make a deal. But this Emily Bradshaw's not the dealing type.'

'I've seen the videos of her shows,' Wayne said thoughtfully, carefully. This was the first intimate or close conversation he had had with his father-in-law, and he didn't want to blow it. He went on, 'Wouldn't call her ladylike, myself.'

'You wouldn't?'

'No, I wouldn't. She's not ladylike, because she *is* a lady. A real lady.'

'They're the worst,' Milt said savagely. 'The worst! Lots of guys would like to get their hands around her fucking arse!'

Wayne found himself actually swallowing, or rather gulping. Uh, he thought with terrible understanding. So that's it! You want to fuck her yourself. You'd like to screw her brains out! He felt the beginnings of a smile ripple his lips, but stifled it.

'I'm losing you,' Milt said impatiently. 'What are you doing, daydreaming or something?'

'Sorry,' Wayne said, then inspiration struck. 'Her husband wants to take her back to London.'

'Say that again. Say that *again*!'

'Simon Bradshaw insists on taking his wife back to London just as soon as she's fit to travel...'

'Who told you?'

'Dr Cowan.'

'So why didn't you tell me that before?' Milt asked, adding affectionately, 'Airhead!'

*

Jake Williams had not yet managed to utter a single syllable; he was quite literally speechless. So far as the expert could see, he was without thought too. It was as if his entire system had shut down, collapsed: even died. He scarcely looked human; he looked more like a waxwork, a rocking waxwork. Only his eyes – wide, staring, confused – and his clammy face and hair showed that he was alive, and a man.

After four hours of this, Lieutenant Tom Janowski gave up. 'He hasn't even peed,' he said miserably.

Tom handed him over to the Bellevue authorities and tentative or 'differential' diagnosis began at once. The media's clamour had become a roar. Dr Steve Ingrams settled on 'brief reactive psychosis' following on 'a highly significant psycho-social stressor'. Clearly Jake Williams had a schizotypal personality disorder which explained his catatonic reaction – a stupor with mutism. Meanwhile he had been hospitalized under heavy guard, and treatment and investigations were in progress.

A statement was prepared along these lines, and beamed round the world.

But questions were being asked.

What was the 'highly significant psychosocial stressor'?

The question reverberated and when Emily began to recover – as she would, very soon – nothing would be able to persuade her that the shape, the form and the design of the 'highly significant psychosocial stressor' was none other than Emily Bradshaw.

For the moment, though, Lieutenant Janowski was obliged to deal with the evidence in hand. There was not much, but it was more than sufficient. The weapon, a Colt 49, was still in Jake's hand when the guards surrounded him. His briefcase revealed his clean undershorts, as well as his annotated copy of *Defending Wives*. The four or five lines that discussed paternity had been carefully underlined in red ink. But the margin notes were pencilled: 'whore, bitch-devil' appeared on page after page. Hidden under the inside flap of the dust jacket were the words: 'Andy Williams is not now, nor ever has been, the son of Jake Williams'. It was signed as well as dated. Here the hand-writing was disorganized and childlike, but the signature appeared clear and decisive. It had still to be compared with his usual signatures.

This led, naturally enough, to a search of his supervisor's desk at the IRS. The signature appeared normal. The drawers were neat and orderly; every pencil had its place, and every paper clip. All his working apparatus was arranged with surgical precision.

The papers all pertained to his work: figures, mostly, and computer printouts. Nothing of any significance.

It was Tom who noticed that two pages looked, or rather felt as if they had been handled more than the others. The symbols, of course, meant nothing to him, but they would be analysed. What else was the forensic department for?

Every document that had ever pertained to Jake Williams would be scrutinized.

Tom's philosophy was simple. Spectacular crime demands standard methods – that was the only way you got lucky. No two men could have appeared more dissimilar than Tom Janowski and ambassador Derek Partridge, yet they were solidly united by a single emotion – patriotism. Despite the bitter disillusionment which could not but be of a piece with their careers – Sir Derek with the UN and Tom with the criminal justice system – each was committed to making the world a better place. And in each case 'the world' meant something different – for Sir Derek it was Britain, for Tom it was America.

*

The combined statement issued by Bellevue Hospital and the Attorney General mentioning 'a highly significant social stressor' had set off a storm of controversy. Geneticists were called in. Paternity, it seemed, had only just been invented. Emily's remark: 'Even if a woman does not know who the father is, she knows she's the mother, and she knows that with a hundred per cent certainty', was hotly debated both in and out of context. Television personalities in France, the Netherlands, Denmark and Germany, keen to make their name, were not above speculating on 'the nature of Emily Bradshaw's curious, one might say quasi-suspicious state- ment . . .' Variations along this theme proliferated, some going so far as to suggest that Simon Bradshaw should try to prove his own validity as a father . . . Militant feminists had a field day.

In London, *Current Opinion*, the prime time programme, said to be one of Mrs Thatcher's favourites, cancelled the show which had been scheduled and hastily assembled a cast of experts. Curiosity about Emily Bradshaw seemed boundless and Keith Summers engaged two new secretaries.

In the end, though, it was *Current Opinion* which scored the real coup, for Lady Rice, Emily's stepmother, had agreed to be interviewed. *Current Opinion* usually aired for forty-five minutes, but tonight – just a little more than twenty-eight hours since Emily had been shot – the show was to be extended by a further fifteen minutes.

That Emily was oblivious to all this pandemonium of interest was of no relevance.

Art Kristol, the president of TAN, arranged for a simultaneous transmission at 1 p.m. eastern time. Naturally enough, Derek Partridge and Simon Bradshaw elected to watch the programme together. 'The world is too small as it is,' Sir Derek said uncomfortably. 'And all this global television is turning us into a suburb, never mind a village.'

'Yes,' Simon agreed, 'a suburban slum.'

'It is a dreadful thing to have one's privacy violated,' Sir Derek said sympathetically. 'The press... well, the entire electronic revolution, I suppose, exposes that which is best kept hidden. Nothing is sacred!'

Staunch, stalwart and sophisticated diplomat though he was, nothing – but absolutely nothing – had ever embarrassed Sir Derek so much as having Simon Bradshaw's paternity questioned in front of the whole world. And what was more, and worse, to have had to sit beside the man while it was happening! Sir Derek was at a loss to know how to handle it; Simon's grim pale face was inscrutable, though once he turned to Sir Derek and said, 'Thank God *you* had the presence of mind to have Danny out of the Embassy.'

But when he saw his stepmother-in-law, Melissa, he said, 'Do you know, I seriously believe I'm going to be sick.'

Sir Derek moved to turn off the set. 'This is scandalous,' he exclaimed. 'Scandalous!'

'Leave it, please.'

When it was over, Sir Derek said angrily, 'So that's what we export now, is it?'

Simon poured himself another drink. He had decided to drop the usual courtesies. 'Tell me. Advise me. How do I handle all this? Shall I make a statement? Have blood tests? Am I to doubt my own paternity?'

'Of course not,' Sir Derek assured him, horribly embarrassed. He paced the room. 'Silence will be your most effective weapon ...'

'I'm not sure I agree. Strong case of libel, there ...'

'Well, that's your field. But I would counsel against, my friend.'

Sir Derek had left instructions that he was not to be disturbed except under the direst circumstances. But he had not thought to mention the newspapers, which were always brought to him at once. The butler brought them in and he cast an automatic glance at the headlines. *New York City News* had been placed at the top of the pile: EXCLUSIVE INTERVIEW WITH HUSBAND OF NEAR-SLAIN EMILY BRADSHAW.

'Well,' Sir Derek said briskly, 'it seems your Christine Slater's got away with a real scoop.'

'To think I thought she was one of us!'

'I think you ought to read this,' Sir Derek said. 'The repercussions will be endless.'

*

Some hours later the butler came in. 'Sir Derek, the hospital is on the line. Mrs Bradshaw is well enough to have asked for Mr Bradshaw and they want to know if they can tell her he's on his way?'

No more than thirty-two hours had elapsed since the shooting, yet Simon felt as if his life had been divided for years and years into before and after the event. Indeed, he could no longer remember the time before it had happened.

Simon was bewildered and angry and jet-lagged. But he must get to Emily. Mercifully, TV cameras and press had been deceived into believing that he was encamped within the hospital, and had taken up positions there.

He had felt himself begin to change when he watched the TV news while he was still in London, and this change had been accelerating ever since. It was as if he had been consciously strengthening his interior muscles, taking them into training, preparing them for a fight to the death.

It was not rage that he felt, but hate.

And hate wastes the hater, as he knew.

Something would have to be done...

*

Flowers filled the hospital. The wards, waiting areas, rooms were all bursting with floral tributes, some exotic, some humble. It was like a carnival or a *fiesta* – it altered the atmosphere and in the gleaming corridors, interns, nurses and patients were more solicitous of one another and more caring. Everyone willed Emily to recover quickly. The switchboards were jammed, extra staff had been recruited to handle the mail. Dr Cowan could hardly be described as sentimental – he called himself a plumber – yet he found all these expressions of goodwill from all those people out there strangely heartening.

Towards noon two days later, Emily began to be able to comprehend where she was and finally connected with Leon's repeated explanations.

'What happened?' she managed to ask.

Leon told her. 'But you will be quite fine,' he said loudly. 'As good as new. You've had the best surgeon and they've guaranteed a total recovery.'

She tried to smile at that and he knew what she was thinking: 'How American!' 'You're thinking, "How American" aren't you?' he said.

She moved her head, and that movement for Leon was like a benediction. Oh God! he thought, oh God, I'm looking at my soul.

Leon sat silently for several minutes and then, as if to drain some of the pain of what he knew he must say, he formed his hands into half-fists and dug the nails – which had already disgusted Simon because they were manicured – into his palms.

It hurt him, all the same, but he forced himself to say, 'Simon

195

and Danny are here. In New York. Staying with your ambassador. Would you like to see them now?'

'Please.'

'I'll stay with you until just before they get here. OK? Would you like that?'

'Yes.'

The nurse came in with a syringe, but Emily shook her head. 'No, please. Want to talk to my husband and son.'

'Are you sure? It's real painful, right now. We know that it's real, real sore . . .'

'I'm certain,' Emily said, but she bit her lip and Leon saw her grit her teeth. What strength, he thought, saying aloud, 'I'll leave you now, but I'll look in again later.'

Leon listened to his own unusually rapid footsteps as he walked down the corridor. Everywhere there were flowers; their perfume mingled with – and only just survived – the sharper scents of antiseptics, which as Leon thought wearily was only fitting. As if to keep some semblance of pace with the speedy twist his life had taken, he walked even more rapidly. It was four o'clock in the afternoon – teatime in London, he thought wryly – and he needed a drink.

Needed one so badly that his throat felt raw.

Somehow he had to stamp out – and crush – that desperate new thought which had crashed in against his will.

His mind skipped, darted, sought a way of escape, of discounting . . .

They had compacted time, he and Emily, turned time backwards in a sense, or beamed it via satellite through space. It had been too quick and too easy, as if they had been required to do no more than touch a button to touch a soul. So soon though, and she had been almost killed and he had almost been free again. Now her death would have freed him. But it was too late.

*

Both Milt and a stiff whisky waited for him in his office.

'The whole world loves her, Milt! The hospital is flooded with flowers, calls. We hired extra help.' Leon took the drink

196

gratefully. 'I'm confused, Milt,' he said with a sigh. 'Mighty confused. Ruthie's death didn't set me free, did it?'

'What do you expect me to say?' Milt replied, rocking his body in grief's immemorial way. 'What can I say to that? The answer's obvious for you and for me. Ruthie, Marcie... My son... What's the use of talking, Leon? What's the use? You tell me...'

Milt's monologue was as familiar as a litany to Leon. Monologue or conversation, it was a recurring theme between the brothers. Also interchangeable.

All the same, it was confusing.

Leon had expected never to be caught by the heart again. He was one of those men for whom 'falling in love' was out of the question and beyond the pale. Because that was the sure way to lose control. What was so unforgivable was that he had not felt anything like this passion for Ruthie.

'Do you feel your age?' he asked, then stopped. 'I don't know what's got into me. Forget it!'

Milt said, 'The Western deal... Problems, problems!'

'Always problems!' Leon said disgustedly. 'At our age, who needs problems?'

'We got problems. We don't make our problems. Teenagers make problems; teenagers don't have commitments.'

Leon stood up and Milt saw on his face a look of rage – even of hate – of an intensity that he had never seen before. 'Don't talk to me about teenagers.'

Milt resorted to an old but seldom used formula. 'Leon?' he said calmly, 'this is Milt you're talking to.'

'So?'

'So, I'm reminding you. We got commitments.' His voice dropped with emotion. 'We *vowed* we would never dishonour Ruthie and Marcie.'

Leon was at the doorway as Milt strode towards him and put an arm about his shoulder. 'Leon, you're the one who's in trouble now. You got problems. But your problems are my problems and I'm going to help you the way you would help me. No matter what it costs, I'll see you through this, OK?'

'OK.'

'She's out of danger, Leon,' Milt went on, 'and she's going to make it. So the major problem's solved, isn't it?'

'That's the problem,' Leon muttered. 'That's the real problem.'

As soon as Leon had left, Milt took out the *New York Post*. Wayne was working on it and there was no need for Leon to see it yet. Let them do their worst, Milt decided. So what if we diverted an ambulance and saved a life. That's what free enterprise is all about!

The phone buzzed. It was Arlene. 'Seen the *New York Post*?'

'Yup.'

'Disgusting. Wendy's seen it too ...'

'So?'

'I hate to disturb you, Milt, but this is hard on Wendy ...'

'It's hard on all of us.'

'But Leon hasn't seen her. Not even a call. Milt, be a honey. Have the four of us meet for dinner tonight.'

'You got it. Consider it done. Talk to you later.'

The *New York City News* made it imperative that the Lerner brothers be seen dining out in their usual way. He buzzed his secretary and reservations were made at the Full Squall, the restaurant of the media stars.

It was a strange new world. But old-fashioned methods still worked best.

You fight fire with fire.

Who the hell was this Christine Slater, anyway?

*

'*Everyone has a dark secret! Everyone. And everyone thinks it is darker than it is.*'

That was what Joan had said on the *Joan Barnes Show,* and that was how Katie's one-sided friendship with her really began. Because Katie had too many secrets – so many that sometimes she had the feeling that she didn't know them all herself.

But the one secret – about Andy – was so bad and so dark, as Joan would have said, that she would have died before giving it away.

When Lieutenant Tom Janowski came, she was ready for him.

'Mrs Katie Williams?' he asked.

'Yes. I know why you're here, I was watching the show. Come in.'

'Sorry about this, ma'am.'

'Honey,' she said to Andy, 'I know that's your favourite show, but we have to use this room now.'

'Are you a policeman?'

'Tom Janowski. Glad to meet you.' He turned to Katie. 'You stay here, son,' he said. 'We could talk somewhere else. What a shiny clean place you have here, Mrs Williams. An unexpected pleasure.'

Tom saw a flicker of gratification cross her pale, frightened face. Poor kid, he thought, poor, poor kid.

'Is the kitchen OK? That would be ... better ... for Andy, you know?'

'I get you.'

Once in the kitchen, she asked, 'Would you like a coffee?'

'Thanks.'

Tom felt awkward. Katie was so frightened – and so brave. He wasn't used to this sort of person and her air of quiet dignity threw him. 'You don't have to answer any questions, you know. We can get you a lawyer. Or you can get one.'

'I know that, from television. But I think I'd be glad to talk to someone.'

'Have you been all alone? All on your own since it happened?'

'Yes.'

'Isn't there anyone you can call?'

'No.'

She spoke and moved so simply, and was so without self-pity and so ... somehow, thin that the hardened Tom – who loved to say that the world was divided into two groups, assholes and cops – found himself taking her hand. 'You poor kid! You don't deserve this. I'll try to help you. Trust me.'

'Yes.'

So Katie told him, but did not trust him. She told him about her series of foster parents, about eventually running away, about meeting Jake, about the grace at meals, about only one of the men she had lived with before Jake. About the family who might only now find out that she was still alive, after all.

Because the publicity might get to them.

She talked about her quiet, cool, safe days. About her bathroom. She even confided her four baths a day. Days with Andy and the television. She talked about her TV friends: Joan, Merv, Virginia, Phil.

Tom heard a nostalgia in her voice, and knew that she realized these days had ended.

Once or twice he interrupted. 'But haven't you been lonely? I mean, Joan and Virginia don't really know you.'

'But I know *them*,' she said firmly.

'I'd like to help you, Katie. You're a good girl.'

One major difficulty overwhelmed all others: the normal difficulty – money. She had no money of her own, only a secret fifty-dollar bill. There was money in the bank, she was sure, but she had no signature and so she couldn't get at it.

'I'll send a social worker,' Tom said. 'She'll fix it . . .'

'No!' Katie begged. 'No! *No* social workers, please.'

'But the legal side of things – you'll have to have a social worker.'

That was when she began to cry. Tom couldn't recall ever having felt so . . . well . . . impotent as her thin body shook soundlessly. He would have done anything to stop it. Anything. 'Tell you what,' he said, 'I'll take care of it myself.'

*

When Tom left, he realized that Katie made him feel better about himself.

In all the violence and horror of his daily life, she was one hell of a clean girl. And she had done it herself. He had only too good an idea of what she had cleansed herself of. He hated to do it, but the usual investigations would have to go ahead.

Tom had been driving for about ten minutes when he turned around and broke the speed limit, so as to rush back to Katie Williams.

When she opened the door, he saw that she was shaking. 'It's only me,' he said. 'I came back to tell you something: don't talk to the media. But if those bastards – excuse me – if they trick you, don't tell anyone what your name was before you were married. Got it?' He turned to leave, but something else had occurred to him. 'How come the media haven't got here yet?' he asked suspiciously.

'I don't know.'

'Haven't they been calling?'

'Our phone is unlisted...'

Now that was something to go on. Those pages of Jake's... some sort of code, he was convinced.

Tom felt cheerful, which was a good omen...

*

Wendy Griffiths had never considered herself authentically beautiful, yet everyone who saw her considered her to be a remarkable beauty. Tonight, she needed to believe that she was beautiful, truly beautiful. She examined herself, but it was no use. If an anxious, insecure woman of thirty-eight cannot possibly consider herself beautiful, then she cannot really be beautiful, no matter what other people think.

Wendy was tired of the struggle, wearied by the whole dreary business of ongoing vigilance. She felt she was like a forgotten concert pianist who still goes on with the finger-exercises, day after day, hour after hour, and fingers her heart out. Exercise, diet, creams and steam. And for what?

Even now, dressing for dinner with Leon, she was exercising. *Squeeze... relax... squeeze... relax.* Inner muscles. She would have turned her womb into a muscle if she could. All for Leon. She was an average, healthily sensual woman. It wasn't that she wanted to be more or less than she was; it was that remorseless straining after excellence which was so cruel. Running against her instincts in a race which, even if there had never been an Emily Bradshaw, she was destined not to win.

A loser.

Of course she could give up – retreat before defeat – in a way. Why couldn't Emily Bradshaw have just *died*?

Dinner at Full Squall turned into a surprisingly glorious evening. Everyone – but everyone – senators, anchor people, even a governor stopped by to explode over the *New York City* article. It seemed Christine Slater's sense of outrage over that ambulance would have gone down better in England, where the undemocratic benefits of privilege receive wide coverage.

Milt found it difficult to conceal his pride. Wayne had done his PR job brilliantly; he didn't know *how* he did it, but it was brilliant. He wondered shrewdly whose pet charity had benefited.

'Oh-oh,' Arlene whispered suddenly to Wendy. 'That bitch Sheila Lyall's got to get in on the act.'

'Evening, darlings,' she said. 'We met at Regines, remember?'

Milt and Leon stood up and remained standing. The four stayed silent.

'Our heroine is recovering well,' Sheila screeched. She poked Leon playfully in the chest. 'You've switched your allegiance, I see.'

'Get lost,' Milt said, sitting down.

'Who the hell do you think *you* are? To talk to *me* like that?'

A scene . . .

And only just beginning.

The maître d' rushed over, but the four were on their way out.

'No,' Milt said firmly, 'we're leaving. You're not careful enough who gets in this place.'

So the evening ended early.

The night when Leon had first seen Emily on television, in his limo, he had suggested that Wendy be dropped off at her place. Tonight he wanted her; Sheila Lyall had been the last straw. 'It's been a nightmare, Wendy, a nightmare,' he told her.

'I know.'

'You're a good girl, Wendy.'

'You're tired, Leon.'

'I know I am.'

'Let's go to bed. We don't have to . . .'

'I know we don't.'

'I'll put you to bed.'

'You will?'

'You're so tired.'

She undressed him and ached with love. What else could she

202

call it, she wondered. But as she stripped him gently and crooned over him, he felt himself grow calmer. 'Sorry about that bitch,' he said.

'Don't think about it. Turn over and I'll get those knots out of your shoulders.'

Wendy was an expert masseuse. She had taken lessons. What had she *not* done to get this man to marry her? How could he stay linked to a vow with a dead woman? It was so unrealistic!

She felt him relax.

Soon he was asleep.

Wendy reached for her sleeping pills. She hoarded them and took them only rarely.

She needed him to fuck her, she always needed him to fuck her. Frustrated and despairing, she fell into a tormented sleep.

Some time later he awoke and made love to her. She cursed the Nembutal that dulled sensation. He was fucking her and her nerve-endings had been neutralized. What a waste! So she fought for more sensation, for herself and not for Leon, and it made her wilder. Wilder still, and wild enough to put herself first.

She stopped his thrusting and pulled away. She had received his cock, big and swollen fat. Now it was his tongue she wanted, the tip of his tongue, the edge to flicker like candlelight over that flaming, tumescence at her pinpointed centre. There. Her raging, miniature cock. His tongue obeyed and connected and flickered. Again and again a rush of separate, split, shattering sensations.

When she could speak, she said, 'I feel close to God, Leon. Do you?'

'I don't know,' he answered, sounding sleepy.

'Thank you, Leon. Thank you for bringing me so close to God. I'll never forget tonight. Never.'

Leon hugged her tight and rolled away.

Because, only two nights ago, he would not have understood what she meant. But Emily had shown him what it meant – in this sense – to be close to God. Or, more likely closer to the devil. Jealousy. The devil, jealousy. How he longed to eliminate Simon Bradshaw.

Then Leon was certain he was going insane. No, he was

already insane. Sleep was out of the question.

He roamed his apartment as if for reassurance that he really was Leon Lerner, one of the great success stories of his era. A man of fifty-five, jealous as an adolescent *girl*, for God's sake! What was happening to him? Why, even this building in which he lived and which he owned had been hailed as one of the architectural triumphs of the century. Built around a simple idea of his, too, one which had led to a minor revolution in engineering.

He knew so much, he had achieved so much. He had known only the jealousy of others.

PART III
Mid-August 1985

Chapter 14

'But what has happened to that poor man's wife?' Emily asked Simon.

'Em, I wish you wouldn't...'

'Wouldn't what?'

'Wouldn't refer to that freak as a poor man. Think of what he has done to all of us.'

'I know that. I also know what I have done to him...' She tried and failed to repress a long, shuddering sigh. 'But what has happened to his wife? What will happen to her?'

It was Tuesday, day five since surgery. The remarkable strength Emily had shown in resisting painkillers had speeded her recovery. She was able to walk quite easily, and but for the sling supporting her right arm, there was little evidence of the victim about her. She had been moved to a larger room in the hospital and it was banked with flowers. An anonymous Texan had airfreighted a huge basket of giant purple orchids; the card read: 'To a brave and beautiful lady. Waiting and hoping to see you back on the *Virginia Byrnes Show*. A well-wisher and a fan.'

The orchids were too tropical and too thickly luscious for Simon's taste, yet he felt compelled to touch one, which he did and then quickly snatched his fingers away. 'Fitting blooms for New York,' he said, his voice laced with sarcasm. 'Jungle blooms.'

'Simon, please. Does anyone know anything about her?'

'Can't say I've given her a thought!' he said impatiently.

'The newspapers said she'd gone into hiding.'

'I also read, Simon. Why can't you understand why I don't want to go rushing home with my tail between my legs?'

At that moment they were joined by Keith Summers. 'What's this I hear about a tail between your legs, my girl? Can't be *the* Emily Bradshaw we're talking about,' he said cheerfully. 'Simon – another deal. At this rate she's going to need a business manager. Full-time, too. You'll have cause to heed my words yet!'

'Yes, Keith. I know Emily's a rich woman now.' Simon's voice sounded dangerous and Emily changed the subject.

'The doctors tell me I could leave in a week.'

'Incredible! But let me not come between husband and wife,' Keith joked quickly.

'Well, Keith,' Simon said irritably, 'what *do* you think? Don't you think she should come home?'

'You're putting me in an awkward position, Simon. Hardly fair, I'd say.'

'That means you think I should stay.'

'Well, since you insist on having my professional – and I warn you, subjective – opinion, you shall have it. I'm your agent. I don't suppose either of you has given a passing thought to how much Emily's incident has added to *my* coffers!'

'To tell the truth, we hadn't,' Emily laughed. '*How* much?'

'A not inconsiderable sum. A sizeable amount. Enough to get my accountant in a tizz.' Keith paced the room.

'Actually, darlings, I think I'll have earned more out of *Defending Wives* than all my combined authors bring in during a single financial year.'

Simon whistled.

'Of course, if Emily stays on a while – and does just a few shows – only one or two – and gives, say, two or three talks on the lecture circuit ... Substantially more thousands for Keith Summers!'

'But we could come back later,' Simon suggested.

'Later? How much later?'

'Next year ... perhaps.'

'Next year? Next month, they'll be saying "Emily who?"'

This is, as Rick would say, the US of A. A month equals a decade here in America. Haven't you listened to the natives when they talk? In the summer they say "way back in the spring," as if three years and not three months pass between spring and summer.' Keith ceased his pacing. 'Why do you think people talk about the Americanization of the world?' he demanded. 'I'll tell you why. Because it's a society of the moment. Seize the moment, obliterate the past because it doesn't exist, in real terms anyway. It is an adolescent society, in an adolescent country. They value change the way we value tradition. As for the past, they've had to invent one, the way they believe they've invented space. We Brits are old and weary... senile. They're adolescent and fresh-hopeful. Who invented the word "hopefully"? The Americans did.'

'Not sure who it was,' Simon said thoughtfully, 'I seem to remember a correspondence in *The Times*.'

'Talking of the riches of America,' Keith said, 'we're dining with the fabulous twins and their ladies tonight, are we not?'

'Don't remind me.'

'I must say, I do think they're fabulous. They have a sense of style – American, but none the less, style.'

'What is American style?' Emily demanded.

'Money,' Keith said emphatically. 'Guilt-free money. Americans are not ashamed of being seen to be fabulously rich, far from it. No hang-ups about ostentation ... they spend with a flair, with talent!'

'Talent?' Simon interrupted scornfully. 'That reminds me, Em. That woman Sheila Lyall has been pestering me.'

'Sheila Lyall,' Emily interrupted. 'What's she going on about?'

'You.'

'Me?'

'She's planning on giving you something she chooses to call a "survival party". Wants to include the people we consider one of us, wants me to tell her who and where...'

Emily was overcome by nervous laughter. Her body shook with it and she seemed unable to control it.

'Oh, oh!' she gasped. 'Stop it now. Stop it! I can't bear this.

A survival party given by Sheila Lyall! As they say, with friends like her, who needs enemies?'

'Is she an enemy of yours?' Keith asked.

'She's rude, aggressively rude. I bumped into her the night before the ... oh, don't let's waste time talking about her!'

'Let's talk about the journalist who conned me on the plane instead: Christine Slater!' Simon said savagely. 'We've made a few enemies, haven't we, Em?'

'Including Lady Rice,' put in Keith, who had encouraged Emily's stepmother to go on the *Current Affairs Show* which had so enraged Simon, and which Emily knew about but had not yet seen.

'Stepmother Melissa is hardly a new enemy,' Emily pointed out.

'Well,' Simon said savagely, 'that's a change.'

Emily shut her eyes. Simon's bitter, she thought. Simon's become bitter. He couldn't possibly know about Leon, could he? But he had changed.

After a few whispered comments, Simon and Keith left.

When they had gone, Emily sat bolt upright. Her fingers trembled, but only with impatience to get at those phone buttons. She longed for Leon, longed to see him so that she could study him yet again. It was for Leon that she had resisted those painkillers. Because during those terrible terror-racked hours she had sensed his presence. Now that she knew what he had done with that ambulance, a sense of timelessness ruled over her connection with him and she felt she had surrendered the soul he had saved to him. *Her* soul ... Several times, now, she had searched deep into her own eyes, in the mirror, but the trace of near-death was as invisible as time.

Emily had Leon's new private line in the hospital. Milt was in despair: Leon spent most of his time in the small office the hospital had set aside for him.

'Leon?' she said greedily. 'Leon?' What a joy to say his name! 'How soon can you get here?'

'One hundred and twenty seconds, give or take a second!'

It took Leon no more than ninety seconds to race to her room.

'What will happen to that poor man's wife?' she asked at once.

'Katie Williams?'

'You know her name.'

'But of course I know her name. When you were able to talk, that was one of the first things you asked about.'

'I've no recall. Drugged, I suppose. I'm . . . anxious about her, you see.'

'Sure I see, so let me set your mind at rest. We're taking care of her. Now, I'll fill in the detail if you promise not to interrupt, OK? You were so anxious that we sent Wayne – Milt's son-in-law, our PR director – to check her out. He had a hard time persuading a Lieutenant Janowski to reveal her address, I can tell you. Had to bring out the big guns of City Hall to do it.

'Katie's only twenty-six or twenty-seven. Has a small son, Andy, who's four-and-a-half. Wayne found a frightened, pitiful young woman. If Janowski had not agreed to accompany Wayne, she wouldn't have talked to him. She'd drawn the drapes, taken the phone off the hook and they were living out of cans. She was smart enough to make it look as if they'd run away. But she trusted Janowski. That guy's a winner; Katie got lucky when she drew him.

'The end result is that she and Andy are living in one of our buildings. Wayne tells me Katie's a good kid. And Wayne, that guy's a winner too. It turned out that her only friends are TV stars. Poor Katie thinks they're her friends. Like Virginia Byrnes . . .'

'I've got to interrupt. I'm not at all clear about what you're saying.'

'God, I love your voice,' he said, leaping from his chair to kiss her forehead. 'You heard it right. Katie was friendless because that crazy man dominated her life. He was a loner, I guess. So Virginia Byrnes, Joan Barnes and Merv and Phil . . . to talk to her, you'd think they were her best buddies. Of course they'd never heard of her!'

'She believes in them, though.'

'True. And you reminded her of the one she liked the most:

211

Joan. The *Dr Joan Barnes Show*. She told Wayne that she was sure the two of you would have become close friends while you were in the States.'

'You can't mean that.'

'I mean every word. To get back to Wayne, he's going to introduce her to Joan Barnes. And guess who is fixing that? "Now here's what I want you to do for me." Rick, bless him!'

'He wants to see you; he's here every day. The guy's got a crush on you. I should be jealous.'

'But you're not?'

'No.'

'You're not the jealous type?'

'I don't know. I wasn't before...' He stopped for a moment, but continued rapidly, 'Rick's fixing it. And she's overjoyed – no shows, no publicity, no kickback for Dr Joan Barnes, either.'

'And him?' Emily asked in that whisper she used whenever she really needed to talk about Jake Williams. 'What is going to happen to him? Rick warned me not to talk about what he called that genetic stuff, but I knew better. Oh, Leon, what's to be done about what *I've* done? What's to be done?'

They had covered this ground over and over again. As far as Emily was concerned, *her* irresponsible chatter had pulled the trigger...

'Emily, I've had a meeting with Professor David Lazar about this. You probably don't know who he is in England, but over here he's ranked with Skinner and Lazarus. Sort of post-behaviourists. They've talked with their people and no one seems to know of any study that's been undertaken to evaluate the effects of radio or television phone-ins. Got that?'

'I know what you mean.'

'Right now LFE are setting the thing up and Professor Lazar will supervise the study.'

'You've done so much.'

'A major gap in our information is all it is, really.'

'In England, you and your brother would have been knighted by now: the twin knights.' Emily bit her lip. Her arm ached. 'My knight in shining armour, Mr Leon Lerner!'

There was a knock on the door – a discreet but determined knock. Rick Cooke, who always made them smile. 'It's me,' he said and Leon gave out his famous snorting, rattling laugh which had not been used for days. Listening to it, Emily felt a great peace come over her. 'How do you like these?' Rick asked, spilling magazines over the bed. 'Emily Bradshaw – cover girl!'

'Careful, you'll hurt her!' Leon shouted.

'Sorry. I'm too excited by all this, I guess. *People Magazine*!' And it was true...

Sheila Lyall's photographs.

People even went so far as to carry an interview with Christine Slater.

Leon's heart raced again. God! she was beautiful, he thought. And smart. And famous. He said so. He said all this even though Rick was in the room and Emily felt embarrassed, but Rick – as engaging as ever, with his usual enthusiasm – merely joined in. Suddenly Emily said, too brightly Leon thought, 'Simon will simply hate this!'

'But it's only in America,' Rick said jokingly. 'None of his kind will see it.'

Emily smiled in spite of herself and was immediately angry with her reaction. She was forgetting not only who she was, but what she was *of*... joining the other side.

'He'll hate it,' she said again.

'Keith Summers called a little while ago. Said he'd just left you, Emily. He told me he'd sorted it all out with Simon, so I'm afraid you'll just have to stay on here awhile. Simon and Danny are flying out on Saturday.'

'Are they?' Leon said. 'You're sure they're leaving Saturday?'

'Sure I'm sure. What's so important about Saturday, sir?'

'I was planning on fixing a meeting with Simon and Governor Brooks,' Leon said, too quickly.

Emily caught the flicker in his eye and knew he had lied. He had not wanted Rick to know how pleased he was that Simon was going. She also knew that she ought to be ashamed of herself. Her son had come perilously close to being motherless and her husband to being wifeless, yet the news that they would be leaving her on her own in New York for a while longer, free of Simon, was utterly and unbelievably wonderful. Her only sadness was that this meant she would be parted from Danny, too. At least there was the telephone and she would be able to speak to Danny more easily from three thousand miles away, than when he would be only a few hundred miles away at the Trevor-Winston School.

*

At last Wendy was convinced that if she had not loved Leon so much, she could have controlled him more. That is to say, she could have had a greater control over her own emotions. Six long abstinent nights had passed since that wild night when Leon had turned her into something like a mystical being.

It would not happen again.

Still, she saw Leon almost every night – their usual foursome at one of the great restaurants. But something had been added to her programme of beauty shops, aerobics, massage and diet. *Coke!* The high that made it all livable.

No problem with money...

And Arlene didn't know.

The insides of her closet doors were pasted with photographs of Emily Bradshaw. She had thought of going to a voodoo expert, but had settled instead on a psychic. It was more spiritual and she felt spiritual... Four years of a steady relationship... Now, thanks to Leon, independently wealthy. No need to work again, ever, nor even to be very, very careful.

But then, how secure could one be with a married man? For that is what Leon was: married for ever to a dead wife. Married to the vow made to a dead woman, witnessed by the brother who had made the same vow to another dead woman. It was bizarre, but more binding than any legal document. You cannot interpret a vow, for there are no shades of meaning nor any precedents to let you off the hook. You obey a vow, the way you obey hunger.

And if you are a Leon Lerner, you squander everything, even the essence of unborn life that is carried in every man. You have a vasectomy – and all in the name of a vow made to a dead woman.

For the thousandth time, Wendy wondered whether Emily knew about this vow.

But even if Emily did know, it would make Leon more and not less desirable. Emily would believe – as Wendy had believed – that it was easier to defeat a vow than a wife.

Of course, Emily was a married woman. How wrong she had been to think that might save her! Leon and Milt had excluded married women on a point of principle. And for Leon, as for Milt, a principle and a vow differ from one another as time differs from eternity.

The sensation of body-minded spirituality and mysticism was with her still, and for its sake she wished she could warn Emily.

But Emily, poor Emily, would scorn the whole thing.

Wendy was certain it would not be long now. A day or two, and Leon would take her to lunch and sign her off. And though his conscience would be clear, he would be generous and send her to a lawyer so that her futureless estate would be protected.

*

Being entertained by Leon Lerner at the newest 'in-restaurant' in New York was the last thing Simon wanted. It was the third time that he had tried, and failed, to catch Keith's eye and he felt disproportionately irritated, not to say betrayed. He had expected Keith to share his disapproval, but instead Keith, star-struck Keith, positively slobbered with admiration. Here was this man, Leon Lerner, this all-star American tycoon unashamedly boasting about the way in which his *Kay-Chow* pet food's newest line in slimming and vegetarian foods was being marketed.

'You really have succeeded in creating a demand,' Keith said in the kind of awed tones which Simon believed should have been reserved for a scientist. He could have understood Keith's awe if he was hearing him say something on the lines of, 'So you really have succeeded in finding a cure for malaria?'

'But surely it's hardly ethical to subject animals to human fads?' Simon drawled. 'Dogs are and always have been carnivorous. My dog wouldn't stand for it!'

'Plant's working at double shift,' Leon assured him cheerfully.

'Dogs seem to like it,' Wendy said. 'It's great; tested it myself. Vitamin and protein fortified, of course,' she added, sensing Simon's distaste. She went on thoughtfully, 'What's your feeling on vivisection?'

Simon smiled. 'And laboratory grown dogs? Another of your American inventions. One of the scourges of our time, I'd say.'

'I get what you mean,' Leon said, 'but to follow the thing through to its logical conclusion, you ought to approve of vegetarian foods for animals.'

'But that's going against nature,' Simon said defensively.

'So is the pill,' Wendy said, adding charmingly, 'I'm sure you're not opposed to the pill, though!'

Leon released his famous infectious laugh and Keith laughed even more enthusiastically than he had done earlier, which sickened Simon. He withdrew from the conversation into his own thoughts. He had never been more confused nor understood less about things in his own life. He had been determined to take Emily home but, as Keith had said, who in his right mind would dream of turning down a minimum of a quarter of a million dollars? In return for an outlay of a few TV and radio appearances, a few talks on the lecture circuit and a pet food promotion? Emily had already made a great deal of what Keith now called serious money, but were the Bradshaws so rich that they could afford to turn their backs on all that lovely lolly?

Simon had countered by saying that they had never gone in for greed, whereupon Keith was enraged.

'*Greed?*' he had shrilled, blinking furiously. 'I'll tell you about greed!' He made a visible effort to control himself, squeezed his eyes shut for a moment and then spoke more calmly. 'Greed is wanting more and Americans are encouraged to want more. Success is fashionable, which is why it's easier to work effectively over here. Do you follow me?'

'Go on. Get to the point, if you can!'

'Rick's a hungry young man. He's hungry for success, isn't

he? Hungry enough to have spotted *Defending Wives* in Frontier's catalogue.'

'You've forgotten that Rick Cooke also got us into the gutter press.'

But Keith went on as if he hadn't heard. 'Anyone who has a chance to make an extra bit of cash honestly, and who refuses on the grounds that greed is indecent, is far far greedier than the man who seizes his chance!'

'Now I'm not following you.'

'Greedy for virtue! I'll put it this way, Simon. If you persuade Emily to accept your line of reasoning, then you and she will be the two greediest people I've ever known. Greedy for virtue!'

'You're going too far, Keith.'

'Not far enough! But when one considers what your sensibilities are going to do to my bank balance, I think you owe me the courtesy of hearing my point of view!'

'I'm listening.'

'Earning a huge chunk is not the same thing as selling an heirloom such as the Ford Madox Brown that hangs on your wall!'

'I wondered how the press got to hear about our Ford Madox Brown.'

'Sheila Lyall, probably,' Keith said airily – too airily, Simon thought.

Wendy touched Simon's arm. 'You look lost,' she said sympathetically. 'It's been a terrible trauma for *you* too.'

'An American nightmare,' Simon agreed with a chilly smile.

'I wonder why I get the impression,' Leon said half-humorously, half-seriously, 'that you don't like Americans?'

'You let us down at Suez . . .'

'And you let us down in Vietnam . . .'

'Vietnam? We did the thing in Malaya without so much fuss.'

'Malaya. What's Malaya?'

'We didn't call it a war, we called it an emergency. *And* we won.'

'Thank God all that's over,' Keith said nervously. 'Let's

drink to continued peace!'

Wendy picked up her glass. 'That's a darling idea, Keith,' she said. 'Don't you think so, Leon? Why don't you call your new vegetarian stuff "Peace"?'

This was too much for Simon. 'You must excuse me,' he said. 'A lag in jet-lag, it's only just hit me.' He folded his napkin.

'Are you going to see Emily?' Leon asked.

'No, I'm going to do what you people call hitting the sack!'

'Sleep well,' Wendy called after him. 'Pleasant dreams!'

*

Simon's chest felt tight and his heart raced too. He couldn't breathe here. America gave him claustrophobia, he decided. Which was probably a damn sight better than all the other phobias he could have caught in this part of the world. Well, he was leaving on Saturday; the day after tomorrow he would be out of this insanity and back in his own known, civilized world.

But Emily was here too... and Danny. The Bradshaw family was here with him in this alien wilderness, yet he felt cut off, disconnected, as if he had fallen completely out of his own sight – out of the self he had known, anyway. It was not like him to leave a dinner party so abruptly, and even less like him to allow any sort of passion to show ... He had never really cared enough about people to have any deep feelings about them one way or another. And now he had what amounted to a hate list: that unscrupulous newspaper woman, Christine Slater, the treacherous bastard Keith Summers and now that unspeakable vulgarian, Leon Lerner.

Hatred was a new emotion to Simon Bradshaw – so new, and so bewildering, that it was as draining as an unexpected physical effort.

Americans poke their noses into everyone's business. What the hell did it have to do with Leon Lerner whether or not he would call on his wife? And because he had said he wouldn't, he could think of no better reason than to see her now, even if it was already nearly midnight.

*

Emily, who had been steadfastly refusing sleeping pills, was awake when he came in and trying to write a letter with her left hand. This was so typical of her, and so comfortingly familiar, that Simon felt his ill-temper begin to lessen. 'Who are you writing to?' he asked, as if writing with her left hand was nothing out of the ordinary.

'My father.'

'About Melissa getting on the box?'

'I can't get over that. You'd think I would have enough on my mind without adding my stepmother to the list!'

'That's funny, Em. I've just been making a list myself . . .'

'What about?'

'Oh, all sorts of things,' he said evasively. 'I'll have a lot to catch up on.'

'I know,' Emily said at once. 'I'm so sorry, Simon!'

'Don't think about it,' Simon said generously. 'Can't say I'll be sorry to get back to civilization, though. What a strange lot they are! That girlfriend of Leon Lerner's thought it would be just darling to christen a vegetarian dog-food "Peace"!' He laughed shortly.

'"Peace"?' Emily said quickly. 'What a stupid idea!'

'Vegetarian dog-food is even more stupid. Imagine marketing a vegetarian dog-food in Britain!'

'I believe there is one already.'

'Sponsored by the anti-vivisectionists, no doubt,' Simon said angrily.

Emily saw that his fists were clenched. 'What's she like?' she asked.

'Who?'

'Um . . . Leon's girlfriend.' Emily hoped her curiosity didn't show too avidly. 'I'm afraid I don't know her name.'

'Wendy, I think she's called Wendy. Not our type at all, Em – Leon Lerner's kind of woman. Nervous, like all kept women.'

'Nervous?'

'Tries too hard and too obviously to be a hostess. You know what I mean? I had the feeling that she thought her days with the tycoon might be numbered,' Simon said. 'But let's not waste our breath talking about them. I've been thinking all evening about what this will do to us, Em. Keith hammered it home all right. It *is* an enormous amount of money for us, isn't it?'

'We mustn't let it ... well, unsettle us, Simon.'

'No,' Simon agreed, 'but it already has, hasn't it?' He began to pace the room. 'I'd made up my mind to take you back home with me. Instead, I'm leaving the day after tomorrow and you're staying on for three or four weeks after you've quite recovered.' He sat down.

'Do you think I should stay on?' Emily asked anxiously. 'We can get out of it, you know. There's still time!'

'Keith told me I was a greedy man. "Greedy for virtue" was what he said. He wanted me to know how much I could cost *him* if I took you home right away.'

'All this ... publicity,' Emily began slowly. 'We can't pretend nothing happened. It's got me thinking.'

'That's too true,' Simon interrupted. 'Our privacy has been invaded. And in a sense, our integrity too. We've been seduced in a way and the thing is that we must decide to get back to normal.'

'Well, of course; that goes without saying, surely ...' She sighed deeply. 'I've been thinking about Danny, about his going away to school. He's too sensitive.'

'That's precisely why he must go.'

She pressed a button and the head of the bed lowered.

'You're tired, Em. I shouldn't have come.'

'I'm so glad you did come, Simon. I couldn't sleep, anyway. Do you think Ophelia will manage? The freezer should be full.'

Chatting about domestic details had long been a cosy accessible source of comfort to the Bradshaws. Pure relief spilled over Simon, spilled like hope.

Emily felt a wave of relief too, though for very different reasons. Simon was not going to be a problem, which meant that she could stay in America not only with his assent, but with his blessing ... Her relief about this displaced but did not obliterate those other nagging thoughts and sensations that she had deceived and betrayed – and would continue to deceive and betray – Simon, their marriage and their friendship in more ways than she could bear.

And it was not only Leon's lovemaking, because her deceptions had begun long before Leon. Her fascination and admiration for the way she believed Americans did things, for the way they thought and felt, was not something she would have wanted Simon ever to guess at. He would have interpreted it as disloyalty. Meanwhile, she would live in the present, or at any rate look no further than the four to six weeks of her extended stay. She had almost been killed, she thought fretfully, so surely she was entitled to that much? She must have earned some license.

But not enough, it seemed, to allow her to tell Simon that she had fallen in love with New York. Which had happened even before that fantastic night with Leon. She had heard people say, 'I went to Paris and fell in love with the place,' but had not understood its meaning. She didn't entirely understand what she meant when she told herself, over and over again, that she had fallen in love with New York. It was a kind of primitive attraction, she supposed – the speed, the enthusiasm and the openly expressive faces were as exciting to her as a new lover might have been. Before Leon.

And Leon embodied the excitement of New York.

Even Jake Williams was part of it. Because excitement was also danger.

Emily did not feel in any way victimized. Of course, if she had died, she and Simon and Danny would have been victims. The whole point, though, was that she had not died. Jake and his wife and their son were victims, and in a sense her victims. It was hard not to think of this. After all, Rick had warned her not to talk about 'that genetic stuff'. But she had gone ahead, stubbornly, and without sparing a thought for what the consequences of this might be for anyone out there. She had wanted to promote her book, that was all. It simply hadn't occurred to her that some among the public looked upon a 'celebrity guest' as an important expert, if only because a television apperance was the stamp of authority. And Emily knew only too well that she was neither an authority, nor even a real writer.

At least Leon was taking care of Jake Williams's wife, Katie, and there was some comfort in that. What a wonderful phrase 'taking care' was. But was the poor girl seeing a psychologist? She would speak to Leon about this. That was another wonderful thing about being in America – you only had to speak about a problem and at once people would begin to think about ways in which that problem might be solved. America was still too adolescent to have any understanding at all of the meaning of resignation...

Simon's unexpected visit, combined with all that she had not said, left her wide awake and restless. It was 2 a.m. She pressed the button, raised the bed, picked up her pen and went on with her letter to her father. She was deep in concentration not only on what she was saying, but on forming the incredibly large characters which her left hand made, when something made her look up.

She saw Leon.

'But it's two o'clock in the morning,' she said.

'I know, I couldn't sleep. So I came.'

'Simon was here, too. He left about an hour ago.'

'He told me he wasn't going to the hospital.'

'I suppose he changed his mind.'

'Simon hates Americans!' Leon exclaimed. 'He says we let him down at Suez. It's absurd, Suez was almost thirty years ago!'

'Oh, did he say that? How like Simon,' Emily replied, wanting to change the subject. 'Don't take it personally.'

'I think you're fantastic,' Leon said, taking her hand. 'Fantastic! Your right hand's out of action, so you calmly use your left hand. I love that.'

'How do you know I'm not left-handed?'

'Because I watched you through the window in your door.'

'Do you know whether Katie Williams is being seen by a psychologist?'

'No, I don't know. Why?'

'I thought perhaps she ought to be. What do you think?'

'I wish I'd thought of that myself. Leave it with me, I'll take care of it.'

'Wonderful words,' Emily said.

'What do you mean?'

'I'll take care of it . . .' Emily gave way to a long, luxurious stretch of her left arm.

'I've watched and watched,' Leon said. 'For six days I've watched and stared. Because you are so beautiful. No make-up. Just naturally beautiful. You know, they wrapped your head in some sort of white stuff,' he went on, 'and somehow it made your features stand out in even clearer lines. I thought you were beautiful, even when I saw you on TV at the back of my limo. I'm proud to even know you.'

'Leon,' Emily said, embarrassed. 'Please.'

'No, let me go on. There's something I badly need to know. It's sort of a confession, I guess.'

'Now I'm really intrigued.'

'People say I've achieved a great deal – and I have, of course. Though only because Milt and I have been such a successful team. Neither of us could have done it without the other, and I don't mind telling you that I am proud of what we've done together. Very proud. But one of my proudest moments was in thinking quickly enough to divert that ambulance to Emily Bradshaw.'

'I don't know what to say . . .'

'Nothing. No need for words. But I couldn't think of a better way to let you know how I feel about you. I love you, Emily Bradshaw.'

'Why do you keep calling me Emily Bradshaw?'

'I can't say. As soon as we can get you out of here, I'm taking you to convalesce at my farm in Connecticut. I've made up my mind – subject to your agreement of course!'

'Oh, I agree. I agree.'

'I'm a clever guy, you see, Emily. It's not for nothing that I included Wendy in my party tonight. Simon saw her with me and he thinks we're a couple.'

'Are you?' Emily asked very softly. When he was silent she repeated, 'Are you a couple, Leon?'

'No,' he said shortly. 'Wendy always knew that. She always knew how I felt about Ruthie. Arlene knows that, too, about Milt.'

'Are you absolutely certain of this?'

'Absolutely.'

'When do you suppose they'll let me out?'

'Don't know. But I won't let you go until we get the OK. You're in my hands now.'

'I know.'

Whatever might or might not have happened in this room, in these past few hours, was something Emily wanted to escape from. So she said, 'I believe I'll collapse if I don't get to sleep now.'

He removed pillows, checked the angle of the bed and helped her settle. When he left, he tiptoed out.

Halfway down the corridor he realized he was still tiptoeing and stopped still. He couldn't remember when last he had tiptoed. He reminded himself yet again that he'd got it bad, real, real bad!

*

While Simon Bradshaw was dining with Leon Lerner, Wendy Griffiths and Keith Summers, Lieut Tom Janowski and his wife Mary were entertaining – albeit much more modestly – Katie Williams and her son Andy. 'The kid's so lonely. She's got no friends, no one. I don't think she's ever been invited to share an ordinary meal with an ordinary family like ours,' he had told his wife, knowing she would extend an invitation at once. Mary thought nothing was more pitiful than a person without a family.

The evening went well. Tom felt expansive, the Janowski children were especially kind to little Andy and Katie's gratitude was ... well, touching was the only way to describe it. And Mary, who was a motherly soul, really took Katie to her bosom. She couldn't bear it that Katie looked upon TV hosts and hostesses as friends. The two women made plans to go shopping and Mary was going to take Katie to a beauty parlour ...

All in all, it was one of those wonderful evenings when you feel you deserve your place in the sun.

They had all piled in the car, seen Katie home and gone to bed feeling better about themselves. Tom and Mary made love, and felt closer even than usual. Somehow Katie's loneliness – in particular, the fact that she did not even know she was lonely – had made them need to draw closer as if to stamp out the knowledge of her terrible, amputated isolation.

Strange, after all the indescribable physical injuries he had seen, that Katie's loneliness should have given him a nightmare. He dreamt he was utterly alone, alone in a corner of milky water in the pond, but as soon as it touched his lips it turned to grease. He began racing through cave after cave of this milky fluid. About to trip, he pressed his foot down, hard. And woke up.

Tom Janowski had been a cop for two months short of twenty years. True, too many things about his line of work made him feel sick and too few made him proud. But he had experienced moments when he had not only been proud of his work, but proud to be alive. There were the lives he had saved with mouth-to-mouth resuscitation, and even one would-be suicide he had prevented with nothing more than a ramble of sympathetic words. He had been proud, too, to graduate as one of the highest in his class at Police Academy. But very little – too little, he thought – made him feel cheerful.

Katie Williams, however, had done this for him. When Mr Leon Lerner's big-shot PR guy, Wayne, had come up with an offer to rehouse her, she had refused to agree to anything unless she could have Tom Janowski's approval. She seemed to respect him even more than she respected this hot-shot smooth-talker.

And, of course, hearing what Rick Cooke had told him about Emily Bradshaw – that she had been worried about Katie – was something else . . . But then Emily was British, and they did things differently. Even so, it had given him a good feeling; he had to admit that – it made him feel better about a whole lot of stuff.

The guys in Forensic agreed with him about these over-fingered pages he had found in Jake's desk. They were a code of some sort, but no one had cracked it so far.

The psychiatrists and psychoanalysts were still busy with Jake Williams, and Tom had not yet been able to interview him. Katie was as helpful as she could be, yet he instinctively felt that she was hiding something . . . something she probably thought was a terrible, murderous secret. Something, the detective believed, that was not so terrible – like Jake not being the kid's father in the first place. But he chose not to press the point; it wasn't crucial at this stage, anyway.

His dream had left him parched and he went to the kitchen to get a Coke. He wasn't given to nightmares, still less to deciphering their content, but you didn't have to be a shrink to know that he was dreaming his own terror of loneliness. What would happen to Katie Williams, he wondered. She would never be lonely again, he decided, not as long as he and his family were around.

He had brought that freak's briefcase home with him. Katie had told him about it – pure leather, she said. He thought he would have another look at it. Yes, it was pure leather – at least the bastard had looked after it.

In six years that poor kid Katie had been able to collect the grand total of fifty dollars! And she was grateful because that crazy husband allowed her to buy things for the *bath*! Why this should offend him so much, he could not have said. A few years younger, and he would have started hurling things. The crashing smashing sounds of splintering glass made him feel better. But he was older now and at forty-two you were either more disciplined or more mellowed. It made no difference, what, except that you did *not* start hurling things all over the place.

The briefcase sat at his feet.

It was only a briefcase.

And he was exploding with rage. The briefcase could stand a short, sharp kick.

He kicked and it went flying . . .

He bent to retrieve it.

Tom had forgotten about his days as a goal kicker and forgotten his force. Which was most fortunate – because if he had not, the briefcase might not have revealed its slender secret compartments.

And so niftily constructed on the left side, on the bottom and on the lid.

A few pages. But more codes and this time initials.
Tom's hands shook.

Well, well, he thought, shows you what a good kick can do! Things were beginning to fall into place.

Chapter 15

Everything about Heathrow appeared not only orderly, but benign. The neat prep-school script on all the signposts was especially soothing and Simon had never felt more patriotic.

Their bags were light, so Danny took charge of the trolley. He responded to his father's obvious sense of well-being – so very different from the grim face he'd seen in New York – and chattered happily. So engrossed were they with one another that neither recognized the excited yelps coming from the labrador puppy straining at his lead.

Suddenly the sounds of their names: 'Simon! Danny!'

They stopped. 'Susan!' Simon said, openly astonished.

The puppy leapt into Danny's arms.

'But how on earth did you know we were coming home today?' Simon exclaimed.

'You are holding us up. Would you mind?' someone asked.

'Excuse me,' Simon said, moving the trolley. 'It's very good of you to have come, Susan. It was announced that we'd be returning tomorrow.'

'Someone from Keith's office telephoned to tell me you'd be home and wanted Hal back.'

'I can't believe this!' Simon said grimly. 'As if I would ever be so demanding, not to say rude. Keith's gone too far; I'm so sorry you've been put to so much trouble.'

'Not at all, Simon. I was delighted. And, looking at Danny and Hal, I was quite right!'

Susan's fawn Mini was cosy and even charming after all

those unnecessarily clumsy-looking cars. 'I'd rather be in your Mini that in one of those over-large "limos",' he said.

'They have televisions in them. Videos, too, and telephones!' Danny put in.

'I can tell you liked America, Danny!' Susan smiled.

'I did. Dad didn't!'

'No, I didn't. And I don't expect I ever will!'

'How is Emily?' Susan asked quietly. 'The papers have been full of her.'

'She'll be leaving the hospital very soon; she's making an excellent recovery. Don't talk to me about the media, though. Emily's been in almost every lurid magazine you can think of.'

Susan was an intelligent, practised driver. She handled the traffic as she handled a violin – darting in and out deftly and smoothly – and they reached Lamont Road in record time.

'Oh, Lord,' Simon said. 'I didn't take the keys with me!'

'Ring the doorbell, Dad. Ophelia's inside, I can tell.'

'How can you tell?'

'She loves Duke Ellington. Can't you hear?'

'That's right, son. I wasn't thinking.' Simon pressed the bell. 'How she could possibly hear this over the sound of Duke Ellington escapes me.'

He pressed the bell harder, then sounded the brass knocker. Still no response.

'I'll go round the back, Dad. And then, if I get in, I'll let you in.'

'No, don't go, Danny. I think I hear footsteps.'

The door opened. 'Cool it, man. Cool it,' someone said – an apparition, Simon thought. You couldn't tell what it was with its mauve cockscomb hair and loose black jacket. It sounded like a male voice though not, as Simon would say later, beyond all reasonable doubt.

'And who, may I ask, are you?'

'What's it to you?'

'Just a moment,' Simon said. 'Just a moment. Ophelia?' he roared. *'Ophelia?'*

A sound of hurried footsteps and then Ophelia, in a black satin dressing-gown and nothing else, was peering out at them through a shield of hair.

'Oh, Mr Bradshaw. You are not here before Monday.'

He pushed past her and the others followed. The place reeked of incense. Simon strode into the kitchen. Cups and dishes were everywhere and here incense had given way to the smell of putrefying cheese. The freezer door was open; a quick look at the contents told him that it must have been open for days. His mind flew to the Ford Madox Brown: had it been stolen? Racing upstairs, he found two other creatures in the drawing room, but the painting was safe.

Susan had followed him. 'Thank God you're here,' he said. 'You're a witness. Because I'm calling the police to get them out.'

'We're leaving,' one of them drawled. 'Just having a bit of fun. Appreciated your Chivas. Coming, Clifford?'

'Wouldn't dream of staying where we're not wanted.'

They fled past Simon.

Downstairs, Ophelia's sobs echoed through the house. 'I'll get our bags, Dad,' Danny offered.

'Good idea.'

'Sorry about all this, Susan. But a jolly good thing for me that you're here. Will you come downstairs with me? I'm going to give her two hours to pack her bags and get out!'

Outside Ophelia's door, Susan paused. 'I don't blame you, Simon. But where will she go? Shouldn't you give her a little more time?'

'No,' Simon said coldly. 'I'm not the slightest bit interested where the hell she goes.'

'I pack,' Ophelia stated. 'I leave in one hour. Not *two* hours!'

'Oh, look at the freezer,' Susan wailed. 'And Emily spent hours and hours planning and preparing.'

'She certainly did.'

'Well,' she said, pulling on one of the disposable rubber gloves she had found among the dishes. 'Clearing this mess could be fun. Don't you think so, Danny?'

'Oh yes,' Danny said enthusiastically. 'Great fun!'

'I can't honestly tell you that we don't need your help, Susan,' said Simon. 'Because we do!'

'Music helps,' Susan said. 'Music always helps.' She switched on the radio and tuned in to Radio Four. Soon Beethoven's 'Emperor' Concerto filled the kitchen. Danny found some dog biscuits and fed Hal, while Simon opened a bottle of wine. The three of them worked happily and well. But the plants had all died and that, Susan thought, was unforgivable.

Simon sat down at the cleared kitchen table and drafted a note for Ophelia to sign. She was being dismissed on the grounds of gross misconduct.

'Once a lawyer, always a lawyer,' Susan marvelled. 'I never would have thought of a thing like that myself.'

'Ah, youth,' Simon said. 'Once upon a time I wouldn't have done either.'

'Do you think she'll sign it?'

'She has no choice in the matter,' he said very formally.

About an hour later Ophelia sauntered into the kitchen. She had got herself up in an amazing combination of reds: tights, shoes, mini-skirt, even a hat, all red. 'I go now,' she said, emphasizing her Swedish accent. Simon gave her the paper to sign.

'My mother, she told me not to go back to the house of a shot woman.'

Ophelia had signed the paper . . .

But the last word belonged to her.

'That wasn't fair,' Susan said.

'Oh, I don't know about that. Ophelia's mother probably dislikes sensational publicity as much as we do.' Simon had flopped back in a chair and now he stretched his legs. 'Tell you what,' he said expansively, 'we're all going to the Chelsea Brasserie. We needn't change our clothes or anything like that, Danny.'

In the circumstances, Simon believed he could not have chosen anything more appropriate. The bistro could hardly have been described as small and intimate – it was dedicated to matters far more serious than the creation of an artificially cosy ambience. The uncarpeted floors, fairly bright lights, wooden chairs and sparkling white paper tablecloths accurately reflected the serious business of honest, timeless French cuisine. The patrons were expected to see their food. And yet, for all the high seriousness of the place, the quality of the food was enough to make it jolly and almost cosy. Besides, in Simon's view, the contrast with the best of New York's plush was perfect. All three made the same choice – leek soup, followed by a *boeuf bourgignon* – a rough peasant meal.

The food, the plain dedication of the waiters in their full-length aprons had an almost magical effect on Simon. The irritations, humiliation and bitterness of the past week began to fade, the constriction about his chest loosened. He was back in his own known, safe world.

They would carry on the 'Operation Clean-Up' – as Susan dubbed it – the next day. She dropped them at home and said she would check on them in the morning.

Simon helped Danny into bed and allowed Hal to spend the night in the boy's room. He wasn't tired enough to go to sleep, and thought a long, hot bath would not be amiss. He had not yet been into his bedroom, but now when he turned the knob the door was locked and there was no key. Simon sighed, but would not allow himself to feel anything more than mildly inconvenienced. He went back downstairs intending to inspect his mail, but instead he looked through Emily's alphabetical household notebook. It was more like a manual – every conceivable emergency contingency appeared to have been included.

Simon turned to 'K'. He doubted it, but there might even be a reference under keys. Emergency locksmiths were recorded under one sub-heading and another sub-heading was entitled 'Spares. Box behind WH.' Directed to the bookshelves, he knew exactly where to find *Wuthering Heights*, behind it an envelope, and in the envelope the clearly labelled key, 'bedroom spare'.

Emily had never let him down. He felt a sudden rush of tenderness and thought of phoning New York to congratulate her on her efficiency. After all, it seemed they could afford that sort of thing now.

But if he called Emily he knew he would tell her about the

Ophelia débâcle and Susan Waddington. He didn't want to do that, didn't want to cause her needless distress. These motives were entirely honourable, but all the same only a week earlier he would have told her at once.

In the fabric of his marriage something had been altered. But he disliked change; his schooldays had made him dependent on established routines. Something unidentifiable had changed, and this made him uneasy. He was not accustomed to doubting his decisions, but now he wondered whether perhaps he should have stayed on in New York for another week?

*

At least thirteen years had gone by since Susan Waddington's formal, though private, recognition that capitulation – once as unthinkable as it had been inadvisable – had come to pass. Since then her life had been divided into two distinct eras – the time when she had believed she would be a concert violinist of the class of Menuhin, and the time that followed. Though not without pain, all that tumultuous hope had been put away. Permanently. It was hope turned into disappointment. And it was a disappointment – because in the end, as Susan learned, however painful failure may be it is *only* disappointment. For all that, it was a disappointment so profound that she became habituated to it and expected nothing else for herself, in any area of her life.

So she turned to the Suzuki method of violin instruction. She was a gifted teacher and produced music-loving if not musically gifted children. But the method – learning to play an instrument without being able to read music – was in itself a travesty of the art she had struggled to master. Disappointment was securely built in and therefore presented no terrors.

One of the many married men in her life, a clinical psychologist with the unlikely name of Blake Mendelssohn, theorized that married men removed all possibility of hope and accordingly made disappointment all the more certain. She dared not tinker with her promise of disappointment.

That jewel of wisdom had been Blake Mendelssohn's farewell gift.

233

From time to time Susan would recall Blake's theories. She did so again now, but defiantly went ahead anyway with her decision to bake her own special brown bread for the Bradshaws. It was a pretty spectacular recipe too, which had never failed her either. Part of the secret was baking it in an old earthenware vase discovered in a junk shop, and the other part was mixing the grains and the wheats herself.

Simon's wife was away. And the current man in her life, Jeremy, was away with his wife. Idly she searched her mind for Jeremy's wife's name. She must have blocked it, repressed it. Ah, well, what the hell, what difference would her name make?

Meanwhile, and for starters, she had the freshly-baked bread. She set off in her Mini and with a tape of Mozart's Violin Concerto for company and the warm sensual smell of the bread for comfort, she certainly enjoyed the drive from Swiss Cottage to Chelsea. She would give Simon and Danny breakfast... She had drawn up outside the house when she remembered the state of their fridge, so she set off again to buy eggs and bacon and marmalade and honey and butter and oranges. Not for nothing had she observed the enthusiasm with which Simon had consumed his meal the night before.

Unannounced, she might appear like an invader. Which of course she was, but though blatancy had its virtues this was not the moment. Before returning to Lamont Road, a telephone call would do the trick.

'730 2434,' Simon answered. 'Hello, 730 2434.' Compelled to raise his voice over the high-pitched pips of the coin telephone, Simon's tone sounded irritable. '730 2434.'

'Good morning, Simon.'

'Susan! You're in a call-box. Where are you?'

'Two minutes away from you. At Coleridge Street.' She spoke in a rush. 'Thought you'd need breakfast. I was on your doorstep a few moments ago actually, but it occurred to me that I might not be welcome at this hour.'

'Couldn't think of anyone I'd rather see. Danny's still asleep but I was about to struggle downstairs.'

'Then it's OK if I come now?'

'Oh, Susan,' Simon chuckled. 'How can you ask?'

Susan hung up.

In the mirror of her Mini, she checked her make-up. Eye-liner and pale lipstick still in place, cheeks bright with the morning chill, and light-brown hair neat in a glistening pony-tail. She could have done more with her looks, she knew. She need not have looked quite so tidy, quite so boyish. However, the openly sexy look was not for her. It might have courted disappointment... Susan went in for the unexpected, for erotic underwear, sometimes even crotchless panty-hose which she was wearing now. This way, she believed she was not at risk. She took the men in her life by surprise. Her earlier assumption that the really sexy ones were those who hid it had been proved over and over again. She looked OK, she decided. And, because there could be no doubt that her glow of anticipation was more effective than make-up, she smiled slowly and sensuously into the rear-view mirror.

'My word,' she said, as Simon led her into the clean kitchen, 'But you must have been up all night.'

'Well,' he said, somewhat defensively, 'there was no shortage of cleaning materials. Just as well – now that you're here.'

Susan laid out her provisions. The bread, a round plump loaf, looked especially inviting on the old oak kitchen table.

'Where on earth did you get that bread?'

'I baked it myself.'

'I can't believe it!'

'This very morning. Shall we wake Danny?'

'No.'

'Now, Simon, if you just sit down, I'll prepare your breakfast. That is, if you'd like me to?'

'Couldn't think of anything I'd like more!'

Simon liked her voice. It was different from Emily's soft tones and surprisingly unmusical. There was nothing soothing about its clipped, concise tones; it was an instructive, sensible newsreader's voice. At the thought of a newsreader, his face blanched.

'What's up?' Susan asked.

'Why?'

'You look pale...'

'Am I so transparent, then?' Simon said, amazed. 'I was thinking of those media vultures again, I suppose. One of their number had the cheek to telephone at the crack of dawn this morning. I'm wise to them now, I told them Mr Bradshaw wasn't expected till Monday. The phone's off the hook now. Glad I didn't do that before you called.'

'So am I!'

There followed one of those mutual stares, part of the immemorial ritual which to one as experienced as Susan ought to have been trite. But it was not trite. The unlocking of a shared gaze is often more exciting than the first connection. Or so it seemed to Susan, as with a fluttered lowering of her eyes she looked away.

Her eyes fell on a cardboard carton of junk. She never could stop herself from being helpful and now she said, 'Simon, you've made a mistake. You've put all these beautiful baskets and burgundy porcelain boxes with the rubbish.'

'No, no mistake, Susan,' Simon said. He strode over to the box, lifted one of the offending ornaments and threw it into the empty rubbish-bin.

The sound of shattering glass jarred Susan. 'You can't be serious. Shouldn't you at least give them away?'

'Would you like to have them?'

'No, but Oxfam might.'

'True. Would you take them?'

'Yes, there's an Oxfam shop very near where I live.' Now Susan went to the cardboard box and peered inside. 'What have you got against them?' she asked.

'It's just that they're phony. Props brought here by an American woman photographer called Sheila Lyall...'

'The one who released all those exclusive photographs of Emily?'

'Yes.'

Simon sat down at the table and pushed up his sleeves.

'What a super sweater you're wearing,' Susan said as she cut her round loaf into plump slices.

'Emily's mother knitted it. Lovely lady, Clara. Wonder

236

what she would have made of all this?'

'Emily's American junket, you mean?'

'That's a good way of putting it,' Simon said, buttering a thick slice of bread. 'This bread is scrumptious! You're a versatile woman, Susan.'

'Thanks.'

'Clara rather encouraged Emily to do this radio television thing. After all, we didn't know anyone over there. She reminded me about Laurence Olivier and his commercials. Did you know about that?'

'No, but I'd like to . . .'

'Can't remember what it was that he was promoting . . .'

'In America? Probably a detergent!'

'Perhaps,' Simon said with an appreciative chuckle. 'But whatever it was, the deal was that none of those commercials were to be used in the UK.'

'I know what you mean.'

'Of course, Clara could never have predicted that Emily would get shot!'

'Who would?'

'Shot on national television. What a fillip to anyone's career . . .'

'Especially in America.'

'The thing is, Emily never had a career. But even that seems to have been changed.'

'I know,' Susan said as she laid her hand over his. 'It has been a dreadfully confusing time for you, hasn't it?'

They engaged in another locking gaze, then heard Danny bouncing down the stairs.

The morning sped by. The three of them went off to one of those supermarkets that stayed open on Sundays and chose all sorts of ready-made delicacies for lunch. Greek taromasalata because it would go deliciously well with Susan's bread, a huge hunk of freshly cut Gruyère cheese, whole artichoke hearts in vinaigrette, smoked salmon and lemon, and all sorts of exotic vegetables for the salad that Susan was going to prepare. When they came upon a few punnets of fresh strawberries, their excitement was such that they might have found them growing wild in a garden in mid-winter. Danny found a round tub of American ice cream, but both Simon and Susan turned it down in favour of a Cornish vanilla. They also picked up a few staples like bacon and eggs and something for Danny's supper; they forgot about oranges and apples, but Danny reminded them.

They opened the champagne that was in the fridge and Simon concluded that it must have been put there by one of Ophelia's men. At any rate, whoever had left it there – as Simon and Susan agreed – had added the perfect touch to their meal.

After lunch, which was long, leisurely and for Simon and Susan, also heavy with sensuousness, Danny was given a violin lesson. But he was jet-lagged, as sleepy as Susan had known he would be and clearly in need of a nap. Simon took him upstairs to tuck him in. Danny fell asleep as quickly as children do, straight away, but Simon stayed beside him for a while to make absolutely certain that he really was sound asleep.

At the moment, though, one minor detail troubled Simon. Very definitely he was going to take Susan to bed – the only problem was where. Which room? The Bradshaw bedroom was perilously close to Danny's room. If anything about this strange and lovely day shocked him at all, it was that he had no reservations about using the Bradshaw bed. The guest room was being redecorated so there was no bed there, and in his experience both drawing-room couches left a lot to be desired. Ah, well, there was nothing else for it; it would have to be Ophelia's room. It was a pleasant room actually, and rather cosy with the yellow and white chintzes Emily had chosen. Ophelia usually kept it in perfect order. Or perhaps she had not managed to tidy it in the short time he had allowed her? No matter. Ophelia's room it would have to be.

Susan was in the kitchen loading dishes. Once again, in his usual way, Simon assessed her body with one of those mechanical glances that he might have given to almost any female form. Susan's jeans were sort of boyish, he decided, but she had a tight little bottom, though she was obviously too flat-chested for his usual taste. Still, one could never be sure –

there was probably a lot more than could be seen.

'Leave those alone,' he said, taking the dishes from her. He took her hand. 'Follow me.'

He led her down the narrow stepladder like stairs which led to the basement. As soon as they were in Ophelia's room, he shut the door and locked it, but did not leave go of her hand.

Simon responded to the shock of her crotchless panty-hose in the same way as all the men she had ever known.

Later, when they were to try being matter-of-fact about what had happened, they would agree that the locking of their bodies had been an extension of the locking of their eyes. There was no seduction, it was a continuation merely. But of what? This they were never able to decide. Because – and here again they were in absolute agreement – neither was the romantic type. But whatever it was, it had altered their lives. And, like all lovers, they would ask themselves again and again how could it have been so incredibly perfect the very first time? True, they had known that going to bed with someone new would be exciting, satisfying and perhaps even highly pleasurable. But to find perfection in passion had been well outside their range of expectations.

But that August afternoon in Ophelia's yellow room, Susan heard herself say, 'I don't mind dying now, Simon. Not now. Not after this . . .'

'I don't think I would either.'

A disturbance . . . they heard Danny calling. They dressed quickly and without regret. The whole night lay ahead of them.

And when Simon told her that he had not been to bed with another woman, not just since his marriage but since he had met Emily, Susan was unsurprised. What astonished her, however, was what astonished Simon. He felt no guilt, not even a particle. Here he was being unfaithful to the wife he loved, and moreover while she was in hospital in New York recovering from a bullet wound.

He felt guilty about *not* feeling guilty.

But at the same time, he felt entirely free.

Because there was nothing, but absolutely nothing, that he

could not say to Susan. Nor she to him.

Their minds accepted – and welcomed – one another as shamelessly as had their bodies.

*

The flowers in Emily's hospital room were positively oppressive, Keith thought. He wished he could open a window.

'I suppose America has affected you, too,' Emily said, or rather interrupted. 'You've changed.'

Keith stopped his pacing. His voice, several tones higher, reflected the pitch of his excitement. He had been talking so much and so quickly that Emily had been unable to take in all he had said, partly because he'd been talking too fast, but mainly because she still linked him to her mother's death.

'I'm not quite with you,' Keith said. 'How have I changed?'

'You're more extroverted and more animated than I would have ...'

'Hardly America, Emily,' Keith said irritably. 'Unless of course one believes that the US dollar is America, in which case I plead guilty. Yes, I might have been – as you put it – affected by America.' He chuckled. 'So, I might add, has my bank manager. Dollars have had a strikingly positive effect on him!'

'America is energy, Keith. Can you deny that you're more energetic over here? I love watching the traffic move; it's fierce, but it's alive, urgent ...'

'In a state of constant emergency, I'd say ...'

'There you go, putting it down. People are enthusiastic even about getting from one place to another. Everything is seen as a challenge over here. For instance, this morning the physio-therapist came to see me; a young man, about twenty or so. The wife of one of his patients had infuriated him. Apparently the man was recovering from open-heart surgery and had to do some chest exercises. His wife objected, said he needed rest. He told me what he'd said to her: "Ma'am, people don't come to hospital to rest. They come to hospital to work to get well." In America, people work at everything – even happiness.'

'I follow your meaning, Emily, but ... Let's get back to business.'

Defending Wives, Keith told her, had been reprinted three times. Fortunately, Frontier Books did not have world rights, so Keith had sold these rights to fifteen countries. In London, Kingsley Publications were about to rush the hardback on to the market – incredibly enough, in less than one month. The paperback houses were bidding furiously. Sheila Lyall was demanding far too much for the use of her photographs. Of course, Leon's pet-food commercials were highly lucrative, not to say outrageously generous. Which would of course, snowball...

Emily managed not to comment on Sheila Lyall until Keith had finished. Then she said, 'You'll have to give Sheila Lyall what she asks, I'm afraid.'

'Why on earth should we? Rick says not over his dead body.'

'I don't think Rick knows that if he doesn't agree, he will be just that – a dead body.'

'Come now, Emily. You're being extraordinarily extravagant, aren't you? I mean, Sheila Lyall's hardly the Mafia, you know...'

'Do you know Sheila Lyall?'

'Haven't met her. Ours is strictly a telephonic relationship, so far at any rate.'

'You won't get away with that. Sheila Lyall is a very demanding woman, I'm warning you.'

'Sounds as if there's something more I ought to know about her.'

'There is, but details are unnecessary. You'll have to cut her in.'

'But...'

'Doesn't *my* opinion count for anything? Who signs the contracts? You or me?'

'Emily!'

'I'll refuse to sign unless she's cut in.'

There was a new and somewhat imperious edge to her voice. Keith noted it and flushed. Frowning, he said mildly, 'Certainly. Have it your own way.'

Restless, Emily fiddled with the belt of her dressing-gown. It was a plain dressing-gown, severely cut and rather shabby.

Once – about ten years ago – it had been a warm royal blue, but it had faded now and become closer to grey. It was made of a soft wool and had been part of her trousseau. Leon said he loved it because he thought it so ladylike and so English . . . 'You'd better give me all the relevant details about Sheila Lyall. Percentages and so on.'

Soon after that, Keith left.

It was difficult for her to believe she had been forceful – as well as assertive – with Keith. He was after all Simon's old school chum, and therefore accustomed to having her defer to him. And now Emily was certain that he would attribute her assertiveness to the fact that she was making so much money. And he would also beleive that she had become tough; the stereotype of the tough American female would be applied to her. Yet neither of these was responsible for her attitude.

The truth was that she knew better than to tangle with Sheila Lyall.

Besides, that photograph on *People* was undeniably brilliant. Somehow Sheila Lyall had summarized – Emily could think of no other word for it – her own image of her subject. The result was a photograph of stunning sexual radiance. Sensuality beamed out of that magazine cover. It might have been the way Emily's intense, emotional eyes highlighted her coldly classical features. Or perhaps it was that her lips turned upwards, in a cross between a pout and a smile. And then her hair, long and full and thick, was lustrous as the coat of an Ascot winner and just as aristocratic. There was no doubt that the burgundy silk blouse had been an inspiration. It gave her a slightly regal yet slightly glamorous look. That cover was the sort that the magazine industry calls 'a selling cover'.

To be fair, Sheila Lyall deserved to make something too. There was enough to go round and in any case, she could afford to pay the woman. Far more important, though, Emily was afraid of her . . . afraid as one is afraid of evil. And aware of the sheer elemental force, the lightning speed of that evil . . .

Paying Sheila a high commission would be a safeguard of sorts, although the danger would not be averted entirely. She would be no safer than if she had taken shelter under a tree during a storm.

As always, the thought of Sheila Lyall made Emily nervous and restless, made her anxious about how Simon and Danny were getting on. She decided to telephone Simon at his office.

'Simon,' she said. 'Darling! It's me.'

'How are you?'

'Getting stronger every minute. How was the flight?'

'Rapid.'

'Oh,' Emily said, taken aback. 'How's Danny? Is Ophelia coping?'

'Everything's under control, Em,' Simon said firmly, masterfully. 'We're all doing fine.'

'All?'

'Danny and Hal and me.'

'Oh yes, of course, Hal. Susan brought him back? It was kind of her to take care of him, wasn't it?' Emily was already noting that down on her pad, having become quite adept with her left hand. She went on, 'You wouldn't have her address handy, would you?'

'No.'

'I'll send the letter to Lamont Road, then. Will you see that she gets it?'

'Of course.'

'You sound ... busy.'

'I am, actually. It's five in the afternoon over here, you know.'

'Silly of me, but I'd forgotten. What did the senior partner have to say?'

'About the publicity?' Simon asked quickly. 'Several of our clients wrote in about it; you'll see the letters when you come back.'

'Shouldn't I reply to them now? Shouldn't you mail them on to me?'

'No, definitely not.'

'I see.'

'The letters are written *about* you. Not *to* you.'

Simon's voice was laced with something Emily could not quite identify. She said, 'Shall I ring you tomorrow?'

'Yes, at seven. Two o'clock your time. Danny would like to speak to you, too.'

After their usual formal 'goodbyes' Emily put the phone down slowly. She felt dreadful, because it was unfair. It was clear that instead of understanding, Simon's partners had rapped him on the knuckles, given him a stern dressing down. In Simon's staid established law practice, it was hardly the done thing for a partner's wife to go off to America in search of publicity in the first place. Now that she had taken so well to the limelight all that seemed remote and yet, as Emily readily acknowledged, there was no doubt that neither she nor Simon would have agreed to such a promotion tour in England. Even so, his partners were being unfair.

It was unsettling.

So Emily dialled Leon's number; he had told her he was deserting the hospital for today and would be in the LFE building. There was no reply to his private line, so she tried the other number and spoke to Leon's secretary. He was in a meeting, she was told, but her message would be handed to him at once.

It was strange, Emily thought, as she waited for the call she knew would come. It was strange the way one could adapt to change . . . if one wanted to. It seemed to her that life was like her left hand – the more you worked at it and yielded to something new, the more calmly adept you became.

Leon, she thought, was like her left hand.

But if he was only her left hand, then she had no right hand . . .

Leon had a lunch date today, one he could not cancel. Emily took it for granted that it was a business meeting, assuming that tycoons like Leon called their own tune all the time. She knew so little about his or anyone else's tycoonery, really.

It was a side of Leon she ought to know more about, she thought, deciding to ask Rick for details. The pet food contract would make her questions seem logical enough.

*

'My brother's turning into a real turkey,' Milt fumed to Wayne. 'It's either that or a case of descended brains.'

'Someone once said that what they call the heart is located

far lower than the fourth waistcoat button,' Wayne dared to say.

'What's that?' Milt asked. But he caught the point before Wayne could reply and broke into one of those Lerner laughs. 'It's not funny,' he said. 'Working on this deal of ours for months – the deal of a lifetime. And he's lunching with Wendy instead of with the president of Kaiser Bank. Can you credit it, Wayne?'

'No, sir, I can't.'

'I've been thinking about calling his kids in Italy. Maybe I should bring them in ... What do *you* think, Wayne?'

'I guess I don't share your view.'

'You don't? Why don't you?'

'Kids don't like to be brought into their parents' sex lives.'

'They're not kids; they're twenty-one and twenty-two ... I'd already seen combat in Korea by the time I was their age. So had Leon.'

'I know that, Milt. But, well, you asked me.'

'Sure, I asked you.'

'Kids don't feel comfortable.' Wayne flashed an adept look at his father-in-law. 'Hell, my father's *fifty* and he freaks out over the woman in my grandfather's life.'

'I get your point,' Milt said impatiently, 'I get it.' He took a long draw from his cigar. 'At his age, going in for women! I don't understand him. It never occurred to me that a day might come when I didn't understand my own brother ...'

These days, Leon was as indifferent to the growing friend-ship between Milt and his son-in-law Wayne as he was to so much else. It was this indifference that Milt resented. They were drawing apart. Before Emily, Leon would have taken steps, unconsciously perhaps, to inhibit Wayne – to prevent him from becoming too close to Milt. The brothers were like that. Both Leon and Milt had long considered Wayne to be smart and his recent dealings with Katie Williams and Lieut Janowski had proved that. He was even smarter than they had thought.

*

Leon's mind was on other matters. On his way to have that final lunch with Wendy, he had chosen a country inn midway between his farm in Connecticut and New York City. He wanted to make certain everything at White Wings was in perfect order for Emily's convalescence.

Although he used his Porsche rarely, he felt that he and the machine were in perfect accord, which helped him to think more clearly. The last time he had driven it had been after his first and only date with Emily. It was strange to think that he and the woman who was now so central to his being had been together only once. Of course, Wendy had never been anything more than peripheral; Leon reminded himself again that Wendy had always known that.

His conscience was absolutely clear. He had never deceived her, nor given her false hopes.

True, they had been good in the sack together. True, their last night together had been a brilliant finale. But it was over.

Over.

Lunch with Wendy would be far from pleasant, but it was imperative that he settle things with her at once.

There was a new sense of immediacy about him now and it had altered the emphasis, as well as the shape, of his life. Perhaps it was the fact that he had come so very close to losing Emily so very soon after he had found her which made him believe – like one who has recently and miraculously escaped an accident or a natural disaster – that life was as precious as it was precarious. It was as if his *own* life had been spared. It was strange, and he knew it was strange, but he had not experienced anything like this before – not even after his cardiac surgery. He had expected to survive that; the surgery had followed on a rational, cold-blooded decision.

But Emily had been almost murdered. Which was at once so shocking and so inexplicable that it was almost mystical. How could he explain this to Milt – or to Wendy – if he could not explain it to himself?

Though he was exactly on time, Wendy would be waiting for him, he knew. She always waited for him, always got to their meetings ahead of time.

But when he arrived, he did not find her. She was not waiting for him.

He decided to go directly to the table; he would not sit alone, at the bar. He ordered Dom Perignon, Wendy's favourite champagne. All the tables were taken, for although it was a Wednesday people flocked to the restaurant – both the truffles and the ambience were legendary and everyone made their reservations weeks in advance. The Lerner twins, however, were always assured of a table – they owned the property. For all that, neither Leon nor Milt would have dreamt of arriving without a reservation. They were resolute about not taking advantage.

The quickening of male interest around him told him that she was on the way to their table, even though he had not yet seen her. She was lovely, he admitted. But now that he knew Emily, he saw that Wendy was unmistakably American, for her immaculately stylish clothes were organized rather than arranged. Emily was the first European woman he had ever known ... well, intimately. Wendy's soft pink tweed suit and the softer silk ruffled pink shirt that went so well with it reminded him of computerized good taste. Whereas Emily ... He realized with a start that except for seeing her twice on TV he had only once seen her fully clothed, in the flesh. And besides that quaint woolly bathrobe of hers, the rest of the time she had been in hospital things. Two more days and she would be with him at his country house. It occurred to him that probably she had not brought the right clothes with her. No problem. He took out his small leather note-pad and wrote, 'Ask Wendy for the name of the personal shopper who replaced her.'

He was just putting the little pad back in his pocket when Wendy arrived at the table. He stood up at once.

She sat down and was unusually troubled about deciding what to eat. Then she put on her dark glasses, which emphasized the sag of her white, drooping face. 'Uh, oh,' Leon murmured to himself, 'this is not going to be easy.' He said, 'Great suit, Wendy. New, isn't it?'

'Yes,' Wendy said sadly. 'You're always so observant. You notice what a woman wears. That's only one of the reasons why women like me find you so attractive.'

'Thank you,' he said. 'Women like you?'

'Women,' she amended. 'Women, period.'

'Wendy...' he began.

'Leon,' she interrupted, 'why did you ask me to meet you here?'

'It's halfway to White Wings. And I'm on my way there.'

'Alone?'

'Yes, for the moment.'

'But you're planning on taking her there?'

'Yes. To convalesce.'

'To convalesce?' Wendy repeated.

'That's right.'

'And you asked me here to tell me that?'

'Partly, yes.'

'And the other part?' An insistent, humiliating sigh escaped. 'It's over. You want me to know that, don't you?'

'Wendy,' he said, making confused movements with his hands. 'Wendy, I don't want anything. And I didn't want any of this, but I must be fair with you.' Almost pleading, he said again, 'Haven't I always tried to be fair with you?'

'Yes,' she said obediently. 'Yes, you have.' She went on, in a rush, 'It was fair for Leon and Milt Lerner. Both of you claiming to be moralists, and both of you no better than married men having standard affairs. Sure, for a man married to a dead woman, it was fair, and more than fair!'

'Wendy,' he said ineffectually. 'Please!'

'No, Leon. Don't try to stop me, for once. *Listen*, for a change, to *me*!' She hurtled on. 'I even respected you for keeping your vow to Ruthie. A vow to a dead woman... We're on forbidden territory, now, aren't we?' she said bitterly. Her voice reeled into the dim, discreetly lit restaurant; for a while she had been almost shrill, but now it sounded used up, beaten. 'That vow is *your* private property. *I* never was allowed to mention it!'

'Wendy, stop this! Stop this at once.'

'I will. In my own good time, I will. Because I'm your friend, you see. That vow left you free to play the field. Subconsciously I always suspected that, but wouldn't admit it to myself.'

'This is a gross distortion.'

'The truth often seems so, Leon – for those who don't like it. You know that, too,' she added with ferocious sadness. 'Goddamn it, Leon Lerner, but I care about you. Care enough to warn you that your precious Emily Bradshaw will not stand for this. You won't be able to fob *her* off with a vow made to a dead wife. Does she know about it?

'I think so,' he said. 'I don't know, I can't remember.' He leaned forward and folded her hand in both of his. 'You are a lovely woman, Wendy. One of the loveliest I've ever known. I didn't ask for any of this; it just happened and right now, I'm overwhelmed.'

'Milt seems to think so, too!'

'Milt is right. Listen, why should *you* understand? When I don't know who I am?'

Wendy stayed silent. She waited, merely.

After a while, Leon continued. 'I didn't want there to be any acrimony in all this, Wendy. It's not your fault, certainly. Not mine either. I wanted to talk to you about the bottom line. Your portfolio's been fattened, you know...'

'You're buying me off?'

'You don't mean that, Wendy. I know you don't.'

'You're right. I'm sorry.'

'Forget it. I'm under no obligation to you, you know. But let's forget that,' he went on smoothly. 'You're a rich woman, Wendy, and if you involve yourself in your financial affairs you could become richer. Now listen carefully...'

His explanation was concise and full, but Wendy barely concentrated. She came alive, though, when he asked, 'By the way, what was the name of the personal shopper at Bloomingdales who took your place?'

'Pat Haines, why?'

'It's not important.'

You *can't* be using her to clothe Emily Bradshaw, you can't be that insensitive, Wendy thought.

Just as they were leaving, Leon said sharply, 'You're not

drinking too much, Wendy, are you?'

'No,' she lied, 'of course not.' Then added reassuringly, 'I'll be OK. Thanks to your generosity, I'll be OK. Don't you fret, now . . .'

'Thank you for that, Wendy,' Leon said.

He made no effort to disguise either his gratitude or his relief.

But Leon's relief was Wendy's humiliation and she could not imagine how to begin to handle it.

It was going to be her season for hell – the longest season of her life, probably. And she honestly began to doubt whether she could go on. He faced her like a stranger, an obligated stranger paying off a debt for having been rescued once. A stranger stranded on a lonely road who might have had his car batteries recharged.

As for the intimacy, and the passion of years – of only a few nights ago – well, there was no hint of any of that.

It might never have been.

It was absent now and would be absent for ever, she knew. It was as if her soul had been annihilated.

*

On Wednesday afternoon, at around three-thirty, the traffic going towards Preston is easily negotiable. For long stretches there were no cars, and as usually happened when the traffic was light, Leon wondered why he didn't visit White Wings much more often.

He loved the place; everything about it interested him, especially the way it had been acquired.

Naturally, neither he nor Milt had ever been anywhere near their home in the Hamptons, the home that Marcie and Ruthie had been flying towards when their plane crashed . . .

Not long after his open-heart surgery, Leon had decided on having a place of his own, in the country. Connecticut sounded like a good idea. Helen Crane, the realtor who had been showing him around, had driven past White Wings. 'That's the most beautiful property in the area,' she said conversationally, 'but it's out of the question.' She went on to explain that it was owned by an eccentric called Stephanie Hunt and in fact it *was* for sale, though at an exorbitant price: one that no self-respecting realtor could possibly endorse. But, as if that were not enough, Mrs Hunt insisted that whoever bought it also had to buy everything in it: paintings, books, glassware, yes, and even the furniture. There was also an old housekeeper by the name of Georgina who went with the place; Mrs Hunt claimed she was also farm manager, though nothing was farmed, but she had promised that Georgina could live there until the end of her days and Mrs Hunt was as good as her word. Not that Georgina was a doddery old woman. Far from it – she was a sprightly sixty-year-old. So whoever acquired the property would be stuck with Georgina.

When Leon asked Helen Crane to make a viewing date, she told him that Mrs Hunt would also have to approve what she called the moral calibre of the buyer. Leon enquired mildly if she was trying to imply that Jews were excluded. No, Helen nervously assured him, that was highly unlikely because Mrs Hunt's husband had once been a Jew himself – that was before he became a Methodist, like Casper Weinberger.

It was bleak and windy the morning Leon went to meet Mrs Hunt once again. For all that its high white colonial columns glistened in the gloom, Leon saw it as a symbol – bright without the aid of electricity. This was one property that would not have all the lights turned on at midnight, to show itself to its new owner. Meanwhile there it stood, unchanged for more than two hundred years, but somehow triumphant. Because the house had nothing to fear from time, it conceded nothing to time. Instead, time accumulated as favourably as compound interest.

So at this stage of his life, still grieving for Ruthie and with reconstituted arteries, he was very much taken by the idea that the sort of concrete timelessness which belonged to White Wings could also belong to him.

The ambience of the land, the carefree pastures, struck Leon at once like a breeze of unexpected hope. And it was that green ambience which made him turn rapidly away from the white house and stride out towards the untended fields. There was a meadow-like softness about the tall grass, though. It made him quicken his pace so that, as he strode through the knee-high grasses, he felt like a swimmer swimming out, out, helplessly. He could neither stop himself nor afterwards say how long he was out there.

When he returned, he was appropriately apologetic but hell-bent on getting the place. Mrs Hunt ordered him to stop apologizing. He had repeated exactly what her husband had done fifty years earlier, she told him. She had watched him from the window and it was as if, in Leon's tall driven figure, she had seen her husband.

So much, Leon thought, for eternity...

So he bought White Wings and the agent thought she had made the deal of her life. She made something in the order of $420,000. Later, when the people from Christie's came to value the paintings, the furniture and the silver, Leon's hunch was confirmed. What Mrs Hunt had openly believed to be exorbitant, not to say extortionate, had been undervalued by several million dollars. Even the bed-linen was worthy of a museum.

There is no doubt that if White Wings had not made sound business sense, Leon would have dismissed the entire proposition at once. And yet, the very obstacle that Mrs Hunt had imposed – her refusal to permit the contents to be separated from the house – was for Leon the most important hidden asset of them all. For the past that was so solidly entrenched in that house was free of nostalgia – it was not his past. He would not be lonely here, living with other people's ghosts.

Milt understood this, and not long afterwards bought a similar place about an hour's drive from White Wings.

When he arrived at White Wings and told Georgina who was coming to visit, she said she had been watching the *Virginia Byrnes Show* and had seen the shooting. Just like Katie Williams, she had loved Emily Bradshaw. She was needle-pointing a cushion cover with red roses when it happened, to present it to Mrs Bradshaw would be a great honour.

Everything would be made ready. Soaps, perfumes, bath

oils, flowers, fruit. No problems about the closets; they were empty and in perfect order. Miss Wendy never left as much as a hairpin behind.

Leon excused himself to call Bloomingdales' personal shopper, Pat Haines. Yes, Pat had seen Emily Bradshaw on *People* . . . Also on the news. That terrible shooting . . . Size eight – possibly even six, now . . . She must have lost weight. Yes, she would send everything – from negligées, to sports, to ball-gowns. Of course, it was confidential . . . Confidentiality was her watchword . . . a lewd, irritating little laugh. Her customers included men in the highest places – Washington, too. A comprehensive selection could be expected at White Wings by noon tomorrow.

PART IV
Early September 1985

Chapter 16

In ten days Emily was to appear again on the *Virginia Byrnes Show*.

Meanwhile, neither she nor Leon could believe that no more than two weeks had passed since their first night together. Since then, compacted moments in compressed days had effectively lengthened the time they had spent together. Dramatic events have a way of opening time and widening it, which was probably why neither felt anything new or strange about being together now, driving out to rest and be together for ten days.

Emily's right arm was still in a sling, so Leon had taken great care to seat himself on her left side in the back seat of the limousine. They sat close: knees, thighs, hips rammed together. All the while in the hospital – or rather, as soon as Emily had become conscious – waiting and waiting for abstinence to end, the power of their sexual connection had intensified. Because their unrequited lust was shared, their need for one another strengthened and turned into absolute trust.

Emily believed that she had discovered trust for the first time. Slowly, though in the temporal sense it could scarcely have been said to be slow, trust stole over Emily, or she gave way to it . . . and found that there was nothing she could not say to Leon. She had been freed of the need to protect anyone or anything from him and exposed her secrets if not gladly, then freely and fearlessly. For she knew that in Leon's eyes she never would be a fool . . .

She still ached for her mother. More than ever. The sad thing, though, was that although her mother had always told her to be her own sweet self, no one had ever known that self. Leon wanted to know everything about her and was openly curious about her mother.

'She would have understood, I think,' Emily said, positively glorying in the knowledge that nothing she could say to Leon would make her seem ridiculous. 'Yes, she would have understood how I feel about Jake Williams. She would have sympathized . . .'

'Sympathy does not always imply understanding,' Leon commented.

'Oh . . .'

'You see, I sympathize. Frankly, though, I never really understood why you felt so bad about that guy. The point is, he tried to kill you . . .'

'That's just the point,' Emily said fiercely. 'He tried *not* to kill me!'

'You've lost me now.'

'Jake Williams mis-aimed deliberately. He chose to aim not to kill.'

'You're too charitable, Emily!'

'No, I'm not being charitable. I'm too objective for that. Lieutenant Janowski found out that Jake was a crack shot, didn't he?'

'Champion of his gun club,' Leon said drily. 'He didn't exactly miss, you know. I almost lost you!'

'What bothers me, Leon, is that I suspect I would have felt very differently if I'd been left severely handicapped. Loss of limb – that sort of thing . . .' Emily shook her head. 'As for what that might have done to Danny . . . well, I try not to think of it.'

'Thank God you weren't!'

'Yes,' Emily said loudly, 'I do thank God. But I must take responsibility for my own actions. I can't avoid that. I wish I could.'

'I know what you mean. It's one of your greatest qualities. But you didn't pull the trigger!'

'I was irresponsible and thoughtless. I'd already had one warning when that man, Norman Maitland, called in. He was furious over what I'd said about fathers not being able to prove paternity . . . I knew that. Rick told me to give it a miss. But no, Emily Bradshaw had to show how clever she was.'

'Have you always been so hard on yourself?' Leon interrupted.

'Oh Leon,' she said urgently, 'I ruined that family's life. And I'm even making money out of it!'

'I'm trying to understand why you think the way you do. But you've got to admit you're not being entirely rational.' He stopped to attend to his cigar.

Emily was silent. Leon was saying she was *irrational* – it made her burn with anguish and disappointment.

'You know, Emily, there will be times when you find me irrational. I hope you'll tell me so, too. I'd be disappointed if you didn't. You're disappointed in *me* now, aren't you?'

'I suppose I am . . .'

'Try not to be. I wouldn't feel free to say so unless I had a very, very great respect for you. Do you know that?'

'Well . . .'

'Yes, you do. Don't be so goddamned modest! It does me an injustice – can't you see that?'

'Yes.'

'Now, to get back to what's bugging you. Jake Williams has been diagnosed as a schizophrenic. Long, long before the world heard about him, he was disturbed. Society throws up these sorts of characters and madness is madness, even if it is a disease. Anything could have triggered it. OK, so go blame yourself for an accident! An accident is no one's fault, don't you know that, Emily?'

'We'll have to talk about this again and again. I'm afraid . . .'

'It will be an honour to be your therapist, Mrs Bradshaw!' Leon laughed then and all tension dispersed. As usual, the Lerner laugh was infallible.

*

Country houses were not new to Emily. Indeed, weekends in the country had been a part of her life for years. And, of course, she had been a house guest in some rather grand English country homes. She had expected White Wings to be somewhat different from those in England. It was bound to be modern, for one thing, which meant that it could hardly be expected to belong to a distant era. Leon had told her it was a tranquil place – perfect for convalescence, and ideal for lovemaking.

An oak-lined driveway – half a mile long at least – led up to the house, and even in the distance the shimmer of the ice-white columns made her heart lurch. She gasped. 'It's beautiful, Leon. It's so white. I've never seen a white quite like it.'

At the front door Georgina, wearing a live white dove on each shoulder, was waiting for them. Leon's English butler Charles, and his cook Laurinda, who had been driven down much earlier, were both standing at attention. It was clear to Leon that Charles, who had been trained at the British School of Butlers, had taken over. He had a quick vision of Georgina's response to all of this and managed not to laugh.

Emily was introduced and everyone, even Georgina, said, 'How do you do?'

Georgina was holding a large, gift-wrapped parcel. 'I was working on this when you were gunned down, ma'am,' she said formally. 'It's a cushion. I was needlepointing it when you were shot. When Mr Leon told me you were coming to convalesce here, I decided at once that you should have the cushion.' She waved the parcel in Leon's direction. 'I told you that at the time, didn't I?'

'Yes, Georgina. You did.'

'Thank you,' said Emily. 'How very kind of you.'

'Tea's ready,' Georgina said.

'Tea? But I was looking forward to your excellent coffee, Georgina,' Leon put in.

'Coffee for you. Tea for Mrs Bradshaw. Charles made it himself.'

'I was not sure which brand you preferred, Mrs Bradshaw.'

'Rose's teabags,' Emily said automatically.

'I don't think they are available in this country, Mrs Bradshaw, but I will do my best.'

'Well,' Leon said, 'Mrs Bradshaw's very tired. We'll have tea, and then go to bed . . .'

The smoky scent of burning apple wood wafted through the house. A huge fire had been lit in the hallway and tea waited in the library. For a moment, but only for a moment, Emily thought she had been transported back to England. The gleam of the silver, of the leather furniture, of the Oriental silk rugs, of the copper at the hearth, might well have been English – only the shine was different, and definitely newer. The fruit in the bowl seemed artificially bright, the crimson apples especially. No dogs rose to meet them, nor was there any sign of one.

Unable to disguise her surprise, Emily asked, 'No dogs?'

'No, no dogs,' Leon replied quickly. 'Not that I wouldn't love to have one or two, but Georgina's allergic to them.'

It made Emily miss Hal, who must have grown during the three weeks she had not seen him. It made her miss Danny, too. Suddenly shocked and ashamed at how seldom she thought of him these days, she longed to speak to him, but to phone now would be unfair when tea and scones waited, and Georgina and Charles hovered.

Emily sank gratefully into the shiny leather armchair. The room felt unsteady and her head fizzed. Almost against her will, her eyes closed and she lay back in the chair. At once a blanket appeared, a stool materialized and someone raised her legs for her. Slowly the room steadied, her head stopped whirling and she opened her eyes.

'Dr Cowan will be checking on her later this afternoon,' she heard Leon say. 'I think I'll get him here earlier . . .'

She revived at once. 'Oh, no,' she said. 'I'm fine now, I really am . . .' But her voice shook. 'I think I'm only just beginning to believe what almost happened.'

'Delayed reaction,' Leon said briskly. 'We've been expecting it; Cowan and I discussed it . . .'

Leon thinks of everything, Emily thought. It made her feel defenceless and somehow naked . . . because she had never been so cosseted, protected or well cared for.

After tea, Leon took her into the huge room that was her bedroom where a vast four-poster bed had been made ready. She tried to take in the detail of the room, but was aware only of the fire in the hearth and of course the bed . . . She was too tired, or too weak, to speak; she just kicked off her shoes and managed to climb the shallow steps that led up to the four-poster. Then, fully clothed, she fell asleep.

When she awoke, she saw that Leon was seated at the bedside. For a moment she could not remember where she was. Then, 'I fell asleep with all my clothes on,' she murmured. 'I've never done that before.' She sat up slowly. 'I wish I could stretch both arms,' she said.

'You've been asleep for two hours,' Leon told her.

'I can't believe any of this – that I'm here, with you, in this lovely room, in Connecticut ...'

'Thank God you are! Thank God you made it ...'

'I can't begin to thank you,' Emily said, very formally. She felt unaccountably shy, even gauche, as if she had forgotten her manners. 'I don't suppose I'll ever be able to thank you ...'

In answer, something that sounded like a gurgle, or a hiccup, escaped from his throat, and he said slowly, 'You are so beautiful, Emily. You've gotten more and more beautiful every day.' He flung himself out of his chair and buried his face in her throat. 'It's been so long,' he murmured. 'So long ... Every minute, at the hospital. I've been watching you. And wanting you ...'

Emily drew him closer, with her good arm. She responded to his kisses with a fierce familiarity, as if she had been kissing him all her life and as if the geography of his mouth was as well known as her own. Her clothes came off and then, when he was at her very centre, fright at how dangerously close she had come to losing him sent her body into a frenzied fight for flight. She would use up her life force, if necessary. Because now, as he met and measured each and every moment with his own, only these movements and only those moments counted.

They shared survival that afternoon, as if each had been reprieved rather than saved. Surely, surely, Jake Williams and the death he had almost forced was there, in the bed with them. It was as if they both knew and understood the permanence of death and were inspired by it. For again and again they came together; death had been delayed, and so they dared little deaths ...

Between these times he fed her fruit, or juices, or biscuits. While she slept, he had moved the trolley up to the bed. In all those hours, he left the bed only once; to add logs to the fire. Towards evening, he asked if she was hungry. 'Georgina's prepared dinner,' he told her.

'Oh, no!'

'She could leave a tray outside the door,' he suggested, reading her mind and understanding that she could not have borne any sort of intrusion.

'Could she? Something cold?'

Leon called downstairs and spoke to Georgina. He asked for a tray of cold things – he hoped she had some of her special asparagus – and reminded her that, barring emergencies, no calls were to be put through. Again, Emily thought fleetingly of phoning London, but then she remembered that it was about eleven o'clock over there and both Danny and Simon would probably be asleep.

It was a long, slow, luxurious night, and though they talked of many things the word love was never mentioned. He showed her the clothes he had had sent, and helped her to decide which she should keep. He had a very distinct taste, she realized; it was obvious that he liked the tailored look. When she demurred about the costs, though no price tags were visible, he told her quite bluntly that he was a very rich man.

'Arab rich?' she teased, because she found his candour utterly charming. She had never met a man who would not have been too embarrassed, or ashamed, to admit to being very rich.

He evaded the question. '*We* put a lot back into the economy,' he answered.

'I know about your Foundation,' she said. 'I know *that*, because the nurses told me what you do for the hospital.'

'Milt and I see things the same way . . .' He tended busily to his cigar. 'May I?' he asked. Then he began to tell her about his business, about how they got started. It had really begun to take off because of Mr Myers, a difficult tenant. The fact was, Mr Myers knew the building he rented from the Lerners had no elevator, which was why the rent was so low. He had a small manufacturing plant, and his staff were objecting to climbing five flights of stairs. For the Lerner brothers, it was a serious matter. They were heavily in debt as it was, and there was nothing academic about the threat of bankrupcy; it was always with them and, moreover, their father had gone bust when they were in their teens. Leon was all of twenty-five then and, to say the least, depressed. After all, Korea was only just behind them. Anyway, he walked round and round the building; even the way it was structured meant that it would be impossible to put in an elevator . . . even if they had the money. And Mr Myers was going to leave, which meant no rent. Walking round, an idea hit him, if Mr Jackson, the owner of the adjacent building, would let them put in an interconnecting door, an elevator could serve both buildings. It took some persuading, but he pulled it off. Meanwhile, Mr Jackson's own factory needed more space and his elevator made the Lerner building very, very attractive. Afterwards Mr Jackson hated himself – it was something of an acrimonious deal – for not having had the brains to see the potential of his elevator. Even so, buying from the Lerners, and paying $280,000 for what had cost $100,000 only ten months earlier, would still be more economical than relocating. Without the elevator, the building was worth $150,000 at the most.

All that was thirty years ago, when there was virtually no limit to the investment potential of $300,000. That amount in cash meant borrowing up to one million. After that, take-off was swift and steady.

But, Leon readily conceded, they had also been lucky. And it was for this reason that they went in for the sponsorship of public parks.

Not bad for a college drop-out, Leon ended, his eyes twinkling.

Emily listened fascinated. She had never been remotely interested in the making of money and had always been faintly contemptuous of people who made rather than earned it. But Leon made it sound more than a skill. It was, she realized, a test of quick thinking . . . otherwise known as luck. She was so much taken with this last idea that she needed to say it aloud. 'What you call luck, others call quick thinking.'

'But it was luck,' he said firmly. 'I can't claim to have foreseen that old Jackson would need an extra building...' He laughed that joyous laugh of his and Emily laughed with him.

But she was not deflected.

'How many times did you walk around his building?'

'Hundreds, I guess. I knew that we were in serious trouble; I'm not good at giving up. I'd already gone to the expense of calling in engineers, you see. I suppose I didn't much go for the way they insulted our building. I was only twenty-five...'

'You make it sound exciting...'

'Business is exciting...'

'Yes, it is,' Emily said enthusiastically. 'It's much more exciting than fees.'

'Fees?'

'Well, Simon talks about fees. And my father hates to talk about money, but I know he has an index-linked pension. No one I know talks about business, unless to sneer at it.' Then, sounding vaguely astonished, she said, 'I suppose you are what is called a self-made man?'

'Well, I had Milt, of course. A partnership of trust gave us the edge over most.'

'Self-made men, then?'

'Yes.'

'That's what I thought.' Now it was her turn to laugh.

'What's the joke?' asked Leon sharply.

'Oh,' she said, spluttering. 'You'll never believe this, Leon, but where I come from "self-made man" is a term of abuse. Did you know that?'

'Yes, I knew that,' he said seriously. A twinkle of humorous intelligence brightened his eyes and he went on, 'You know the guy who sent me a telex about you – Sir Roger Wilbury? Well, he made a bundle – sold some stock option. He was sort of embarrassed about it, like he thought it was unfair...'

'I know what you mean,' she said. But her eyes darkened. Mentioning Sir Roger reminded her of Simon and Danny. She said, 'Simon was with Sir Roger on the day of the shooting. What time is it? I should phone him...'

'Ten after one...'

'When did I wake up?'

'At two-thirty.'

'Do you mean to say we've been talking, non-stop, for twelve hours?'

'Well,' he said, with that wonderful laugh of his, 'we didn't only talk. A lot of fucking went on. Remember?'

'Yes,' she murmured. 'A lot of beautiful – fucking.'

Which was the signal for more.

They made love slowly, patiently, compassionately. Once, she said, 'I need *both* arms for this,' but other than that they did not say anything. And then, moments before they fell asleep, she said, 'The earth didn't move. It stopped.'

Some time later she awoke, agitated, and remembered that she had not phoned Simon. It made sleep difficult, but the thought of disturbing Leon was unbearable. She lay quietly while her mind zoomed.

It was crazy, she knew, and absolutely went against all the rules. Well, her rules, anyway. But she could not imagine life without Leon. She was being ridiculous, she knew. Yet she could not stop herself. Which was also ridiculous and made her feel shockingly insecure. Being ridiculous went against her nature.

*

Lieutenant Janowski hoped that his dislike of the thin neat man in his office, who sat on the opposite side of his desk, did not show. The man was called Vic Porter and it was that monotonous sing-song voice which irritated like an itch in the eyes. He had come to associate that voice with a certain type of do-gooder, those who had no doubts about their own superior qualities, those who believed that because they had been gifted with an excessive capacity for love they were duty bound to despise the police. From time to time Vic Porter's head nodded in agreement with his voice, and Tom found even that irritating – which made him feel disgusted with himself. Vic Porter had come to the precinct because he had valuable, vital information on Jake Williams, but he, Tom Janowski, was allowing the man's starry-eyed, inflexible belief in the perfectibility of mankind to get in his way.

Which meant that he had to start all over again. From the beginning.

'Mr Porter, I believe you said you'd been out of the country for four weeks?'

'Yes, I went to Europe. On a Sunaway Package. That's how I happened to read *People* magazine. I read it on the plane coming back to the States. As I've already mentioned, it's not my sort of reading material . . .'

'I know,' Tom agreed hastily. 'You already told me.'

'I'm not a magazine reader. But if I hadn't picked up *People* I would never have seen that picture of Joshua Winston . . .'

'Jake Williams, you mean . . .'

'Sure I do. I keep forgetting that Joshua Winston is a pseudonym.'

'The initials are the same . . .'

'I noticed that myself,' Vic Porter gushed. 'That clinched it for me. Joshua and Jake had to be the same man, I said to myself. I called the police from Kennedy, you know.'

'I know. We're very grateful. If there were more citizens like you, there'd be less need for citizens like me . . .'

'I do have a highly developed sense of civic responsibility.' He broke into high-pitched titters which drove Tom crazy. 'I guess if I didn't have that, I'd have a totally different vocation.'

'Like I said,' Tom said wearily, 'society needs people like you. Now, if you would just fill me in on more detail about your job . . .'

'It's not exactly a job, see. It's more like a calling.'

'OK, your calling. I'd need to know more about your calling.'

'Did I tell you how I got into it?'

'Jesus!' Tom exploded.

'We mustn't blaspheme, you know. 'Course, I used to do that a lot myself . . .'

'Mr Porter, please. Stick to the point!'

'OK, OK. Don't get so excited, it makes me nervous. I'm the director of an organization called Homes for Hope. We have two so far, both in New York State. We're hoping to expand into the State of California.' Vic Porter tittered again. 'Come to think of it, this Jake Williams situation could bring Homes for Hope into the public eye.'

'Right. Certainly. You've got something there. 'Course, we'd need more details.'

'We've been operating now for about six years. The total idea wasn't mine; it was more like an inspiration from on high. It was after I was rehabilitated myself. I had a flash of light. I knew I wasn't the only kid who'd been deserted by his father. The name of the place was given by the Reverend Aiken. You've heard of him?'

'Can't say I have . . .'

It took at least two hours for Tom to get the full story. The core philosophy motivating Homes for Hope, aside from the belief in human perfectibility, was to help kids who had been abandoned by their fathers. The homes were restricted to boys; they had twenty adolescent boys in each home and, of course, they were always short on finance. Their mothers could have them on weekends, whenever that was possible. The prevailing philosophy was that these boys needed a male influence, a male environment. The boys went to regular schools, but their time was ordered for them. They were encouraged to participate in all sorts of regular masculine activities such as the martial arts, carpentry, even fishing. All the boys had a history of some sort of minor misdemeanour, which is why the organization was called Homes for Hope.

Vic Porter surely hoped Tom would understand why it was difficult for him to refer to Joshua Winston as Jake Williams. Joshua had always seemed hyper-sensitive – he hid behind glasses and a beard. He was always neat, though, and it was obvious that he didn't waste any money on clothes. He looked sort of . . . ordinary. Vic had assumed it was because he was too modest to want to look like the rich man he had become.

It was easy to tell that Joshua Winston was the symbol of the American Dream of Success. He never knew how Joshua got to know about Homes for Hope. All Joshua told him was that his life had been loused up because he thought his father had left him when he was two. He had spent all his life hoping his father would return. He was always looking for him. Then, just before he graduated from college, his mother died and he went through her documents and discovered his father's death certificate. All those years he had been searching, and hoping, his father had been dead. It was true that he had abandoned Joshua when he was only two, but he had died three years later. He had found his father's suicide note, too, but he didn't want his son to know about that. So he brought the money in dollar bills...

He was such a fantastic benefactor that he had to have made it in a big, big way. Who, in this day and age, would give amounts totalling *half a million in dollar bills* on condition there would be no publicity?

Yes sir, that's how much that man had given! It was on the basis of this that a new Home for Hope was already in the planning phase.

All the while that Vic Porter had been speaking, Tom Janowski's mind had been turning somersaults. *Blackmail!*

It was fantastic, but it looked as if Jake Williams had been playing a modern Robin Hood. Robbing – no, extorting – from the rich to help the poor. But probably not the super-rich – too much power there... No, only those who had made just enough to risk cheating Uncle Sam. There were at least sixty different numbers on Jake's list. Sixty poor slobs...

Everything began to make sense...

The details fell beautifully into place. So far, Jake Williams had not yet uttered one word. The doctors and psychologists were fanatically certain about the diagnosis – schizophrenia... Well, Tom thought, we'll see what sort of schizophrenic he is when Vic Porter calls on him...

A sigh whistled through Tom's teeth. It was within the power of those doctors, those ego-maniacs, to prohibit such a visit. Sometimes Tom suspected that he was even more allergic to doctors and to social workers than to criminals.

Vic Porter had dumped a bundle of dynamite in his lap.

From the very beginning, this case had been something of a minefield. And now this new information was dynamite. The media would turn Jake Williams into a hero – an IRS agent blackmailing taxpayers to fund Homes for Hope. He would have to be super-smart if he wanted to make sure that Jake Williams didn't get a medal! At the same time, his deepest gut feeling was that this was the career opportunity of his life...

What he needed was to coordinate a *strategy* . . . He was in over his head and he needed help: needed it real, real bad. Tom had never been shy of asking for help or advice.

A strategy.

Television and the press could tear him to shreds. Or he could use them, and to his own advantage.

Suddenly it came to him, and again it was a gut feeling. He knew where to go for expert help, even if it was outside the rule book.

He would see what Rick Cooke had to say . . . Rick had done so much for Katie, fixing for her to meet Dr Joan Barnes, taking Katie and her kid out.

He believed he could trust Rick Cooke, so what more could he ask for?

Tom let out another low whistle. 'Mr Porter,' he said, dropping his voice to a confidential tone, 'it sure looks like your benefactor is guilty of a felony. Which might implicate you.'

'Me?' Vic Porter squeaked. 'Me? What've I done?'

'You're innocent, I can see that,' Tom sighed. 'The courts might give you a hard time. So, I'm going to process everything you've told me myself. I'm not allowing any junior to take your statement – I'll take that myself, too. I may be stepping out of line, but I don't meet too many people like you. People with a social conscience . . .'

'I sure appreciate what you're doing for me.'

'You'll be OK if you keep your mouth shut . . .'

It was time to go home, but Tom could not face the rush hour. He needed to go in for some hard thinking.

This had never been an ordinary case . . .

To begin with, there was Emily Bradshaw. He had interviewed her several times and still he could not understand why she should feel not only responsible for Jake Williams' action, but blame herself for it. Yet there was no doubt that she was anything but a sane and sensible woman. And she was so nice, modest and charming as well as beautiful. And such a lady.

Tom and his wife talked about it, and talked about it. Emily remained convinced that even in his blind rage, Jake Williams had taken care *not* to do her a mortal injury. After all, as she pointed out so reasonably and so charmingly, Jake's gun club had confirmed that he was a crack shot, an accurate marksman. Emily told him that she prayed for Jake's recovery for many many reasons – not least because she wanted to apologize to him. It was her fault, her thoughtlessness, which had exposed that raw burning nerve of savage suspicion.

She was grateful to Tom, and to Rick Cooke, for taking care of Jake's wife and son. Because, that way, her conscience had been more than a little eased.

Her conscience... he had had to deal with women who thought that way too often. Battered wives who insisted on taking the blame for having been beaten up. But then they were neurotic disturbed women, and it was obvious that Emily was neither neurotic nor disturbed. Only British.

It was equally obvious that Emily was sincere about her need to have him understand how she felt. She believed she had had a duty to consider the consequences that her words might have on other people. Instead, the awful truth was that she had been too light-hearted and too casual... which meant she had been delinquent in her responsibility.

And, looked at from her point of view, Lieutenant Janowski had to admit that it made some sense.

After all, Emily had conceded that she probably would have reacted very differently if she had been maimed, or paralysed, or even blinded.

She believed she had got off lightly...

Which, as his wife agreed, was beyond all understanding. But troubling all the same. Deeply troubling.

Suddenly Tom laughed out loud.

Because there was a lighter side to all of this. The IRS would come in for some pretty fierce criticism. Jee-*sus*, who would have believed that he could ever have felt sorry for those IRS bastards?

This was rich, real, real, rich. He felt better about the world.

*

Simon had suggested that Emily should not phone him before seven-thirty in the evening. It had been a suggestion only, and a mild one at that, which was why Emily knew that he could not have been more emphatic. It meant, though, that she had to wait until well after lunch to phone. And she had not spoken to him for three days, which would put her in the wrong at once as soon as he heard her voice. It was this and not her infidelity that made her feel horribly guilty, as well as unnecessarily careless.

She began to dial London. The sooner war, the sooner peace, she said to herself. And it was only then that she realized she had begun to dread calling him. It made her nervous. 'Simon?' she said when he answered. 'How *are* you? How is Danny? Is Ophelia pulling her weight?' Her own babbling irritated her, but Simon's silence made her add, 'Is everything going smoothly? I hope Danny's keeping up with his practising...'

'Susan's pleased with him...'

'Oh, good. I'm at White Wings now. You have the phone number?'

'You gave it to me before you left the hospital. You've been there since yesterday, I believe?'

'Yes, but I fell asleep almost as soon as I arrived. And then it was too late to phone you.'

'I see,' Simon said pleasantly. 'For the whole afternoon?'

'I suppose the journey tired me.'

'You're feeling rested now?'

'Yes, thank you.' She tried a laugh, but sounded breathless. 'I'll be doing the *Virginia Byrnes Show* on Friday.'

'So I'm told.'

'Oh, who told you?'

'Keith. He's back in London; I thought you knew that. More publicity of course...'

'I suppose so.'

'I'll save the clippings for you. I've a mountain of those, as it is.' His voice, tinged with the purest anger, dropped. 'You ought to be very satisfied.'

Furious, Emily said, 'Simon! That's unfair!'

'Did you want to speak to Danny?'

'Of course.'

'He's out with your father...'

'What?' Emily said, shocked. 'On a week night?'

'They're at the Festival Hall. Menuhin's playing the Mozart Concerto . . .'

'Oh, I see,' Emily said doubtfully. 'Will you tell him I called?' She hesitated. 'Tell him I've written to him,' she lied.

'Certainly . . .'

'Well, goodbye then.'

She hung up at once, her nerves positively jangling. The physiotherapist was waiting for her. And Simon hadn't even *asked* about her arm! But the truth, she knew, was that this insultingly callous behaviour of his was something of a blessing. It eased things; it lessened guilt; it allowed her to tell herself that Simon made her turn to Leon for consolation.

He didn't even ask about my arm, she thought again.

Meanwhile, the physiotherapist waited.

Keeping people waiting went against Emily's nature.

But she wanted Leon now. No, she needed him, needed the certain sympathy of his arms. After Simon's chill, more than ever now, she needed Leon's warmth.

Perhaps Simon had sensed the truth of her relationship with Leon.

Because if he had, then . . . But before it could be completed, Emily banished the thought.

'I've told you, Milt,' Leon said, making his exasperation clear, 'I'm *not* coming to the office. Right now I don't give a shit about the Western deal. Or any other deal.'

'You're crazy, man, crazy.'

Leon held the phone away from his ear. 'You'd better get a hold of yourself, Milt,' he said coldly. 'You're losing control.'

'*I'm* losing control? You're pussy-whipped!'

'Never talk to me like that again, Milt,' Leon said softly. 'Have you got that?'

'Come on, Leon . . .'

'Listen, Milt, get this straight. Before I let you talk to me like that again, I'll see you in hell.'

'Leon, this is *me*. This is your *brother* Milt you're talking to.'

Speaking even more slowly, and making it clear that he was measuring every word, Leon said, 'Exactly. *You* should know better than to talk to *me* like that.'

273

Leon slammed down the receiver. It was rare for him and Milt to quarrel, very rare. But somehow exhilarating. It added something extra to Emily. Leon knew what it was, too. Power – pure power ... It gave her even more power over him. Because, if he was ready to go as far as to fight with his brother over her, then she must be one hell of a special woman.

He had never been in anyone's power before ...

Power, he thought, power is the greatest aphrodisiac of them all ... He wanted her now, and wanted her now, immediately, at once. This minute! He had a hard on.

But she was with the physiotherapist. Surely the session was almost over? He would knock on the door of his gymnasium.

The gymnasium, which was perfectly equipped, was in the basement – a fair distance away from his study on the top floor. It would be quite a while before he could reach it.

Of course, poor Milt had never experienced anything like an Emily Bradshaw, so he had no idea ... Even so, he had no right to attack Emily. Leon was forced to protect Emily, even from his own brother ... He grew angrier.

How dare Milt insult Emily?

At the same time he felt a stirring of compassion for his brother. After all, every man wanted her. Milt couldn't help it.

He knocked at the door. 'Almost through?' he called.

'Almost,' Emily answered. 'But please come in.'

'She's doing well,' Alison Bowles, the physiotherapist, said proudly. 'Thanks for sending the car for me, Mr Lerner ...'

'Is there anything you need? I mean, any suggestions about what could speed the recovery process?'

'I was just saying to Mrs Bradshaw that a jacuzzi might help ...'

'I should have thought of that,' Leon said quickly. 'Don't know why I didn't. How long would it take to instal one?'

'I'm not sure, Mr Lerner. A day or two, I guess.'

'You going back to New York right now?'

'Yes.'

'Could you take care of it? My secretary will go with you, if you like. 'Course, I expect you to bill me for all your time, expenses and so on.'

Emily felt as if she were eavesdropping on a conversation between people who were utter strangers to her. It was not only that the jacuzzi was being acquired specifically for her that made it all seem so unreal. She wanted to ask how all this could be possible. Here they were, deep in the country, in a house more than two hundred years old, and not a mention of plumbing or any other difficulties. They might have been making arrangements to order a bowl of flowers.

Leon hurried the physiotherapist to the door. When he came back he sat at the edge of the high, narrow massage table where Emily lay. 'Was Alison really good?' he asked. 'She's got the greatest reputation for sports injuries. How do you feel? Does it feel better?'

'She's wonderful,' Emily said dreamily. 'I missed you . . .' She thought of Simon, thought how he had not asked about her shoulder. It made her voice shake. She said, 'I resented her, though.'

'You resented her?'

'For taking me away from you. I couldn't wait for her to go. I wanted to be with you.'

'What've you got on under that towel?' Leon asked.

'Take it off and see.'

Emily was naked, powerfully naked. Leon groaned and stood up. He grabbed her hand so that she could feel his erection. She tugged at his fly. The zipper caught his underpants, and stuck. She forced his trousers down. Neither could wait for him to step out of them, and the trousers did not get in their way. The narrow table restricted their movements gloriously and forced them into a closer union, into swifter rhythms. Or so it seemed to Leon.

She felt her body rip and churn until it was all sensation, as if ecstasy had skinned her body, leaving her raw and exposed and utterly alive, the better to receive him. And more still, and still more, as ultimate exceeded ultimate. Her mind slipped. Stripped of reason, stripped of emotion, greed was allowed its fullest rein until it peaked.

Greed equalled greed. As they came together she felt his hot tears mingle with hers.

Opening her eyes to look at him, she found him pale and white, deathly white, with whiter polka dots about his mouth.

She remembered his heart condition.

Terrified, she screamed, 'Leon, Leon! Speak to me. Speak to me.'

He moved his head and the light changed, and the polka-dots disappeared. He said, 'Are you OK, Emily?'

She was about to tell him she thought he had died, but managed to stop herself. Instead, she said, 'I thought I had died.'

*

Thanks to Emily Bradshaw, Rick Cooke was about to move to a more elegant suite of offices. Finally, finally he would be on Madison Avenue. He was attempting to tidy his desk. He had given up hoping to stop smoking until after Emily went back to England, so those empty Coke bottles filled with cigarette stubs should have disappeared. He lifted a pile of papers and found one. Disgusted, he flung it into a trash-can. He was still trying to work out why Lieutenant Janowski wanted to see him...

When Tom had asked to meet him, Rick had put forward several alternative meeting points. His office did his image no good. But Tom had been adamant. It was to be a confidential meeting – strictly confidential, was what he had said – and Rick's office was the safest place...

Rick had to admit that he was kind of excited about this meeting. It had to be connected with Emily, or else why would Tom want to see a small-time publicist like Rick Cooke? Not that Rick Cooke was very small-time these days. That shooting episode, as he called it, had gone over big for *him*. It was his big break, he was damned if he was going to kid himself on that one...

Tom was five minutes early. Rick let him in and seated him in his own chair behind the desk. 'You're so tall. My office kind of shrinks with you in it...'

'So what's with me sitting in your seat, behind your desk?'

'Respect,' Rick said at once. 'Respect. It's a better chair, too...'

276

'OK, let's get to business. Why would I come and see you, huh?'

'I tell you, I'm honoured . . .'

'Cut the crap, Cooke.'

'What the fuck is this?' Rick said, his voice high. 'I make an honest statement and you tell me to cut the bullshit. What's going on here?'

'I guess I'd better tell you what brings me here. It's all off the record, understand?'

'Listen, Tom, you can count on me. I liked the way you handled Katie Williams.' Rick paused to scratch his head. 'This might sound kind of crazy to you, but I'd sure like to help if I can. You're here on account of Emily?'

'Nope.' Tom Janowski released one of his longest whistles, which reminded Rick of a creaking door. 'It's Jake Williams. Listen, what I've got to tell you is dynamite. Shit. I'm going to tell you stuff before I even talk to the DA.'

'Tom,' Rick said seriously, 'you'll have to trust me, I guess. How can I reassure you?' Suddenly, as if he had had an inspiration, he said, 'Emily Bradshaw trusts me . . .'

'You're right,' Janowski said miserably. 'I will have to trust you more than my own wife. And, let me tell you, I've got a lot of faith in her. But I didn't tell her I would be coming to see you.'

It was Rick's absolute candour which finally persuaded Tom to speak. He told Rick about Vic Porter's visit, about how much Vic Porter resembled Jake Williams – both wore heavy horn-rimmed glasses, both wore beards. He told him his theory about Jake as a blackmailer. He wanted the people who had been blackmailed to come forward. They would need to be . . . seduced, of course. *But how to reach them?*

Tom was ready to admit that he could have gone to police psychologists, to police media consultants who were available to him. But those guys were disillusioned and there was a real emotional shutdown going on amongst them. He couldn't blame them for that . . .

So, instead of going to the cops for help, he was obeying his own gut feeling and going to an outsider. For two reasons:

number one, he believed that if he, Tom, could become a sort of unofficial spokesman, he could do a whole lot to improve the police image; the other reason, number two, was more personal...

Here Tom whistled again. He stopped talking.

The guy's shy, Rick thought. He said, 'Shit, man, you're not going to get all embarrassed on me now, are you?'

Once again Tom responded to Rick's simple candour. All his reservations fell away and he whistled again. This time, however, the whistle passed through a smile. 'Hell, man,' he said, 'I trust you now. I'll get to the point. The right sort of public relations could do a whole lot for my career. Got it?'

'Sure,' Rick said. 'Listen, I don't mind telling you that Emily Bradshaw's the hottest property that's come my way.' His rolling, throaty voice deepened. 'I'm making such a bundle out of her – got contracts with other publishers – that I'm already negotiating for new offices!'

'OK. So we understand each other. Only...' Once again Tom paused. He looked troubled.

At once Rick asked, 'What's the problem?'

'How much will it cost me?'

'Not a cent. Not one cent,' Rick said slowly. 'Now here's what I want you to do for me. I want for you to listen to every word I'm going to say. Concentrate hard. OK?'

In a few days' time, Rick told him, Emily would be appearing on the *Virginia Byrnes Show*. Emily was on billboards everywhere. The show format was going to be exactly the same as when she was shot. Only, right now, that had been changed – he was going to put Tom on the show. 'Because if you tell whoever you have to tell – the DA, or whatever – on Thursday night, the night before the show, it will make *all* the national network news and Virginia Byrnes will have the biggest scoop of all time!' Rick could no longer contain his emotions. He jumped up and literally rubbed his hands with glee. 'TAN's president, Art Kristol, will roll over and die for me, now! Do you know what a break this is for *me*?'

He sat down again. 'After the show, I'll have a whole lot of classy print interviews lined up for you. One or two editorials

They'll have to promote you and before we're through, President Reagan will personally award you a presidential medal!'

'Jee-sus, I sure knew what I was doing when I came to you!'

'Right – now as of this minute you have severe gastritis. You're getting cramps every fifteen minutes. You're doubling up in agony. Just as soon as you leave here, you're going to your doctor, as an emergency. Got that?'

'I got it ...'

'A few days' rest will be good for you.' Rick added. 'It'll be a vacation and you'll have time to read. Have you read *Defending Wives?*'

'*Defending Wives?*' Tom repeated. 'I don't read much ...'

'You'll read this one,' Rick said, handing him a copy. 'It's the book Emily Bradshaw wrote. You know something? You and me never would have met without this book ...'

*

Emily looked about her while Leon buttered her croissant. Everything at White Wings glitters all the time, she decided. Though the autumn gloom entered the dining room, the log fire sent a peculiar sparkle to the silver – as if the table, set for breakfast, was on display in a shop. Equally, it might have been on a film set. In a silver tureen, scarlet apples shone, and again there was an almost artificial sparkle to them. Georgina had taken orchids from the hothouse, and they formed a ring around the tureen. On Emily's lap the linen napkin that matched her breakfast mat crackled. She loved the feel of the linen so much that she was glad it also had a sound to it ... reminding her of the feel and sound of the silk dress she had worn on her first date with Leon.

It was pure happiness she was feeling, she knew. Happiness pure as the linen on her lap; pure as the silk of her dress. She said, 'I'll never understand how Mrs Hunt could have borne to have parted with all these exquisite things. It's quite beyond me.'

They had discussed this before. Patiently, Leon said again, 'She didn't want the headache of deciding which of her three daughters-in-law should have what.'

'Yes, but...' Emily was thinking of their Ford Madox Brown, of their Chippendale desk; of the hardship of holding on to them. But that had changed too, now... She tried to move the thought away, but it persisted and she frowned.

'My theory is that Mrs Hunt disliked all her daughters-in-law so much that she preferred to offer them to a stranger.'

'Except that everything belongs in this house. In England it would probably be declared a national monument...'

She listed to Leon's infectious laugh – she loved it so much that it made her afraid. 'I'm restoring the wall, you know,' he said. 'We've been working on it for two years. Two experts are laying stone on stone – no cement, no technology of any sort...'

Emily made no effort to hide her enthusiasm. That was the incredible thing about being in America, with Leon – she could be as enthusiastic and as blatantly excited as she liked. About everything, too – and in every way. 'Gosh,' she said, 'that's wonderful. What an imaginative idea!'

'Not really,' Leon said, 'I can't take any credit for that idea. Restoring historical structures makes the best tax sense.'

But Emily found this equally engaging. It was all part of what she thought of as the way she had been liberated. 'So very liberating,' she would tell herself. 'This freedom to talk about money without ever feeling ashamed...' It wasn't such a giant step backwards, really, but of course Simon – and for that matter, everyone she knew – would see it as a colossal leap backwards into untamed jungles.

But for Emily, going against her nature – or what she had always believed was her nature – was incredibly liberating. The awful thing was that it was also disloyal. But she could never quite rid herself of a constant inner argument. Now, she defended herself, perhaps her newly acquired taste for making her *own* money was no more disloyal, really, than her newly acquired taste for fragrant – rather than strong – tea.

A whiff of Leon's musk aftershave came to her. 'Oh,' she said aloud, 'I think I prefer the aromatic life...'

'What are you talking about?' Leon asked.

'You smell so good. It's your aftershave.' She left her seat, suddenly – to sniff him. His smooth morning skin was irresistible. Her nose snuggled until it found his mouth, then she could not stop herself from drawing a long, deeply tongued and fairly noisy kiss.

The butler coughed . . .

Emily and Leon drew apart like guilty teenagers.

'I beg your pardon, sir,' Charles said, 'but Mr Milt is on the phone. He asked me to tell you that it is most urgent.' He handed Leon a cordless telephone, repeating, 'Most urgent.'

'Sorry, darling,' Leon said, 'I'll have to take this call . . .'

He sounded angry, Emily thought. But he *had* called her darling . . .

'No, I will not come in for another meeting,' Leon was saying. 'And I don't give a damn if Al Bishop has offered 110 million or 510 million, for only twelve and a half per cent of our company. There's no way that I'll agree to any deal, of any sort, whatsoever. Why? What's going on with you, Milt . . . You're talking to me about principles . . . Do you know what you're saying . . . ? What's happened to your memory . . . ? Sure, sure I'm talking about twenty-five years back. I'll remind you . . . As far as *I* know, for the Lerner brothers vows count, no matter when they were made . . . What's that? I resent your calling me an immature adolescent . . . You just talked to me about principles . . . In my book, vows are principles. No – there's no deal . . . no discussion . . . No, that is not my last word . . . You're waiting for it . . . You're sure? The only message I've got for you is . . . go to hell!'

With that, Leon flung the small instrument into the fire.

Throughout the entire exchange, Emily had held her breath. It was dynamic. It was exciting. Above all, it was passionate. She had never seen such a dazzling display of strength. Admiringly she said, 'You are a strong man, Leon.'

Although Leon smiled, she saw that he was still furious. She could tell . . . He said, 'I was about to apologize to you for my bad manners.'

'What was it all about, Leon? What vow? I'm dying to know.'

'Twenty-five years back we had a cash-flow problem. It was pretty dire, I can tell you. This guy, Al Bishop, knew all about it; he told us we could double our money if we invested in his stock.'

'And you lost everything?' Emily interrupted.

'No,' Leon said, his voice edged in ice. 'No, that's just the point. We didn't lose one cent because we didn't invest one cent. The bastard was telling the truth. In less than six months his stock doubled. And we could only watch, helplessly. That bastard laughed at us. You see, he knew we wouldn't be able to lay our hands on the stock, no matter what we were prepared to pay. He and his nominees held it *all*. There were no sellers.'

'Business excites me, as you know,' Emily said, 'but I don't quite follow . . .'

'It's very simple, really. A matter of simple cruelty, you see. Al Bishop wanted us to break our necks trying to get hold of the stock. We were only beginners then; we didn't know that if a man was serious about that sort of offer, he would also have to offer to get the stock for you. Got it?'

'Yes. What a dishonourable, devious way to behave . . .'

'Well put, Emily. Except that I call it sick – a sick way to get kicks – so you understand why we made a vow never to do business with that rat . . .'

Another of Charles's elegant coughs disturbed them. 'I'm extremely sorry, sir, but Mr Milt is on the line again . . .'

A second cordless phone was handed to Leon.

'OK, OK, I accept . . . Forget it . . . just as long as we agree that a vow's a vow. Couldn't trust Al Bishop, anyway . . . Sure . . . So I apologize myself . . .'

Emily could not help noticing how Leon's tight voice eased, melted even, while he spoke to his brother. She had heard about the twin-tie, the bond between twins. But she had never known a twin before. Yet she had sensed Milt's antagonism towards her . . .

'You're very close to Milt, aren't you?' she asked.

'Closer than close.'

Emily felt like an outsider.

Again, she could not identify what it was that made her uneasy. But she had a strong feeling that she was . . . well, temporary.

Charles brought more coffee and Emily drank it gratefully.

Her throat felt painful, as if it held her heart, and any hot liquid would have helped.

The breakfast table gleamed, reflecting the orchid centrepiece as accurately as a mirror. Something about their thick, fleshy petals reminded Emily of a tick. Overtaken by a nameless dread, she was scarcely aware of her nervous shredding of the orchids.

'You don't like orchids, do you?' Leon asked mildly.

'I loathe them . . .'

'So do I.'

'Why do you ask me about orchids, Leon?'

'You've been tearing them apart, and orchids are not your style. Roses . . . you should always have roses.'

'You know me too well,' she whispered. 'I wasn't concentrating. I didn't know . . .'

Leon stopped her. He said, 'I'll never know you well enough.'

*

Emily had never woken up beside any man other than her own husband. Now, of course, there was Leon . . . Now it was as if even the texture of her own skin was felt through his. It was late afternoon and he had insisted that she take a nap. It was too easy to get used to Leon's sort of cosseting, Leon's sort of tenderness. It made no sense, yet even the bed itself was like an ecstatically tender embrace. On the other hand, it made all the sense in the world – because when Leon had stayed at the Ritz in Paris, he had slept on that mattress and liked it so much that he had gone to great lengths to buy it. Perhaps he was able to care for others so well not only because he had the means, but because he cared about himself . . . Leon and Simon were very different. Simon never shaved in front of a mirror. Simon would have sneered at Leon's array of impeccable suits under their transparent dustcovers. Simon would have seen so many clothes as proof of self-love – and what could be more shameful and more vulgar than that? Once, in another life, Emily would have thought so too.

But that was before. Before America.

The bedside phone buzzed. 'Sheila Lyall is here to see you, Mrs Bradshaw,' Charles said. 'I am extremely sorry to disturb you . . .'

'Sheila Lyall?'

'She said to tell you she was in the area, so she dropped by . . .'

'I'll be right down.'

Thank God Leon's here, she thought. He'll handle Sheila Lyall. He knows all about the frozen peas . . .

'Darling,' Sheila drawled. 'Aren't you superstitious about wearing green? Don't you know it brings bad luck?'

'Of course not. I'm not the superstitious type.'

'Aren't you? But you've got so much to lose, I see.' She paused and shot a pointed glance in Leon's direction. 'I'll withdraw that. As possessions . . . women are wasting assets.'

'You should wear green. It's the colour of jealousy, isn't it?' Emily retorted bitterly.

'Sheila Lyall certainly is jealous,' Leon said mildly. 'She's just been telling me that giant billboards of you are all over New York.'

'Billboards?'

'You Brits call them hoardings, I believe,' Sheila said.

'Hoardings?' Emily repeated. 'What would I be doing on hoardings?'

'Don't sound so coy, it doesn't suit you,' Sheila replied. 'No one can take two steps in New York without seeing a huge billboard of Emily Bradshaw, screaming about the *Virginia Byrnes Show* . . .'

'You can't mean that.'

'But I do mean that,' Sheila said, mocking Emily's accent. 'My photographs, too! That's why I'm here. To congratulate you!'

'Why don't you give up?' Leon said reasonably. 'Emily doesn't want you!'

'Because she's got *you*!'

'Sure.'

'Just because she's your whore—'

'Now see here, you fucking dyke,' Leon said, his voice raw with anger, 'get the fuck out of here this instant. I'll see you off myself.'

Emily sat, paralysed, straining after each sharp footstep. Then she heard Sheila call out, 'You'll pay for this. The both of you. I'm warning you. No one talks to Sheila Lyall like that – but no one!'

'Who does she think she is?' Leon exclaimed when he returned. 'The Mafia?'

'I don't know,' Emily said softly. 'I only know what she called me.'

'Forget it,' Leon said. 'Forget her. You've gone pale.'

Training, years and years of training (*don't make a fuss, Emily*) made her say: 'I'm quite all right, Leon. Really I am.'

Emily bit her lip hard. She was humiliated and, even worse, afraid, because every instinct told her that Sheila Lyall would not forget what Leon had said.

'Wouldn't you like to see those billboards?' Leon asked. 'I'm dying to see them myself.'

They didn't have to drive far before Leon stopped the car. The hoarding was enormous and Emily thought she looked ... well, amazingly large. Leon thought she looked stunningly beautiful and said so. He also said he was bursting with pride because, 'Emily you've made it. You're big-time ...'

But Emily's instincts were concentrated on the certainty of the terrible price Sheila Lyall would exact.

*

Within less than twenty minutes he had actually bitten through and spoilt two pre-Castro Cuban cigars. There could be no more accurate index of Milt's rage than that and he contemplated his mutilated treasures with amazed horror. He and Leon had acquired several hundred uncontaminated Havana cigars at a Sotheby's sale when Dunhill had been forced to close down their famous humidifier room. And now he was treating them as if they were cigarettes! This, combined with Leon's obsession with a woman, and with his refusal to consider taking an offer way in excess of the true value of those pieces of real estate, was too much.

'I can't take it,' he said to his son-in-law, Wayne. 'I'm not going to stand for this.'

'But you told me you called him back and apologized,' Wayne said. He allowed his hard-won discipline to slip. 'That was crazy. Just crazy.'

'It looks that way to you, huh, Wayne?' Milt smiled weakly. 'You think I'm as crazy as my brother, huh?'

'It does look pretty dumb to me, yes.'

'You've got a lot to learn, my boy. A lot to learn.'

'Teach me,' Wayne said patiently, as if he were humouring a very old man.

'You think I've gone senile or something?' Milt said, reading his mind. 'Come on, admit it.'

'I'll admit no such thing,' Wayne felt himself flush. 'I asked you to explain, you know.'

'Sure you did,' Milt said smoothly. 'Would you like a cigar?'

'Thank you. But it would be wasted on me.'

'I hoped you'd say that, Wayne.' Milt gave Wayne a shrewd, nearly affectionate look. 'You know how I feel about my brother... Leon thinks he's won this round, and he's quite right, of course. He's putting principles before business, because he can afford it. We all know that. But business, *our* business anyway, has always been a matter of negotiating with outsiders. Because LFE is private – no shareholders, no boardroom personality clashes – none of that shit to get in the way of decisions. Got it?'

'Sure, though I would like to know where all this is leading...'

'You're short on patience, Wayne. I'll get to the bottom line, but in my own good time.' There was a silence while he took several more energetic puffs on his cigar. 'To get back to what I said about Leon being able to afford it – sure, it will get around that Lerner brothers refused 110 million dollars for a mere twelve and a half per cent of their real estate.'

He paused again, making it clear that he was considering each word. 'Real estate only, mark you. None of our other stuff...'

'Turning down *110 million*!' Wayne broke in. 'Anyone who does that has got to be crazy.'

'Negotiation, Wayne, is the science and the art of business. How do you think Wall Street will view this? I'll tell you. Rumours will fly, and before you know it we'll get a higher bid. Because no one in their right senses would turn down such a generously overvalued offer. They could only have been refused because the Lerner brothers know its true value.'

'I see,' Wayne said slowly. 'You're right. I sure have got a lot to learn.'

'One day I'll tell you more about negotiation,' Milt said. 'Right now, there's big negotiations and there's small negotiations. I want for you to call in Blue Print Consultants and two or three others. I want in-depth reports on the kind of damage Emily Bradshaw could do to us.'

'Damage? How could Emily Bradshaw possibly hurt us?' Quickly Wayne amended this to, 'Hurt our products, I mean?'

'I know what you mean. Negotiation – remember – or are you too slow?'

'I see,' Wayne said. He smiled suddenly. 'I see the relevance of danger . . . she could hurt us real, real bad. Consumers associate Emily Bradshaw with danger, and that image would spin off on the product. Of course if she hadn't been nearly assassinated, we'd have been stuck with her. But right now – she'd be the kiss of death to any promotion.'

Milt put out his hand. 'Congratulations, my boy! You're a great student.'

'Hey, wait a minute. I just thought of something – we've contracted with Keith Summers and Rick Cooke.'

'Keith Summers? I met Rick Cooke at the hospital. Who's this guy Summers?'

'Her British agent. He'll never let us get away with this, he's got his commission to think of.'

'Negotiation, remember. We'll strike a deal. Calculate whatever the maximum would have made, add ten per cent and he's got the deal of his life. What's in it for us? Product protection, of course. We'll submit out reports along with our offer. There'll be more negotiations and then, when we think it's the right time, we'll add that ten per cent I spoke about. Summers will make, and she will make, and everyone will be happy.'

'Except Leon,' Wayne said, his voice tight. 'Leon won't . . .'

'Yes, I know. All of a sudden Leon's busy with principles.' Milt leaned across his desk. 'A principle is also a consequence,' he said bitterly. 'Never forget that. Leon forgot it, I think, or he never would have talked to *me* about principle . . .' He studied the framed photograph on his desk, then suddenly he handed it over to Wayne. 'Ruthie and Marcie and Leon and me,' he said, as if Wayne didn't know. 'Leon talks to me about principles; I'll talk to him about *vows*.' He walked round his desk, and seated himself in the chair beside his nephew. 'You see, Wayne, Leon says principles and vows are the same. I'll remind him of that. I'll have to remind him of that...' He clapped Wayne on the shoulder. 'And when I do ... that will be the ultimate negotiation.'

*

Rick Cooke was coming to dinne. at White Wings. Emily looked out at the dusky light. In the distance, in an emerald field, the white horse reminded her of white sails on a calm lake. The place was as peaceful and as gentle as a croquet lawn. Leon called it his retreat, and it was true they were cut off. Yet it was cheerful, and for Emily it was like being snowed in and praying for more snow.

Emily looked forward to Rick's visit. His presence would somehow authenticate her idyllic life...

Rick had called to ask whether he could come and see both of them about the *Virginia Byrnes Show*.

'You've sure got a great place here, Mr Lerner,' he said in that deep rolling voice of his. 'This is a castle.'

Though Rick was alone, his lively enthusiasm made it seem as if he had brought a group of appreciative party-makers with him.

He had some serious things to talk about, he told them. But all of that could wait. Right now he just wanted to look at Emily, because she looked so good and so relaxed.

He had brought a selection of the newest Reagan jokes, and rolled them out one after the other. It was this, more than anything, which made Emily aware of New York speed, of the pace of New York change. In New York a day equals a season, she thought, as even the speed of their laughter made her feel very far from home.

It made her think of a day when she had been driving into London from Heathrow after an absence of three months. Snarled in traffic because of some Buckingham Palace ceremony, she had been comforted because there had been *no* real movement, *no* real change. Now she thought: in London there are only yesterdays, in New York there are no yesterdays. If you were away from New York for just nine days, you were aware of it; all the changes were felt at once, just as soon as you returned. She remembered that return to London very well – all that had changed was that the elderly newsagent's shop had been taken over by a Pakistani.

Both Rick and Leon were on constant starter's orders – as she had been, until she had been gunned down and stopped. For the first time she felt a twinge of resentment.

Rick showed them some snapshots of Katie Williams and of Andy. He was proud of the way Katie had changed since Tom Janowski's wife had taken her under her wing. Katie was a whizz at dressmaking, so Rick was checking out one or two designer schools for her. Katie was really coming on, she was learning not to apologize every five minutes, he said. Now, that was progress for you . . .

All his jollity, all this warm camaraderie stopped when Charles said, 'I'm sorry to disturb you, Mrs Bradshaw, but Sir Thomas is on the line for you from London . . .'

'Oh, my God!' Emily cried, jumping out of her seat. 'Something's wrong! My father's not the sort to go in for long-distance calls.'

'Will you take the call in the library, Mrs Bradshaw? You can be more private there.'

'Daddy? What's wrong? Is Danny—?' she asked as soon as she got to the phone.

'That young man's in very good form. I had tea with him this afternoon.' Sir Thomas indulged in a brief chuckle, then he went on rapidly, 'When are you coming home?'

'In about three or four weeks. It's not definite, yet . . .'

'Pity,' Sir Thomas said pointedly.

'Why?'

'I think the boy's pining for you.'

'Simon says he's coping – and Ophelia's pulling her weight . . .'

'Yes, well. I thought long and hard before I made this transatlantic call, you see.' He paused and Emily could hear his breathing. 'That woman – Susan Waddington – she seems to be hanging around an awful lot.'

'But Daddy, Susan's Danny's violin teacher.' Freed of all anxiety, Emily laughed delightedly. 'She teaches Danny the violin. You met her yourself . . .'

'I am aware of that,' her father said coldly, 'but I thought I ought to warn you . . .'

'*Warn* me?' Emily repeated.

'This is rather . . . awkward. You're making a mistake if you think you can leave your husband to his own devices . . .'

'Oh, Daddy,' Emily said, laughing helplessly. 'Simon is perfectly capable of looking after himself. Besides, I left the deep-freeze stocked up with enough food to last for months!'

'I see. Well, I wouldn't mention this call to Simon if I were you. How's the arm?'

'Improving.'

'Good. Well, goodnight, Emily.'

'Goodnight . . .'

Emily walked slowly back to the dining room. She told Leon and Rick that everything was fine, only Danny was pining . . . She didn't mention Susan . . . Simon had always been rather scathing about her. Still, coming from her father, that phone call had been uncommonly extravagant.

But Rick was talking about the *Virginia Byrnes Show*. He had come to a major decision and proposed to take them into his confidence. So he told them about Tom Janowski, about Vic Porter and Jake Williams. The show would be sensational. Sensational!

'Now here's what I want you to do for me.' His voice was low and urgent. 'The first thing you knew about this was just before the show – Got that?'

'Yes,' Emily said, 'but why?'

'Because Tom told me before he told his chiefs . . .' He looked at Emily. 'We owe him one. He took care of Katie for you . . .'

'I'll be grateful to him to my dying day,' Emily assured him earnestly.

'I don't like it,' Leon said. 'I want TAN to tighten security. I'll talk to Art Kristol myself.'

'Don't do that,' Rick begged. 'Please. You could blow the whole thing. Believe me, Tom's taking super security...'

'Frankly,' Leon said. 'I'm against it. I don't think Emily should go on the show.'

Rick showed dismay and seeing that, Emily said with a light laugh, 'Of course I'll go on. It's no more than my *duty* to go on.'

'Duty,' Leon repeated. 'Duty?'

'Well, of course. It's the way you behave when you know you're frightened, but don't want to let others down. You don't even want to let *yourself* down. It's like getting on a horse immediately after you've been thrown. Besides, I owe it to them.'

'The producers?' Leon snorted. 'You owe them nothing.' He was almost shouting. 'This is America, we don't go in for the stiff upper lip over here.'

'It's not that at all,' Emily said. 'When things go wrong, we shrug our shoulders and get on with it...'

'That's cool,' Rick agreed, nodding his head. 'Real cool...'

Making it clear that she did not want to talk about this, Emily went on, 'My father told me Danny's pining for me.'

'Tell you what we'll do for Danny,' Rick suggested. 'We'll have a video converted to the British system.'

'Thank goodness Simon's not here,' Emily said brightly. 'He'd hate those hoardings!'

PART V

Mid-October 1985

Chapter 17

Emily and Leon spent the night before the *Virginia Byrnes Show* apart. Emily returned to the Pierre and Leon to his own apartment. After all those delicious days and nights enjoying Leon's endless capacity for attention, the night was as lonely as it had been long.

During their time at White Wings, Leon had taught her to play chess, so she tried to read her book on chess games. But she couldn't concentrate or think about anything; she could only feel. And she had discovered emptiness.

The TAN people had booked her into the Pierre, and she and Leon had thought it best to go along with this. Twice during that long night Leon called – once to remind her to take her vitamins, and once to say that he missed her. But he sounded rather preoccupied, almost distressed. He had had dinner with his brother, and Emily had the feeling that things had not gone too well between them.

Now, at last, at last the *Virginia Byrnes Show* . . .

Emily's pulse throbbed in her throat. She was chatting to Rick in the Green Room and her shapely legs, swinging in time with her pulse, betrayed her nervousness. She wanted to run away . . . and she wanted to stay. Unbearable, and at the same time thrilling, her excitement was at its highest pitch, as if each nerve ending had come ecstatically – and alarmingly – alive.

She was thinking of Leon, thinking of the wonderfully enthusiastic way in which he would watch the show. She would not see him, which of course was only natural. And yet, to be seen and not to see – that was not natural. It made her feel a fraud. Made her wonder again about the author of *Sixty Seductive Salads from Fifty-one States*, about that nameless accident which had brought her to America, and brought her alive...

And then Tom Janowski was in the Green Room, his large muscular body encased in the tight uniform on which brass glinted. He told Emily and Rick that, at the very last minute, Vic Porter's nerve had failed him – he would not be on the show.

Emily's legs swung ever more wildly, 'You'll be very telegenic, Lieutenant Janowski,' she said. 'I can tell!' She turned to Rick. 'What time is it?'

'About twelve minutes to go,' Rick answered. Emily could hear his tongue click against his palate – it was obvious that his mouth was dry.

'You're nervous, Rick,' she said accusingly.

'Aw, too much coffee, I guess...'

Emily tried to study the posters of the stars who had appeared on the show, but her eyes kept returning to the poster of herself.

'Katie will watch the show with my wife,' said Tom Janowski.

Dazed, Emily asked vacantly, 'Katie?' The tension in the Green Room made it difficult for her to connect.

'Katie Williams,' Rick said. 'Remember how *worried* you were about her?'

'Your mouth has gone dry, Rick,' she commented.

Suddenly Tom was overtaken by a fit of nerves and his coffee cup rattled against the saucer. He stood up too quickly, the cup lost its perch on the saucer and hot coffee spilled over his leg. 'Ouch!' Tom called out. 'Jee-sus, that burns!'

'It won't show up on the screen,' Emily assured him. 'You can cover it with your other leg.'

'Are you all right, Tom?' Rick asked. 'Can I get you anything?'

'We're going on. Now,' Emily said.

The three of them followed the production assistant through the labyrinthine corridors, Emily keeping up a patter of conversation all the way: 'I hope your leg won't be scalded... I always feel as if I'm going in for an operation before I do a

296

show. It's like going in for elective surgery . . . In a way, it's like anaesthesia . . . you lose all your options, you see . . . Once you're on air, you're on . . . and there's nothing you can do about it . . .'

Emily's too nervous, Rick thought. She's freaking out – she thinks there's another fucking crazy out there – she'll be better when the show's out of the way. She looks great . . . but what if she makes a fuck-up of this?

*

Milt looked at his brother with acute distaste. Leon sat at the edge of the couch tapping his foot, and according to Milt, his breathing didn't sound right. 'For God's sake, Leon, relax,' Milt said. 'I've never seen you like this . . .'

'I didn't want her to go on,' Leon said. 'I don't like it.'

'You told her that?'

'Sure I told her!'

'So. Looks like she's a tough lady . . .'

'What have you got against her, Milt?' Leon asked impatiently.

'What have I got against her?' Milt laughed bitterly. 'Nothing. Why should I have anything against her? She only keeps you away from the office, from meetings. I mean, she's your boss now! It would be a waste of time if I had anything . . .'

'So I took nine days off. Nine days in a lifetime . . .'

'And did me a favour to give me two minutes on the phone . . .'

'Ah, Milt,' he said. 'She's a fantastic woman. Fantastic!'

'OK, so you're a love-sick teenager.'

'She's on!' Leon shouted. 'She's on. Doesn't she look great? She's beautiful, isn't she?'

*

In Sheila Lyall's apartment, both her guests – Wendy Griffiths and Arlene Roberts – were showing the effects of all that vodka. They had dispensed with tomato juice, but not with ice. Though indisputably the worse for wear, their analysis of Emily's appearance was cute.

'It kills me to say so,' Wendy said, 'but the bitch looks great.'

'She ought to,' Sheila drawled. 'You know what that little Adolpho costs?'

'The hell with that!' Wendy said. 'That blouse is a Chanel – costs twice as much.

'Pat Haines has got the best taste,' Sheila put in.

'Pat *Haines*?' Wendy said immediately. 'What's Pat Haines got to do with Emily Bradshaw?'

'Why, darling, didn't you know?' Sheila said sweetly. 'Leon had her send a van load of stuff to White Wings. So Emily could choose . . .'

'Oh, Wendy!' Arlene wailed. 'Wendy! How *could* he? How could Leon do that to you?'

'Leon's in love, didn't you know?' Wendy said, pouring another drink. 'Everyone out there will be crazy for her. With that arm in a sling – why, they'll just die for her!'

'He'll never marry her, though,' Arlene burst out. '*Never!*'

'Emily Bradshaw just happens to be married herself. Leon's her American fling . . .' Sheila Lyall spoke authoritatively.

'So far as Leon is concerned, Emily could be a virgin and marriage would still be out of the question,' Arlene stated.

'Come now, darling,' Sheila said scathingly. 'Just because you're even younger, and Milt hasn't married you . . .'

'That's the point,' Arlene said, her soft New England voice going softer. 'It's because of that vow. The Lerner brothers can't remarry – ever. It's a vow they made, to their wives.'

'You've got to be joking, Arlene! Come on, those wives are dead and buried.' Sheila's tone was scornful. 'Arlene's trying to pull one on me, isn't she Wendy?'

'No,' Wendy said wearily. 'No, she's not. Only Arlene's wrong about one thing . . .'

'But . . . Wendy . . .'

'It's not the vow they made to Marcie and Ruthie that counts. They're dead; they can't enforce it.' A brittle laugh escaped. 'The brothers made that vow to each other – that's what makes it so goddamn sacred.'

'They even had vasectomies,' Arlene put in.

'Vasectomies?' Sheila repeated sharply.

'Arlene shouldn't have mentioned that,' Wendy said. 'Listen,

Sheila, none of this leaves these four walls, OK?'

'Wendy, you shouldn't have said that,' Arlene said drunkenly. 'If *you* don't trust Sheila Lyall, I'm damn sure I do!'

'You're drunk, Arlene,' Wendy said.

'Why shouldn't she be?' Sheila said. 'She's adorable when she's drunk. She's adorable anyway.'

She lunged after Arlene, her bracelets tinkling and jangling. Her plait hung down her back – like a hangman's rope, Wendy thought.

Sheila was saying, 'Let's get out of here. Come and see Sheila's darling bedroom. We don't need Wendy, do we? We don't go for rejects...'

Wendy desperately wanted to see the show. Giggles came from the bedroom as she looked around Sheila's black and white living room. The black walls seemed to be coming down on her and she longed to scream, but couldn't even begin to weep. She felt she'd lost everything, even tears.

Even the living room is cruel, Wendy thought; she longed to escape. The sounds coming from Sheila's open bedroom door made her feel nauseous – she had to get out of here. But she had to watch Emily on that show... she forced herself to cross the living room and shut that bedroom door.

Suddenly Wendy remembered that she was recording the *Virginia Byrnes Show*, so there was no need to stay in Sheila Lyall's terrible black and white apartment. On the television, Emily Bradshaw was saying something about needless divorce. This was too much for Wendy and she picked up an empty vodka bottle and hurled it at the screen. Glass shattered all over the black and white check carpet.

She was about to leave when her eye fell on a lamp: Sheila Lyall's proudest possession. It was a genuine Tiffany glass Wysteria lamp, the only object in the room which was not black or white. Its soft, gentle lilac did wonders for that stark decor. Sheila Lyall really cared about that lamp; she boasted about it. She had an ongoing, intimate relationship with that lamp, she had said.

Scattered all over the carpet, Wendy thought it was much more beautiful... It certainly made her feel good. As highs go, this one beat every high she had ever known.

The black bile of her life began to thin, and lift.

There are worse things than being alive, she told herself.

*

At Bellevue Hospital, a collection of experts had gathered to watch the *Virginia Byrnes Show*. After many conferences, it had been decided that seeing Emily on the same show might well be an excellent form of shock therapy for Jake Williams. Amongst those assigned to his case, opinion was still divided over whether he was unable or unwilling to speak. Three days before the show, Jake had been moved out of his private room into a six-bedded maximum security ward.

For three days Jake's responses to television had been carefully monitored, but now a large team of doctors and psychologists had been assembled to study his reactions to Emily Bradshaw. Both diagnostically and therapeutically, it could be a useful experiment.

So far, Katie's and Andy's visits had been ineffectual. Either Jake had had no reaction, or he had fooled the experts into believing he had no reaction.

Unaware of Vic Porter's revelations about Jake and Homes for Hope, the experts sat back to watch the show...

*

In London, Simon Bradshaw was equally unaware of this new development on Jake Williams. And even if he had known, it is doubtful whether he would have been more than vaguely interested. Susan Waddington was spending more and more time at Lamont Road, and frequently spent whole nights there. They let it be known that she was helping out until a new *au pair* could be found, but in the meantime Emily was not to be worried about her family's domestic arrangements. Accordingly, Emily was unaware of Ophelia's departure.

Meanwhile, it was really rather pleasant having Susan around. Besides, Danny had made great strides with his violin.

So it was that while Danny was practising upstairs in his room, while Simon and Susan were settling themselves for a

300

pre-dinner drink as they watched the evening news, that they saw a brief clip of the *Virginia Byrnes Show*.

It seems a blackmailing tax-collector was considered newsworthy... *More* British publicity for Emily. More snide remarks from his partners... Clearly, Emily did not know when to draw the line.

And Susan listened sympathetically. She too abhorred sensationalism. For a man in Simon's position, it was quite the wrong thing. Which was why she couldn't help saying that Emily was really rather selfish.

*

One of the consequences of the shooting of Emily Bradshaw was the instant increase in ratings for the *Virginia Byrnes Show*. The consensus of press comment on this was that it was unsurprising. After all, Emily Bradshaw was not only stunningly beautiful, but as the daughter of Sir Thomas Rice she had a visible aura of aristocracy. She recalled a more graceful era, a more gentle culture. Some papers went so far as to remark on her resemblance to Princess Di – her voice, height, colouring and style were similar. The significant difference, however, was that she was a Princess Di with a formidable blend of the smarts.

Some papers carried favourable reports on the history of the *Virginia Byrnes Show*. Thanks to Emily Bradshaw and Jake Williams, the show received infinitely more coverage in one week that since its inception six years previously. Now that it had become newsworthy, it was considered to be a caring, courageous show which explored and exposed sensitive and crucial human issues.

Virginia Byrnes was profiled in *People* magazine. A full-page photograph focused on her legs. Banked by TV screens, standing tall, knee lifted so that an exceedingly shapely foot could be displayed over a high pile of mail about the shooting, Virginia was now a card-carrying member of the media elite. Nor could she have asked for a more glamorous – or sexy – credential.

Well before the negotiations about Emily's reappearance had been concluded, Virginia had been insisting on having more say in the format of the show. The shooting had been Virginia's lucky break – the consequences of that shooting could not be left to chance...

And then on the day before the show, in the late afternoon, the producers were advised of the newest developments. It was Rick Cooke who told them that Jake Williams was an extortionist and a blackmailer. Rick's strategy was devastatingly effective; from the president down, everyone at TAN entreated him to get Tom Janowski and Vic Porter on the show.

The gift of a second sensation having fallen into Virginia's lap, she determined to have her own way about the order of events on her show. Virginia pulled out every trick she knew; she even suggested that they find someone else to take her place...

Virginia won.

The *Virginia Byrnes Show* was on from noon until one. But when you got down to it, there were only forty-seven on-air minutes. The 'hour' was divided into three segments of thirteen minutes and the entire first segment would be given over to Emily. Halfway through that, both Emily and the audience would be warmed up by viewing a brief clip of the shooting itself. Virginia staked her all on her instinct that Emily was not the type to have asked to see it. As it was, Emily's arm in the sling would create sympathy and then, after her reaction to viewing her own shooting, Lieut Janowski would be introduced. Virginia would question him about the gunman, about gun control and so on, and then at a strategic moment – with only two or three minutes to go before the end of the second segment – she would inform the world about Jake Williams, the blackmailer. The tension would be carried over into the third segment.

Virginia gave the performance of her life and ratings soared. Even the president of the entertainment division looked at her through new eyes. Virginia Byrnes had earned the kind of in-house studio reputation they understood best. She was tough and she was mean.

*

Dr Alex Levy had only recently received his PhD in clinical

psychology and was regarded as something of a prodigy at Bellevue Hospital. His was the only dissenting voice on using the *Virginia Byrnes Show* as a diagnostic and therapeutic tool. Dr Levy was nothing if not pompous. He had written a paper entitled 'Information Overloads: Non-communication in the Communication Industry'.

When his advice was disregarded, Dr Levy pleaded for compromise. He suggested that before subjecting Jake to this technique, the content of the show should be monitored. After all, they had recourse to technology – the show could be taped.

Levy typed out an official statement dissociating himself from the procedure, and let it go at that. As far as he was concerned, he was covered.

No one, not even Levy, considered whether the original shooting would be screened again.

No one in the team was against technology, however. All the patients in the ward had their neurological responses measured and Jake Williams registered the maximum stress-response that could be recorded. Still Jake did not speak. The diagnosis of a 'brief reactive psychosis' – a schizotypal personality disorder, with catatonic reaction – a stupor with mutism' was in jeopardy.

Jake was removed to a single-bed ward. Levy considered it to be a dangerous form of punitive solitary confinement and said so, loudly, clearly and often.

By the time the experts recognized that out of sheer obstinacy they had allowed Levy's pomposity to stand in the way of their assessment of his opinion, it was too late.

Jake believed it was real crazy – but at the same time, unsurprising – the way everyone had got everything wrong about him. Everyone, that is, except for Emily Bradshaw. Somehow she had understood that he had aimed to miss – she had said so on the *Virginia Byrnes Show* – and although he wasn't absolutely sure about this, he had the feeling that she was probably right. Anyway, since being at the hospital he had thought very little of Emily Bradshaw and all her talk about genes and blood tests which had compelled him to pull that trigger. His mind had skidded away from all that and then gone into endless reverse: and when it did not escape into sleep, it took refuge in its own distant past. Sometimes, though, he would try to understand what he had done, but his thoughts would not connect, for he could get no closer than struggling to remember why he had not taken the train from Queens to work that day.

Because if he had not heard Emily Bradshaw on his car radio, his life would not have broken down the way it had. But here his mind would cut out, or swoon away from the realities of Katie and Andy. Shock takes many forms and, in those rare moments when he was able to bring himself to think at all, he was fixated on why he had driven to work.

It came to him, of course, during the *Virginia Byrnes Show*. He had been meant to collect $7,000 from Dr Sam Purdy . . .

Until then, though, his entire being had been concentrated on dredging up memories of his father. He would contemplate his navel and see his father; he believed he could still see his father's large round, hard stomach. He remembered the stomach and not the face. The face was a photograph, merely – the stomach though, was an authentic memory. Which was strangely comforting.

Jake's body rocked back and forth, back and forth. For years and years he had believed he would find his father, and instead, just before his mother's funeral, he had discovered his father's death certificate. *Suicide!* Betrayal – his mother's lifelong betrayal – had compounded his silent, terrible grief, but at the same time his mind continued to deny that his saintly mother had lied. After that, his life was a series of black moods and blacker doubt. Even now he hesitated, fumbled – his mother had told him a half-truth and not a whole lie – after all, his father *had* gone away . . .

Back and forth his body rocked, back and forth – tender as a cradle. In all that anarchy of Jake's endless confusion, the rhythm of his own body was his only comfort. Abruptly, the rocking stopped. Janowski's absurd lie that he had been ripping off the government in order to give to the poor, was as illuminating as truth. Everything was being polluted, even the purity of his proudest achievement – Jake Williams had never defrauded the US government, nor even violated the IRS code of conduct.

That had been the whole point – his trick had been entirely honourable. He had merely induced those taxpayers whom he called his contacts to be charitable. Was it not written in the Bible that charity shall cover a multitude of sins?

Sure, his contacts had paid him, and paid their taxes too. Take Sam Purdy and the way he lied to his poor wife about his earnings.

If Sam Purdy was a hundred times richer than his wife suspected, he got to keep his secret at a bargain-basement price. For the Sam Purdys of this world, seven thousand dollars – a quarter – was peanuts. All those countless adulterers who had the cheek to believe they had every right to get Uncle Sam to pay for their whores! So far, Jake had only netted six of those sinners: a total of $150,000. Not bad when you considered that on the strength of this alone, there would be a new Home for Hope. These bastards were cheating on their wives and kids, so there was nothing immoral about inducing – or forcing – them to become involuntary contributors. Far from immoral, he, Jake Williams, a Lamb of God, had given them a secret redemption: *Behold the Lamb of God which taketh away the sin of the world . . .*

All this was his secret too, a hidden private joke that made his insides glow.

True, his mother had wanted him to be a senior corporate executive. And but for Don Cooper, who had been sent to Brookline College Accounting School to recruit for the IRS, he never would have tasted real power. In a way, Don Cooper had reminded him of his mother. For one thing, he called Jake 'son', and something about the shape of his shoulders and chest had been reminiscent of his mother's ample bosom. But besides that, it was his thick gold wedding ring and chewed nails which had been eerily like his mother's hands. Like Don Cooper was his mother's messenger . . . His hands constantly stroked his pearl-grey tie, or fingered his broad brown belt as, lovingly, he recounted his first taste of pure power. That was when Don Cooper, only twenty-four, had the senior partner of one of the big eight accounting companies call him direct. 'Hell, son,' Don Cooper said. 'When that man wanted to talk to me, he didn't get his secretary to make the call for him.' Here Don Cooper rolled his fat hands into fists and put one at his ear, and the other at his mouth, and conjured up an image of a telephone. 'No, sir! The senior partner was on the line himself. I tell you, son, that was the big time. It gives you a good feeling, you know? Sure, they'd put in thirty years' work on a deceased estate, and it was all taken apart by a kid like me, get it?' Don Cooper's oversized hands thumped the desk as he went on with his sales pitch. 'See, you get power and you get security, in the Service. You're one of a group of fifteen, you report to a group supervisor and you can do your own thing.' Don Cooper had looked at him shrewdly. 'I keep to myself, don't mix if I don't want to.' Then Don paused and stroked his tie and, in a subtle way, puffed out his chest. 'Know what, son? When you have the ability to cause distress to others, you don't need to depend on company.' He went on smoothly, 'Course you only work a forty-hour week and *you* have the authority to determine the correct tax. The people you deal with – well, son, you're their boss. Because it's all based on fear, son; it's all based on fear. And when you get senior partners who deal in billions of dollars shit scared of you, well then, you know you've tasted power.'

Alone in a narrow, clinical hospital bed, Jake had a revelation. Don Cooper was everything he had imagined his father to be. His stomach was the same shape as his father's stomach and that shape was the only solid memory he had.

Ten years in the Service, and still Jake had not come into contact with a senior partner of one of the big eight, but he had his power just as he had smelt their fear. No, Don Cooper had not exaggerated.

Charity shall cover the multitude of sins...

Still and all, he was willing to admit that he wouldn't have got on to the charity angle if he hadn't met Annette Burg, Dr Gray's secretary. The irony was that he was working at dentist Dr Calvin Gray's office at the time, conducting an audit on the premises. On Jake's first day there, Annette had been full of smiles. But the next day her lips drooped, as if her mouth had fallen in because she'd suddenly had all her teeth pulled. It turned out that after four years of promises, promises, she had been dumped by Dr Gray... Annette thought there was something Jake should know – she had some information.

Of course he had been trained to accept information so, when they met at a bar the next day, he had the official form right there with him. Annette was shaking, he remembered, shaking and pale, and knocking back the martinis.

But what struck Jake even more forcibly was that Annette had not known there was anything in it for her. She was totally ignorant of what the IRS referred to as the reward/incentive system. She wasn't doing it for the money – she hadn't expected to make a dime. It was only then that Jake realized it was revenge she was after, revenge and nothing *but* revenge. That was way back in '81; he'd been with the Service for six years, yet every detail of that form was with him still, including Annette's blood-red nails against the black ballpoint pen as she filled it out and signed it. Especially the way her pen had stabbed *no spouse* where the form stated name of spouse.

Jake had no need to close his eyes to bring the form back into sharp focus. His lips moved imperceptibly as he recited the details to himself.

The form itself came before him, clear, exact and quick – as if he had pressed the enter key on a computer and flashed it on the screen.

Application for Reward for
Original Information

This application is voluntary and the information requested enables us to determine and pay rewards. We use the information to record a claimant's reward as taxable income, and to identify any tax outstanding (*including that on a return filed jointly with a spouse*) against which the reward would first be applied. We need social security numbers on this application in order to process it. Not providing the information requested may result in the suspension of the processing of this application. Our authority for asking for information on this form is derived from 26 USC 6001, 6109, 6011, 7623, 7802, and 5 USC 301.

Name of claimant: ANNETTE BURG	Social Security number 46382
Name of Spouse: NO SPOUSE	Social Security number

Address including ZIP code	504 HYLTON ROAD NY11672

I am applying for a reward in accordance with the law and regulations, for original information furnished, which was of a violation of the internal revenue laws of the United States and which also led to the collection of taxes, penalties, fines and forfeitures. I was not an employee of the Department of the Treasury at the time I came into possession of the information nor at the time I divulged it.

Name of IRS employee to whom violation was reported JAKE WILLIAMS	Title INTERNAL REVENUE AGENT	Date violation reported (*Month, day, year*) — 7.30.81

who committed the violation
DR CALVIN GRAY

Address, including ZIP code	4441 E. 65th ST. NEW YORK NY10072

Under penalties of perjury, I declare that I have examined this application and my accompanying statements, if any, and to the best of my knowledge and belief they are true, correct and complete. I understand the amount of any reward will represent what the District Director considers appropriate in this particular case.

Annette Burg   4.12.81

--   ----------------------
Signature of claimant   Date

Of course he never did get to see the completed form – it came under the direction of a special department.

So that was how he started in on Homes for Hope. Because when the form was signed, Annette promised that if she got anything he would get half.

Annette kept her promise.

Jake got twelve and a half thousand dollars!

And if he donated every single cent to a charity, he could not be accused of violating the IRS code of conduct.

Of course, if the dentist hadn't dumped Annette, he would have got away with half a million dollars of capital gains he'd made on some stocks. He had tried to offset those gains against a painting he'd bought. So Annette's information was that he had back-dated the real date of purchase – and with penalties and so on, the IRS collected a quarter of a million dollars: ten per cent of that came to twenty-five thousand dollars. Once

Jake donated his share to a charity, he wasn't required to pay any tax.

It was beautiful because it was clean.

Lieut Janowski had got him all wrong, but that no longer mattered. What mattered now was that he had lost his private joke and his inner glow – the trick that made his life tick was gone.

He understood now that his way had been pointed the day he had held his father's death certificate in his hands. He had placed the choice of his timing on hold, that was all.

His dark trick – that anyone else would have called blackmail – the trick that had blasted through his darkest days was finished.

It was the exercise of other people's fear that made his life relevant and set him apart from the masses. Of course, Katie and Andy were afraid of him too, but that was the sort of ordinary power given to most husbands – most fathers.

But *was* he Andy's father? Was he a father? There was no certainty, no absolute proof, which was a good thing. There were no roots to hold him down, hold him back.

Thanks to Emily Bradshaw, he was free.

*

To the very end, Jake Williams had outwitted all the experts. Even the method of his suicide mocked them, as it had mocked their skills. It was as easy as bending, twisting and then breaking a hairpin. For a hairpin can easily be made to be sharp as a needle. Even though only a few nurses used thick, heavy hairpins, exactly which nurse it had belonged to remained a mystery. But it was obvious that Jake had found a harmless hairpin, bent it, wound and wound the bent area of the pin until it broke. Then he had plunged it into the radial artery in his wrist.

The humiliating thing was that it was one of those avoidable suicides. The experts agreed that Jake's move to end his own life probably began no more than twelve hours after his *Virginia Byrnes Show* treatment. Levin was vindicated, but even he saw it as an unwelcome victory.

Chapter 18

The following morning found Emily still at the Pierre. She and Leon planned to drive out to White Wings as soon as he and Milt were through with their breakfast meeting.

Emily was entirely alone, and altogether unprepared for the journalist from *New Lights* who broke the news of Jake Williams' suicide. So it was that the questions about her role in his life and death were raised by Emily herself.

As soon as Rick heard he tried to call her, but of course her line was busy. He ran all the way to the hotel and was racing towards her suite to bang on the door, when he was stopped by security guards. Then he had to persuade the manager of the hotel to allow him to interrupt Emily's call.

All Emily's calm had left her and she was hysterically inconsolable. In desperation, Rick called Dr Cowan who came at once and administered a sedative. He also left some barbiturates.

*

Leon was in the habit of using his Porsche whenever he went out to White Wings. But Dr Cowan suggested that Emily would be more comfortable in the limo; she might even be able to sleep. She was very quiet, and with her head laid back and her eyes closed, so peaceful that he thought she was asleep. He stared at her wan face, noting that her complexion seemed yellow rather than pale. He caught himself checking on her breathing, as if he half-expected it to be as weak as she looked. I could kill Jake

Williams for what he's done to Emily, he thought, and then realized his utter stupidity. Of course, Jake Williams had killed himself.

But though she looked peaceful, rhymes and jingles jangled in her mind: *When my back began to smart, 'twas like a penknife in my heart. When my heart began to bleed, 'twas death and death and death indeed,* competed or merged with *Don't care was made to care, don't care was done. Don't care was put in a box and stewed till she was done.* At the same time she was carrying on her lifelong habit of engaging in an interior dialogue with her mother. She ached for her mother, and like a *mantra* or a slogan, the jingles were a way of short-circuiting thought – also a return to childhood, where suicide was as unmentionable as swearing.

Though she was convinced that she would never get over Jake's death, she was nevertheless determined to pull herself together. She longed for her mother and couldn't help noticing how much more acute her longing became when she recalled – and obeyed – her mother's teaching. *Don't make a fuss, Emily! . . . Think of the burden you are putting on others and you will lessen it for yourself . . .* But Emily cared about nothing except what she had said on that show . . . So, again and again, that nursery jingle ran in her mind.

Of course, Penny had been a childhood friend and, but for Penny's suicide, *Defending Wives* might never have been written. Penny, whose life had drained out of her on her married man's bed, the bed in which he and his wife still slept. Penny had slashed her wrists, and Jake had made a longer and more agonizing slash, all the way down from elbow to wrist. And Emily's own arm was in a sling.

She wished she could rest her mind in a sling the way she rested her arm. She wished she could stop thinking. Her head ached and her brain felt swollen. At White Wings she and Leon played chess, and though it soothed, the jangling continued. She found herself reciting those rhymes to Leon – also telling him more about her mother, about her childhood and about Melissa. The warmth of his interest made it possible for her to talk about herself without feeling in the least shy or self-indulgent.

She talked about Danny, about his tousled blond hair, his angelic blue eyes and his violin lessons. She told Leon how she dreaded her son's having to go away so soon to the Trevor-Winston School. 'He's not boarding school material,' she said sadly. 'Of course it will be hard on me, but I'm thinking of Danny. I know it's the wrong thing.'

'Surely your opinion counts for something?'

'Not when Danny's father and both his grandfathers went to that school!'

'How does Danny himself feel about going?' Leon interrupted.

'I don't know. I'm not sure.'

'But you've asked him?'

'Not directly.'

'Then you'd better ask him directly!' Leon exploded. 'This is crazy, sending a small boy away without even discussing it with him. It makes no sense,' he said, shaking his head. 'It sounds like outright cruelty to me.'

'We've talked about taking Blue, his teddy-bear, with him.'

'Talk to *him*, Emily,' Leon said angrily. 'Talk to Danny, not to his teddy-bear.'

Once, and only once, Leon mentioned Milt's son's suicide. But he would not discuss it because he had not come to terms with it. 'Because coming to terms with what Martin could – and did – do to himself, would be the ultimate self-destruction.' His voice sank to a whisper and Emily had to strain to hear.

'I think I understand what you mean,' she said slowly. 'Not long after Penny's suicide, Simon and I had a disagreement. I wish I could remember what it was about, but I can't. Anyway, we were in the kitchen and all through that long row I thought of the bread-knife, of plunging it into my chest. I remember playing with it, pointing it towards my heart. That knife got me through that quarrel. For a long time, it got me through all sorts of things . . .'

Emily's mood shifted. There was only one thing her mind refused to consider, and that was going home – to London. Talking about the knife had hurled her into her own kitchen.

This made her aware that it was some time since she had

spoken to either Simon or Danny. She had received a letter from Danny, though: a few lines really, with coloured drawings – painstakingly done – of Hal playing the violin. Strange how little she missed him, it made her feel almost unnatural.

That was why she wrote to him so often. Left-handed letters, she thought.

*

And then it was back to New York and once again she found herself walking faster, thinking faster. She understood now what was meant when people said: 'She thinks on her feet . . .' In New York, everything – even emotions – appeared to be so much enlarged that, like an enlarged heart on an X-ray, they showed.

Meanwhile, there was business to attend to.

Suddenly Emily wanted to make money for its own sake. She had become passionate about this and it was both an urge and an obsession. She found it strange, yet did not try to understand it. It was a fever and she had caught it – it could not be cured, only satisfied.

Emily had discovered ambition, and ambition makes its own laws. She called her ambition New York fever. Which meant many, many hours with Rick in his new suite of offices on the forty-first floor. Sometimes Emily felt she was in an aeroplane, the lift went so fast. It was movement all the way – movement accelerated and accentuated by negotiation and counter-negotiation.

Emily overcame her reluctance to work with Sheila Lyall. Because as Rick said, if she wanted to get anywhere with her own show, *Family Mix*, she could not allow a dumb personality clash with Sheila Lyall to get in her way . . . Before the New York fever hit her, Emily would have thought nothing of turning it down. Once, the alternatives to serious money would have merited serious attention. Now, however, there was no alternative to consider . . .

Jake's suicide had sparked intense debate. The producers of *Perceptions* were planning an entire show around this and, of course, Emily had been invited to take part. That was in three weeks' time and after that . . . but that was where Emily's mind cut out – it seemed it could go no further.

In New York, Emily did not live in Leon's apartment, but at the Pierre. It seemed only right and proper – she was, after all, a married woman. She saw him almost every night and whenever she returned to the hotel, she would find messages from him. Typewritten messages in their envelopes with cellophane windows continued to excite her; there were always surprises.

As soon as her arm had come out of the sling, she adopted the practice of New York career women – walking in jogging shoes while carrying her high heels. She was still holding her shoes when she opened the envelopes. She found not one, but two glorious surprises. The first was from Leon: *Invited to dinner at the White House. Pat Haines, the personal shopper at Bloomingdales, is expecting your call. Hope you are as pleased as I am. Leon.* The second was equally exciting: *Em, dearest, please call Rebecca Pelham at 935 4141.*

Thirty seconds later Emily was speaking to Rebecca. 'I just happened to mention to Derek that I saw you on the cover of *People*, then he calmly told me where you were staying.'

'Oh, Rebecca, what super luck! When do we meet?'

'As soon as you like.'

Emily glanced at her watch. It was five o'clock and she had planned to wash her hair – later she was meeting Leon and the Kristols. She said, 'How about now? This minute? Could you come to the hotel?'

'I'm on my way. Can't *wait* to see you!'

Rebecca was as good as her word. It was two years since they had seen one another and only a few months since Emily had wanted to write and tell Rebecca about that incident with Sheila Lyall and the frozen peas. Rebecca was reassuringly unchanged. Slim and immaculate in her serviceable suit, she reminded Emily of herself and the insipid looks that she had once preferred.

Both women were equally impatient to talk about Emily.

But first they disposed of the usual news about husbands and children; then Rebecca had to tell her why she was in New York. Her husband, Tim, been transferred from Spain to the British

Consulate, because of all things, he was an expert in textiles.

'What's this I hear about you and Leon Lerner?' Rebecca asked with a mischievous smile. 'I'm dying to hear *all* about it!'

If they had been in London, Rebecca would have said nothing. But being far from home altered things. Their intimacy intensified, and if their usual constraints were not dismissed, they were lessened. Besides, they had been at school together in the same year. Even so, Emily blushed. 'What *have* you heard? Who told you?'

'Derek Partridge. We lunched today. You know he's our ambassador – Simon stayed with him.'

'Of course I know Derek. He visited me when I was in hospital.'

'I gather Leon Lerner is a spectacular tycoon, even by American standards.'

'What on earth did Derek tell you?'

'He said that you and Leon Lerner are having a thing. Does Simon know?'

'Of course not. At least I hope not.'

'Tell me about him.'

Emily leaned forward in her seat and bit her lip. 'He's the kindest man I've ever known,' she said.

'And fantastic in bed, I suppose,' Rebecca said sympathetically.

Once again Emily blushed. 'I never knew it could be like that,' she said slowly, as if she were still trying to make sense of her emotions. 'He's so extraordinarily tender. He cares so much.' She laughed weakly. 'He even supervises my vitamin intake.'

'You *have* gone American, Emily. Vitamin intake! I never thought I'd live to see the day when I would hear you – a Cambridge double first – talk about vitamin intake!'

But Emily would not respond to criticism. 'I love America,' she said, allowing her enthusiasm to show. 'The American language is seductive, too.'

Rebecca, in turn, allowed her curiosity to show. 'He's a Jew, isn't he?' she asked.

'Yes.'

Rebecca's avid eyes narrowed with excitement. 'Is it true that they're more passionate?' she asked. 'I don't think I know any Jews. One simply doesn't meet them.'

'You'll meet them in New York,' Emily said seriously. 'I'd never met one myself until I met Leon...'

'He's obviously very generous.' Rebecca threw an assessing glance around the sitting room of Emily's suite. 'Installing you in a suite...'

'Leon's not paying for any of this,' Emily said quickly. 'TAN is putting me up here.' She paused for a moment and went on, 'But yes, he *is* generous. Remarkably generous. Do you know, he's set up a trust fund for Katie Williams? She's the widow, you know. It was her husband who...'

'I know that. I read about it in Spain – but you know that, of course; I wrote you at once.'

'I didn't know, exactly. I suppose you wrote to Lamont Road?' Emily did not wait for a reply. 'It's odd, isn't it? I wasn't keen on this promotion thing, but Simon persuaded me. And then over that... incident... and all the publicity – well, he wanted me to give the whole thing up.'

'That must have been rather awkward,' Rebecca said. She added shrewdly. 'How do you feel about Leon? He hasn't a wife... So...'

'I don't honestly know,' Emily answered, looking away. 'I'm not thinking beyond my last commitment. My TV show. That sort of thing...' She turned toward Rebecca and her chin tilted upwards as she said resolutely, 'I'm living for the moment.'

*

Living for the moment is a blessed way of abolishing fear. Besides, the pace of life made living for the moment a necessity. Meetings began at breakfast. For those who need to postpone the future, to postpone thought, the split-second life is the safest life. Living for the moment also eliminates the past – only the immediate present remains.

Until one hectic, crowded day when Emily realized that though her telephone calls to Simon had diminished, the split-second life did not entirely guard her from her distant reality.

For Simon sounded so remote and, Emily thought, so resentful, that she phoned as seldom as possible. She detailed her tight schedule and when Simon suggested – as she had hoped he would – that she restrict her calls to two a week, she had been relieved. She continued to send notes and cards to Danny.

Once, she had believed that she could not have survived being parted from Danny for so long. And here she was, not only surviving but thriving.

Yet her conversation with Rebecca had forced her to acknowledge the future. But only fleetingly, for the future, she told herself, does not exist – and in any case, she had no time for that now.

Above all, how could she think of the future until after she and Leon had dined at the White House?

*

Emily was on her way to her appointment with Pat Haines at Bloomingdales. These days she walked fast enough to look like a real New Yorker. Seeing Rebecca yesterday had been exciting enough, but then, on top of that, there had been last night. Such happiness could scarcely be borne – it was almost terrifying. Emily, in her lace-up jogging shoes, walked faster. Then suddenly she stopped still. How could she explain away last night's gift of a diamond necklace and matching bracelet? Well then, she would never wear it ... except, of course, that rhinestone was at the height of fashion now: it could be mistaken for fake jewellery.

On the other hand, might this not be some sort of declaration – or commitment – from Leon? He had bought them, he said, because he happened to have a meeting with Alf Herzog, a jeweller as well-known as Cartier who was also one of Leon's tenants. As for the annual insurance premium – well it didn't bear thinking about.

Just before she entered Bloomingdales she exchanged her jogging shoes for beige high heels. She had grown to depend on how she looked. The state of her appearance affected the state of her mind and her own hair could influence her mood. She thought of her sensible walking shoes at Lamont Road, but reminded herself that she was now in New York where it was not unfair to be fortified by the right clothes, the right hair style...

Pat Haines was businesslike and efficient, yet not at all brisk. Choosing the right clothes was a serious matter – no less important, say, than choosing a place in which to live. The main thing was not to feel harassed. Pat already had an excellent idea of what Emily would like, because she knew what she had chosen from the selection sent to White Wings.

When she was shown into Pat's den, Emily felt as if she had been ushered into a secret room. For there, hidden behind a door marked 'private', was an enchantingly cosy living room. It was hard to believe she was not visiting Pat in her own apartment. The room was elegant rather than opulent – two sofas faced one another across a coffee table which held magazines and books and coffee. The doors leading off it might well have been those of bedrooms.

A copy of *Defending Wives* lay on a side table. 'I read your book,' Pat said.

Emily said, 'Oh...' and let it go.

'It was honest,' Pat continued.

'Thank you,' Emily said. The book, or rather its content, had become irrelevant in her life. It was the consequences of the promotion and not of the book that concerned her now. Emily was not one to delude herself; but for Jake Williams, *Defending Wives* would not have been on that coffee table.

'It sure is an honest book,' Pat repeated. She looked at Emily appraisingly. 'It's just adorable to dress women like you,' she said, her hoarse voice reminding Emily of Sheila Lyall. 'You should be in *Dynasty*...'

'You're very kind,' Emily said.

An assistant approached warily and there was a whispered consultation. 'Excuse me, Emily,' Pat said, standing up. 'This is one call I have to take.'

Emily watched her tall form glide away. Pat smiled a lot and Emily imagined her practising that brilliant smile in a mirror. She was tall, graceful and glitteringly fashionable. Yet every movement, even to the widening of her eyes, struck Emily as being studied, artificial. Emily could hear squeals coming from the fitting rooms and a few moments later two girls aged between ten and twelve emerged. Each carried a great bundle of clothes. Emily listened to their chatter – apparently they had found things that would be 'just darling for Palm Beach'. 'You don't need twelve pairs of panties,' their mother said. Through an armoury of wire bands, the older of the two responded, 'Daddy's picking up the bill . . .' The child sounded tired, Emily thought, also bitter. She wondered who they were.

One of them noticed Emily. 'I know you,' she said. 'I'm Candy and this is my sister, Nancy.'

'She got herself shot,' her sister said, sounding bored. 'On the *Virginia Byrnes* creep *Show*.'

'Oh yeah, I saw it.' The child turned away. 'Janie will just eat her heart out when she sees how many designer jeans I got . . .'

Pat and her brilliant smile were back. 'Let's go,' she said. 'I've alerted the sales people.'

Fascinated, Emily followed Pat as she glided through the store. The sensual sweeping way Pat handled the clothes and then draped them over the assistants' arms reminded Emily of a ballerina.

Suddenly Emily said, 'Forgive me asking you this, but were you in ballet?'

'Yes, I was with the Martha Graham Dance Company . . . a long time ago!' A twitch of suspicion: 'Why did you ask?'

'You have extraordinarily graceful movements.'

When all the clothes had been chosen and the decisions made, Emily believed that she had made a friend. Later, over coffee in her personal shopper's den, Pat said, 'You're a lucky woman, Emily. I've known him for years and he's a good man. I knew his late wife, you know . . .'

'Oh,' Emily said. She wanted to ask for details and sensed that Pat expected this, too. But she could not. It would have been a kind of disloyalty, and that went against her instincts. Instead she said, 'You've been wonderfully kind to me.'

Pat shrugged.

*

Small wonder, Rick was flying high. Emily had been a hot property, now she was the *hottest* property.

Negotiations with TAN for Emily's own show were under way. Rick had dreamed up the show: *Family Mix* – the nuclear, the extended, the single . . . A whole new world was opening up to Rick; clients were coming to see him from Texas, for God's sake . . . And from Great Britain, too. The money wasn't great, but Emily was ecstatic. Charles Sutherland, the executive producer and a great power at London Television Company, wanted Emily to host a new show: *The Emily Bradshaw Show*. Rick was currently negotiating a co-production between the UK and the US.

At night, Rick took his pocket calculator to bed with him. Dreaming that he had miscalculated, he would wake up. Again and again he checked his projections . . . for Emily, for Keith and for himself. It was mind-blowing. Undreamable heights! He became obsessed with that simple, tiny and infallible piece of technology. At first it was something like a good-luck talisman, then more like a magic wand. One compulsive night was spent calculating how much Emily was generating into the economy – a million dollar paperback sale, serialization and foreign rights, to say nothing of the *Kay-Chow* products. To top it all, film and TV bids were being negotiated. As for Europe and Britain, well – *wow* . . . Because one way or another, through his complicated deals he would get seventeen per cent of Emily's gross.

He had backed his instincts, even before he had seen Emily's fragile, glowing complexion. More than a hot property, Emily was priceless.

So why was he afraid to congratulate himself? He was neurotic, that's what he was, a neurotic of the 'things-are-too-good-to-be-true' variety.

It was no good, he couldn't kid himself.

It was her affair with Leon that bugged him. It was bad news, that affair. It ripped his guts.

He damned his instincts which insisted that affairs of the heart have a way of turning winners into losers.

When Emily arrived at his office wearing her luscious new

320

Russian sable coat, Rick's fears were confirmed. Even so, he rushed forward to wrap her and the coat in his tightest hug.

'It's mind-blowing,' he said. 'Just mind-blowing!'

'I know,' Emily agreed, 'it's adorable.'

'Hey, America is getting to you, Emily! You talk different.'

'That's precisely what an old school-friend of mine told me the other day . . .'

'The coat's from Maximillian?'

Emily looked away and Rick could have sworn that he saw her blush. He sighed. She looked like a movie star, he thought. But she was losing something; glamorous instead of elegant, the dignified *English* lady was vanishing. Yet she was even more beautiful. She glowed, she sparkled, she was a beam of energy.

Emily Bradshaw could easily pass as an *American* star.

'I've got a surprise for you,' he boomed. 'Now here's what I want you to do for me. Listen!'

He switched on a tape and lit another cigarette. Soon the soothingly romantic sound of a gentle harp filled the room.

'What's this?' Emily asked.

In answer Rick held his finger to his lips.

The high, sweet soprano of a boy chorister entered the room:

> Switch on the night
> Night's loving light
> By Heavenly Emily
> Only night only
> Easily, sexily
> With heavenly Emily
> Switch on the night.

'So,' Rick demanded when the tape ended. 'So what do you think?' He didn't wait for her to reply, but rushed on, 'Corny, but great! They'll roll over and die for this one.' He checked himself. 'Hey,' he said, almost shouting and reaching for the typewriter at the same time. 'Wait a minute! Wait a minute.' He handed her a typed sheet. 'Read this aloud; he said, 'like – recite it . . .'

'Why?'

'So read it to me.'

Emily laughed but complied.

'Fantastic!' Rick exclaimed, jumping up. 'Now here's what I want you to do for me! I'm going to play the tape again, and when the music comes on without the words, I want you to read it. I'll record that on another recorder. OK?' He laughed. 'This is exciting, exciting. Know why I want you to do this for me?' Again he didn't wait. 'Residuals, see? Residuals . . .'

'Rick,' Emily said, 'calm down. Explain. I don't know what's going on.'

'Of course you don't,' Rick said, suddenly serious. 'I've just been fooling around. You know Wayne, Leon's nephew?'

Emily nodded.

'Wayne said that if I could come up with the right jingle and the right product name, I'd make a bundle. So I heard about this fantastic group of kid harpists and choristers. I was fooling around with names and one of them was Heavenly Emily. Those dumb kids thought it was for a cosmetic!' Rick began to laugh wildly. 'A cosmetic – shit! So that's a few bucks gone!'

'I'm sorry, Rick,' Emily said, trying not to laugh. Then she said, 'It's hilarious.'

Rick laughed with her.

'We'll have you do the voice-over, anyway,' he said. 'When we get the right jingle. It's residuals – like every time your voice is used, the bucks add up. I've been adding it all up. See, I have this fantastic . . .'

'Calculator' Emily finished for him. 'I have one, too. I decided I needed one.'

'Emily Bradshaw working her own fucking calculator,' Rick said, his voice high with amazement. 'I can't believe it. When I think of the dignified English lady you were . . .'

'English women do use calculators, you know,' Emily said stiffly. 'Not all technology originates here. This may come as a great shock to you, but the pocket calculator was invented *and* developed by a Englishman!'

'Keep your cool,' Rick said anxiously. 'You're getting nervous and that makes *me* nervous . . .'

But Emily would not be placated. She had sensed something

322

of Rick's calculations. She said, 'Yes, I confess it. Yes, I do want to make money...'

'So what's new?'

'Oh, Rick!' she said breathlessly. 'Won't you try to understand?' Overcome by emotion, she continued, 'The hallmark of civilization – in America – is wanting to make money. People even talk about it. In England, it would be regarded as greedy.'

Rick sighed. 'I guess where you come from is less competitive; a smaller population means smaller potential.'

'That's not the point,' she snapped. 'Take Simon. He wants enough. It's only the ill-bred – who have bad taste anyway – for whom enough is too little...'

'Simon knows how much is enough?' Rick asked, sounding doubtful. 'What will he make of that Russian sable?'

A look of dismay crumpled Emily's features and slowly, as if listening and speaking at the same time, she said, 'At the moment, thinking about things like that is out of bounds.'

'Let me tell you what to do when you're in doubt,' Rick said. 'When in doubt – worry.'

Emily laughed and laughed and laughed.

Rick's laughter echoed hers. When he could speak, he said again, 'When in doubt – worry!'

And yet they both knew that, for the moment only, they had converted fear into laughter.

Suddenly Emily remembered and handed an unwrapped box to Rick. 'Leon sent you these,' she said.

His tone rising with every syllable, Rick cried, 'Pre-Castro Cubans! Why?'

'Because of the way you watched over me with Sheila Lyall.' Her blue eyes were brilliant. 'Leon knows about the frozen peas...'

*

Emily was nothing if not honest with herself. She supposed she ought to have felt some sense of shame, or at least an awkwardness, even if not outrightly troubled by Leon's persistent and versatile generosity towards her. Still, she did not take it for granted, nor did she consider it to be more than her due. Somehow, Leon had made her believe she was his guest of honour. This was his country, after all. And yet he had given her more than hospitality – and much, much more than generosity. He had given her his love, and his generosity went with it, as an accessory like a shirt and tie. For her part, any expression of disquiet or distaste would have been not only graceless, but indelicate.

Sometimes Leon spent whole nights with her at the hotel, and sometimes not. They studied one another minutely, and their lovemaking gained intensity as well as expertise. It was a fusion of bodies that led to a fusion of minds. Neither mentioned the future; they concentrated on the past and the present, and it may have been that the absence of a future put the seal on that moment, so that in their own private world there was a mutually touchable horizon. Only the future, which did not yet exist, had the power to injure them. So they avoided it.

True, they were lovers. But they were also friends. And friends *shared* things. Leon's gifts – or rather her acceptance of them – were a measure of that sharing, and not entirely unconnected with the way she and Rebecca had once borrowed one another's clothes.

From time to time Emily's other life intruded: a telephone call from her father, demanding to know when she would be back to attend to her God-given responsibilities. When Emily couldn't say because she wasn't sure, her father, triumphant, said, 'Melissa wants the flat and you have to see to Mummy's things! You wanted to sort them out...'

'Tell Melissa to put them in storage!'

'But that will cost the earth.'

'I know that.' Suddenly, an entirely new idea occurred to her. 'If you were to put the flat on the market, how much would you ask for it?'

'It hadn't occurred to me to sell. Why?'

'Perhaps I'll buy it from you myself.'

'Emily!'

'Get a price from an estate agent and let me know, will you?'

'Look, Emily, I didn't put through a transatlantic call to talk about that.' He paused and there was a short silence. 'Are you listening?'

'Yes...'

'Simon ought not to be left.' Another meaningful pause. Then, pompously, 'He's a man, you know. I'm against interfering and always have been, but you're my daughter and I'd be failing in my duty if I didn't warn you!'

'Tell me about Danny,' Emily interrupted roughly. 'Is he still pining?'

'Pining? Danny?'

'The last time you phoned, you said he was pining,' Emily said impatiently. 'But I'll be late – I'll call you soon. Must go...'

She would probably have to fly home after the *Perspectives* taping, which would be after the party announcing the paperback sale, the night before dinner at the White House.

Lunch with Rebecca was another intrusion – and, if she had not had Leon to insulate her, an insulting intrusion at that.

Emily and Rebecca met at the Pierre. As soon as they entered Rebecca, making her embarrassment very plain, said, 'We won't be dining with you and Leon next Thursday.'

'That's all right. We'll set another date.'

'I'm dying to meet Leon,' Rebecca said, putting her hand to her eyes, 'but Tim says it wouldn't be right and proper.'

'You can't be serious!'

'Sadly I am. It *is* rather awkward... for everyone. But, as Tim says, we are friends of Simon's too. And Simon doesn't know about you and Leon.'

'Well then, couldn't you have a drink with us on your own? Without Tim?'

'I suggested that to Tim myself,' Rebecca said miserably, 'but he positively forbade it.'

'I see. Well, I quite understand. It's par for the course, I suppose...'

*

On the evening of the anniversary of Ruthie's death, Leon and Emily did not meet. Leon explained that this was not the actual but the Hebrew anniversary. He would light a candle – the *jahrzeit* candle, that would burn for twenty-four hours – and then he and Milt would go the synagogue to recite Mourners' Kaddish, that ancient prayer praising and glorifying God. He had been seeing much less of his brother than usual and this left him feeling more than somewhat deprived. He had severe withdrawal symptoms. 'People who don't understand us would call us neurotic, I guess,' he had said. 'And I wouldn't blame them . . .'

So it was that Leon made it clear that he didn't care what anyone thought of his relationship with his brother. Emily understood that he had joked over withdrawal symptoms only because he was being entirely accurate about his feelings.

Emily understood, but felt abandoned all the same.

She decided to spend that night on her own. Rebecca had been horrified to hear that she found American television exciting, believing it put her in touch with Americans. She should have been enraged by the American perspective of Britain as a suburb, which was anyway a hick continent, but instead she felt more worldly and more sophisticated. Also disloyal – even unpatriotic. Because she had come to share their thinking. In common with everyone she had known before she came to America, she had always accepted unquestioningly the view that if Europe was civilized, Britain was most civilized, and the rest of the world uncivilized. But now she saw that what passed for 'most civilized' was a veneer of justification for endemic indolence.

But these were half-thoughts, unformed thoughts, thoughts brought about by her general sense of well-being. For all that, this kind of vague ephemeral thinking was highly pleasurable. Because it was not only that she had earned enough to buy that flat from her father that so delighted her. It was evidence that, like mountain air, America was good for her.

A large turquoise envelope was lying under her door and as soon as she saw it, her mood changed. She wondered how long it had been there, and bent to pick it up at once. Even so, she poured herself a cup of coffee and then waited for a while before she opened it. Inside the envelope there was another; she opened that and found another. It was like opening one of those Russian dolls sold to tourists. Trust Sheila Lyall to do a thing like this, she thought! When she reached the last of the envelopes, she was tempted not to open it. Sheila always meant some sort of mischief, some sort of malice. On that last envelope she had written: 'Alone tonight? Read this for your own good.' Curious about the newest shape of Sheila Lyall's spite, Emily opened the envelope:

Darling Emily,
I don't hate you.
I know you hate me.
You are alone tonight. How do I know?
None of your fucking business *how* I know.
Now I've offended you. Again.
Don't be offended. Be warned.
Leon will never marry you. He has a vow to keep. He will never marry you. Never. Never. *Never*.
If you won't take this warning, you will lose everything.
Yours in good faith,
Love and kisses,
Sheila Lyall

What an immature childish thing to do, Emily thought. Sheila Lyall is mad. Of course she's mad. Sheila Lyall is a witch. It was ridiculous to pay any attention to this. Intending to tear it to shreds, she carried the envelope to the wastepaper bin, but at the last minute she changed her mind.

And yet she was not the sort who thought along the lines of superstition, or witches, or evil. She was, she reminded herself, too sensible – above all, too intelligent – for that sort of thing. And intelligence overwhelms irrational fear.

Look at facts, not at fears. And the fact was that Leon had told her about that vow on the very first night. Since then, so much had happened that it was perfectly understandable that she had brushed it aside.

Now, thanks to that letter, she was forced to ask herself some hard questions. Had she been nurturing the hope that Leon would break his vow and marry her? Had she been *that* sure of herself? Was she really contemplating leaving Simon, she asked herself savagely, and breaking up her family? Was she going to force that kind of suffering on Danny?

She could not be certain. There were no absolute answers. And she was sufficiently honest with herself to admit that she was not yet ready to face the questions, never mind the answers.

Strange, though, that thinking of Sheila Lyall as a witch had tempted her mind along the primitive path of superstition. Next, she would be believing in the malignant glance and the evil eye – and before she knew it, she would be wearing amulets or blue beads! All her life she had excluded and despised the superstitious – could it be that this was superstition in itself?

And Leon, sitting beside the memorial candle that would flicker from sunset to sunset – surely that was also superstition? The fact was that his dead wife added to Emily's general sense of confusion.

Her mind darted back to Sheila Lyall. Just what had she hoped to achieve? There had to be some motive behind those evil forces.

One way of outwitting Sheila was to say nothing of this letter to Leon, or to anyone . . .

Chapter 19

The days that followed whirled at a dizzying speed, and there was no time to think. In a replica of fast-forward, the commercial was shot, her voice-over recorded (Rick got his way), more clothes fitted, new contracts negotiated. All was action, action, action. Emotion was in recess.

One day, rushing between appointments, Emily stopped outside a jewellery store to tie the laces of her jogging shoes. As she glanced idly at a display of turquoise jewellery, a small charm caught her eye. Fashioned in varying shades of blue, a single eye had been set into the stone, like stained glass. It was one of those superstitious eyes, designed to deflect the glance from an evil eye back to the sender. Blindly, Emily followed an impulse and bought it. Of course she was not superstitious, but she kept it hidden and made sure that the charm was always with her. It was silly, she knew, but like a well-worn seashell, pleasant to touch.

*

The future started too early and the night of the paperback party seemed to arrive ahead of time, probably because she had not been able to bring herself to decide when to leave for London. The producers were delaying the taping of *Perspectives* and this was something of a reprieve.

Now, Emily was dressing for the launch. She had chosen a moonlight-coloured, gossamer silk dress. Cut in the classic style of a Grecian toga, it emphasized and flattered her femininity.

Flowers and messages arrived constantly; she found herself almost numb with excitement, and too dazed to read any of the greetings. The first flowers to come were from Leon – before breakfast, dozens and dozens of roses. Now she was running late, Alfredo had behaved like a prima donna and taken too long over her hair. There was no time to read the messages on the cards, so she would take them with her.

At last she was at the restaurant – on the top floor of the tallest building in New York, at the Windows on the World. The launch was on and there was Rick, unashamedly emotional, his eyes brimming with prideful tears. Katie Williams was with him too, still shy but radiant. Rick had not forgotten Tom and Mary Janowski – there they were, wide-eyed and bewildered, but joyful. The ambulance attendants of that fateful day, Dr Cowan and some of the nurses, the British Ambassador Sir Derek Partridge ... Rick had remembered them all. Even Virginia Byrnes made a brief appearance. Eartha and Art Kristol were among the last to leave – a good sign for *Family Mix*. Pat Haines, elegant and graceful, came too. Emily felt she was at a surprise party in her honour and it took all her reserves of discipline to conceal her own emotions, but despite a constant catch in her throat she managed to conduct herself with the kind of dignity which was expected of her.

And then it was over, and the guests left. It was generally agreed that the Windows on the World had been the perfect venue for Emily.

After the party, which ended well after midnight, Emily and Leon stopped off at the Pierre so that she could change into something more suitable for travel. As they left the hotel, she was handed more messages.

They would be in Washington before morning, having decided that it would be better to wake up there the next morning rather than travelling on the same day as they were expected to dine at the White House.

So at about three in the morning, Emily and Leon checked into their Washington hotel. Understandably enough, Emily could not sleep, so she left Leon and went into the living room to watch television. Unable to concentrate, she then decided to read the cards which had come with the flowers. She half-hoped and half-feared that Simon might have sent her flowers, yet it was only when she was quite safe – when she was certain that no card had come from him – that resentment tugged at her lips. She was sorry, in a way, that she had brought the cards with her – now she couldn't tell which flowers they belonged to. Well, she shrugged, that couldn't be helped now.

The first two messages that she opened made her smile. The third, from Simon, was as terse as it was simple: *Danny admitted to the London clinic with suspected appendicitis. Surgery likely. Simon.*

Even as she read it, she began dialling London; it was now about nine o'clock in the morning there. No reply at Lamont Road. Cursing herself for not dialling Simon's office, and at the same time rifling through the other envelopes in case there was another message, she tried his office.

'No,' Simon's secretary, Mrs Evans, said. 'I'm afraid Mr Bradshaw is at the clinic.' Her reproachful voice plunged several levels.

'I see. Do you happen to have the number of the clinic?'

'Certainly.'

'Thank you.'

Emily dialled again, feverishly. No reply. No one ever answers the phones in London, she thought fretfully. Eventually, however, the phone was answered and she explained that she was phoning from the United States. No, she didn't mind how long she would have to hold on ... Yes, she knew it would be terribly expensive ... But could she please, please, *please* speak to her husband. Or the doctor or the sister in charge. Or anyone who could tell her how her little boy was – please ...

Finally, finally Simon was on the phone.

'Ah, Simon!' she cried. 'Thank God I got you! How is he? Has he had the operation?'

'Yes.'

'When?'

At five o'clock yesterday afternoon. We tried to get hold of you. Where are you?'

'In Washington.'

'That explains it, then.'

'But I only just got here. Just got your...' Emily was babbling. 'Simon, how *is* he? For God's sake, tell me!'

'The doctors are perfectly satisfied.'

'Thank God for that!' Emily said, breaking into tears. 'I only just read your message. Do you think I should fly back? I could get a flight this morning?'

'What are you doing in Washington?'

'I'm meant to dine at the White House tonight.'

'I see. Moving up in the world, aren't we?'

'Who operated?'

'I beg your pardon?'

'What is the name of the surgeon who operated?'

'Reginald Thresher. He's a paediatric surgeon. Fine fellow, too.'

'Do you think I should come home?'

'That's up to you, Emily. No medical necessity, however. This is the doctor's line, so I shall have to ring off. Let me know your plane – Danny will be pleased to see you...'

The phone clicked.

Emily dialled again and an emphatic voice told her that Mr Thresher was operating. She wondered if she should wake Leon. No, not yet. She dialled again. This time she would ask to speak to the sister, and if she couldn't reach her, she would ask for a nurse. But she had to talk to someone who would give her more detailed information. In a squeeze of guilt, her heart raced and contracted as her fingers fiddled nervously with her soft silk negligée. Remorse mounted and with it, panic. Presently she heard the sister's high treble. 'Danny's holding his own... An exceedingly brave young man... Oh, yes, I'm sure he would be much happier if he had you with him... Sometimes... No, *no* medical urgency... I shall most certainly tell him of your telephone call... Goodbye...'

An exceedingly brave young man. That could only mean that Danny was in pain. Oh, God! Danny deserved to have his mother with him. What sort of a mother was she, anyway? She hated herself, and it was a greedy hate. Because her father had warned her that Danny was pining. Danny had made himself ill, it was psychosomatic. A childhood friend of hers had actually died having her appendix out – it was the anaesthetic. Oh God – if anything had happened to Danny, it would have been her fault.

Post-surgical complications? She told herself to stop it, to stop that panic, that inner hysteria and pull herself together. But that phrase, *exceedingly brave*, haunted her.

The blue amulet was in her coat pocket, her Russian sable coat. She fetched it and fingered it restlessly, hoping for guidance. So what if she was too intelligent for superstition? Because there was a dilemma to face. Should she take the first available flight to London, or should she go after dining at the White House? She had been not only too busy but too self-involved to bother to read her messages. The plain truth was that she had become selfish . . . Twenty guests were expected at the White House. Of course she wanted to go – anyone would and she couldn't fault herself for that. On the other hand, not going would be something of a noble sacrifice.

Now, when she most needed to think clearly, her mind was performing tricky arabesques. Never mind, she told herself, she would think more clearly on the plane.

And that was when she realized that no decision had been necessary. Leon would be disappointed, of course, but he would understand.

Meanwhile there were reservations to be made. She would not tell Leon about Danny until all this had been attended to. The snag was that she would have to fly to New York to pick up her clothes . . .

*

'But Emily, you say there's no medical need for you to go back.' Leon sounded puzzled.

'I know.' Emily pressed her hands against her stomach. 'I know. But I must go. If only I'd read my messages . . .'

'What would you have done? Miss the launch?'

Negotiation always makes his eyes gleam, Emily thought irrelevantly. She said, 'I don't know, Leon, I honestly don't know.'

'It's quite something to cancel dinner at the White House.'

His voice was cold and bit like a whiplash.

'Oh, I know that, Leon. But this is an emergency.'

'Don't give me that, Emily! The fact is that it is *not* an emergency,' he said gravely, taking her hands. 'You are not being honest with either of us. You are letting guilt get in the way of reason . . .'

'Leon . . .'

'No, Emily, let me make my point. Haven't you just been talking about unopened messages? You are ready to cancel dinner with the President of the United States because you neglected to read your messages.'

'He's my son, Leon,' Emily said, her voice tight and despairing. 'I've got to go to him.' She clenched her fists. 'I'm sorry, but I have no choice. Danny's expecting me now, anyway. I phoned Simon – gave him my flight number . . .'

'Surely,' Leon said, 'surely you understand how important this is to me? I can't stand this . . .'

'I hate to let you down.'

'Just so long as you know that that is precisely what you *are* doing.' He tapped her chest. 'You are being self-indulgent. Surely you see that you are doing this just to show what a great mother you are?'

'Perhaps,' she said, impatient to leave. 'Perhaps you're right. I don't know. I've *got* to go . . .'

Emily tried to telephone Leon from the airport. She wanted him to know that if her mother had not died, it might have been possible for her to stay.

PART VI
Early November 1985

Chapter 20

Once she was on her way to London, Emily was almost relieved that she had been unable to reach Leon on the telephone. She was far too engaged with the hypothetical, anyway. There was no more point in asking herself what she would have done if she had had a business commitment than there was in asking what Leon would have done if it had been his small son who was lying in hospital. For all that, she continued to put questions to herself to which there could be no answers. In any case, she was vaguely disappointed in Leon. She had expected him to be entirely sympathetic, entirely understanding and entirely supportive. Yet she could not but understand and even sympathize with him, because as a woman she was in the habit of understanding ... Leon was only a man, after all. Maternity and childbirth, and the ache in the womb – these were beyond Leon, as they were beyond most men. Emily now understood that when things failed to go Leon's way, he clenched his teeth and talked through them. She had the strongest feeling that, as far as he was concerned, his wishes had become directives. Well, she had now seen another and commanding side of Leon Lerner. She had taken his absolute understanding for granted because she had expected his reactions to match her own.

'You want to show what a great mother you are!' She burned at this, at the heartlessness of it – and because the awful thing was that it was also partly true. She longed to retreat into sleep, but her mind whirled between Danny and Leon and would not let her be. And all the while, hovering bleakly at the back of her mind was the thought that for the very first time her mother would not be there to welcome her.

She had not been certain whether or not Simon would be at Heathrow to meet her, but even before he saw her, she glimpsed his new moustache. He was blinking furiously and the grim muscles of his jaw warned her.

Simon knew!

She felt his stiff lips and the new moustache brush against her cheek. Then he took the baggage trolley from her and led her towards the car. Emily saw at once that his approach to her would be scrupulously and exasperatingly polite. He told her that apart from a slight rash due to an allergic reaction to his sedatives, Danny was making excellent progress. He might have been talking to one of his clients about another of his clients, Emily thought. His neutral tone was nevertheless guarded.

'You've grown a moustache,' she commented. 'You didn't tell me . . .'

'Well, there's a good deal more to tell, I suppose.'

'It suits you,' Emily said.

Simon was silent.

Emily fidgeted. 'The traffic,' she said quickly, 'it's bumper to bumper. It was good of you to come and collect me.' As if she had just thought of something vitally important, she added, 'Have you had breakfast?'

'Certainly. Bacon and eggs and hot fresh, home-made wholewheat bread!' Then, in a poor imitation of a Texan accent, 'Yes, ma'am! Gen-u-ine home-made, fresh out of the oven.'

'How nice for you.'

'So you gave up going to the White House?' Simon said bitingly. 'What a little angel of mercy you turned out to be!'

The bitter sarcasm in his voice made Emily flinch. 'Why didn't you send me a cable? How could I answer the phone when I was out?'

'Come now, Emily. I left perfectly good messages. How could I have dreamt you wouldn't answer them?'

Another and uglier silence filled the car.

It was broken by Simon. 'Tell me, Emily, is it one of those

intimate, exclusive, ten-thousand-dollar, plate dinners for five thousand guests that you have given up?'

'I was to be one of twenty guests,' Emily said, and immediately regretted it.

'And no doubt Mr Leon Lerner was another of those twenty?' Emily was silent.

'You're in love with him, aren't you?' Simon asked. 'It's a perfectly civilized thing to be in love, it happens to everyone. Of course the big romance, in capitals, is rather less civilized!'

'What *are* you talking about?'

'Don't play the injured innocent, my love. Your big romance, in capitals, is quite unlike mine. And yet mine will take me to the altar.'

'Oh, Simon!'

He took one hand from the steering wheel to point his finger at her. 'He'll never marry you, Emily, you know. You're not his kind.'

'You mean I'm not a Jew, don't you?'

'Hardly that,' Simon laughed contemptuously. 'I know that!' He pointed his finger at her again. 'I'm indebted to one Sheila Lyall for . . .'

'What?' Emily interrupted roughly. 'Sheila Lyall?'

'Yes, ma'am, that sho' is what I did say – Sheila Lyall.' Once again Simon mocked her with his self-styled Texan accent.

'Simon! Do be sensible, please,' Emily begged miserably, her tone openly supplicating.

Satisfied now, and briskly businesslike, Simon said. 'Yes, Sheila Lyall wrote to me. I'll quote exactly: "Leon Lerner never will marry your wife because of a vow he made to his dead wife." Does that make sense to you?'

Again Emily said nothing.

'In case you're wondering about me and my fresh, home-made bread,' Simon went on pleasantly, 'if you're interested, I'll tell you all about it . . .'

'I'm interested,' Emily said. 'Most interested.'

So, with his meticulous lawyer's concern with chronology, Simon recounted the chief events. He told her about Ophelia and her drunken, drugged soldiers, about the freezer and the state of the house when he and Danny had returned, about the humiliation of all her publicity. He went into endless detail about that confidence trickster, Christine Slater, the journalist who had tricked him on the Concorde. Only then did he tell her about Susan and the home-made bread that she had brought for their breakfast.

From time to time he took his eyes off the road to look at Emily, but she just stared straight ahead, willing him to go on until he had told her everything.

A traffic light seemed to have stopped functioning. Simon stopped talking, but drummed his fingers on the steering wheel.

'The light's turned green,' Emily told him.

Simon's foot went to the accelerator. 'Thanks,' he said, 'I wasn't concentrating ... uh ... this next bit's a bit ... ropey.'

'Then you'd best get it over with ...'

'The thing is, about two weeks ago Susan moved in with me.' He threw Emily a hard look. 'I'm disinclined to ask her to move out just because you decided to fly home. I'm going to marry her. It would, of course, have been much neater if you and Leon could have teamed up.'

'Oh, Simon!' Emily said. 'Spare me your sarcasm, please.' Her leg had gone to sleep and she jiggled it awake, her voice low and effortful as she said, 'You can hardly expect me to stay at Lamont Road. I'm not the *ménage-à-trois* type.'

'Aren't you?' he came back at her. 'What sort of type are you?'

Emily flung her eyes upward. 'I'm not going in for a slanging match,' she said calmly. 'I suppose I could stay in Mummy's flat ...'

'That had occurred to me,' Simon said.

The rest of the journey was completed in an impassioned but thoughtful silence.

When they reached the hospital, he said. 'You realize of course, that I will not permit Danny to leave the country ...'

'Oh, Simon,' Emily said sadly. 'You're way ahead of me. You really are.'

Whatever doubts Emily might still have had about returning to London vanished as soon as she saw Danny. The delicate bones of his flushed face stood out frighteningly. He smiled weakly, and thrust his arms towards her, and she knew why the sister called him a very brave young man.

'They took the drip out,' he told her proudly. 'I didn't even squeak.'

'Did it hurt?'

'No.'

Emily sat on Danny's bed and stroked his forehead. He drifted back to sleep again, and awoke when Simon entered the room. In that new cold and injured voice of his, Simon said, 'I've left your luggage with the porter, Emily.' He stood at the foot of Danny's bed. 'Mummy missed a dinner at the White House,' he said, 'just to see you, Danny. Aren't you honoured?'

Emily sent him a pleading glance – *Not in front of Danny! Please!* She said, 'I got on a plane as soon as I heard.'

'Oh, did you?' Danny said. 'I'm glad!'

All that day Danny drifted in and out of sleep and Emily sat beside him. The nurses were kind and helpful; they plied her with tea and sandwiches, and every one of them made some sort of reference to the shooting. This took Emily unawares – beyond the reactions of Simon and his senior partners, she had given virtually no thought to the possibility that people in London would know about it. At one point she suspected that nurses from other floors were popping in to view her as they would a specimen.

'Well,' one of them said tartly, 'it made you famous, getting shot, didn't it?' Astonished, it occurred to Emily that this nurse might even have been envious.

At about four o'clock her father came to see her. Danny was asleep again, so she tiptoed out of the room.

'Simon phoned me,' he said, sounding agitated. 'What's all this about your wanting to sleep in Mummy's flat?'

'Simon and I are having... difficulties.'

'That's obvious. What sort of difficulties? It's that music teacher. I phoned you about her – you can't say I didn't warn you...'

'Oh, Daddy, I'm so very tired. I really can't talk about anything now.'

'You do look pale. Simon should have told me about Danny, you know.'

'Oh, didn't he? I'm sorry.'

'We didn't put the furniture in store. I brought the keys – don't think you'll find anything to eat, though.'

'I'll manage.'

In so far as she felt anything for herself at all, she felt sordid.

It was late when she arrived at her mother's flat in Austen Gardens. At least the porter was expecting her, and there was some comfort in that. He too knew about the shooting. 'Damned Yanks!' he snorted. 'Uncivilized...' Again, Emily was astonished; all that now seemed to have happened in another life, and to someone else. Shocked, she understood that it was madness to have believed that if she dropped out of her own world, it would drop her too...

The furniture was shrouded in dust-covers, but miraculously, the electricity functioned. Leon, she must phone Leon... But the phone had been cut off. She removed the dust covers, found sheets, unpacked and, longing for her mother, collapsed on the bed. Towards dawn she awoke and a sudden inspiration took her downstairs to the porter's desk – she would telephone Leon on reversed charges. There was no need to change, for she had slept fully clothed.

The porter stared at her through bleary eyes. 'Of course, Mrs Bradshaw. The phone's here.'

It seemed ages before Leon's phone was answered and Emily heard Michael's voice saying, 'Most certainly. I would be happy to accept the charges, but Mr Leon Lerner is unavailable...'

The operator cut in. 'Would you like to speak to the party on the line?'

'Yes, thank you.' And to Michael, 'Please tell Mr Lerner my own phone is out of order. I'll telephone again later...'

Then Emily phoned the clinic and was told that Danny had spent a fairly restful night.

In her mother's flat once again, she remembered: of course, Leon was still in Washington. Lovable, discreet, perfectly trained, Michael never gave away any information...

Unable to bear being alone in that flat – it felt oppressively

342

eerie – Emily returned at once to the clinic. Suddenly she was grateful to Simon; at least he had enough medical insurance to cover the costs of private treatment and she could visit Danny whenever she liked, or call him on his bedside telephone. She must arrange for her mother's telephone to be reconnected.

*

Though Katie Williams was only twenty-three, life had taught her enough to know that she was not the first woman to find it more comfortable to be a widow than a wife. To be sure, she had started counting her blessings on her wedding day; life as a wife was a dramatic improvement over the unremitting horrors that had gone before. Then, as a bride of seventeen, she had expected her life to improve – but she had never as much as hoped for happiness, or anything like it.

For Katie, the absence of dread meant happiness of the purest sort.

She had dreaded Jake's moods, Jake's smouldering silences and the hate she sometimes heard in his voice when he spoke to Andy. She was glad he was dead, and felt no guilt. She was gladder still over the manner of his death – his suicide meant that she was compelled to tell Andy that Jake was not his real father. Otherwise, if Andy believed that both his father and his grandfather had ended their own lives, he might also believe that he too carried the germ of suicide in his own veins. Of course, she would never tell Andy the whole truth – he must never know that he was the product of a rape. No, Andy must never know that he was the son of his mother's foster-father, Pete Chesser.

She was not quite ready, yet, to discuss this with anyone. In time she would get advice, but in the end the decision would be hers. The great thing was that now she had people to whom she could turn. She trusted the Janowskis and she trusted Rick Cooke. But in her heart of hearts Katie already knew who could give her the best counsel – and that was Emily Bradshaw, the woman who had transformed her life. Even now, Katie could not get over the fact that Emily cared about the family of the man who had nearly murdered her – it was the sort of behaviour that made her believe, really believe, in God. The Janowskis knew this and wanted Katie to be received into the Catholic Church. But she was terrified of the confessional.

The funny thing was that she had only met Emily Bradshaw twice. And now Emily's little boy was ill in hospital, in London.

It was two days since Rick had given her Emily's London address, and for two days Katie had been thinking of the letter she would write to her. Understandably enough, Katie was somewhat inhibited – this would be the first real letter she would ever write. Should it be handwritten or typed? Should she mention the similarity of their sons' names – Andy and Dany – they used the same letters? She could have asked Rick as she could have asked Mary Janowski, but chose not to do so. Not that she wanted to keep the letter a secret, but somehow it was private. In the end she decided to send a Get-Well card, because this meant she need only add a short note:

Dear Emily,

Andy and me are praying for your son Dany. Dany and Andy have the same letters in their names?

I will never forget what you have done for Andy and me. We are all much happier now, including Jake. You are a beautiful person.

I am going to typing classes. TAN have promised me a job.
Love from Katie and Andy

P.S. Andy and me are going to change our last name to Shaw.

When Emily received Katie's card, she wept. Until then, the knowledge that she had wantonly brought the destruction of her family on herself had forbidden tears. Of course, she knew it was ridiculous to feel so desperately hurt by Simon and Susan – she had asked for it, hadn't she? After all, it was no less than she deserved. Even so ... *divorce*!

Whatever she had done, and however much she had been swept away by Leon and her own passion for him, she had always believed that her relationship with her family was as fundamental as that between vocal cords and the voice. But her mind and her body had been engaged in moments, and not consequences, and it was too late to learn that nothing is so fundamental that it cannot be destroyed.

Emily felt frighteningly alone; she heard herself weep, and wished there was someone she could talk to.

It was then, at midnight in London, that she decided to phone Katie. First she took a vodka to steady her nerves. These days, vodka was becoming quite a habit.

'Katie? Emily Bradshaw.'

'I didn't know you were back in New York already.'

'I'm not, I'm in London.'

'You're calling all the way from London, England?'

'Yes,' Emily laughed. Katie reminded her of those transatlantic calls from Rick. It seemed as if four years rather than four months had passed since then. 'I phoned to thank you for your card.'

'You're welcome, Mrs Bradshaw.' Katie sounded bewildered.

'Emily ... please call me Emily.'

'You're welcome, Emily. Is Danny better now?'

'Yes, he is.' Emily's voice shook, but she rushed on. 'Your card meant a lot to me – more than I can say.'

'You're very welcome, Emily,' Katie repeated.

'I like the name Shaw. It's a great compliment to me.'

'Shaw is from Bradshaw.'

'I know that.'

'Rick said you wouldn't mind.'

'I'm flattered.'

'You know, Emily,' Katie burst out, 'Jake wasn't Andy's daddy!'

'I didn't know that.'

'No one knows. But one day, I'll tell Andy. You see, he mustn't think suicide runs in his blood.'

'Katie, you are wise beyond your years.' Emily sighed into the telephone and it echoed back at her. 'Thank you for telling me. Thank you. See you soon. In New York.'

'Take care now, Emily.'

'Thank you. Goodbye.'

Emily felt calmer when she put down the receiver. She could not have said exactly why she had phoned Katie, nor could she guess why Katie had written her phone number along with her address on that Get-Well card. Emily was certain, though, that she had done the right thing. Nothing else mattered.

But for the excitement of talking across the Atlantic, Katie might not have been so trusting. Emily hoped she had no regrets, but above all – and whatever the cause – *Katie had trusted her.* It occurred to Emily that this was probably the most satisfying as well as the most comforting of all her achievements.

Because out there, someone believed in her. Katie Williams, soon to be Katie Shaw, believed in her.

Which was something to hang on to . . .

Emily found a lawyer, or rather her father found one for her – Miles Grayson, who had just begun a new practice in the West End. 'A newly married man,' her father said. 'Dynamic, forward-looking, not a tradition-bound fuddy-duddy firm like Simon's.'

Miles Grayson took matters in hand. Emily was vague about her finances, so he took Keith Summers in hand as well. It was clear that Emily could now afford to buy something much grander than her mother's little flat, but it was sound business to buy it since her father was selling at such a fair price. However, when Emily told him that she proposed to pay the entire sum at once, Miles Grayson drew the line. 'Now that doesn't make any sort of business sense at all,' he said. 'Your money won't be working for you. Of course, if you acquired another property and tarted it up a bit, and then sold it at a tidy profit, *then* you'd be making sound business sense.'

'You're talking about real estate,' Emily said.

'Yes, that is the American term for it. Why do you ask?'

*

Leon was altogether unused to having a request turned down. Part of his spectacular success as a negotiator lay in his skill at couching unreasonable requests in reasonable terms.

But a personal request was, of course, quite different. For

years, decades even, people had flocked and scurried and vied for the blessed opportunity of fulfilling – or better still, anticipating – his every wish, reasonable or otherwise.

Now, with the best will in the world, Leon could not persuade himself that his request to Emily had been anything but reasonable. Since there was *no* medical emergency, she need only have returned to London on the day after the White House dinner.

Accordingly, he was forced to conclude that because his intelligent, sensitive – and above all sensible – Emily had disregarded the consequences and given way to an hysterical impulse, he had seriously overestimated her. He took this further and was now convinced that Emily Bradshaw was more headstrong, more stubborn than was good for her or anyone else. The memory of the way she had agonized over Jake Williams was nauseating...

The following day Leon and Milt decided to have lunch in Milt's office, at his desk. They did this from time to time, usually when some serious soul-searching was necessary.

'I may as well come clean, Milt,' Leon said, somewhat apologetically. 'I miss her like hell.'

'Sure you do,' Milt agreed. 'She's some doll.'

Leon flushed angrily. 'She's no doll, Milt, and you know it!'

'What do you want me to say, Leon? I tell you she's a beautiful girl and you take offence.'

'I guess I am touchy about her.'

'You can say that again.' Milt tilted his chair backwards, placed his feet on the desk and took a deep draw from his cigar. Flinging out his arms, he said, harmlessly enough, 'This office turns me on. I tell you, Leon, it turns me on!'

Leon looked around the room. It was unusually large, of course, and on the highest floor; but the architect had somehow managed to effect an illusion of endless space and anyone who looked out at New York – as Leon now did – had the sensation of floating on top of the city, on top of the real world. Several million had been spent on the art in this office, and it was the Lerner brothers' most flamboyant homage to their combined egos.

'You know what she said about this?' Leon asked with the same sweeping gesture as his brother. 'She said it was like having a permanent and personal capsule in the sky.'

'She's not wrong,' Milt said. He turned to safer territory. 'That guy, Rick Cooke, is really something. I tell you, the guy's got world-class smarts.'

'So?'

'His company is growing. I said I'd talk to you, of course, but I knew you'd go along with it.'

'Go along with what?'

'It's not a big deal, backing him. You see, Leon, I thought it best to have him on our side.'

'Who's talking sides?'

Milt went on imperturbably, without answering, 'Wayne's smart, too. We sort of lost you, Leon, and Wayne stepped in.' The brothers exchanged a flicker of a glance which instantly affirmed their bond. 'Wayne called in Blue Chip Consultants on the Windsor commercials. Kiss of death, they said. Rick Cooke drives a shrewd bargain, is what I'm saying; that's why I want him on our team.'

'And the bottom line?'

'According to Rick, when they signed with us they missed out on Sunlife cereals. So he had us over a barrel. So, Wayne and I decided to cut our losses.' Milt attacked his cigar again. 'Half a million.'

'Does she know?'

'Rick probably called her in London.' The way we're not mentioning it, you'd think her name was classified material, Milt thought. But he said, 'Course, if it had been anyone else, anyone less compromising, we'd have seen them in hell before we parted with a dime, never mind half a million—'

'OK, OK. No need to rub salt into the wound,' Leon said irritably. 'You want to buy into Rick's company? So buy into it.'

With an abrupt movement, Milt removed his feet from the desk. He asked mildly, 'What are you going to do, Leon?'

'How do I know?' A mixture of a shrug and a sigh. 'I don't know.'

'How old is her kid?'

'Yeah, you don't have to tell me. Only eight. But, Milt...' Now Leon leaned across the wide desk and with each word, jabbed his brother's chest. 'She's one hell of a woman, Milt. One hell of a woman.'

*

Emily and Simon were agreed on one thing. There was no question that in their new circumstances Danny would suffer as little injury as possible. To this end, they would be both civilized and amiable. Emily said that she would prefer not to see Susan just yet, and Simon accepted this. It was only logical that Danny would not go home to Lamont Road, but to Austen Gardens.

Emily took to wearing her mother's velvet dressing-gown. She felt less insecure, almost protected, when she had it on. Mostly though, she was aware of having lost her bearings, as if the real Emily Bradshaw was in a temporary state of suspension, or in cold-storage. She was still a mother, though not purely... Sometimes she felt as though her personality – or her mind – was splitting. As if she had been an actor who, having taken on the role of Emily Bradshaw, had performed as a talk show guest, on radio and on television and in commercials. Sometimes, most times, she felt as if she and the woman who had written *Defending Wives* had no connection. Worse, she had nothing in common with the woman she had been. Whoever or whatever she was, or had now become, had difficulty in remembering whoever it was that she had once been. It was all very confusing.

One night, she dreamed of the film *The French Lieutenant's Woman*. When she awoke, she understood why when the actor's on-camera and real-life lover was leaving, he had called out after her, confusing her own name with the role she played. Because she felt the same sort of confusion about herself – which was the real-life Emily, which the on-camera Emily...? Or had it all been an interlude only, an interlude that turned into a long breaking point?

*

Emily took care of Danny, but was no longer a wife.

One rainy afternoon while she and Danny were playing Scrabble, Emily found the courage to ask, 'How do you really feel about going to Trevor-Winston School, Danny?'

'I have to go, don't I? Daddy went.' Danny looked away. 'Christopher won't be going with me now. His father can't afford it, he says. I think he's lucky.'

'You'd rather not go, wouldn't you?' Emily said slowly. 'You can tell me the truth; I won't tell Daddy.'

'I wish we were poor!' Danny burst out.

The entire Bradshaw family, Emily's father and even her mother had taken it for granted that Danny would go to the Trevor-Winston School. Two hours after he was born, Simon had rushed to put his name down. It had never occurred to Emily to question this, or even to question Danny later as to how *he* felt about it. And but for Leon, she never would have done . . .

The telephone kept her in touch with Leon, but she felt as out of touch with him as she felt with Rick and even with Simon. Everything merged and entangled. It was futile even to try to sort things out.

Emily constantly expected to hear her mother's footsteps. She found nothing odd about this; it was an absolute and persistent expectation. Of course, it was because she was in her mother's flat, surrounded by and using her china, her silver, her linen. Every cupboard and every drawer released the lavender scent which had been as much a part – perhaps even more a part of Emily's childhood than going to school. For her mother's imminent return seemed more likely than her own return to New York. The *Perspectives* programme had finally been scheduled. She was in shock, she supposed – an inner secret shock, or a shock driven so deep that it was invisible from everyone. Outwardly, of course, there was no evidence of any confusion.

For the moment, she was certain of only one thing: where once she had lived *for* the moment, she now lived *by* the moment.

One night, by appointment, Simon came to see her after

dinner. He had asked her to ring him when Danny was asleep. Emily changed out of her mother's dressing-gown for this meeting. He announced his intentions at once: he had come to advise her to find herself a lawyer to represent her. There was no point, he said, in delaying their divorce. In that tight, dry voice she had come to dread, he began, 'The point is . . .' and stopped speaking.

'You were saying?' Emily said pleasantly.

'The point is, Susan's pregnant.'

'I see.' Emily suppressed an urge to giggle. She said, 'And when, may I ask, is that happy event expected?'

Simon did not answer, but burst out, 'Well, *you* wouldn't have more than one child!'

That's not true, that's not fair, Emily wanted to say . . . It had been a mutual decision based on school fees; they simply could not afford to educate more than one child. It was Simon who had first brought that up, Emily thought resentfully. Now she said only, 'That's unfair, Simon!' In a forced, mild voice she went on, 'And you know it's unfair . . .'

'That's one problem you haven't got,' Simon exploded, blinking furiously. 'Your Mr Leon Lerner had a vasectomy . . .'

Again that hysterical urge to giggle, replaced by a long, shuddering sigh. 'Another of Sheila Lyall's titbits, I suppose?' She clenched her fists. If it killed her, she would be civilized. Besides, Simon was looking at her with that familiar look of his, the look she only saw when he wanted to take her to bed. She thought this consciously, and her legs echoed her thought as she uncrossed and then slowly crossed them again. She definitely didn't want him and certainly felt no desire for him. Wanting to seduce him, however, was entirely different from wanting him. She had heard how maddeningly desirable a man could find his own wife simply because another man had made love to her. Still playing with this idea, she looked down and fiddled with her skirt, then quite deliberately raised her eyes, beamed him a long, hard stare and twiddled her tongue about her lips. She murmured, 'That moustache of yours is really sexy.'

A harsh, dry, pained sound escaped him. '*Emily!*' he said, grinding her name between his teeth. '*Emily!*' Now he was beside her as she turned her mouth to meet his, a flicker of warning came. He might be cruel. Over the ripping of her shirt, she heard him say, 'So that's what your scar looks like!' He tore her clothes from her and threw her on the floor. Then he flung himself at her with all his strength and – again with all his strength – entered her. Stripped, yet Emily's body was further stripped of feeling, which was probably why it was so easy for her to control it . . . Even down to the finest nuance – its every movement.

Emily directed her body thoughtfully and with passionless skill. A lurching, clutching, grinding permanent attack on his memory was what she intended. This was one fuck he would never, never forget. He would hanker after her for ever. On and on it went as her muscles teased and tantalized, tightened and widened. Emily was giving the most determined – and because it had to be unforgettable – the most inspired performance of simulated ecstasy of her life. Her body served him and served her mind; it did not give way and serve itself.

And then it was over and at last, at last, Emily could lie still. But not Simon. Though spent and still on top of her, he kicked his feet like a child in a temper tantrum.

As if he were a child, Emily patted his back. At least he had not been cruel.

Suddenly Simon flung himself away and looked at her. Then Emily made a mistake. She smiled.

'Damn you, Emily,' Simon said. 'Damn you to hell!'

But for Emily it was the kind of curse that was even better than applause after a decisive victory.

Chapter 21

Even with the help of the human conveyor belt, it is a long walk at Heathrow's Terminal 3 to get to the departure gate for flights to America. Emily's left shoulder ached and it still wasn't possible for her right shoulder to carry the weight of her hand baggage. *New York. New York. Leon. Leon.* Emily quickened her pace to the quickening inner rhythms of these words. *New York. New York. Leon. Leon.* Suddenly her heart raced. It couldn't be, yet there it was – a huge poster of herself: *Defending Wives by Emily Bradshaw.* She had stopped walking, but continued to move – a human package on an inhuman conveyor belt. When the belt stopped, she got off and, sweating and trembling, stood quite still.

An airport luggage trolley was coming towards her and she smiled at the driver. 'You're not by any chance going in the direction of Gate 18, are you?' she asked.

'No, miss, I'm not. But hop on, and I'll change my direction!'

Sitting on that comfortable, smooth trolley, Emily laughed out loud. The driver laughed too and sounded his dull horn; he drove faster and made Emily's hair fly. Oh, Emily, she thought, at last a good omen! Her fingers sought and found her small, small, soothing charm.

Leon was there to meet her and seated close beside him – thigh to thigh behind fogged windows, at the back of his limousine – Emily felt almost, almost as if she had come home. True she was in another time zone, but the minutes were taking too long. Because nothing mattered, nothing except being in bed with Leon.

He was taking her to the Pierre and not to his own apartment, but the thought skidded off her mind. She didn't care where. What mattered was to get there, to be there with Leon.

Still, they were forced to wait. Her baggage had not yet been brought upstairs. At last – it seemed an eternity – that petty detail was out of the way.

She wanted him now, as she had made Simon want her. And it showed, all this wanting, it showed. She was without tenderness, without delicacy. As if her white-hot heat could weld him to her, his body was her weapon. She needed it, so she took it and took it again and again. When he had had enough and cried out that he could stand no more . . . it was too much, too much . . . she stroked and sucked him into another erection. He was fifty-five years old, veins had been taken from his leg and grafted into his heart, yet within the space of two hours he had four orgasms.

'What are you trying to do, Emily?' he asked. 'Kill me?'

'Not you, darling,' she said sadly. 'Me.' She got up. 'Would you like a cigar?' she asked.

'I sure could do with one,' Leon said. 'There should be some fruit. I'd like an apple.'

Emily busied herself with these things. However successful her lovemaking had been, there was no sensation of achievement in it for her. All the desperation and survival-like urgency had been on her part, not on his. It couldn't even begin to compare with the way he had made love to her after the shooting. Then, it had been soon after she had been in danger of losing her life. Now she was in danger of losing her soul. She had lost Simon, and with him her family. It was not the loss of Simon but the loss of her *family* that tore at her, and sent her lusting after bodily oblivion. Now, it seemed, even that was out of reach.

'Oh God,' she murmured, 'I wish you hadn't saved me. I wish you hadn't sent that ambulance.'

'What's that?' Leon asked. 'Can't hear you . . .'

'Nothing,' Emily said. 'Nothing important.'

*

If Leon couldn't help her to sort herself out, vodka could and did. So many advantages to vodka, Emily decided. The breath didn't smell and neither the calories nor her problems were of such overwhelming importance.

Nothing was as she had expected it to be. Not that she knew what she had expected. 'You see, Emily,' Leon explained, pushing his fingers against her chest as was his habit whenever he was emphasizing something, 'if you were just an ordinary model, Milt wouldn't have had a leg to stand on. But it's been our policy never to do business with family.'

'But I'm not family,' Emily said, bewildered.

'Not in the strict sense, I know,' Leon agreed reasonably.

'What other sense is there?'

'Doesn't sexual intimacy count for anything with you, Emily?'

'How you can even ask such a question is beyond me.'

'Of course we are honouring our contract,' Leon told her. 'That made a big hit with Rick, I can tell you. Residual fees are included.'

'Oh, Leon. I can't possibly accept that...'

'It's out of your hands,' he said.

*

It seemed to Emily that a lot else was out of her hands. Her own projected television show, *Family Mix*, had been shelved. 'They've been dragging their heels, Emily,' Rick said. 'That fucking article in *Plush*, I guess...'

'What article?'

'Didn't I tell you?'

'No, you fucking well did *not* tell me. What article?'

'Now here's what I want you to do for me.'

'Oh, Rick,' Emily burst out, 'for Christ's sake, stop it! Cut the crap and stop trying to humour me!'

'About you and Simon. *Plush* said it was rich, considering your views on needless divorce.'

'But Leon's not even married!'

'I know. But *you* are.' Rick shifted uncomfortably and lit another cigarette. 'I mean, you were...'

'You've already got one cigarette burning in the ashtray,'

Emily said. 'Can I see that article?'

'I tore it up. I'll get you a back issue.'

'How did *Plush* find out about the divorce?'

'Search me! Sheila Lyall, I guess.'

'And how did she find out?'

'Sheila Lyall and Arlene are having a big affair. Didn't you know?'

'No, but I seriously think I'm going to kill that woman...'

In that capsule of uncertainty in which Emily now lived, time acquired an agreeable distortion. Which was why the third successive night that she and Leon were dining in her suite multiplied in her mind into a time-worn habit. She said – just like a wife, she thought, 'I saw Rick today...'

'So what's new?' Leon said, just like a husband, she thought.

'Rick told me about that article in *Plush*.' She hoped she did not sound as reproachful as a wife when she added, 'I wish you had told me about it...'

'Ugh! Gossip!' he said. 'Why repeat gossip?'

'I suppose I should have told you that Sheila Lyall wrote to Simon.'

'Why didn't you?'

'Too ugly...'

'I can imagine...'

'Can you? I wonder,' Emily said, too pleasantly. She saw Leon's interest quicken. 'Sheila told him about you and me. She also managed to include a few of your most personal details...'

'Such as?' Leon asked quickly.

'Your vasectomy, for one.'

Leon laughed then, and it was one of his full-hearted funniest laughs. And when Emily decoded the laugh, she again thought she was thinking like a wife. Before she could stop herself, she said, 'Sheila Lyall also told Simon about your vow...'

'My vow?'

There... it was out.

Too late to take it back.

A confrontation now was the last thing she wanted.

'Your vow never to remarry. Simon flung that at me when he was driving me into London.'

356

'Why are you telling me this now?'

'I don't know why. I don't know why I'm telling you this now...' She bit her lip hard. There was nothing worse than a begging, tearful wife, yet she went on, 'You never thought Simon would divorce me, did you?'

Leon made no attempt to answer, he merely sighed.

Was it impossible for her to hold her tongue? She was thinking this even as she said, 'You didn't ask me to stay with you in your apartment because your children are coming back from their semester in Greece.'

'Semester in Italy.'

'Sorry, semester in Italy. But I've hit the nail on the head, haven't I?'

'You make it sound as if I've misled you,' Leon said angrily. 'I told you about my feelings for my wife. I told you that the very first night we were together...'

'I know. I remember.'

'I could never marry again,' Leon said, almost shouting. 'Never! You of all people should understand that...'

'I do, that's the trouble. I do understand that.'

'I love you, Emily.'

'Perhaps.'

Now Leon leaned forward over the table to take her by the shoulders. Dishes crashed to the floor, the shoulder ached and she winced, but he ignored all that. 'I love you, Emily, and you know I do. We could live together, you could even take my name. It's just a simple procedure.'

'Then why can't you marry me? *Why?*'

'I can't marry anyone ever again. You know I can't do that to Ruthie...'

'Ruthie's *dead*,' Emily shrieked. 'A dead woman's ruling you from the grave.' Pausing between each word, she added, 'Your... wife... is... dead.'

'Milt's not dead,' Leon shouted. 'I would lose him, too! Would you want that? Would you want to divide my brother and me? Don't you understand anything about the tie of blood?'

Emily did not answer because she could not speak.

'Blood ties mean nothing to you,' he said bitterly. 'Nothing!'

357

'Oh, Leon,' she said. As if his name were a prayer, she repeated, 'Leon.'

'Know something? You've changed, Emily,' Leon said slowly, 'You sure have changed. You used to be subtle... gentle... British. Now you sound like...' He stopped abruptly.

After a silence, Emily asked, 'What were you going to say I sounded like?'

'Like a macho, female New Yorker! I want you to think about this very, very carefully. If you loved me enough, you would understand. If you could love *enough*.'

When he stood up to leave, Emily didn't even try to stop him. She wished that she could cry, but it seemed that tears were as remote as hope.

At first Emily thought she was being silly, but once it had taken hold she could not rid herself of the idea that if he loved her enough, he would make her his wife. Unoriginal, conventional, call it what you will, she argued with herself – however outdated, it remained an ancient truth that there *could* be no adequate substitute for an offer of marriage.

Emily Bradshaw a second-rate, common-law wife? No, it was an absurdity and was not to be contemplated.

The taping of *Perspectives* was two days away, there were meetings to attend and, once again, Emily tried to put her soul on ice.

But she took Leon's advice very seriously and thought very seriously. Danny would be going away to school later, so she could live with Leon ... She considered her other options – she could avail herself of her tempting cache of sleeping pills. Meanwhile, there was always, always vodka. Also, should she return his gifts?

At the same time, an unwelcome question nagged and niggled at her brain. Did *she* love Leon *enough*?

She had fallen in love with or been seduced by America long before meeting Leon. Because even more than Leon, it was America which had made it possible for her to know herself, her ambitious self. Pitiless though her ambition was, and however much more costly it would turn out to be, she could not bring herself to give in to regret.

On the other hand, groundless ambition was inexcusable.

*

'Emily, there's something I want to ask you,' Katie said shyly. 'Would you be Andy's godmother?'

'I'll be honoured,' Emily answered at once, rising to kiss Katie's cheek. 'Deeply, deeply honoured.'

They had lunched in Emily's suite at the Pierre. Andy was in the bedroom happily piecing together the jigsaw of Buckingham Palace which was among the many gifts Emily had brought for him.

'You've been a fairy godmother to both of us,' Katie said soberly.

Emily turned away, not wanting Katie to see the sudden tears that she was unable to control. Katie's appearance had altered. She glowed as a healthy twenty-four-year-old woman should glow – she was no longer sallow and ageless. Her hair – long and shiny and straight – was tied back from her face with a bright yellow bow, and the fringe she now wore highlighted her soft brown eyes.

'You saved us, Emily,' she said fiercely. 'You saved us!'

'Oh, Katie, you make me feel . . . I can't put it into words,' Emily said brokenly. 'Andy reminds me of Danny – he's such a good-natured little chap. Danny's leaving home next September; he's going away to school.'

'Leaving home? At his age – *eight*?'

'Well, his father and his grandfather went to the same boarding school at the same age,' Emily said defensively. 'And they tell me it did them no harm. I try not to . . .' To change the subject, she said, 'I like your dress, Katie. Yellow suits you.'

Katie's simple wool dress looked as soft as silk, and she could easily have been taken to be an elegant young matron who had been cosseted and protected all her life. Looking at her, and reflecting that Leon's generosity had been responsible for all this, an affectionate smile hightened Emily's reflection.

'There's something I want to tell you, Emily,' Katie said slowly. 'It's about Andy.' She paused for a moment and then, in a rush, the words came. 'I told you Jake was not Andy's father. His father was my foster-father – you can guess the rest.'

'Oh, Katie, how terrible for you!'

'But Andy will hear the truth one day. Suicide sometimes runs in families, and I'd like him to know that the man who committed suicide was not his father.'

'I told you before that this was absolutely right,' Emily said staunchly. 'Andy must be told.'

'Emily, you are the only person who knows,' Katie went on. 'Andy's real father must never know. If anything happens to me will you tell Andy for me?'

'Of course I will,' Emily said, rising to hug Katie. 'Nothing will happen to you, but I understand how you feel. I'm deeply honoured to be Andy's godmother.'

'You are the best thing that ever happened to Andy and me,' Katie said passionately. 'We want you to know that.'

As soon as Katie left, Emily cancelled her hair appointment with Kenneth. She needed to think about everything Katie had said, because unknowingly she had touched on an almost fatal weakness in Emily, a weakness she was now forced to confront. She had been giving too much serious thought to her supply of sleeping pills. She realized that she had been playing with the idea of suicide as if it were a safety-net, but she had not thought of the effect this might have on Danny. Feeling horribly ashamed, she flushed the pills down the lavatory.

*

But it was not until *Perspectives* had been taped that Emily allowed her fears of groundless ambition to fall away. Besides, things had changed. Rick was now utterly confident that her own show, *Family Mix*, would be signed. She did not plan to leave America until the deal was signed, or until she and Leon had sorted themselves out.

That night, Emily planned to have another serious talk with Leon. It was going to be one of their usual dinners *à deux* at the Pierre.

The phone rang and Leon said, 'Darling.'

As soon as Emily heard him say that – he usually said 'Emily' ... she was on the alert and quite literally stood to attention. 'Yes?'

'Can't make it tonight.'

'I see.'

'Looks like this meeting will go on till hell freezes over!' He laughed. 'I'll call you in the morning.'

Emily stared at the phone.

That laugh, again that wonderfully useful jingle of a laugh, Emily thought. Then she caught herself staring at the phone. 'This won't do,' she said aloud. 'This won't do.' Very slowly she poured another vodka.

She stared at the transparent liquid in the glass, just as only a few moments before she had stared at the telephone. The colour of the vodka reminded her of the life-saving liquids that had been dripped into her veins. No, she thought again, this time silently, this won't do at all. It struck her that the phone and vodka connection was nothing other than the mistress connection. She was one of all those women who were eternally available, and always waiting.

Because the day before, and with the same useful laugh, Leon had cancelled a lunch date. He would cancel others too, and just as carelessly, though always with that laugh ... that laugh in which she had once loved to drown – that laugh was Leon's personalized commercial.

In the end, Leon would always do what suited him. It had suited him to call her a macho, female New Yorker; that insult had found its mark, and she still smarted from it. He had meant to be hurtful, she was sure, but even so the insult was as revealing as it was cruel. It told her more about him, about his thinking, than he had intended – a kind of intelligence of the heart. She understood that he had mistaken her insecurity, her unhealthy lack of confidence for the kind of subtle modesty which conformed to his notion of British gentility. She had never been less self-deprecating than she was now, which also made her less attractive to Leon ... which was quite a thought.

Glancing at the vodka again, she was reminded of those colourless liquids which had kept her alive. Surely, surely, she had earned her life – paid for it, so to speak. Of course, without Leon's ambulance there would have been no life to earn back again. To let it go now, to reject and then to strangle her exhilarating interest in his, her own life, would be a kind of slow suicide ... the ultimate waste.

Leon was right. On the face of all the evidence, she had changed. Yet she felt that *if* she had changed, it was because she had been cleansed. It was as if, in coming to America, she had been plunged in a great solvent which had caused the lifelong collection of sticky wraps with which she had plastered and squashed her intellect – and her enthusiasm and yes, even her sensuality – to merely float away. Until then she had expected, just as she had been expected, to drift into the drab-trap. Well, well, she preferred primary colours; it seemed they suited her best.

Emily got up slowly, slowly, almost measuring every drop, and because she was concentrating so fiercely, she dripped the vodka from the glass back into the bottle. She had no idea how long she had been staring at the telephone, but this was some sort of action at least and it broke her spell of staring. It also broke her growing affection for vodka itself. Such a small, trivial thing to do – pouring a half-filled glass into a bottle – yet by the time it had been done, Emily had taken a decision on something she had not known she had even been considering.

As long as she was in New York, she would not be able to leave Leon.

So she would return to London.

The decision gathered momentum.

Now she was definite, almost obsessional about leaving New York at once. The very next day.

True, she had been – and would continue to be – punished for her ambition. Looked at sensibly and from her point of view, her successes offered no consolation for the broken family which lay on her conscience.

She would leave New York.

But she would tell no one.

She would be back soon, she knew. In the end, and before very long, *Family Mix* would get off the ground and on the air.

And yet before leaving New York, she had to make the acquaintance of one woman. Curiosity can be dangerous, but Emily needed to meet the author of *Sixty Seductive Salads from*

Fifty-One States. So she did. Which turned out to be an unnerving experience, to say the least. After that, she went straight to the airport.

She felt very bad about not letting Rick know that she was leaving New York.

PART VII
Early December 1985

Chapter 22

Emily fastened her seat-belt and resolved never to take flying by Concorde for granted – it was so gloriously conducive to thinking.

She had always liked flying; it eliminates options and restricts freedom – if only because, barring the unforeseen, no alternative direction is possible. Up in the sky, overflying, outreaching the world – or her world – was one way of approaching clarity. And there was no doubt about it, she needed to think things through, to sort out and then try to make sense of the direction her life had taken. So she had followed her instincts, not so much to run away from Leon as to cut out and cauterize their sensual connection. She was not going to allow herself to stand in perpetual readiness, hoping to catch whatever cast-off crumbs Leon might care to fling her way. For, as she told herself, lives built on crumbs must crumble.

Still it was odd, Emily thought, how the decision to break with Leon had left her tearless. And yet she had been happy with him, wildly and greedily happy. A phrase from one of those announcements that appeared regularly in *The Times* flashed through her mind: *The engagement has been cancelled and the marriage will not now take place* . . . Except that – as she now understood it – there never had been an engagement, nor a commitment on either of their parts. The prospect of marriage had never been a factor until she had introduced it. The truth was that, along with his vow and his vasectomy, went Leon's freedom. It was she who had if not automatically, then thoughtlessly, made that ancient insistent leap from attraction to marriage. That she might prize her own freedom had not, at the time, occurred to her. Passion, and then Jake Williams, had whirled them into one another's arms and it had been easy to believe in a special destiny. Even in the pitiless light of loss, Emily could not bring herself to regret Leon. When he learned that she had gone, if he felt anything at all it would probably be relief.

Emily's mind turned towards Simon. Gradually, over the past weeks, she had come to recognize that her marriage had conformed to her earliest expectations of what it would be. Consequently she had been neither happy nor unhappy, but comfortable. Perhaps Simon had felt the same way about his marriage... True, she had felt so strongly about needless divorce and the destruction of the family, that she had written a whole book about it. Now Simon's Susan was pregnant, but she conceded that even if there had been no pregnancy to consider, she would not have tried to go back to him.

She made a small, clicking sound with her tongue. The ironic truth was that Susan's pregnancy had set her free.

Something troubled one of her eyes and she took out her mirror to check whether it was a speck of mascara, but could find nothing. She used her eye drops expertly, and then put the mirror away. Which was the real Emily, she wondered: the glamorous, ambitious one of four or five months which she saw in the mirror, with the lustrous, gold-flecked hair – or the neat, ordinary one she had been for the previous thirty-four years? She had heard how cosmetic surgery alters people. Had she changed from the dutiful Emily to the ambitious Emily only because her appearance had changed? Was she really so shallow? Well, yes, partly...

But not entirely.

Ambition is passion without mercy and realizing this, Emily gave an inner shrug. If once she had despised all those whom she considered shallow and synthetic, it was because she had known nothing of ambition.

Yet, if she wanted to be fair to herself, she ought not to forget that when she had agreed to go on a coast-to-coast publicity tour she had known no one in America, and therefore both she and Simon had believed that no harm could come to her privacy, her integrity or her anonymity. The whole thing was meant to be a brief, working interlude, after which she was to resume her usual life...

Her fingers cradled the turquoise amulet in her pocket. The other Emily had been as contemptuous of superstition as of ambition. Sheila Lyall had only once to mention that green brings bad luck, and Emily had never worn green again.

She acknowledged her debt to Sheila in the same way as she acknowledged her debt to Jake Williams. Jake's murderous attempt had catapulted *Defending Wives* to the best-selling list, and Sheila Lyall's photographs had gone a long way towards keeping it there. Emily knew that she was nowhere nearly as lovely as Sheila's pictures – which, as she told herself, was proof of how malice triggers genius. She had a momentary spasm of guilt over her uncompromisingly cruel rejection of Sheila.

Sometimes, and usually when she least expected it, she would hear again the radio phone-in when the caller had cried out, 'Hell, man, I know I'm my kid's daddy...' She heard it now and it made her wince. Her hand flew to her injured shoulder.

Fortunately, she was beginning to feel a little less guilty about her role in the life and even the death of Jake Williams, though nothing could alter the fact that her own life was now intimately linked with this dead stranger. As time went on she became more rather than less involved with Jake, finding to her astonishment that she had developed a certain affinity with him – with his Robin Hood tactics, especially. Now Katie had asked her to be little Andy's godmother, and she loved the child as if he were a member of her own family. She hoped he and Danny would become friends.

At any rate, as Emily now consoled herself, there would be no problem with financing Danny's entire education at Eton. Simon would not have to part with his beloved painting, nor his Chippendale desk. In just eight months, Danny would be a boarder at the Trevor-Winston feeder-school to Eton.

The thought of a new but, oh, so obvious possibility made Emily tremble. Danny need *not* go to Trevor-Winston School, and she did *not* have to submit to Simon's decree. She could and would oppose it – through the courts, if necessary. True Simon was a lawyer, but she had the funds and she could fight him. Leon had been right – sending a child like Danny to the Trevor-Winston School would be an act of cruelty. She blessed Leon, for it was thanks to him that she had discovered Danny's terror of the whole idea.

Meanwhile, there were custody details to sort out. Emily's mind, which had been rushing anyway, now began to race. Danny and Simon were close and nothing must disturb that, yet *she* needed Danny, too.

And then it came to her.

Unlike herself, the author of *Sixty Seductive Salads from Fifty-One States* was a real author, and Emily was heavily indebted to her. It was one of those uncanny happenings – a case of accidental ambition, and Danny was its major casualty. Though it would be an incurable heartbreak for ever, it was one she would have to learn to live with, much in the way that others learned to live with a permanent disability.

Whoever the real Emily was seemed irrelevant now, because accidental or not, her ambition was real. Also solid. Emily snapped on her calculator. She was a woman of means now, an emancipated woman with a network of career contacts. For all that, her own emancipation was the last thing she would have chosen. Yet she could now *choose* to use her own resources to get *Family Mix* and herself off the ground.

Ideas fell about her in tumbles of disorder. She opened her notebook, but wrote nothing. Instead she closed her eyes and bit her lips, the better to concentrate.

She started to make plans.

That contract with *Kay-Chow* – her fee could go towards a part sponsorship of *Family Mix*. Frontier Books? She had made them so much that she was sure she could count on their participation. The Lerner twins might be persuaded to do business with an ex ... Rick could handle the publicity; *gratis*, to begin with. Tom Janowski was a real expert on crime – he would be her crime consultant. Sheila Lyall would make a perfectly brilliant set designer ... Emily believed she had the perfect secretary in mind too – Katie! She had the nucleus of her own network already! But based in London to fit in with Danny. Rick was already negotiating with the London Television Company. She would form a transatlantic company and call it just that.

And all because, though still utterly amazing, she could inject some of her own capital and even get a loan.

Her lips felt chapped.

She realized she had been biting them, though in a new kind of passion; the passion which came from an understanding that she had enough faith in herself to risk bank-rolling herself. Which incidentally would be certain to attract other investors to her own production company which she had, only just this moment, decided to create!

It was then that Emily understood that despite the loss and the pain, the faithlessness and the seduction, she still saw herself as a potential winner.

In America, Emily thought, ambition is rewarded rather than punished.

As the plane landed, she tried to imagine what her mother would have made of all this. She hoped Clara would have been proud of her, if only because at last she had become her own person.

A soon as Emily was in the airport building, she broke into a light run.

She needed a telephone urgently.

And as she ran, a slight breeze lifted her streaming hair. Aware of appreciative stares, Emily smiled with the self-confidence that makes a beautiful woman still more beautiful. She saw no reason why she should delay telephoning until she had been through passport control. Charming an airport official into allowing her to use his telephone was as easy as it was pleasurable and she rejoiced in the powerful sensuality that her American seduction had released.

She called Rick. Collect.

'Katie!' she heard him shout, while the international operator was still speaking to him. 'It's Emily, calling from London.'

Emily giggled.

'Emily! What the fuck are you doing in London?' Rick sounded indignant. 'The Pierre said you'd checked out and Leon's going bananas. Thank God you called! Katie's smart; she told us you'd gone to London. Are you OK?'

'I'm phoning from Heathrow,' Emily said impatiently. 'I was trying to sort myself out on the plane. Then I had this idea. Rick, how does Emily Bradshaw Trans-Atlantic Productions sound to you?'

'It sounds great to me. Just great—'

'Rick I'm putting all my capital into it. A not inconsiderable sum, as you know...'

'Sure, I know,' Rick said with an appreciative chuckle. 'I can think of one or two guys besides myself who would jump at the chance of going in with you.'

'It's like old times, talking to you like this, calling collect,' Emily told him affectionately.

'Now here's what I want you to do for me,' Rick said. 'I want you to stop worrying, OK?'

'I'm not in the least worried,' Emily declared emphatically. 'As long as there's ambition, there's hope!'

PART VIII
August 1986

Epilogue

BRADSHAW *v.* BRADSHAW

Before Mr Justice Wilcox in the Family Division of the High Court.

[Judgement given 6 August 1986].

Mr Justice Wilcox said '... having regard to a pending divorce hearing, and having regard to the Court Welfare Officer's finding that at the tender age of eight, the boarding school environment could be potentially harmful to the boy, the Court rules that Danny is not required to take up his place at the Trevor-Winston School ...'

'We won, Emily, we won!' Rick said to her.

Emily nodded.

'Now here's what I want you to do for me,' he said with a crooked grin. 'Wait for me, OK? I gotta go to the john.'

Emily waited on the steps of the High Court. Simon and Susan walked out slowly, Susan still pale only two weeks after the birth of their baby daughter. Simon stalked past Emily – his expression and his body taut with hatred. Thank God Rick is here, Emily thought; she could not begin to imagine how she would have got through these past months without him. Her father had been so opposed to her Court action that he had given an affidavit in favour of Simon.

Nothing mattered now, not her father's betrayal nor Simon's undying enmity. Danny and she would be together in their new home.

Wanting an immediate escape from the tense court atmosphere, Emily turned around to look for Rick, but what she saw made her heart lurch. No, no, she told herself rapidly, it was impossible; it was only her usual fantasy that Leon was coming towards her. But the fantasy came closer and silently took hold of both her hands.

'I couldn't sleep last night. I got this gut feeling, so I called Leon. He just made it in time from his office to the Concorde,' Rick said, his deep voice unusually high.

He watched Emily move towards Leon and snuggle against him. She sure had come a long, long way, Rick thought. She had had to learn to want what others took for granted. Emily had learned, at last, to make the most of herself and to do the best for herself.

William J. Coughlin
Her Father's Daughter £2.95

When Hunter Van Horn is killed in an air crash, everyone assumes that both control of his mighty but ailing empire and his seat on the Vault – the secretive group of New York power brokers – will pass to his feckless son, Junior. But Hunter chose as his true heir the daughter from whom he'd been estranged for years . . .

Victoria Van Horn, beautiful and rich in her own right, she cannot resist the challenge, even when she discovers that her father's enemies are now set on destroying her . . .

Cecilia, Junior's scheming wife who will do anything to improve her wealth and social position . . .

Chilton Vance, Hunter's trusted right-hand-man who ruthlessly sets Victoria up to further his own ambition . . .

Barry Lytle, the smooth-talking Congressman who uses Victoria in his quest for a Senate seat . . .

Lucas Shaw, the youngest member of the Vault whom Victoria hires to build her waterfront development and who shows her there is more to life than wheeling and dealing . . .

Sweeping from glittering Manhattan to the sleazy Hudson River waterfront and the hustle and bustle of Hong Kong, this is a spellbinding story of power and passion at the top.

Cynthia Freeman
Illusions of Love £1.95

They had parted many years before in despair and bitterness, lovers
sacrificed to a star-crossed destiny. Now she was back in his life —
threatening his marriage, his family, his heritage. Sweeping
dramatically from lavish San Francisco mansions to the devastated
villages of war-torn Italy, from the glittering thoroughfares of post-
war Manhattan to the present day, *Illusions of Love* is an epic story
of astonishing emotional power and stirring human drama.

Unity Hall
The White Paper Fan £2.95

Jade had just made love in the jacuzzi in Aspen, Colorado with the
big blond American when she got the phone call. The man who'd
always been her father, who'd adopted her and Poppy when they
were just tiny Chinese baby girls, had been killed in a hit-and-run
accident. He bequeathed them not only money, but many
unanswered questions. Who were those names in his address book?
What did the clippings from the Hong Kong newspapers mean? And
who were Poppy and Jade, anyway? The answers lay in Hong Kong,
in a labyrinth of drugs and death, sinister Triad connections and dark
secrets — hidden behind the white paper fan.